Praise for Virginia Swift's
BROWN-EYED GIRL

"A dazzling, dangerously funny debut from Virginia Swift, *Brown-Eyed Girl* has a rich voice, a wonderful sense of the modern West, and tons of attitude. With this book, Virgina Swift threatens to do for Wyoming historians what Janet Evanovich has done for New Jersey bounty hunters."

Stephen White, author of *Cold Case*

"A sexy novel set in the wide-open town of Laramie, Wyoming. Bawdy and suspenseful with a wonderful literary mystery buried in the middle, this debut novel promises a solid career ahead for Ms. Swift."

Margaret Maron

"A soaring debut from Swift, who combines a bittersweet romance, resumed after a twenty-year hiatus, with academic infighting, paramilitary paranoia, and a puzzle dating back to WWII."

Kirkus Reviews

"Sally and the mysterious, marvelous
Meg Dunwoodie are great characters."

Toronto Globe and Mail

"A delightfully heterogeneous cast . . .
This witty, warm, engrossing first
novel is highly recommended."

Library Journal

"Entertaining . . . Swift certainly provides plenty
of color in terms of characters and setting."

London Times

VIRGINIA SWIFT

AVON BOOKS
An Imprint of HarperCollinsPublishers

This is a work of fiction. Names, characters, places, and incidents are products of the author's imagination or are used fictitiously and are not to be construed as real. Any resemblance to actual events, locales, organizations, or persons, living or dead, is entirely coincidental.

AVON BOOKS
An Imprint of HarperCollins*Publishers*
10 East 53rd Street
New York, New York 10022-5299

Copyright © 2000 by Virginia Scharff
ISBN: 0-06-103030-9
www.avonbooks.com

First Avon Books paperback printing: April 2001
First HarperCollins hardcover printing: April 2000

A Disclaimer, and Many Acknowledgments

This is a work of fiction. Laramie is a real place, and some of the places in and around Laramie are real, but the people are pure products of my own fevered imagination.

Many thanks:

To Maria Montoya, for an evening in a cabin in the high Rockies when I told this story, and who said, "Oh, you've gotta write it." To Beth Bailey, Melissa Bokovoy, Hal Corbett, Henry Levkoff, Jeff Limerick, Valerie Matsumoto, Harriet Moss, Craig Pinto, and Peter Swift, who read the book and gave me all kinds of suggestions, which I should have taken.

To Kathy Jensen and Audie Blevins, who've offered me a home away from home for twenty years. And to more Wyoming friends: Katie Curtiss and Hal Corbett, Karen Marcotte and Jon Myers, Colin and Roxanne Keeney, Bev Seckinger, Janice Harris. All this is made up, of course, but it kind of rings true, don't you think?

To Tom Baumgartel, Catherine Kleiner, and Jon "Mad Dog" Myers for keeping the music alive.

To Richard White, for giving kindly hardheaded advice and the chances of a lifetime. To Elaine Koster, my agent, whose faith in this book and me amazes me still. To

Carolyn Marino, my editor, who is teaching me how to write. To my excellent colleagues in the History Department at the University of New Mexico and in the Western History Association, who keep me crazy after all these years.

To Sam and Annie Swift, the world's finest children. To the Swift, Scharff, and Levkoff families, who matter most of all.

To Peter "the Rocket" Swift, companion on all twenty thousand roads, and off-road for that matter, my love.

Part One

1

Twenty Thousand Roads

Three days from LA. Almost there.

Over the high country, late afternoon sun glinting off the rocks and shining grasslands where Colorado rose into Wyoming. Sally fiddled around trying to pick up a radio station (Broncos 17, Patriots driving, stupid exhibition season football) and put up with static until she could see the Monolith Cement Plant. Then she could indulge herself and slip the tape in the slot. She caught sight of some antelope loping dark shadows across the golden meadows, with day waning into night, lights flickering on in the Laramie valley and the tiniest August chill in the air.

She'd had the hammer down since Longmont, where the traffic thinned out, and found the cutoff that put Fort Collins behind her. She could never resist the urge to see what kind of time she could make between the Denver Mousetrap, where I–25 and I–70 snarled, and the first sight of the lights of Laramie coming on in the dusk. Two hours and twenty minutes, for what some people called a three-hour drive. She sang, loudly, along with the tape, along with Gram Parsons and Emmylou Harris and her whole life. Sang her way down twenty thousand roads. Maybe, finally, heading straight back home.

The sun painted the hills pink. The air got just a taste chillier. Sally could really get nostalgic now, if she weren't obliged to history, so adept at remembering the bad with the good. How they'd all headed west, to grow up with the country . . .

Shit!

Where the flaming hell did that cop car come from?

So much for the peaceful fading glow of day in the high country. Now it was bubblegum lights in the rearview, and Sally's perfect certainty that she'd had the Mustang doing better than seventy passing the Holiday Inn, and despite her most earnest efforts, over fifty as Route 287 turned into Third Street. What was the statute of limitations in Wyoming? She looked again in the mirror, knew she was cooked, slowed and pulled over to the right, heart pounding.

California plates. A '64 Mustang, restored to sleek perfection by the Mustang King of LA, doing maybe fifty-seven miles per hour in a thirty zone entering Laramie, Wyoming: She was dead meat, looking at a ticket for a hundred bucks easy. She turned off the tape, composed her face. She wondered again about ancient outstanding warrants, looking at the police cruiser in the rearview. She leaned over slowly and opened the glovebox.

The Laramie cop did things with his brake, his radio, his clipboard, his hat, got out of his cop car, walked up to her window, peered down at her through predictably mirrored sunglasses, and drawled genially, "Well, Sally, guess you'd better slow that Mustang down."

She stopped in the middle of getting out the registration slip. Freakin' Dickie Langham. Guess this was Road Number 20,000 after all.

He didn't give her a ticket. Instead, he gave her the biggest hug she'd had since the last time, sixteen years ago. He hadn't gotten any shorter than the six foot four inches he'd been back when he'd been tending bar at Dr. Mudflaps, and he hadn't gotten any lighter. Back then, Mudflaps had the gall to pretend to be an upscale restaurant and lounge but was really a place with orange plastic booths (red leatherette? Sure.) and a brisk trade in bad white stuff. Dickie had been carrying maybe thirty pounds less than now, had been a completely different color (greenish gray-white to his current reasonably tan) and extensively more jittery. That's what living on Dr. Langham's Miracle Diet (booze and blow) would do for you. He'd been unerringly decent then, in his own way, and funny as hell, but not so much so that four big guys from Boulder had seen either the humanity or the humor of his coming up a little short of cash one time when they were in town.

"The Boulder guys were drinking black coffee," Dickie explained to Sally, "and they weren't enjoying being squeezed into one of those orange booths. I had experienced their form of persuasion the year before," he recalled as they looked at the plastic-covered menus in the Wrangler Bar and Grill. "My shoulder still aches sometimes from where they simulated ripping my arm off. Extremely frightening guys. So, lacking the money to pay them, I told them I was going into the back room to get something and, well, I came back eleven years later."

By the time he returned to Laramie, Dickie said, as he requested a double cheeseburger, an order of rings, an order of fries, a side salad with blue cheese dressing, and an iced tea, the Boulder guys were who knows where, and the sensible people who ran the Wyoming Law Enforcement Academy had use for somebody who'd personally seen law enforcement from a variety of different points of view, but upon whom nobody could seem to make a particular rap stick. He had picked up some valuable skills along the way, including familiarity with a range of firearms, fluency in Spanish, and intimacy with the rigors, rewards, and limitations of twelve-step programs. Now he was an Albany County deputy sheriff with four years in, likeliest candidate for sheriff when the incumbent moved on to the state legislature this November. Dickie was a lucky man on his way up in the sometimes forgiving (or at least forgetting) state of Wyoming.

"You know, I don't know how Mary did it, or why she took back a lowlife like you," Sally said, thinking of Dickie's wife. Sally told the waitress she wanted an order of rings, a dinner salad with Italian dressing on the side, and a Budweiser. You did not order chardonnay, even if this was the Equality State.

Mary Langham, it turned out, was most forgiving of all. Fifteen years ago, when Dickie took a powder, their daughter Brittany was six, Ashley was four, and Mary was pregnant again. On the day their son was getting ready to be born in the Ivinson Memorial Hospital, Dickie, on the lam but knowing the time was near, called Mary collect from a pay phone at the Corn Palace in Mitchell, South Dakota. He was crying. Mary started to cry, too, and said, "Tell me what you want me to name him, you bastard, and if you don't get your shit together and come back, I'll hunt you down and take your balls off with the nail scissors."

There are so many ways to say, "I love you."

Fortunately for Dickie, Mary was an unaccountably loyal wife. Her kids had inherited something of her quality of mercy. Josh first met his father when he was eleven, but he looked up to him anyway. Brittany and Ashley seemed to be perfecting ways of making Dickie pay, as they had every right to do, but now and again, he said, they made him think they might somehow end up all right.

Their food came, and they dug in. Wrangler onion rings: nothing else possessed the sheer grease power to soak up seven or eight tequila and grapefruits.

"You know, I've never understood those curly fries they have at the state fair," Dickie mused, stuffing a huge forkful of dripping lettuce into his mouth in hot pursuit of a giant bite of burger. "I mean, you've got your fries, and you've got your rings. One is for potatoes; the other is for onions. Seems to me curly fries are a mixed metaphor."

Dickie had earned a master's degree in English from the university at the same time Sally had been getting her own master's over in the history department, quite a few years ago.

"You have to admire that machine, though," Sally told him. "The way it just keeps curling 'em out." They ate awhile in silence, the waitress refilling Dickie's iced tea and eying Sally's disappearing Budweiser. "Well, I'm glad you came back, Dick. I feel safer knowing that the deputy sheriff has such an intimate acquaintance with the criminal mind."

"Thank you very much for that extravagant vote of confidence. Helps me out a lot when I'm looking for lost dogs and chasing speeders," he said modestly.

"Come on now. I bet you get your share of criminal mischief, or at least hunting accidents and one-car rollovers. Aren't those the main causes of death in Wyoming?"

"We do get a few, what with the interstate going through here. But it's a lot worse up around Jackson these days. They seem to be killing off tourists right and left, and even the locals are running off the road and shooting themselves to beat all hell. Teton County sheriff told me about a guy from Dubois who drove his Range Rover off a cliff in Togwotee Pass last fall, and wasn't even drunk. Guy named Mickey Welsh. Pillar of the community—a church-going, big-money accountant, big deal Republican. Used to be only the reprobates terminated themselves in their cars." He shook his head and considered ordering more food.

"Yeah, it's a real pity when even upstanding Republicans buy it," Sally commiserated.

"They're dropping like flies, I understand," said Dickie, who would run for sheriff, of course, as a Democrat. "Especially in Teton County. Have you ever heard of Walt Flanders?" Sally shook her head. "He is—or was—a lawyer in Jackson Hole, personal buddy of George W.

Bush." Sally whistled in admiration, and let Dickie continue. "He was only *forty-two*, a real Republican rocket, and last hunting season he went out to get his antelope and never came back. Big NRA activist, and he still managed to shoot himself in the head with his own rifle!"

Sally looked askance. "Tax problems?" she asked. "A little cowgirl on the side?"

Dickie chewed, shrugged. "Not my problem." Albany County was plenty enough for him to handle, he was thinking. Two weeks previously, he'd been called out to investigate an abandoned vehicle in the Snowy Range west of Centennial. A remarkably aged Ford Fiesta with a flat tire, Arizona plates (stolen), and nobody home. He'd rummaged around in the woods nearby and found a young couple, two Mexican nationals probably on their way home from illegally making beds and running leaf-blowers in Jackson Hole. They'd been beaten horribly, burned with cigarettes, and shot again and again. Dickie did not like to contemplate what kind of people did such things to other human beings.

He changed the subject. "Do you still pick up a guitar now and then?"

Sally wagged her head. "My Martin's in the Mustang."

"Well whatever it is you're up to, it sure made headlines here. You should have seen the story in the *Boomerang* about you coming back to be an endowed professor," Dickie continued, squirting ketchup all over his fries. "Mary cut it out of the paper, but I don't think she saved it." The last part was true technically. There was no reason Sally needed to know what Mary had done with the clipping, that she'd mailed it off to someone in Tucson. Although Dickie didn't know what had become of it upon arrival in Arizona, the clipping had been read, crumpled, tossed away, straightened out, crumpled again, thought about, and incinerated. "She was so excited about you coming back, so proud of you. Even prouder than when 'The Going Home Alone Again Waltz' was such a big hit."

"Yeah," Sally said. "Sally and the Mustangs' wonderful one hit. That was the highlight of that band's career, honey. Although we did have a steady Bay Area following at gay cowboy bars with names like The Rainbow Cattle Company. Guys in tight jeans and western shirts and Stetsons, drinking cans of Coors and dancing with each other, went insane when I sang 'Crazy.' I wonder how many of those good-lookin' boys are still around?"

Dickie looked down at his plate.

"So after all, I wasn't sorry to leave it behind. The whole thing didn't mean much, when you think about it from a distance. What did it cost me to kiss off too much cigarette smoke and tequila shooters, too much time among scumbags, dope everywhere and one-night stands that were hellishly scary, when I think about it too much? It's a lot safer and more peaceful sitting in a quiet library, or in front of a computer screen, or performing lectures for students who don't usually send up cocktail napkins with handwritten messages reading 'Why don't we get drunk and screw?'"

Dickie let her know precisely how far Laramie thought she'd come from the hell-raising chick singer she'd been. "I think the headline on the story about your new gig said something like, 'Former Bar Singer Returns as Dunwoodie Chair.'" He laughed.

"Sounds like Dunwoodie Barstool," she declared dryly. Dickie snorted. "Nobody is ever supposed to be anything except what they were the last time," Sally said, pouring viscous yellow salad dressing out of a little plastic cup onto a pile of iceberg lettuce and a hard, pale pink wedge of tomato. "Well, maybe it's not that big a leap from the Gallery Bar to the special collections, trading in the ought-to-be-dead for the literally deceased. Officially, I'm now holder of the Dunwoodie Distinguished Chair in American Women's History, which also makes me chair of the Dunwoodie Center for Women's History. I never expected to have a named piece of furniture."

She ate an onion ring, considered. "If you want to know the truth, the whole thing is a little bit strange. Usually when colleges hire professors, they do a search, let anyone who wants to apply for the job, interview the people they think they might want to hire, and then choose somebody.

"But this thing didn't work that way. Last fall, I got a call from Edna McCaffrey—"

"Sure, the one who got the MacArthur genius grant. Dean of the college now. Her kids were at Laramie High with Brit and Ashley," Dickie said.

"That's her. She was calling to ask me if I'd be interested in applying for this new endowed chair, funded by a bequest from Laramie's most famous poet et cetera.

"I said, 'Whoa Edna, what's this about?'

"She said, 'Sally, the university has just received a bequest from the estate of Margaret Dunwoodie, in the neighborhood of five million dollars. You remember Miss Dunwoodie—she taught in the English department for forty years or so. Didn't start publishing her stuff until she was an old lady, and she died before they gave that last collection of poetry the National Book Award. Her gift includes an endowed chair in women's history. You've been nominated.'

"Imagine me, an endowed professor at the University of Wyoming. Do you remember, Dick: the biggest thing I'd ever done as a student here was to walk into the history department office, get hassled by that pickle-sucking powderface of a secretary who never did any work. That day I got so fed up with her losing my mail that I told her to go fuck herself. That asshole professor, Byron Bosworth, was standing there listening to the whole thing, and when that secretary died of a stroke a month later, the Boz told everyone I had caused it."

"I took English Comp from Margaret Dunwoodie," Dickie interjected. "She told me to give up writing before

I hurt someone." Polishing off the last of his onion rings, Dickie wiped his hands on a disintegrating paper napkin, reached in his shirt pocket and extracted a pack of Marlboros. He shook one out and lit it without asking Sally whether she minded. Ah, Wyoming.

"So Margaret Dunwoodie died rich and left a bundle to charity," he said.

"And I'm one of her charity cases. The Dunwoodie women's history chair is a special appointment in the college of arts and sciences," Sally continued. "The history faculty has absolutely no say in what we do with the very nice chunk of discretionary money that comes along with the salary and the title." She bet they were good and pissed off.

"Everybody knew Meg Dunwoodie came from Texas oil money somehow. But nobody figured she'd be worth millions." Dickie understated the point. The whole state had been dumbfounded at the alleged size of her estate, rumored to be twenty-five million dollars give or take a few million more. And she'd given a good fifteen million to charities—to the American Friends Service Committee, Planned Parenthood, the Wyoming Symphony Orchestra, the Nature Conservancy, and to the University of Wyoming. "And that Simon What's-his-name thing," Dickie added.

"Simon What's-his-name? Dickie, you'd think by now you'd know enough to get it right talking to a Jew about the guy who found Mengele."

Dickie shrugged; Sally went on. "Anyway, I told Edna, 'I bet Byron Bosworth and some of the guys in the history department will love this.' Edna thought that was pretty funny. But she admitted that there had been some, uh, negative feedback, as they say these days. In fact, the hiring committee had decided that since I was far and away their top candidate, they'd fly out to LA to talk to me."

"They were probably afraid that if they flew you to

Laramie, somebody would poison your T-bone," Dickie interjected. "So what did you say?" He mopped up blue cheese dressing with a bunch of fries.

"I knew it was fishy. I asked her how much money we were talking about," Sally returned in a reasonable tone of voice. Dickie waited. Sally was coy. "It was enough. Put it this way. On the way up here, I stopped in at John Elway Toyota down in Denver to have a look at the new Land Cruisers. They say you get a personally autographed football if you buy a car from him." Dickie was impressed. "I've also been wondering where I oughta take everyone in town who still considers me a friend out for a steak dinner to celebrate my great good fortune. What do you think—the Old Corral or the Cavalryman?"

Dickie tried to calculate what that meant, starting merely with the bar bill from the steak dinner, and decided it meant that she would be making more than enough to infuriate the average chronically underpaid Wyoming history professor. He'd taken his share of domestic disturbance calls involving faculty families, and usually the victim tried to explain that they'd just been having a loud family argument about money. How much worse that Sally Alder had once put herself through a master's program in history by singing songs like "Up Against the Wall, Redneck Mothers."

"So one week later, I met them in a suite at the Beverly Wilshire Hotel," Sally continued, dipping a ring in what was left of his salad dressing and crunching happily at the memory. "Edna was there. So was Egan Crain from the archives. Part of the Dunwoodie Center money is supposed to pay for them to acquire collections in American women's history. There was only one other person—this Denver lawyer, Ezra Sonnenschein, very cool dude in a very expensive suit, who is the executor of the Dunwoodie estate, and who said he was there on behalf of the Board of the Dunwoodie Foundation, whoever the hell they are.

"Anyhow, we chatted for a while, then they called

room service and ordered up drinks, then we went out to dinner at an incredibly expensive restaurant, and over a dessert that should have been in a museum somewhere they asked me if I wanted the job. Just like that."

The whole thing seemed pretty slippery to Dickie, who knew something of the extreme pettiness of academic politics. "So basically, you said okay, shower me with money and I'll come on back to Wyoming and not worry about anybody who ever saw me puke on my own shoes."

"I never puked on my shoes—that was you. And you puked on the cop's shoes. And he told you to drive on home," Sally retorted.

She sat back, watching Dickie smoke. She had hated cigarettes ever since quitting herself almost twenty years ago (all right, nineteen). Annoyingly, after nearly two decades of aerobic exercise, part-time vegetarianism, antioxidant supplements, and meticulous application of number 30 sunscreen, watching him suck smoke made her feel like bumming one. Really Wyoming.

"So did you take it, just like that?" Dickie asked, measuring her covertly.

"Not just like that. I thought it over for a couple of weeks. But then, I figured, this was probably the best college gig I'd ever be offered. I was sick of LA. I thought about who around there would miss me, really, and after ten years, decided there wasn't a soul in the whole city who couldn't live without me. LA's a lonesome town. I needed to get out."

Sally did not tell Dickie that she'd given herself a way back to LA. This unorthodox Dunwoodie bequest could easily end up in court, or in the toilet. She hadn't quit her old job, but instead had taken the classic academic back door, a year's unpaid leave from UCLA. She could get another year, if she needed it, to make up her mind. If, in the meantime, the University of Wyoming decided that it couldn't, in good conscience, continue to take the Dunwoodie money, she had a job to go back to.

"When I left here, I thought I'd had enough of places where everyone you know knows everyone else you know. But the more I thought about it lately, the more that seemed, I don't know, comforting."

"That wasn't how you felt when you lit out of here," Dickie reminded her.

"I wasn't looking for comfort then—I was just escaping." Sally'd made a career of escaping back then. "But now, sixteen years later, who's going to remember me?" She thought about that *Boomerang* headline he'd mentioned. "Well maybe some people will, but people *change,* don't they? Live and learn, forgive and forget, absence makes the heart—"

"Forget it," Dickie said. "If nobody else in this town remembers you, Bosworth and some of those happy people in the history department do. And of course Mary and I do, and Delice and Dwayne, and then there's Sam Branch—"

"Enough, Dick. I just got here. Give me at least an hour before I have to start worrying about who around here wants me tied up and whipped. You know, Dunwoodie must have had to deal with that every day of her life! She wasn't exactly Miss Congeniality, either."

"Have you read the poetry?" Dickie asked.

"Actually, I read it when it first came out. I thought it was, I don't know, raw and warm and plain and . . . "

"Troubling. Seductive," Dickie finished. "Terrifying. Furious. Hilarious. Surprisingly sexy. Seems like she knew everyday things we don't even suspect."

"Seems like," Sally agreed, dismembered phrases of Dunwoodie's work flitting in and out of her mind.

"I tell you one thing—she was one hell of a pissed-off woman." Dickie chuckled. The collection of poems had been titled *Rocks and Rage.* "But who would have predicted that some old maid would have such a feel for sin? Anyhow, it's probably all for the best that she didn't get famous until after she was dead," Dickie allowed, "because nobody around here had read the poems until they won the award." He ground out his cigarette in the round glass ashtray and grinned. "My particular favorite was 'Still Life of Fascists with Herefords.'"

Sally grinned back, going to work on her second beer. "Yeah, those poems weren't intended to be flattering. And the five million dollars she left UW has so many strings attached that she'll have the satisfaction of making life crazy for everybody around here for years to come."

Dickie snickered. "Well, you've got to figure, leaving her money the way she did, she meant to see one or two of 'em get their drawers in a wad."

Sally sipped her beer. "They're going to be even more ticked off when they hear what I'm supposed to be doing with my first year as Dunwoodie Professor."

"Which would be?" Dickie asked.

"While everyone else is punching the time card on the industrial teaching assembly line and trying to figure out how they'll retire on thirty K a year take-home, I'll be living for free in her beautiful house, going through her papers, writing her biography." Dickie looked amazed as Sally continued. "I just met with her lawyer in Denver to get the house keys and find out what I'm supposed to do. Nobody except her housekeeper—not even Egan Crain at the archives—has been allowed in the house. There are forty boxes of assorted stuff in there, full of God knows what. I have the whole year off from teaching to organize things, arrange publication for her stuff, do whatever other research I need to do, and figure out how to write her life story. I have the option of asking for another year of research and writing time if I need it.

"Some of the conditions are weird. I'm not supposed to talk about anything I've found out until Dunwoodie's work is safely in press and the biography is published. When I'm done with her papers, they're to be given to the archives, but until then, nobody, not even Egan Crain, gets a peek but me. And I had to promise to live in her house until I'm done!" Sally looked amused, and a little bit worried.

"That's fairly strange, don't you think—live in her house?" Dickie asked.

"Yeah, it's a little twisty, but it's a great deal. The place is supposed to be a museum of upper-class '20s and '30s taste in furniture and art, very deco, very elegant, very comfortable, very Carole Lombard. I could get used to a little luxury after the pest-hole I had in Westwood!"

"I can think of a number of people who would be real pleased to get into that house and have a look around," Dickie replied, a crease appearing between his eyebrows. He didn't find it necessary to tell her that since Margaret Dunwoodie's death, the sheriff's department had already collared three or four punks trying to break in and steal Dunwoodie's television set, or whatever. Dickie himself had heard the rumor that Dunwoodie had stashed a fortune in gold and jewels somewhere in Wyoming. It was a ridiculous rumor, of course, but it didn't have to be true to cause problems for Sally. It only had to be believed. "I'm going to have to keep an eye on you, and that house."

"You always did watch out for me." Sally smiled, grabbing his hand as it moved to his pocket to get another cigarette. "Even when you needed some looking out for, yourself. I wouldn't worry too much, though, Dick. Just think about it," she said, by way of changing the subject. She gave him a hard look. "It's a miracle either one of us is alive."

2

The Wranglers' Club

A sudden shriek disrupted the sentimental moment, as Delice Langham came barreling through the archway between the restaurant and the bar, clattering straight for Sally.

"De-*leeeeece*!" said Sally, leaping up. Then they were both hollering and hugging.

Delice was Dickie's sister. She'd hired Sally for her first Laramie gig. Dickie and Delice also had a brother named Dwayne, who had been working at the Axe Attack Guitar Shop the day Sally happened into Laramie back in 1977, needing picks and strings. Dwayne sold her three sets of strings and a dozen picks and asked her if she wanted a gig, and she figured, why not? He'd sent her to see Delice at the Wrangler. She'd walked in that cold and windy May afternoon, gotten out the Martin and sung three songs. Delice took her on, paying her twenty-five bucks a day for two weeks of happy hours in the cavernous dance hall. This was big money for somebody who had open-miked and Tuesday-nighted her way through two hard-luck years of the Bay Area music scene. Sally looked in the paper, found a cheap apartment on a month-to-month lease.

One afternoon when Sally was playing, Dickie had come in to talk to Delice. He told her he could get her a gig at Mudflaps for two consecutive Thursday through Saturday night solo shots: fifty bucks a night. Bliss among the orange plastic booths. The second Thursday, Dwayne and some of his reprobate musician friends had come by Mudflaps for various reasons of their own. That led to five years of hauling a pickup full of P.A. equipment all over Wyoming, Colorado, Montana, the Dakotas, and hell, following the music and the money around.

She'd gigged by herself and with partners and with bands that formed and re-formed under names like The LowDowns, Lost Cause, Saddlesore (no kidding), and her personal favorite, a short-lived western swing band she'd fronted with the amazing Penny Moss, the Sister Brothers. Through poor judgment, however, Sally'd mostly been hooked up with Sam Branch and Branchwater. Along the way, she'd written maybe two hundred songs, including possibly a dozen good ones. Including seven good songs about Hawk Green, but she didn't want to think about him just now. Hawk was a long way back in her Laramie past.

Over five years of raucous hard living, Sally and Delice had come to depend completely on each other. They'd formed a club, the Wranglers' Club, consisting of themselves and Dickie, conducting bleary meetings on Monday mornings over eggs and hash browns. Both women had managed to get into sticky situations and to fish each other out again, most of the time anyway.

Langhams had been running the Wrangler for more than fifty years, and Delice was the latest of the Langham women to take over Laramie's most revered combination greasy spoon and sleazy dance hall. It was a matter of pride with Delice that the food at the Wrangler had not improved in over five decades, although she admitted to a light twinge of guilt every time one of her regulars wound up in the Ivinson Memorial Hospital with a coronary episode. Delice was secretly negotiating to open up a

Nouvelle Southwestern Pacific Fusion Arugula place on Ivinson Street, which would be managed by cousin Burt Langham, who had run off from Cheyenne to San Francisco and returned with a degree from the California Culinary Institute and a slim, brilliant partner named Frank Walton, whom Burt affectionately insisted on calling John-Boy. John-Boy was a wizard with wasabi: he could probably figure out a way to put it on elk steaks and sell it in Laramie. Delice preferred not to have it known she'd ever heard of wasabi.

Delice looked pretty much the same, give or take the usual wrinkles. She was wearing her Levi's 501s tight, with a black T-shirt with the sleeves cut out and a little bit of tummy showing. Her jet-black hair (jetter than it had been in her youth, truth told) hung down to her ass, and she wore so much silver jewelry she jingled even while hugging.

"I knew it I knew it I knew it," she exclaimed, eyes closed, enveloping Sally in a shockingly familiar cloud of Chlöe perfume. "I told Dickie you'd be back today! I figure he picked you up speeding somewhere near the Holiday Inn." Sally and Dickie exchanged glances but said nothing. "And then I saw that Mustang with the California plates parked right out front and I thought, I am *always* right. I'd have been here sooner, but I had a Historical Society board meeting I couldn't walk out on."

Delice had always had a thing for Laramie's Endangered Architectural Heritage, beginning with the Wrangler itself, which she had managed to get on the National Register of Historic Buildings, roaches in the food preparation area and slime in the ice machine evidently being no barrier to historic preservation and its attendant tax breaks.

"Can I buy you a beer, Dee?" Sally asked, slapping her on the back and shoving her into a chair.

"Nah," said Delice. "I know the owner." Without asking, the waitress brought her a shot of Cuervo Gold and a

Budweiser. "Saving our precious past always gives me a thirst."

"So what *are* you saving these days, Delice? Ought to be about time you put the cement plant on the register— it's been puking out pollution more than twenty-five years now, hasn't it?" Sally thought historic preservation was an oxymoron and a real estate scam.

"Still a riot, Sally," Delice answered, mouth puckering as she licked her hand, shook salt on it, licked it again, took a hit off the Cuervo, took a bite out of a lime wedge, took a pull off the Bud. "But it takes fifty years. In a couple of years we could get Dickie nominated." Dickie appeared not particularly glad to hear this. "Actually, I bet you'll be delighted to know that we're hoping to put together a Register application for Margaret Dunwoodie's house!" Delice said the last as if she truly believed Sally would be thrilled and raring to help out, although why Sally should care one bit was anybody's guess. "What with all the attempted break-ins while it was empty, a bunch of us were getting ready to take turns sitting on the porch with a shotgun to discourage prowlers."

Historic preservers with shotguns? And what was all this about break-ins? Evidently this research project had some unanticipated complications, Sally decided. But after all, she'd spent ten years in LA, where every decent stereo she'd ever bought had been stolen within a month of the date of purchase. "Don't shoot anybody on my account," she said, setting doubt aside and putting an arm around Delice for a half-hug. "At least not until I've had the chance to give you a list of who I want dead."

"I could probably come up with a short list on my own," Delice remarked, and cackled until the clanging of her jewelry deafened three nearby tables full of customers. Dickie pulled at his earlobe as if he was trying to work something loose, and suddenly Delice remembered that her brother was there. Abruptly, she settled her arms on the table and her bracelets jangled to a halt. She looked a pointed, silent question at Dickie, who carefully acted as if he were still ignoring her. Sally was suspicious.

"You didn't tell her, did you?" Delice narrowed her eyes at the fidgeting Dickie.

"Tell her what?" Dickie asked, feigning an innocence so guilty it might have been endearing, had the hairs on Sally's neck not stood up in apprehension.

"You big lard-ass goat-sucking shithead," Delice yelled at Dickie, who was by now very busy shaking his Bic and trying to light a Marlboro. "You haven't *told* her."

"Told me what?" Sally asked, her voice rising and the three tables of customers now leaning over to hear. "What?! What haven't you told me, Dickie? Goddamn it, *what*?"

Delice threw down the last of the shot and looked straight at her, eyes shining with what might have been tears and might have been tequila shock. "You're back, and we are glad, darlin'," she said quietly, sitting very still. "But you're not the only one." Sally waited, going hot and cold and hot again, knowing what Delice was about to tell her. "You might as well hear it from me," she said. "Hawk's back, too."

Sally choked down the last swallow of Bud, muttered, "Who gives a damn anyway?" and explained that she was beat and had to go get settled in Meg Dunwoodie's house.

Delice just shook her head and said, "My my. Here we go again."

Dickie insisted on driving along behind her the nine blocks over to the Dunwoodie place, getting the suitcase out of her trunk, walking her to the door, stepping inside to look around as she turned the key in the lock and walked into the dim foyer. Margaret Dunwoodie's housekeeper, Maude Stark, had turned a few lights on. In fact, the house was subtly lit for nighttime welcoming. In the foyer, a black and gold lacquered 1920s deco table held a silk-shaded lamp and a crystal bowl full of fragrant sweet peas, reflected from behind by a matching lacquer-framed mirror. "Guess they're expecting you," Dickie said.

Sally noticed, for the first time, that he seemed to have his hand on his gun.

She thought about Delice's remark about break-ins. "Would it make you feel better to walk around and check the place out?" she asked him.

Doughboy Dickie, big and strong and serious, strangely quiet and graceful, drew his gun, stepped into the living room, glanced around, pushed through the swinging door into the kitchen, satisfied himself, and returned to where she stood, staring wanly at her reflection over the flowers. "I'm going to look over the rest of the house and check out the backyard. You go on out and get the rest of your stuff, then come back and stay here until I tell you it's okay for you to move."

"For Christ's sake, Dickie," she said, trying to sound brave but succumbing, suddenly, to the feeling that she'd never been so tired.

"I mean it, Sally. This house has been more or less empty for three years. Now you come tearin' in telling me it might be full of priceless manuscripts and deep dark secrets, not to mention more antiques than they've got in the Ivinson Museum. Shit happens, girl."

God knew it had happened to him. She would be stupid to resent him for being careful when she didn't know herself quite what all of this was about. Had she maybe heard something in the bushes when she went out to the car to get her guitar? She was too beat to tell.

Dickie walked out the back door, into the yard, but reentered through the front. He went through the whole house again, clomping up and down the stairs. He pulled out a business card, wrote his home phone number on the back, and handed it to her. "Call us in the morning. Call us anytime," he said, bending over to give her a gentle squeeze and a kiss on the cheek. "Mary will be dying to talk to you."

"You're the best, Dickie," Sally said, putting her arm around him, glad to feel his big, pear-shaped body.

He chose not to tell her that in looking around the backyard, he'd found a cat that had had its throat slit. "I mean it, Sally. This Dunwoodie thing is extremely cool for you." He tried a smile. "But even if Laramie doesn't have but four interstate exits, as you may recall, it does have its share of thieves, punks, shitheads, and pissed-off people."

Driving down Sheridan Street, away from the Dunwoodie house, Shane was feeling a little short of breath. It had been a long time since he'd harmed an animal. Slitting the cat's throat had made him temporarily sick and ashamed, but not sorry.

He'd nearly pissed in his pants when he saw the cop car driving up Sheridan, but when the patrol car failed to hang a U-turn and scream after him, his heart slowed down a little. He'd left a little calling card for the new bitch at the old bitch's house, and the thought that somebody, probably Sally Alder, would soon find the cat, cut through the shame and gave him a nice little rush.

He needed a bigger fucking rush. He had money. The afternoon of hanging around that day care center parking lot, waiting for some mother to leave her purse in the car while she went in to pick up her kid, had paid off. Maybe it wasn't exactly robbing banks, but shit, those women deserved it. Why weren't they home taking care of their kids anyhow? Fuck 'em. They'd only been good for seventy-three dollars, but that was enough for a buzz good enough to enjoy thinking through his possibilities.

Somehow, he'd get his chance at whatever there was in that house of old lady Dunwoodie's. Meanwhile, he'd wait. And watch.

3

Good Coffee

It took Sally's brain three tries to figure out waking up. Impressions shifted, shuffled around seeking some kind of jigsaw fit, and finally came to the astounding resting place of Meg Dunwoodie's cool and peaceful bedroom, Laramie, Wyoming.

The last thing she remembered seeing was the taillights of Dickie Langham's Albany County patrol car, shrinking off down Eleventh Street. She had a vague memory of dragging herself up the stairs. The housekeeper had turned on a lamp on a bedside table in the master bedroom. Sally walked toward the light, kicking off her Birkenstocks in the hallway, yanking her shirt over her head as she crossed the bedroom threshold, throwing the shirt into a corner. She sat down on the bed, hauled off her jeans and underpants in one move, unhooked her bra and tossed it on the floor. She turned down the covers, switched off the light, and slipped under a sea green satin coverlet between cool, fine, clean sheets. She was asleep in seconds, stone dreamless for hours.

Pearly pink light filtered in the windows on three sides of the spacious bedroom. She was pleasantly warm, her face cool in the chilly mountain morning air. She

stretched, rubbing her body against the soft sheets, and realized how much room there was in the carved mahogany
queen-size bed. Why would an angry spinster poet need a
queen-size bed?

She pushed disorder into sequence, willed thoughts in
line. She had learned to be good at thinking a thought
from one end to the other. She had woken up in this bed
because her new day job put her here, in Laramie: scene
of some of her most unforgiveable crimes. She had come
back in order to be paid excellent money to read and write
and talk and think. To do exactly what she was good at,
and happy doing. Dickie and Delice had welcomed her
gladly, but she didn't deserve gladness, welcome, gratitude, or, for that matter, forgiveness. She was a professional. She couldn't expect love, but she could demand
respect.

And the fact that Hawk Green might be five walking
minutes from where she lay was of no significance whatsoever.

Sally swung her legs out from under the covers. She
wiggled her toes, stretched her back, and decided she'd
better start out her new life in Wyoming by going for a
morning run. She was far from used to the altitude, and
figured she'd spend more time walking and gasping than
running, but at forty-five, she meant, when possible, to
follow the path of wisdom, health, and responsibility, even
if it was Laramie out there. She laughed. It occurred to her
that all twenty thousand roads had been paved with such
intentions.

Still, a run couldn't hurt. She brushed her teeth in Meg
Dunwoodie's gleaming bathroom, a palace of vintage
mirrors, crystal cabinet knobs, and tiny sea-green tiles.
Washed her face, put on her running tights and bra, and a
holy relic T-shirt from the Sleeping Lady Cafe in Fairfax,
California. Pulled on her socks and shoes and clipped on
her Walkman, flipped on the tape, and stepped out into the
crisp morning.

Her legs felt surprisingly good after four days in the car, and the first song on the cassette, taped off a broadcast of the hallowed KFAT radio in Gilroy, California, was the Grateful Dead's cheerfully fatalistic "Box of Rain." The tape was a wildly eclectic mishmash of stuff—from the Dead to Wanda Jackson, Leadbelly and Steve Earl and Spike Jones (way too much Spike Jones) and her own Van Morrison anthem, the one about the brown-eyed girl. Half an hour of unpredictable and uneven music later, she was rounding the Washington Park bandshell for the third time at her usual snail-paced jog, feeling a little light-headed but strong enough to damn well keep on running, soundtracking with Simon and Garfunkel (God, they sang good together).

She started back toward Meg's house, meandering through neighborhoods to look at everybody's flowers. Marigolds and zinnias, purple asters and shasta daisies, petunias and cosmos delighted her from front yard plots, windowboxes, hanging planters on front porches. So many people in the old neighborhoods south of the university gardened madly in the brief summer, with something of the same spirit Sally had heard in "Box of Rain." She knew that in dozens of backyards, somebody was tasting a gold morning and thinking about harvesting lettuce and string beans and way too many zucchinis. The first frost could come any time after Labor Day, maybe even before.

She passed Delice's house, near Fourteenth and Kearny, a brown brick with four gables and tidy dark red trim. Dickie, Delice, and Dwayne had been raised there. When Doreen Langham followed her husband to the grave, she willed it to her daughter, and Delice had lived there ever since. A handsome, lanky teenager and a slightly younger boy stood in front of a basketball hoop in the driveway, shooting free throws. She recognized them from the family Christmas card pictures Mary had sent every year, even when Dickie was on the run. Josh, the older one, was Dickie and Mary's boy. The younger had to be Josh's cousin, Delice's son from her short, spotty marriage to Walker Davis: Jerry Jeff Walker Davis. He was the image of his feckless long-gone father, but looked as if he might have more of a clue. She waved at the boys, then realized that they could have no idea who she was. Still, this was Laramie, not LA. They waved back, smiling uncertainly but smiling anyhow.

It still cracked her up that Delice had made good on their pledge to each other, that they would name their first-born children after their favorite singers. Jerry Jeff had been Delice's first and last, all that remained of a marriage Delice had described as an extended, sometimes pleasurable, often ludicrous mishap with mixed consequences. Sally remembered long, expensive phone calls from Laramie to California and back. Walker, who had lost what there was of his mind over Delice, had finally left his wife and moved into the house on Kearny. Jesus, he was handsome, a great big gray-eyed ranch boy with steer-roper's shoulders and a bull-rider's ass, but Sally had never regarded him as that big a prize. All summer long, he rodeoed around trying to shatter his pelvis in quest of a big belt buckle. How intelligent was that? He had reached the peak of his career potential driving a truck for the state highway department.

Sally knew the story. One winter morning when Jerry Jeff was five, Delice got a postcard from Houston, Texas, with a picture of the Baytown Ship Channel on the front ("Eighth Wonder of the World"). Walker was in Houston for the rodeo. On the back was a message in his tiny, childish handwriting, explaining that he'd fallen in love with a barrel racer from Belle Fourche, South Dakota. Wyoming was too cold. They were heading off to Florida to live in a trailer and work cattle for some sawgrass ranch operation: Did she know that Florida was the biggest beef-raising state in the US? He hoped he could eventually get on with a road crew there. He wouldn't ask for half of Delice's property if she wouldn't contest the divorce. In all those years he'd been married to her on the road amid the stock pens, this was the longest postcard he'd ever sent.

That night, Delice put on her felt-lined Sorel boots and her down-filled jacket and walked into the clear, frozen world. It was twenty below. The door handle on her truck was so brittle it broke off when she pulled it. She left Jerry Jeff with Mary, went into the men's bathroom at the Wrangler. She bought a pack of condoms from the dispensing machine, stopped to warm up with a cup of coffee and a shot of peppermint schnapps. Then she went out and got shit-faced at the Cowboy Bar, danced with a trucker to "Faded Love," and had a cramped, half-clad, freezing but relatively satisfying revenge fuck in the sleeping cab of his idling rig. She'd gone home, dialed California, and poured the whole story out to Sally before passing out and leaving her phone off the hook. The telephone bill was even worse than the hangover.

All this flashed through Sally's mind as she made the turn onto Eleventh Street and slowed to a walk coming up on the Dunwoodie place. The front yard was a testament to Meg's green thumb, rampant with every kind of flower. A big cottonwood tree presided over a small, lush grass lawn.

Sally hadn't bothered to lock the door. Undoubtedly that was stupid, given what Dickie had told her about attempted break-ins, but she'd never locked a door living in Laramie, and she really didn't want to start now. It was one of the things that was supposed to make it worth coming back. She reflected on her own attempt to keep the pledge with Delice. Since she'd never had kids, she'd been forced to settle for naming a dog George Jones. When she first moved to LA, she rationalized getting a puppy, not because she was suffering from loneliness so severe it verged on disabling, but because she lived alone and getting a dog was a security thing. Jones was a typical black lab, dumb and rambunctious but sweet and loyal, and about as much use against home-invading strangers as a Welcome Wagon full of Jaycees. He'd been hit by a car on Hilgard Avenue. Sally hadn't had so much as a tropical fish since.

Thirsty. Water. She threw open the screen, powered down the hall and into the kitchen, and ran straight into the formidable person of Maude Stark.

Margaret Dunwoodie had been tall, almost six feet. Even in advancing age she had been big enough to command notice, and respect. Maybe she had required a house-keeper who could look her in the eye. If so, Maude Stark filled the bill. She towered over Sally, who claimed to be five-foot-six (claimed), staring down at her mildly through eyes so pale they were almost transparent. Her steely hair was pulled back into a ponytail. She was a fit sixty-something woman wearing faded Levi's, worn Nikes, and a red T-shirt with a picture of Susan B. Anthony on it and the slogan FAILURE IS IMPOSSIBLE.

Sally had once owned the same T-shirt, along with a purple one with the slogan SISTERHOOD IS POWERFUL. There had been moments among feminists, over the years, when she had thought they could use T-shirts that said SISTERHOOD IS IMPOSSIBLE. Still, you kept on.

"You must be Sally," Maude said in a voice that was amazingly soft and friendly. "I saw you take off running just as I pulled up." Sally now recalled the new silver Chevy Suburban parked out at the end of Meg's front walk. "I took the liberty of making some of the coffee you brought—how about a cup? There's cream and sugar if you want it."

Sally looked skeptical. She had never in her life had a good cup of coffee in Wyoming; that was why she'd brought beans from Peet's and her own grinder. Even Dean Edna McCaffrey, the goddess of gourmet cooking, had had a Mr. Coffee that she filled with Folger's. The best thing about that Mr. Coffee was how it moaned when you turned it on, like somebody having the best sex they'd ever had in their life, right there in Edna's kitchen. But even though Sally had become finicky about coffee to the point that it was embarrassing, she didn't want to get off on the wrong foot with Maude.

"Great!" Sally said, smiling with what she hoped looked like gratitude. "Thanks." She poured in half-and-half (that might help) from a little china pitcher.

It was good. Damned good. Maude made good coffee. A sign from heaven.

"Meg got to where she couldn't live without Peet's coffee. A friend in the Bay Area used to send her five pounds at a time," Maude explained, blowing Sally's mind. A tea kettle whistled on the stove. Maude moved to pour boiling water over a Celestial Seasonings tea bag. "I myself gave up caffeine ten years ago—you know it's been linked to breast cancer." She *tsk*ed slightly. A sign from hell. "But I'm not one to tell people what they should or shouldn't do," she finished implausibly, taking tinfoil off a pan of fresh blueberry muffins. She dumped the muffins into a towel-lined basket, passed it and a china plate to Sally, and gestured at a pot of Tiptree's Summer Fruit preserves. If this was purgatory, make the most of it.

"Meg's lawyer, Ezra Sonnenschein, told me you live out in West Laramie," Sally said, biting into a still-warm muffin.

"Actually, it's a little west of West Laramie, out by Wood's Landing, off the grid," Maude told her proudly. "Solar panels, wind generator, and a greenhouse for heat exchange and, of course, for getting garden stuff going. Meg always got her seedlings from me," she explained, consuming two muffins in four bites without dropping a crumb. "I write a Sunday gardening column for the *Boomerang* and do a little consulting for the Albany County Agricultural Extension Service. I'll give you a tour of the back garden in a little while," she said, digging into another muffin, polishing it off, and wiping her hands daintily on a linen napkin. "I assume you'll be composting."

Sally was speechless. She broke her muffin in half and put some jam on it.

Maude saw that she'd need to jump-start the conversation. "So when do your things arrive?"

Relief: frittery life details. "They left LA last Monday, but since this is only a partial load they're making a couple of stops on the way. The moving company said they'd be here Tuesday," Sally told her, taking another swallow of wonderful coffee. "I don't have much. Some basic kitchen stuff. My furniture was sh—uh, secondhand junk, so I got rid of it all. It's mostly books. Aside from that, it's my other guitar, records and tapes, sh—uh, stuff like that." Sally really had to work on not cussing.

"I'll plan to be here to help you, if you want," Maude offered. "I've cleared out some bookshelves."

"That sounds fine," Sally said, smiling, "and I'd be glad to have you help me move things around up here, so I don't fu—er, mess the place up."

"You won't. You may have been liable to do that a few years ago," Maude told her wryly, letting on that she knew more about Sally than she saying, for the moment. "But you're a big girl now, in spite of that nasty mouth on you." She stood up. "I hope everything here is to your liking. Since the estate is paying me, I've tried to keep the house in the kind of shape Meg expected." She gave Sally a long, inspecting look. "I don't need the money, as you probably know."

Sally knew; Sonnenschein had told her that Margaret had left Maude a two-million-dollar trust fund and a sizeable annual sum. Maude was a hell of a lot richer than Sally was.

"I knew Margaret Dunwoodie, and kept house for her for nearly thirty years, and I'm not about to quit now, even if she is dead." Maude drank the rest of her tea standing up, moved to the sink to wash her cup and plate, and set the clean dishes in the rack. She turned back to Sally, fighting strong emotion. "Meg used to have me in three days a week—wouldn't cook a lick or wash a towel to save her life, spoiled brat," she muttered. "But you probably don't want me in your way while you work on her stuff. If it's okay with you, I'll come once a week, on Fridays, to do a thorough cleaning. The yard sprinklers are on timers, but I'll be around an hour or so three days a week this summer to keep up with the gardening, more when it needs it. I'll do whatever else in the way of cooking or cleaning you see fit. That's it."

"I appreciate it," Sally told her, liking her and meaning it but not quite knowing what else to say, and trying to keep from saying anything that might lead to further heedless cussing.

"That goes two ways," Maude offered graciously. She headed for the back door, then turned to say more. "Listen, Sally. I don't know how much you know about Meg, or her life, or how folks felt about her or how she felt about them. I don't know exactly what's in her files," she said, nodding her head in the direction of Margaret's locked office. "I haven't looked at them, because I wasn't asked to do so. When she died, they were all over the place. I just looked at the things she'd written on the folder tabs and put them in boxes. I didn't even read the loose papers—just stacked them up and boxed 'em. Dealing with that stuff is strictly up to you.

"But I do have an idea of some of the stories you're going to find in those boxes. I lived through them and heard more. It's not going to be easy." Maude looked sober, apprehensive. "Various people will see to it that it's just about as hard as it can be. Lots of people hated her. She was a liberal and a feminist, and they don't exactly win popularity contests around here. Byron Bosworth hated her guts for more than thirty years, and from what I hear some people have hated yours for almost twenty. When Bosworth found out she'd endowed a chair in *women's* history, and that his department didn't have anything to say about who would be hired for it or how much they'd be paid, he screamed his head off. He isn't about to give up on the idea that the money she gave the university ought to belong to him and his friends.

"Meg wasn't always, well, nice. And then there's her life, her *life*. Meg had an interesting life. Do you really know what that means? It's a Jewish curse to wish an interesting life on somebody."

Sally knew a version of this old saying, but didn't want to interrupt.

"Are you ready to try to understand the things she chose? Are you sure you have the imagination?" Maude caught herself in mid-tirade, and shook herself. "Sorry I got carried away. I don't even know you."

Sally remained silent, eating the delicious muffin, the delectable jam.

Maude apparently decided she'd raised enough heavy issues over a muffin and a cup of coffee. And she looked like she had plenty on her mind. "I don't really know what you're made of. But writing her life will be the most important thing you ever do with yours." She pulled a bandana out of her back pocket, wiped her eyes, squared her shoulders, worked up a smile. "I'll be in the back when you're ready," she said, walked into the mud room behind the kitchen, and stepped out the back door into sunlight and green.

4

Her First Visitor

Sally wanted to see the garden, of course, but she had not yet explored inside. She took her cup of coffee now, and walked toward the front of the house. One odd feature of Meg Dunwoodie's house was that the front door was off-center, practically in one corner, and now Sally saw why. The living room, huge, high-ceilinged, and stretching across most of the front, looked like something out of a Fred Astaire movie. Tall windows stretched almost wall-to-wall, hung with sheers and silk. Creamy wool carpet, soft low sofas, overstuffed chairs, gleaming coffee tables, built-in bar, ashtrays the size of your head. Debonair silver floor lamps with sleek silk shades. A huge fireplace, faced with polished, pink-flecked gray granite Sally recognized as the same rock that composed the formations up at Vedauwoo in the Laramie Range.

A lot of stuff, but not a trace of clutter. There was even a gigantic silver cigarette lighter, and a hinged silver book-shaped case full of ancient cigarettes, on one high-gloss black lacquered end table. A huge crystal vase of pink gladioli presided over the coffee table. She thought she caught a faint whiff of Joy perfume. She could imagine Ginger Rogers in a marabou-trimmed silk dressing gown and high-heeled slippers, tapping a cigarette on the table, leaning over as Fred snapped open the lighter for her, stretching back into a chair and saying, "So tell me about the show, Johnny."

It seemed impossible that anyone had lived like this in Laramie. It was assuredly not possible that Sally could live here. Imagine some snowy afternoon dumping her wet book bag on a silk chair, throwing her down coat on the sofa. Her apartment in LA had been something in the nature of an extended sleeping bag.

To the right of the front hall table, an arch into a narrow hall led to glossy wooden stairs carpeted with an oriental runner. She went up the stairs, noting that the ceiling in the second floor hallway had a pull-down door to an attic. On the left was a small spare bedroom and bath. She turned right into Margaret's study—functional, but still remarkably large and graceful. A French empire desk, and matching chair with a needlepoint seat, was set out from the wall, freestanding on a large, pale oriental rug, facing windows that framed the canopy of the cottonwood in front of the house. Once again, Maude had added a touch, fresh garden flowers in a Spode teapot. No filing cabinets. Double doors on the wall behind the desk held a walk-in closet. She tried the doors, knowing they would be locked—the lawyer Sonnenschein had said he'd send her a key. A sofa sleeper covered in figured silk. Over the couch was a grouping of four framed pen and ink drawings. They were exquisite renderings of hands in different positions on the keys of a piano, etched in black on white, then washed with streaks of vivid red and blue watercolor, signed by someone named Blum. The cabinets held books (including all three of Sally's!), a television, a modest stereo rig and records, mostly classical and jazz instrumentals. Lots of piano music. No piano in the house, though.

Meg's books were, of course, on the shelves, two thin, fine volumes from beautiful little presses, and of course the larger, slick-covered National Book Award collection, *Rocks and Rage*. She took it off the shelf. It fell open to one of Meg's minor poems, one Sally happened to like particularly, "Between Memory and Hope":

A trembling tussle between memory and hope.
Moment to moment, transposes:
Tender brush of an
    unsuspected key.

Quickens, jars,
Awakens, appalls,
One word whispered.
One flickering

Flash of the blade,
Brush of the key,
A shifting half-step
Transforms, plays out.

I was born of
an irresistible monster.
Bloody born alive,
Hope's poison in my veins,
Remembering the
    brush of the key.

Sally closed the book, turned to go back down the stairs. She was ready, now, to have a look at Meg's (and Maude's) garden, to listen to Maude describe, as she undoubtedly would, every plant variety, every weed and pest, the shapes of leaves, and where caterpillars hid in the crannies of the cauliflowers. And then she heard, for the first time, the sound of Margaret's door chime, a sound that made her feel as if the person ringing the bell expected someone a hell of a lot more gracious and stately and important to answer the door. She was sweat-soaked, disoriented, and noticed she'd spilled coffee on her T-shirt on the way up the stairs. But then she remembered that the real lady of the house had been dead for three years. Whoever was at the door had come to see Professor Sally Alder, sweaty spandex, coffee stains, and all.

Her heart gave a flop, but then she reminded herself that there was absolutely no reason in the world Hawk Green would come to see her. In fact, if he was even aware that she was coming back (was he? Had Delice or Dickie or Mary or anybody told him?) he was probably using his excellent brain to work out ways of not running into her, in a town of twenty-five thousand people where the numbered streets ran out at about Thirtieth.

Don't think about Hawk. Had he changed much? Had he gotten fat like Dickie, or would he still be tough and sinewy and rangy in the hips? Would he have wrinkled in nice crinkles around the eyes like Delice, or would he have furrows in his forehead and commas around his mouth, like Sally? Would he have that beautiful hair, long and thick and black, or had his hair begun to thin? How would he think she was looking? Oh God.

As she went downstairs, Sally eyed the big splotch of coffee on her T-shirt and missed a step and almost fell flat. Catching herself, she took a breath, opened the door, and peered through the storm door glass into the watery-eyed, chin-challenged face of Egan Crain.

"Sally, old girl," Egan chirped, brandishing a cellophane-wrapped bouquet of purple-dyed daisies straight from the Safeway. "Heard you'd been sighted at the Wrangler last night. Simply smashing to have you back!"

As long as she'd known him, which stretched back just about to the bicentennial, Egan Crain had used terms like "old girl" and "simply smashing." He'd still not managed to perfect a real British accent (which would have made it impossible for any American to understand a word he said) but he had apparently not given up working on his half-perfect impression of an English twit.

Egan had been born, educated, employed, and empowered in the state of Wyoming, but he came by his claim to Brithood semilegitimately. His great-grandfather had been an earl of some kind who had gone to Dubois to try his luck at ranching in the 1880s, and had managed to last through the terrible winter of 1886–87. Lord Crain had left his heirs a serious spread in the valley between the Absarokas and the Wind Rivers. Lady Crain, Egan's great-grandmother, had been a German girl with Hanover blood. Everyone remarked that Egan bore an unmistakable resemblance to his cousin, H.R.H. the Prince of Wales, and that the biggest problem with Egan was that he didn't realize that the resemblance was unfortunate.

Sally opened the storm door and stepped out on the porch, permitting Egan a stiff, near-miss hug. They had been graduate school gossip acquaintances rather than hugging buddies before, and Egan had always been good for the latest dirt. But he must figure that the Dunwoodie Center had brought their relationship to a new level.

"Thanks for the flowers, Egan," she said. "I'd invite you in, but I just got here last night and don't quite know what the house rules are yet."

"Quite all right, my dear," he twittered. "I mean, I think it's up to you, something about possession and nine-tenths of the law don't you know, but I wouldn't want you to go to any bother."

She stood staring at him a beat too long, then realized that it was probably a good idea not to antagonize him before she'd even figured out why she felt like doing it.

"Actually, I've just come by to welcome you on behalf of the archives, and to see if I mightn't steal you for a spot of lunch next Thursday. Give you time to settle in, then we can have a nice chat about those moldy old papers of Meg's," he told her.

"I hope to hell they're not moldy, Egan. The house seems tight enough." Careful, Sal. No need to be irritated.

"Just a manner of speaking, ducky. But I do so want to

talk to you about how to treat Meg's precious legacy. After all, you'll need some professional advice on how to make your way through the mess. I don't mean to speak ill of the dead, but Meg was never what you'd call a compulsive organizer. I hear that when they unlocked the door to her office in the English department after she died, the place was knee-deep in books, papers, half-dead aspidistras, and I don't know *what*! They say Maude Stark showed up and just started *throwing* things in boxes and carting them out. I can only begin to imagine what she's left us!" he finished with a heavy sigh, rolling his eyes skyward.

Sally took a deep breath, and found the sense to wonder why she was already feeling defensive on Meg's behalf, why it bugged the crap out of her to hear Egan refer to Dunwoodie as "Meg," and why Egan's offer to help shouldn't be seen as sensible and generous, even if self-serving. "I appreciate the offer, Egan, really I do." She even laid a hand on his arm, thinking she'd learned something about diplomacy after two decades in academia. She'd find a wall to kick soon. "And I'd love to have lunch Thursday. I really need any advice you can give me."

"Well, dearie, I do have one piece of early advice," said Egan. Sally hoped he wouldn't bring up the idea of moving the papers to a secure room in the archives. She really didn't want anybody else deciding when, where, and how she could get to the papers and do her work. Fortunately, Maude appeared from around the side of the house. She was carrying a basketful of perfectly shaped zucchinis, glowing carrots, slender green beans.

"Do you mind if I take a few veggies home, Sally? There's lots back there—I'll show you as soon as you have time. Oh, hello Egan—I didn't know you were here."

"Maude, ever the faithful retainer," Egan greeted her, automatically patronizing, but evidently uncomfortable. Egan was not blessed with great height. He had to crank his head back to look Maude in the eye, so he settled for looking in the direction of her neck. "I've just come by to

welcome our new Dunwoodie Professor on behalf of the
Archives, and to be on my merry way. Do take care of our
girl, won't you?"

"You can bet on it Egan. And she'll take good care of
Margaret's papers, I'm sure."

Maude made it a dismissal, and Egan hustled to leave.
He turned to Sally, saying, "I'll ring you about the details
for Thursday, old thing. Cheer-o."

Watching him walk down her—Dunwoodie's—front
walk, Sally remembered that she'd always thought Egan
walked as if he were trying to keep a cork from popping
out of some critical orifice. "Thanks for saving me,
Maude," she told the housekeeper, and meant it. Then she
said more, knowing she shouldn't and not knowing why
she couldn't seem to stop herself. Why trust Maude? "I realize I have to deal with him, but to tell you the truth, he's
always driven me bat-sh—uh, crazy."

"Think nothing of it," Maude said, "he drives me bat-
shit, too."

5

Katmandu Calling

Sally developed a provisional routine. Dawn came early. Through the east window of Meg's bedroom the sun came up and poured in just as the winsome young Joni Mitchell had imagined, so very long ago, on some butterscotch Chelsea morning.

Get the coffee going, return upstairs to shove on running gear, head to the bathroom to brush teeth. Slip on those Birkenstocks. Back down to the kitchen for coffee, and then out the back door. This great Laramie garden, in full late summerburst, made her forget she had a lot of work ahead, dissipated worry about angry academics and greedy burglars. She walked between the rows of beans, along the low pea fences and admired the high trellises of scarlet runner beans, festooned with red blossoms, dripping with dangling green pendants. Lettuces and spinaches, cool multicolor bouquets of cauliflowers, broccoli, and pale and purple kales. Heaped mounds bursting with huge flat leaves that shaded squashes.

Wyoming vegetable gardens had few pests. Pests weren't stupid. Why try to survive in a place this hard? Did horn worms, zucchini beetles, stinging caterpillars, and their brethren care more about a view, or were they practical enough to opt for a place where it wouldn't freeze eleven out of twelve months? Well, maybe they were stupid, but they wouldn't pick a place where they would die before laying their eggs. Sally liked a view, but she figured it took a big brain to care about whether you could see the mountains from town. Big brain, yeah, but not necessarily a smart animal.

She carried a knife, a huge canning kettle, her coffee cup. Walking among the rows, she cut this, chopped that, pinched the other, drank coffee. She walked back to the house with the big pot piled full of vegetables. She shed the Birkenstocks at the back door and left the heavy kettle on the kitchen table.

Now she put on her socks and shoes, her Walkman, and headed out running. Then it was weird KFAT music, more coffee, a day of reading over the stuff she'd gotten from the Dunwoodie Foundation, browsing Meg's books, picking idly at her guitar, eating Maude's vegetables, pouring a Jim Beam to watch the sunset. For three days it went like this, but on the fourth, Monday, something changed when she returned from her run.

The phone rang.

"Katmandu calling," said a voice.

Less than twenty-four hours after last spring's graduation, Dean Edna McCaffrey and her second husband had been on a one-stop flight from Denver to New York, the first leg of the marathon air trek to Nepal, via London, Istanbul, and New Delhi. After spending three months as a working guest of disciples of the Dalai Lama, she and Tom had returned late at night, conked out, and woken to discover a dead lawn, a houseful of shriveled ferns and a nightmarish parade of answering machine messages. Some messages were welcome: "Hi, Edna. This is Sally. I'm here, ready to have a beverage and talk about Dunwoodie chairs and whatever. Your place or mine?" This made Edna smile.

The next message, which touched on something like

the same subject, was substantially *less* welcome. "Hello, Edna. This is Byron Bosworth. We need to talk about the History Department's role in administering the Dunwoodie bequest. The department has met to discuss this matter, and I've sent a memo outlining our funding needs for the year to your office. I've had your secretary set up a meeting for Wednesday afternoon before school starts." Click. Far be it for the Boz to waste words on the likes of Edna. Edna smiled at this one, too, but it wasn't a very nice smile.

Eighteen years ago, Byron Bosworth had told Edna's then-husband that he thought there was "no room for faculty wives in a university that has real standards." It was a shame that the anthropology department had seen fit to hire Edna as a part-time adjunct instructor. Edna nevertheless instructed along for another year, publishing articles and writing grant proposals, then accepted a two-year appointment at the Institute for Advanced Study at Princeton. Her children went with her to New Jersey, while her husband remained in Laramie. They pretended the separation was only temporary.

At Princeton, Edna had worked closely with Rodney Wertz, the king of cultural anthropology. Her own field work had taken her all over Asia and later to Los Angeles, and it seemed to her that every time she tried to imagine pristine "natives" who inhabited "homelands," she met a Trobriand Islander wearing a ZZ Top T-shirt. People didn't stay put, she surmised. This stunning observation had led to three prize-winning books on refugees, exiles, expatriates, and diasporas, and had eventually won her a MacArthur Foundation genius grant. Byron Bosworth probably thought she got his MacArthur.

During her time in New Jersey, her husband had taken up with a University of Wyoming cheerleader. It was a rotten divorce. But when she finally got tenure in the anthropology department, she did as she damn well pleased. There was plenty of oil money in the state then, money enough, even, to fund a fledgling women's studies program. A small, merry band of feminists kept a lot of balls in the air, year to year.

She became a community builder. Edna was an avid concertgoer and patron of the arts, a member of every commission and task force in the state. And she was known to her lucky friends as the best and most creative cook in Wyoming (what, they asked, was the competition?). Her dinner party invitations were treasured. Her kids went to Laramie High, and Edna ended up falling in love with and marrying her daughter's green-eyed American literature teacher, Tom Youngblood.

Friends from Cambridge and Berkeley and Palo Alto had come to visit during the occasional summers Edna remained in Laramie, and wondered why she didn't move someplace civilized. They didn't realize that despite her warmth, wit, and graciousness, despite her good-looking new husband and MacArthur cash in mutual funds and all the good things that had happened in her life, Edna Mc-Caffrey still lived with the bitter urge for revenge. One big reason she had stayed at the University of Wyoming, turning down much better jobs in much more prestigious places, was that she planned someday to have enough power to really stick it to the bastards who'd messed with her all those years ago.

So Byron Bosworth and the boys had "needs"? Edna grinned nastily. She and the Boz would hold a fake-cordial conversation on the matter. Like the best administrators, Edna specialized in appearing sweetly reassuring while being as insulting as she chose, and filing all information for future use.

She went into the kitchen to look up Margaret Dunwoodie's number in the Laramie phone book, a volume smaller and slimmer than Edna's daily planner. She wanted to call to invite Sally Alder to lunch at El Conquistador and to a little dinner party on Saturday night. Sally and Edna had become friends years ago when both had needed the solidarity of sisterhood and the solace of a good laugh. But Sally was also, at this point, a highly expensive property that could be an asset, or a definite liability. She could be—had been—a bit of a loose cannon.

It had not been entirely Edna's idea to recruit Sally Alder for the Dunwoodie Chair; in fact, by the time the Foundation and the University had decided to move on the bequest and had brought Edna into the process, Sally was already the clear first choice for the job. Sally was a fine scholar, but there hadn't been the slightest effort to do an open search. And it wasn't just that there might be equally qualified candidates. Back in the days she'd lived in Laramie, before starting school, Sally Alder had been best known as a hard-living bar singer. Who wanted her? Really, why?

The Foundation was secretive. (And who was the Foundation anyhow? There were rumors, of course. Only the lawyer, Sonnenschein, seemed to know.) The president's office was unusually discreet. Edna had done considerable digging and run up against one stone wall after another. Failing to find out anything useful, Edna had decided, in her sensible fashion, not to sweat the details. It would be fun to hang out with Sally again, and to revel in the certainty that the return of Mustang Sally Alder, on a tidal wave of Equality State bullshit and Dunwoodie money, would infuriate precisely those benighted fools who would be powerless to stop it.

Tom came into the kitchen, kissed Edna on the back of the neck, poured her a cup of the fancy coffee he insisted on drinking. She would have been satisfied with Folger's, and she rather missed the suggestive moaning of her grungy old Mr. Coffee, but Tom was picky about coffee. She took a sip and her jet lag rolled back like a Bay Area fog at noon. She punched in Dunwoodie's (now Sally's) number. Sally answered on the third ring.

6

The Best Restaurant in Wyoming

As Sally recalled, Hawk and his friends had developed a
scale for rating Wyoming restaurants, based on how sick
they made you. One star for a visit to the hospital, two for
a week on Pepto-Bismol, three for a sleepless night, four
if eating there hadn't made you sick lately. A five-star
Wyoming restaurant had not made you sick at all, to the
best of your recollection. Delice had not found this particular example of wit at all amusing. And Hawk had never
even told her how he rated the Wrangler (two stars, based
on an unhappy encounter with an improperly handled
chicken-fried steak.) Hawk and Sally used to say that the
best restaurant in Wyoming was in Colorado.

But they all knew that the best restaurant in Wyoming
was, in fact, El Conquistador, the unpretentious Mexican
place down on Ivinson Street. It was still there, sixteen
years after Sally had savored her last chile relleno and
chicken taco lunch combo. Like the Wrangler, the food
hadn't changed, but in this case, that was heartwarming.

When Sally walked in to meet her for lunch on
Wednesday, Edna McCaffrey was already there, sitting at
a corner table with a menu, a yellow plastic water glass,

and a basket of chips with scorching hot sauce. Sally was wearing Levi's and a T-shirt and her Birkenstocks. Edna was wearing a costly cherry red silk suit with a tight short skirt and black pumps that showed off her endless legs. Sally knew that if she had tried to eat chips and salsa in such an outfit, she would glop grease and tomatoes all over the silk jacket.

Another hugging scene, this one a pleasure. Edna and Sally had been in the women's studies trenches together during the two years Sally had been a graduate student at UW. Sally imagined the two of them as Union generals who hadn't seen each other since the Mexican War, bent over a much-unfolded map fraying at the creases, plotting out a near-final assault on the tattered Confederate Army.

From Edna's point of view, it was fairly simple. Edna was in charge of an endowed chair, and Sally sat in it. Edna didn't much care for some aspects of the arrangement, like the stipulation that Sally and the papers stayed in the Dunwoodie house. People had tried to break in. That was disturbing. The shadowy Dunwoodie Foundation attached strings to the money. That could cause difficulties. But Edna was willing to play. If anybody wanted to bitch about the way the money was offered and spent, they could deal with that later. Sally could be a problem or she could be a solution, and both of them had reason to see to it that she was not a problem.

Sally Alder had once been a loudmouthed feminist graduate student with undeniable talent and an attitude that terminally ticked off half the men in Wyoming. Edna liked that in a woman, as long as the woman was honest, intelligent, and funny. Sally was, and she appeared to have mellowed in useful ways. She had written three good books, plenty of scholarly articles, had a national reputation in women's history. Now, the two of them would memorialize a brilliant Wyoming woman writer, would make a place for women's history at UW, would have some great dinners, laugh a lot, get in some skiing. The Boz types would hate it, and that was fine. Edna ordered beef flautas and a Dos Equis.

From Sally's point of view, many puzzles remained. She had read the too brief, intriguing biography Margaret Dunwoodie had prepared for public distribution shortly before her death. Sally was mulling over what she'd read. She would soon go down into the basement and into the locked office closet and wade through the boxes in Meg's house, to touch more remnants of this perplexing and deceptively well-documented life. She would help the foundation to spend money, would write and read and speak as she had for twenty years. Eventually, she would either teach courses on women's history at the University of Wyoming, or she would return to Los Angeles. There were advantages and disadvantages to either plan. At UW, the people who claimed to be in charge of explaining the past didn't believe that history had women in it. UCLA was in LA.

Hawk Green was in Laramie.

Don't think about Hawk.

Sally sat down at the table, reached into her daypack and pulled out four glowing trophy zucchinis, gifts for Edna's kitchen. Edna exclaimed over the squashes (something about ratatouille) and swept them into a large black suede tote bag. Sally ordered a relleno and a chicken taco and a Dos Equis. "Tell me what you know about Margaret Dunwoodie," she said to Edna, "and then tell me what bodies need burying."

The bones of the story were familiar to Sally from the Foundation biography, which Edna had of course read. But Edna had her own version. In the first years Edna had been at UW, she was a young feminist ethnographer who was sure every woman had an important story to tell. It had occurred to Edna that *somebody* ought to do an oral history with Professor Dunwoodie. Meg was willing to be interviewed; she wasn't famous then, though she had published some poetry in little magazines, even one poem in *The New Yorker*. And so Edna had gone to Meg Dunwoodie's house one coppery October Saturday morning in 1976, battery-operated tape recorder in hand.

Now she handed Sally copies of the interview transcript and tapes, saying, "Peruse at your convenience. Maybe they'll help you navigate your way through the papers—Meg was notoriously disorganized, and the word has it Maude Stark just threw things in boxes and shoved them in a closet."

"Maude gave me a slightly less frantic version of the same story." Everybody seemed to be an expert on the job Sally was about to do. Actually, everybody she'd talked to since she'd arrived knew more about it than she did, and she reminded herself once again that it was better to listen than to bristle. "Thanks a million—I can't wait to hear the tape. If I could have picked anybody in the world to interview somebody I want to write about, it would be you." Edna had an international reputation as a careful and gifted interviewer, a person who knew how to establish rapport, who always managed to ask the right questions.

"Meg Dunwoodie was a magnetic woman, Sal, even in old age. She was so tall, with those blues eyes that could look right through you. And she had this, oh, old-fashioned kind of graciousness—offered me terrific coffee and apple cake Maude must have baked.

"Of course she was gracious like a calculator. When she answered my questions, she seemed so wide-open and direct that I almost didn't notice that she wasn't telling me much I couldn't get from reading the entry for her in *Who's Who in the United States*. She gave me more elegant renditions of the same information, of course." Edna dipped and ate another chip, immaculately. Sally had salsa spots all over her Hot Rize T-shirt. "But as I thought about it, it felt like she was a master at *seeming* to reveal, while actually concealing all kinds of interesting and troubling stuff."

Their delicious lunches came, with iced tea. Sally spooned a little of the torrid salsa into her taco, took a bite and blessed her own senses. "Look, Ed, I know I need to figure out ways to do some public talks to keep the trustees and the president and the Foundation happy. But I'm not real sure how much I'll be able to talk about the project. I don't want to do anything that violates the terms of the bequest, and to tell you the truth, I think maintaining deep, dark secrecy, then telling all is one of those great book-marketing strategies I've never quite been able to cash in on. I don't mind telling people I can't discuss work in progress."

Edna tried to bury her disappointment. She had, reasonably enough, seen the Meg Dunwoodie project as a collaboration. She also suppressed her surprise at the fact that Sally could be so deliberate about strategy. The Sally Alder she'd known had been damned smart, but spontaneous to a fault. It wasn't just a question of going for the short-term pleasure over the long-term gain. Sally had seemed incapable of calculating her interests, period.

But Edna was a patient woman, and she knew that Sally, in the end, was not a discreet one. Eventually what Sally knew would come bursting out in a cathartic confession, and Edna was a logical person for her to confide in. "Yeah, you've got to play this one conservative," Edna agreed. "You might as well do this right and make some money while you're at it." Edna took the last swig of beer, reached for her iced tea. "But I don't think you'll have to cook up a mood of mystery." She savored another bite, thinking about how to give Sally some rather strange information. "There have been rumors around here ever since Meg died about her hiding some kind of treasure somewhere."

Sally almost choked on her fire-breathing relleno. She took a drink of water, fanned her face, and said, "What?!"

"The way I heard it," Edna explained, deftly catching a glob of guacamole before it could fall off her flauta and into her lap, "it had to do with her father, old Mac Dunwoodie, who got pretty paranoid at the end of his life. He had some money, of course, and the story is that he cashed in his securities, traded them for gold coins. Supposedly buried a fortune in Krugerrands somewhere, or she did. I wouldn't be surprised if all kinds of people around here have the idea that there's a treasure map somewhere in those boxes. Or maybe just a big trunkful of gold, stuck away in her basement or something. There've been some attempted break-ins. The police have been keeping close tabs on the house."

"I've heard about the break-ins," Sally said, "but I've assumed they were the typical thing—nobody home and plenty of stuff to steal. What's this treasure business?"

"Ask your friend Deputy Langham. I wouldn't be surprised if Byron Bosworth showed up there in a ski mask and a black turtleneck. That self-righteous prick probably thinks he's entitled to burglarize her house. He's put me on notice that he expects the history department to have some 'role' in disbursing the bequest. One or the other of us will be in hell first," she said softly.

"Boz? He's too chickenshit." Ludicrous. Still, the scene seemed at that moment uncomfortably plausible, no matter how ridiculous. Sally considered another beer and decided against it, sipping her own iced tea.

Why the hell hadn't Dickie mentioned a treasure, she wondered. She was less panic-stricken than pissed. No, that wasn't it. She was strangely exhilarated. Imagine having to move from LA to Laramie to get a thrill. She ate another chip, drank some more tea. "Well, I guess I need to look on the bright side. I mean, being a historian isn't usually all that exciting—hanging around in silent rooms, waiting for the dead to speak and all that. At least this will add a little spice to my pathetic, barren life."

Thinking about Los Angeles, Sally decided, put the

whole thing in perspective. "I guess you have to expect that people are going to try to get into a vacant house—especially one that was owned by a person who died rich. I mean, in LA, if I went away for the weekend, I'd always end up having to pay some student a hundred bucks to sit around watching my TV, just so nobody would steal it. I seriously doubt anybody in this town would actually bust in when I'm there, and Maude will be around and she's terrifying enough, God knows."

Edna laughed and polished off the last morsel of her flautas. "The important thing is to fulfill the terms of the bequest, get the book out, use the money, and defeat the cretins. And most of all, to have fun. I've got to go to a meeting with the Cretin King," she said, rising gracefully, shedding not a single crumb. They hugged again. "Thanks for the squash. We'll see you Saturday night at seven. Bring wine—whatever you can find around here."

Sally thought that was pretty funny.

Edna spoke once more, softly. "Lock your doors, Sal," she said, "and watch your back."

7

The Multiple Listing Service

At forty-five, Josiah Hawkins Green had never owned a house. He owned a number of mining claims, controlling interest in a working mine, and had even invested, unwisely, in several unproductive oil wells. But never a house. He'd always picked his dwellings based on convenience and cost. He had never wanted to get tied down. He'd lived a lot in trailers and motels with kitchenettes, in damp rented basements and leaky cabins. He'd lived out of a frame pack and spent months in a tent, slept in his truck for weeks at a time, eating at Denny's. It could get fairly disgusting, but it hadn't much mattered to him.

Now here he was on a fine August morning, waiting to be picked up by a Realtor named Sheila Czerny. She was the cousin of the geology department chairman's wife, and they'd asked him if he wanted to talk to someone who could help him find a house. He hadn't said no; he hadn't said anything; he'd just let them do what they wanted. So Sheila Czerny, his chairman's cousin-in-law, had called him at the Holiday Inn, made an appointment to show him some houses, had told him on the phone to look for a red Jeep Cherokee. In any town bigger than Laramie, that woman would have been cruising for a carjacking. Hawk had read in the Arizona *Daily Star* not three weeks ago that red Cherokees were the most popular vehicle among the nation's car thieves.

Sheila Czerny pulled her Cherokee up in front of the Holiday Inn office. Hawk was standing there, a tall, bony man with big shoulders, a ponytail, and round, wire-rimmed glasses, wearing jeans, a faded black twill shirt, and scuffed cowboy boots, carrying a clipboard.

"Oh, Dr. Green, Dr. Green!" Sheila hollered, waving gaily.

Hawk sized her up as a typically calculating Realtor. He noted a quick look of surprise on her face: No one had told her about the ponytail. But then, Hawk had influential friends in Laramie. Dwayne Langham down at the Centennial Bank had prequalified him for the loan. If the check for her commission didn't bounce, Hawk knew that Sheila Czerny wouldn't care if he had a mohawk. He folded himself into the front passenger seat, gave her a small smile, and told her he hoped to find a house by noon, and to close the deal as soon as possible. The Realtor wouldn't mind. The less time she wasted on each client, the more she made for every hour of work. He knew he looked impatient to the point of desperation. Yahoo for her.

"Have you owned a home before, Dr. Green?" she chirped, patting his hand with her own plump fingers.

Hawk shrugged and stifled a recoil. He didn't like having his hand patted and he hated it when people referred to houses as "homes."

She ignored him, lumbered on. "Well, what we do is every week we get a printout of homes on the market in your price range from the multiple listing service of the Wyoming state real estate board. Now I know you're looking for something in the tree district near the university, but I want to start out by showing you some of the *real bargains* just a wee bit farther out, where you get so much more square footage for the money!" She was heading east on Grand, out of the trees and into the tracts.

Hawk forced himself to speak. "Mrs. Czerny, I don't really need a big house, living by myself."

"Well, just wait until you see a few places, and then you can decide," she told him firmly. "I've selected a nice range of homes to give you some choices. Don't hesitate to ask if you have any questions about financing, or inspections or any of that stuff. After all, that's what you're paying me the big bucks for, ho ho!"

Hawk said nothing.

The first place was one of those plywood and plastic houses erupting like boils every year in the outer reaches of every western city. It had four bedrooms the size of packing crates. The window frames were vinyl-coated aluminum. The mauve carpet smelled like every dog and cat in Laramie had peed on it, and then some idiot had come in and sprayed it with a firehose. "Now don't think of this place as it is now, picture it with your own things in it," advised Sheila Czerny. Five minutes and they were gone.

The second place, way the hell out in West Laramie next to a gas station, was dark as a tomb and freezing cold even in August. Every room was painted a different muddy color. "Visualize!" she exclaimed. Hawk visualized that the hot water heater was in the garage. He'd lived in a similar house one winter long ago, and woken up one morning with his undershirt frozen to a glacier that had crept down the wall overnight. Five more minutes.

Hawk was openly unimpressed with the bargains she'd presented him. Now she'd give him what he wanted, but at a slightly higher price. He could almost hear the noise in Sheila Czerny's head, the sound of the cash register: *ch-ching*. "Well, I do have one place here," she said, peering at the printout from the M.L.S., "that's only about four blocks from the U, right on Eighth Street. It's small, though, and pretty pricey for the square footage."

Who used words like "footage" besides Realtors? But it was time Hawk bought a house, took advantage of the tax laws and put some of his savings into a place to live. He'd be out in the field a lot anyway. "Okay," Hawk said, gritting his teeth and hoping wildly that he wouldn't be stuck in a Jeep Cherokee with a Realtor for the rest of his life. It had been less than an hour, hellish.

He knew from the moment he saw it. It was a small white frame house with a big window in front.

Sheila Czerny unlocked the lockbox, opened the door, sniffed. "The owners did some remodeling recently," she said, "so they want more than they should, given the square footage."

It smelled like varnish and fresh paint. The floors, recently and brightly refinished, were blond oak, the walls were white. The living room was washed in morning sun, with floor to ceiling built-in bookshelves. The bedroom had windows on two sides, with a view of the Snowy Range to the west. The sun streamed in large, new, wood frame, double-paned windows. The bathroom had real tile in it. He could throw down a sleeping bag anywhere in this clean, well-insulated house. Hell, he could get a bed. He might even buy a chair and a TV.

"I'll take it," said Hawk, standing in the bathroom, looking at a big tub with whirlpool jets. "Offer them the asking price."

"Oh, I just *knew* this cute little place would be *perfect*, Dr. Green," Sheila gushed, dollar signs lighting in her eyes, tabulating her commission for forty-five minutes' work. Just then, the front door opened, and the next thing Hawk knew, he was face to face over a toilet with an already chattering Natalie Charlay Langham.

"Why, Sheila honey, I knew you had an appointment to show this house, but nobody told me you were showing it to my dear old friend Hawk Green," she squealed, throwing her arms around Hawk, who found himself grateful for the toilet between them. He'd known Nattie twenty years back, but "dear old friend" was a stretch. "You're lucking out here, Hawk. I've only had this adorable place listed a week, and I'm expecting two offers to come in by Friday."

She handed him a business card that claimed she was a "board-certified Realtor" working, Jesus, for Branch Homes on the Range. He really hated to think of that son of a bitch Sam Branch getting any of his money.

Nattie caught the grimace of surprise and distaste he shot at the card. "Oh, you must not have noticed our sign in front—Sam's very big in Laramie real estate these days—residential, commercial, why he's even started getting into new developments! Remember that place everyone used to go up to to watch sunsets on Ninth Street Canyon? Well, Sam's just about closed a deal for a gated community of over fifty mid-priced homes!" Hawk looked faintly sick.

Sheila Czerny seemed confused. She said, "So you all know each other? How sweet! Did you used to live in Laramie, Dr. Green?"

"Well, actually, I've lived mostly on the road," Hawk began, but Nattie interrupted.

"Oh now, Hawk, you did too hang out here, on and off, for years. Sheila, he was part of the Gallery Bar gang, in the wild old days before everyone settled down and got serious about making money. Hawk, you should see the house me and Dwayne built, up in Alta Vista? We had it designed by the same guy that did the Gem City Bone and Joint Clinic, you know, all primitive granite and rough-hewn pine, very natural. Five thousand square feet. 'Course, I don't suppose college professors ever actually get *rich,* do they, Hawk?"

No, they didn't. Hawk didn't answer.

"Unless of course," Nattie said slyly, "they cut some kind of inside deal for one of those endowed chairs, huh,

Hawk? Who do you think old Sally had to pork to get *that* gig?"

Hawk simply stared, imagining her head exploding. Perhaps sensing the tension, Sheila Czerny discreetly went into the kitchen, mentioning something about seeing whether the hot and cold water faucets in the sink worked.

Nattie herself looked considerably richer than she had back in the days when she'd sex-baited and guilt-tripped customers into leaving folding money on the bar at the Gallery. She wore about six gold chains with ugly charms dangling off them, diamond earrings the size of green peas, a shockingly noticeable gold watch, and enough orange lipstick to spray-paint a baseball bat. Hawk remembered her saying that she liked to put henna on her hair because it made it, ooh, so shiny. Today she looked to Hawk as if she'd been soaking her head in a bucket of mercurochrome.

He remembered the night he'd first met Nattie. He'd been prospecting for uranium, working a crew out of Saratoga that summer. They had come over to Laramie one Saturday, as one guy delicately put it, "to eat some meat and get laid, or at least meet some women." They had a good steak dinner at the Cavalryman, and walked around downtown until they heard music coming out of the packed Gallery. They'd waded through the crowd to the bar, ordered beers and shots of Beam while looking straight down the low-cut shred of a tank top on the bartender, Nattie Charlay. Inside of five minutes, one of Hawk's friends was asking her for her phone number, and she was telling the guy that if he stuck around long enough that night, she'd show him the whole phone.

The band was the Sister Brothers. Hawk said he thought they were good, and Nattie had said, "Yeah, if you like lesbos." Hawk watched Sally Alder and hoped to hell Nattie was a liar as well as a gossip.

During the break, Hawk told Nattie to buy the band a round. Sally came up to the bar to get another tequila and grapefruit, talking to seven people at once. He hadn't had the nerve to do then what he felt like doing, which was putting both of his hands on both of Sally Alder's hips to see if they felt as good as they looked.

They hung on through three sets to close the bar down. Sally and Penny sang and played, Hawk drank, shot a little pool. Biding his time, he went back to the Cowboy Motel, assuring himself that there would be plenty of time later to see about this Sally Alder. In that, at least, he'd been right.

Her hips did feel as good as they looked. So did various other parts of her.

He shook off the memory and regretted the present, vise grip over-toilet hug. The year before he'd left Laramie, Nattie Charlay had gotten her hooks into Dwayne Langham. Their marriage had, miraculously, lasted. Hawk looked at her enormous wedding ring, did a little calculation based on what he knew from his own experience with diamonds, and thought of what his father would say about it. Crawford Green, who was in many ways a worthless piece of work but who assuredly knew diamonds, would have judged Nattie's big ugly stones as proof that "not all the rich were smart." Crawford was proof that not all the poor were dumb. Poor Crawford. But at least he had Maria. Poor Dwayne.

Now her purse was ringing. Nattie rooted in the depths of her gold-trimmed white leather bag and extracted a cellphone. (Why the hell would anyone in Laramie need a cellphone? You could be face-to-face with anybody in town in under ten minutes.) She flipped it open, tapped a button with a long orange fingernail, and spoke. "Oh hi, Sam," she cooed, listening for a moment. "Why, you'll never guess who wants to buy that little bitty bungalow on Eighth Street. . . . C'mon, guess. . . . C'mon . . . all right, Sam . . . remember, it's money in the bank . . . okay, okay, the guy who's writing the check is old Hawk Green!" She listened a moment, then turned to Hawk and smirked at him. "Sam says he didn't know you were the bungalow type. And he hopes your check is good."

Sheila Czerny took Hawk back to her office on Grand Avenue, made him fill out about sixty pieces of paper, and dropped him back off at the Holiday. She said she'd phone Nattie with a formal offer that afternoon and start in hounding Dwayne Langham for a closing date. He'd already prequalified for the loan and this was Laramie, so it wouldn't take as long as it would in, well, cities. Hawk kept trying to impress upon her that he wanted to move in as soon as possible, and that, since the place was empty, he would be willing to rent until the sale was final. He'd lived in plenty of Holiday Inns and worse, but he'd just as soon get settled as close to the beginning of the school term as possible. His father, Crawford, and stepmother, Maria, were storing several dozen boxes of books, papers, rocks, and tools in a Tuff Shed behind their trailer outside Tucson, and he wanted his stuff shipped up early in the fall semester. Hawk imagined unpacking about five hundred black widow spiders amid his notebooks.

By the time he got back to the Holiday, it was only eleven-thirty in the morning. He ran up to his room, took off his jeans and shirt and boots, put on sweat shorts and a Tucson Toros T-shirt and a pair of high-top Chuck Taylors. He pulled the coated elastic band out of his hair, regathered and tied his ponytail tighter, stuck his room key in the pocket of his shorts. He stuffed his wallet, some clean clothes, and a bar of soap in a Ziploc bag into a daypack and ran out the door. Fifteen minutes later he was at the university gym, looking for a noontime pick-up basketball game.

As long as he'd hung around Laramie, there had been men of various ages milling around on the basketball courts, dribbling, shooting, lackadaisically checking each other out. Acting as if they weren't paying any attention, they formed into teams, half-court today, three-on-three.

Hawk played on a team with a short, blocky, muscle-bound black guy who looked like he might once have been a leg-pumping running back, and a gangly, sweet-faced, green-eyed white guy whose specialty shot, could you believe it, was a Kareem sky hook! They played against three tanned, toned white boys whose combined height was about twenty feet and combined age probably didn't top sixty-five. Hawk was six-one and admitted to being forty-five years old, but he was sneaky. Twice he had dropped his special move on the opposition: Pick your spot, three slow dribbles, a head fake right, a quick crossover dribble left faking out the defender, elevate, sink the jumper. They even fell for it the second time. He shoots. He scores. They win! High fives.

"Haven't seen you around here before," the green-eyed guy said, showing Hawk where to pick up a towel on the way into the locker room.

"It's been a while," said Hawk, wiping off his glasses and stopping at a drinking fountain.

"Tom Youngblood," said the guy, sticking out his hand.

"Joe Green," said Hawk, shaking it. He'd been introducing himself that way forever. He hated "Josiah" and his father and Maria had called him Jody (so had one other person, intermittently, at particularly intimate moments). Only his friends from way back knew him by the nickname the preppies at college had given him: Hawk.

"Nice crossover dribble to the jumper," said Tom.

"Nice Kareem," said Hawk. Gosh, guys knew how to communicate.

They got cleaned up and ended up going to the student union to get plastic-wrapped ham sandwiches and sodas. They took their lunches out onto the broad green rectangle of Prexy's Pasture. Hawk learned that Tom taught American literature, a subject Hawk had studied in some detail, long ago when he had been an English major at Yale. Tom learned that Joe had just been hired as a professor of earth sciences, specializing in economic geology. But really he'd been hired because they were trying to cash in on his experience as an exploration geologist. They evidently thought he could go out prospecting and dig up jobs for their graduates.

"And can you?" Tom asked, washing a desiccated bite of sandwich down with Minute Maid orange soda.

"If they're willing to move around, live in weird places, and get laid off a lot," said Hawk.

"What kind of weird places?" Tom inquired.

"Oh, about everywhere from Pioche, Nevada to places in Peru that nobody's ever heard of," Hawk said, flattening his Coke can.

"Try me," said Tom. "I've been to Peru. Great climbing."

They talked about the Andes. Tom had done technical climbing all over the world. Hawk offered the opinion that when you walked off-trail up and down mountains to make a living, you were less inclined to spend your weekends trying to die hanging off a precipice. But he didn't mind walking some to get a good view. Tom moved on to ask a number of personal questions. Hawk gave short answers. He'd been born in Connecticut. Gone to high school in Arizona. Gone east to college. Gone west to grad school. Worked exploration in South America and Europe and all over the West, including Wyoming.

Tom returned to familiar turf: basketball. He was a member of a perennially victorious city league team, which was made up of wily aging jocks who called the team "Old, But Slow." He asked Hawk if he was interested in joining, and Hawk said he'd think about it.

Then Tom tried the personal angle one more time. "You married?"

"Nope."

"Significant other?"

"No."

"You free Saturday night?"

Hawk considered. "I could be."

"My wife," said Tom, "is the best cook in southern Wyoming, possibly the whole state. We're having some people over for dinner. You want to come?"

Hawk smiled a little. "Do I look like some kind of lonesome bachelor who'd do anything for a home-cooked meal?"

Tom put up his hands. "Hey, for all I know, you could be a psycho-killer, and I've just made a really stupid, indeed fatal mistake."

"No," said Hawk, "I'm a man of peace. And I'd do anything for a home-cooked meal."

8

A Wyoming Girlhood

Sally had returned from El Conquistador to Margaret Dunwoodie's house full, nervous, and curious. When a mood like this came on, all she could do was read and write. She went to the office, sat down at the beautiful desk, put on her funky LA-hip reading glasses and opened the folder labeled DUNWOODIE FOUNDATION OFFICIAL BIO. Candor and contrivance leapt out at her this time: Meg had written this brief account of her own long life in the third person. Sally read it, then opened the folder Edna had given her and read through the transcript of the interview. Then, checking against the transcript for discrepancies, backing the tape up to repeat things she couldn't quite make out, she listened to Margaret's surprisingly steady old-lady voice on tape, answering Edna's warm but pointed questions with an appearance of forthrightness that left much out. Sally paid close attention to the speed of Dunwoodie's words, the hesitations, the places where she laughed and where the phrases sounded canned.

Then she booted up her laptop, with the folders open in front of her on the desk. Sally opened a file she titled "Meg1" and began to construct her own first narrative of Margaret Dunwoodie's life story.

Margaret Parker Dunwoodie was born in Odessa, Texas, in 1904. Her father, McGregor "Mac" Dunwoodie, had been a wild West Texas cowboy who rode the range and the rails into Wyoming as the twentieth century bashed into life. Mac Dunwoodie found himself working cattle in the Saratoga and Centennial Valleys, and on his rare days off rode high into the Sierra Madres and Medicine Bows of southern Wyoming. He liked the wide sage basins, the switchback trails, the solitude, the feeling of thin, cold air and the look of frozen gray peaks. But he also liked the company he found in noisy barrooms, the prospect of greater comfort than a bedroll on the ground next to a fire that died long before dawn. He mended Wyoming fences, branded Hereford cattle, and resolved to find a way to make a fortune.

So he took the stake he'd squirrelled away and went to the town of Laramie, to the infant state university. He'd decided to take a bachelor's degree in science. He figured he'd learn enough about geology to go back to Texas and find himself a big old oil field. He could come back to Wyoming a rich man, have his pick of beautiful valleys, and spend the best years of his life as a gentleman rancher.

Sally made herself a note: This was Mac's Young Man Dream. As a rich old man, they said, he'd gone bitter and paranoid. How did he change along the way, if he did? When? What changed him?

Gertrude Parker fit right into Mac Dunwoodie's plan. She was a ranch girl with eyes as wide and blue as the Wyoming sky. Her folks had a place out south of Albany. Mac had seen her at the college, but never much talked to her until a box lunch picnic the first week of his last year at the University.

She was finishing up, too, taking courses in history and political economy, tall and straight and smart and blond and fired with the cause of woman suffrage.

OK, Sally noted. Height, hair, and feminism ran in Meg's family.

At that picnic, Mac had noticed that Gertrude wore a purple and gold VOTES FOR WOMEN pin on the bodice of her starched white shirtwaist. He'd made a joke about it, and she'd let him have what-for. They loved to argue with each other, to match wits. Mac proposed in April, and Gert said she would marry him after graduation.

They graduated in May, and married at her parents' ranch on a brilliant June day in 1903. The next morning, they awoke to ten inches of snow. The lilac bushes in the ranchyard, heavy with blooms, were bowed to the ground. Gert got up, went out, shook the heavy white clumps off clusters of blossoms that sent out grateful bursts of perfume. Then she went inside, made coffee, woke her husband, dressed. There was no hope of getting a wagon to Laramie to catch the train that would take them, ultimately, to a new home in Texas. A week passed before they could leave.

What was she thinking? What did he promise?

Gert never learned to like flat, dry, dusty West Texas in the five years they were there, working on Mac's fortune. His family were all dead. The young couple were on their own, a hard thing in a hard country. Wyoming was a hard place too, but she knew its bleaknesses as her own, and there were Parkers everywhere to lift some of the weight of the long cold time. Mac swore to Gert that once his wells came in, he'd take her back home to Wyoming and start buying up every pretty piece of property for sale in the entire state. They'd ranch some of it, and leave some of it for the deer and the elk and the moose.

She must have loved him. Must have shared that dream. Watch it, Sally, you dim-witted romantic.

They'd both seen Meg's birth, barely a year after they'd married, as a blessing, but it had come at a cost. Gert had a hard time. The doctor told her that baby Margaret would be her last.

A lonely way to be born, no?

Meg had only one dim memory of her first years in Texas. She had later asked her mother if the remembered moment had actually happened, but her mother couldn't say for sure. Meg couldn't have been much more than three. It had been a typical West Texas summer day, windy, sere, no prospect of relief. Her mother had been doing the wash, hanging it up to dry. Meg remembered how hot and gritty her skin had felt, how she had toddled over to her mother and fallen beside the basket of heavy wet linen at her feet. Her mother had snatched her up, wrapped her in wet sheets, and stuck her in the shade of a lone spindly cottonwood tree, brought her a cool cup of water and held it to her dry mouth. She had grown cooler, drowsy, slept.

Sally's semidistracted thought: So that's what they did before air-conditioning!

Meg was awakened by her father's voice, whooping in exultation. She opened her eyes to see him jumping up and down, covered with filthy sticky black stuff. His first well had come in.

They were off to Wyoming within the year.

Mac and Gert took out extended homestead claims on land shading up into his beloved Sierra Madres, not far from the town of Encampment. Though he had to spend time in Texas tending his oil-fields, he bought up range land and mountain mead-ows scattered across Wyoming: in the Bighorn basin, on the south flank of the Absarokas, in the shadow of the Tetons. But the Woody D Ranch, just a day's ride from Bridger Peak, was the place Mac determined to call home. He paid a neighbor to come in with a mule team and grade a dirt road in to the place he built his ranch, and started hounding the Carbon County com-missioners to lay down gravel on the road to Baggs. He bought himself a 1908 Maxwell touring car, which sat idle in the barn nine months of the year, waiting for snow to melt, then mud to harden.

The winters were just plain horrid, the summers ambrosial. Meg went to a one-room school, when she could get there, doing her lessons in a classroom where the ten pupils ranged in age from five to fif-teen. By the time she was twelve, she had become the teacher.

Gert knew that her daughter was far too bright to be deprived of a proper education, so for high school, Meg was sent to live with Parker cousins in Laramie. She loved the fine brick school building, the smart, strict teachers, the town kids who invited her over to bake gingerbread and throw snowballs. But she missed her mother and father and the near-ness of the great, brooding mountains. As far as she was concerned, the Laramie Range to the east of town had some nice rock formations, but was really little more than an overeager hillock. The Snowies, to the west, were too far away to walk into in an afternoon. The minute the school year was over, she hurried back to Mac and Gert and the Woody D. Her home in the Sierra Madre was safety and sameness to her, even if, one year when she returned, she found they'd graveled the Baggs road.

At sixteen, Meg graduated from high school, and it was clear she should go to college. She had grown tall and lanky, nearly six feet, with a diamond-shaped face and Gert's cascading blond hair and big blue eyes. She had inherited her mother's insistence on looking a man in the eye, and boys found her too formidable to court. It was 1920, and she was full of life but the furthest thing from a flapper, sturdy and studious and incapable of flirting.

As her mother had, she went to UW. And much to Gert's delight, many of Meg's university teachers were women, some of whom had been there back in Mama's time. She took classes on the Civil War from the serious Laura White, in political economy from the outspoken and controversial feminist, Grace Raymond Hebard. Both encouraged her to pursue a teaching career, or perhaps to enter social work. Meg wanted to be useful, above all, and earnestly joined the Red Cross and the League of Women Voters, the Society for the Prevention of War. But her inner rhythms thrilled not to reform, but to create. She was a superb student in all her classes. In Professor McIntyre's class on British po-etry, her mind sang.

Clara McIntyre and Laura White shared a two-story frame house near the campus. Each fall when the students returned, they hosted a tea for women students in their spectacular gardens. Meg ached to please them with her knowledge and her imagina-tion. She would be invited again, in the bare-branched snowclad days of winter, for hot apple cider and conversations on poetry.

The year Meg graduated, they invited her over for a chat about her future. Meg admitted she wanted, well, to write. "You should write," Miss McIntyre agreed. "You have the brains and the courage to do it. But if you want to write, you've got to get out of here, Margaret. You simply have to leave," she told Meg, sipping sweet tea from an eggshell china cup. "And I can help."

The computer screen offered only faint light in the dusky office. Sally couldn't read the pages in the folders. She looked up, dazed, and realized that she'd written through the purpling blaze of a sunset. Now it was time to turn on a light and keep going, or call it a day. She switched on the lamp on the desk, and decided to stop working anyway. She knew where to start in the morning; a good time to quit. She saved the file, backed it up on a diskette, closed it, tap tap tap and out. Took off her reading glasses, rubbed her eyes, and stretched. The job was begun.

She realized that she was starving. Thought about what she had to eat in the house. Blessed Mary Langham had sent her home from dinner the other night with some leftover lasagna. She had a cold bottle of California sauvignon blanc in the fridge. She could heat up dinner, have a glass of wine, turn on the television and watch summer reruns of shows she'd never been that excited about in the first place. Sounded like another monster night in the life of the artist formerly known as Mustang Sally.

After making themselves a frozen pizza for dinner, Josh Langham and his cousin Jerry Jeff Davis had ridden their bicycles from Jerry Jeff's house to the Diamond Shamrock on north Fourth Street to rent videos. They were currently working their way through the collected film work of John Candy, and tonight they were taking on *Volunteers*, which neither had ever seen, and *Wagons East*, the fateful last Candy movie. They cut south on Eleventh Street, pedaling hard, with the videos and more than four pounds of junk food, soda, and candy in Josh's backpack.

Jerry Jeff was in the lead; his bike was newer. Josh had his sister's old hand-me-down bike. As he puffed along, Josh saw the light go on upstairs in the Dunwoodie house, the one that was supposed to be haunted, or at least to be full of cool stuff including a map to buried treasure. Jerry Jeff saw it too, slowing as they passed and pulling alongside Josh. "Josh, look!" he stage-whispered. "A light just went on in the haunted house. What the heck?"

"Aw, it's just that friend of Dad and your mom's," Josh explained. "That Professor Alder. She probably just got home or something. J.J., you don't really believe in ghosts, do you?" he scoffed, shaming his cousin.

"'Course not," said Jerry Jeff.

Neither did Josh. But as the son of a police officer, he did believe in noticing odd things. He also knew his dad had busted people trying to break into the old lady's once-empty house. The light in the window wasn't particularly odd, but the guy sitting in a parked car, across the street from Meg Dunwoodie's house, was a bit out of the ordinary. Creepy. Josh glanced in the car as he pedaled past, registering a twenty-something guy with a shaved head lighting a cigarette. He didn't dare circle back to check the make and model of the car, but knew it was some kind of big old shark of a sedan, maybe late sixties, early seventies, dark color. In-state plates.

Jerry Jeff, reassured, was powering those pedals for home, inspired by the prospect of popping open a Pepsi or two, slamming bigtime junk food, and video-vegging. Josh decided he'd call his dad as soon as he got to his Aunt Delice's house and tell him somebody might be casing the Dunwoodie place. His dad would probably want to know.

9

All You Care to Eat

Delice had always made sure that no matter how bad the food at the Wrangler was, at least the canned music was good. You could be sitting there eating a soggy BLT on Wonder bread with Miracle Whip, but you'd still be listening to Hank and Patsy and the Amazing Rhythm Aces, if you wanted to listen. El Conquistador didn't bother to change the one tape they played all the time, which was a greatest hits thing by the Texas Tornadoes ("Hey Baby, Que Paso?"). Instead, El Conquistador relied on the food.

Most Laramie restaurants weren't particular about either the food or the ambience, so the places that pretended, vainly, to either were especially disappointing. The ones that claimed both and delivered neither, and had the balls to charge a fortune for spewing up a good case of entrée poisoning, rated a special narrow-eyed negative star or two on the Hawk Green scale.

The former Mudflaps had closed down when the owners torched the kitchen for the insurance money. In its place now was a pseudo-Italian place called Hasta La Pasta! which had an unpromising sign out front that said, BEST LUNCH BUFFET IN LARAMIE, ALL YOU CARE TO EAT, $8.95. Bad omen number one. Sally was no novice. She knew you should never eat at an Italian place that has an exclamation point in the name. But this was where she was supposed to meet Egan Crain for lunch.

Bad omen number two slammed her in the ears the minute she entered the dim, smoky entryway. The Muzak was the Hollyridge Strings, assassinating "Light My Fire." Bad omen number three followed quickly. She turned into the dining room and saw Sam Branch, a man she had once tried to run over with a truck, sitting at a black Formica table, having lunch with a big man in a pin-striped suit. If she had still been a die-hard baseball fan, she would have thought the count had gone to three strikes, and retired to the dugout, cursing perhaps. In the past two decades, she'd switched to football (even if it was the Broncos). No mercy. After three downs, you were supposed to punt.

She pretended she hadn't seen Sam, and strode up to the hostess's station to say she was looking for the Crain party. The hostess, who was doing her nails and talking on the phone, didn't even look up: time to punt. But Egan saved her the trouble of announcing herself, hollering from a table with one of his patented "I say, Sally, over here!" fake-Brit remarks. She went to his table, hard by the pasta and salad bar (so convenient for refills!) and thought instantly about ordering an alcoholic beverage. For almost sixteen years in California she hadn't drunk booze at lunch more than a couple of dozen times, and now here she was, back in Laramie, going on two for two. Maybe this endowed chair thing wasn't such a good idea. "Iced tea," she told the pierced-nosed waitress, feeling careful.

Sam acted as if he'd just noticed that she happened to be in the room, a ludicrous sham given that he was sitting approximately eight feet away from her, pretending not to stare at her over the rim of his Heineken bottle.

Sam looked good. Still had the sandy hair falling over one blue eye, still had the guileless, lying smile. He was wearing a denim shirt and Dockers. He'd obviously taken up working out. But then he'd always had a nice hard body, a miracle of biological design when you thought about what he'd done to it.

He waved, grinned. She mouthed a little "Hi, Sam" and flickered limp fingers.

Egan tittered at her obvious discomfort. "Guess you can't go far in this town without running into old chums, eh wot, Sal?" he chortled. "Isn't it just jolly, though, that we've all come up in the world so? Why, who would ever have thought that we'd live to see the day a chap like Sam Branch would be having his elevenses with the governor of Wyoming!"

Hey, thought Sally, she'd had an elevenses or twelveses or more often two A.M.-ses with one or two Wyoming governors along the way, as had most musicians who ever made a buck playing bar gigs in the state. Twenty years ago, the best place to see the governor, as anyone knew, was a bar. Sally had personally seen one governor at the airport bar in Cheyenne at two o'clock in the afternoon, and at the Holiday Inn twice when she was playing happy hours, and even once at the Wrangler, though, thankfully, never at the Gallery. Some things were just beneath a governor, no matter how devoted to bars.

This governor, a Republican, she recalled, was drinking something clear in a glass. She couldn't remember if he was born-again or not, so she couldn't decide whether he was loading up on water or vodka. Sam said something that made the governor laugh. She should have known he'd eventually be yukking it up with Republicans. Hell, he was probably a member of the NRA. He probably belonged to the militia.

The waitress finally returned and took their lunch orders. Sally ordered a caesar salad, a mental lapse she regretted almost immediately but was unable to correct, since the waitress fled quickly and didn't show up again for some time. (She imagined Hawk explaining that they should have spelled that salad "Seize Her," as in the first two words of a sentence that ended "before she orders something that stupid again!") Egan ordered the Pavarottiburger (menu: "It's a BIG ONE." It oughta be, Sally thought, for eleven bucks!)

It took forty-five minutes for their lunches to come, by which time they'd nearly exhausted their store of reminiscence and innocent current gossip. The waitress, who obviously had something more important to do, nearly dropped the plate in Sally's lap. Rescuing her lunch, Sally looked down at a mound of browning romaine lettuce, drenched in bottled dressing and blanketed with stale industrial bread cubes. Egan dug into his huge burger, but judging from the vigorous way his undershot jaw was working, it had the consistency, if not the actual taste, of Styrofoam pellets.

"So do we have business to do, Egan?" she asked, wanting to get to the point of the lunch and get the hell out of there.

Egan swallowed a bite of his burger and drank half a glass of water. "Since you're supposed to be advising us on special collections we might purchase with Dunwoodie legacy funds, I thought it'd be a good idea if I brought you up to date on our plans for the archival acquisitions," he began. "We've identified a number of donors around the state whose collections would be *superb* contributions to the archive. They include papers from some of the first ranching families in the state, really top-drawer stuff. I've a list right here," he said, digging in his briefcase and coming up with a typed sheet. "You'll see that they're all over the place—Pinedale, Gillette, Green River, Torrington, what have you. Not all of the donors have agreed to give their collections to us, yet. We'd really like to have the Flanders papers, but of course the family is so distraught, what with Walter having that tragic hunting accident last fall—"

"Egan," Sally said testily, sensing a major digression

coming on. Time to show him who was sitting in the endowed chair. She pushed aside her untouched plate and got her reading glasses out of her big leather bag. Egan's list featured the names of ranching families she'd heard of, including his own.

"Let me get this straight," she said. "You're proposing to use Dunwoodie money to acquire, transport, catalogue, take care of, and store these collections, and you want me to help you get them nailed down?"

Egan's face fell. She'd deliberately started right up by using the word *money*—it made everything seem so tawdry. "Righto," he answered brightly, as if she must surely see what a fine idea this was.

"But Egan, these look like Wyoming collections you guys would have wanted anyway. They may be interesting from the point of view of ranch life, but they're not especially pertinent to women's history—"

"Come on, Sally. Families have women in them!" he sputtered, setting his teeth so that his jaw receded even more than usual. "Why, none of the great ranches could survive without strong, determined women keeping the home fires burning . . . "

She waxed him with a brown-eyed glare. "Spare me the hearth-and-home routine, Egan. You're trying to scam the Foundation to pay for stuff you already wanted. I'm not saying that Dunwoodie money shouldn't go to acquiring materials on Wyoming women—that's reasonable. There could be some interesting stuff in the collections you've listed. But I would advise you to think more carefully before you start going around spending Dunwoodie *money*." She took a sip of iced tea to cool herself down. She nearly choked on a lump of undissolved instant tea powder.

"Now Sally," said Egan, seeing his opening as she reached for her water glass. "You're no archivist. I'd really thought your role with us was to offer suggestions, not try to interfere with the integrity of our collections," he grandstanded.

Sally turned diplomat. "Of course you guys are the experts. But I do have some understanding of what the bequest is supposed to do, and I'm advising you to be deliberate and conservative with Foundation money."

"Deliberate? Conservative?" The dust-dry burger had stuck fast in Egan's throat, but the idea of Sally Alder advocating caution and care was impossible to swallow. "Sally?" he wheezed, as if it really couldn't be she, but some middle-aged Machiavellian look-alike cousin come to cash in on her big break. They laugh alike, they walk alike, at times they even talk alike.

"First of all, Egan," said Sally, who was after all herself just a bit older and more knowledgeable, "you're going to have to pay for processing Meg's stuff, and you'll want to acquire more materials on her—letters in other people's hands, correspondence with publishers, maybe even do some oral history work with people who knew her. That'll cost big bucks. Just the letters—since she's become famous, letters from her are probably going to be auctioned off, and they're liable to be expensive. I read that an Emily Dickinson letter went for ten thousand dollars last month at Sotheby's."

"I hardly think Meg Dunwoodie's in a league with the Belle of Amherst!" Egan said huffily.

The Belle of Amherst? "Look, Egan, you haven't even thought about this. All I'm saying is, let's take some time to think about what a really damned good collection of Dunwoodie papers might look like, and what it might cost to put it together. That strikes me as the logical first investment for the acquisitions money." Egan was pouting, so she played her ace. "And I'm sure that if I called Ezra Sonnenschein and asked him to take it to the Foundation officers, they'd agree."

Egan gave up on trying to make lunch out of the humongous hamburger that had been cooked to the consistency of a briquette and then left to cool slowly. He obviously had to concede that she was right. And Sally was sure he knew that the moment the Foundation stepped in to micromanage the archive money, he could kiss off any thoughts of having some say in how it was spent. It must be galling him that the Dunwoodie papers themselves were still sitting in Meg's basement, at the Foundation's insistence, at the mercy of everything from mice to mildew to murderers, for all he knew. He was stuck.

"Yes of course, you're right," he told Sally. "I hadn't really worked this through. It might be well to wait until you've had a look at what's in those bloody boxes. And do have a go at getting Maude to have a burglar alarm installed."

"I'll do that," she said vaguely. "And I intend to get to the boxes as soon as possible." She threw him a bone. "Of course I'll be grateful for any advice you can give me if I run into any problems." He gave her a small smile. She worked up a smile of her own, laying her napkin over the Seize-Her salad and rising to make her escape.

She reached for her wallet, but Egan shook his head and insisted, "No no nonononono. My pleasure." He had to be kidding.

"Thanks for the lunch, Egan. I'll be in touch."

Escape denied. By the time she was on her feet, Sam Branch had gotten up, shaken hands with the departing governor, and come over to their table. "Just a little chat with the gov," he told Egan. "Asked me if I want to be on the state party committee. Nobody's been appointed since we lost Mickey Welsh."

"Terrible story," Egan told Sally. "Mr. Welsh was killed in an automobile accident in Togwotee Pass. Leading citizen and all. His poor family."

Sam cut him off. "Mustang," he said, turning to Sally, his raspy, low voice annoyingly familiar after sixteen years. "Heard you were back in town. You look good."

"Thanks, Sam," she answered, flushing, but got hold of herself. "Last time I saw you, you were running for your life down Grand Avenue."

He thought that was hilarious. "You had a shitty aim with a Chevy, Sally."

"It must have been that," she returned, "because I was really trying to kill you. Listen, great seeing you again, but I really have to be going . . . "

Egan goggled, enjoying the show.

Sam picked up left hand and inspected her fingertips. "Wimpy calluses," he remarked. "Aren't you playing anymore?"

"Not much. Just for fun. Really, I gotta—"

"Well, you'll have to get back in shape. Dwayne and I've been putting jams together now and then. We've got a little band we call The Millionaires. Probably get together in a couple of weeks—you'll have to sit in." He gave her his Look. It was a long way from melting her as it had, once or twice. Instead, it brought back a strong, guilty memory of melting: Sally Alder as the Wicked Witch of the West.

Sally and Sam hadn't exactly parted on the best of terms, but he'd evidently chosen to overlook her attempt at vehicular homicide. She was still not sure whether she had really meant to injure or kill him, though at the time she'd been quite sure he'd deserved to be harmed. He had managed to escape unscathed, laughing.

He was still holding her hand, smiling in a way that made her vastly uncomfortable. The calluses on his fingertips were thick and rough from intimate knowledge of a guitar neck, reminding her of other things with which his fingers were closely acquainted. She removed her hand and gathered up her bag. She ought to try to be reasonable. Whatever was bugging her, it had been over a long freaking time ago. She was a middle-aged college professor, holder of the Dunwoodie Chair. And at the same time, she was definitely ready to get back into playing some tunes. "Yeah, maybe. Give me a call. I'm in the phone book under the listing for Meg Dunwoodie."

"Oh, I know, I know," Sam said, running his now-free

hand up and down her arm. "I heard all about the big endowed chair. Fact is, Sal, you and I might be seeing each other around campus—the governor tells me he's thinking about appointing me to the University Board of Trustees next spring." He dug a card out of his wallet, gave it to her. Branch Homes on the Range. Mr. Laramie Real Estate. Work phone, pager, cellphone numbers. He pulled a fancy pen out of his pocket and wrote his home number on the back, but said, "Cellphone's best. Most private." He patted the phone hanging from his belt, like that ought to reassure her that they could have intimate conversations which would be conducted, on his end, at Hasta la Pasta! Sheesh.

"Wow. Uh. Wow," she managed. Time to split, really. "Thanks again, Egan. See you around, Sam." Byron Bosworth and one of his cronies walked into the room, freezing at the sight of her, and she realized it was long past time to punt. She was a quarterback who'd just been brutally sacked in her own end zone, being taken off the field in a motorized cart.

Egan tried the hug thing again but she made him settle for squeezing her shoulder. Sam was a lot smoother, managing to swoop an arm around her waist before she knew it, to wrap his sure, hard fingers around her ribs. Why the hell had she worn a spandex T-shirt? She felt as if she were getting a chest x-ray. The Boz and his friend glared at her from the hostess station, openly hostile. The hostess blew on her nails and thought about seating those two losers sometime, if she felt like it. The waitress bore down suddenly on Sally and Egan, hoping to act like she cared before Egan could stiff her on the tip. Sally backed out of Sam's grasp. Sam made a pistol with his thumb and forefinger and pointed at Sally, a gesture that shouted "Realtor."

"Call me anytime. Soon, angel," he purred, unloading his Look one more time.

10

She Never Married

Waking up Saturday morning to a clear sky, a clean house, and Maude's banana bread, Sally felt she inhabited fresh space. She drank coffee, she ran. She had no trouble clearing her mind for a day at work. She had all day Saturday to herself, and an Edna dinner party to look forward to that night. It was time for a quick summary of the second phase of Margaret Dunwoodie's life.

Clara McIntyre had a friend, who had a friend, who said he could get a well-educated, hardworking college graduate like Meg a job as a copy girl at the *New York World*. Miss McIntyre had another friend who had a spare room in her apartment. Meg told Gert and Mac that the apartment was "in a nice neighborhood in Manhattan," gambling that they wouldn't ever visit her and find out that it was in notorious Greenwich Village. But from what Miss McIntyre's friend said, the newspaper business would see to it that Meg didn't have much time to stay at home and be corrupted.

She'd left West Texas as a little child, and after that had never been out of Wyoming. What could Meg possibly have thought, Sally wondered, of New York? Her biography didn't say. She hadn't told Edna.

There weren't many women in the newspaper business in those days, and most newspapermen prided themselves on a citified vulgarity they mistook, in Meg's opinion, for honesty. They tested her, cursing and spitting and telling rude stories, smoking repulsive cigars and talking endlessly about vicious boxing matches, big bloody steaks, women who wore their clothes a little too tight. They claimed to love nothing better than running out in the middle of the night to see a gun-shot corpse splattered on a sidewalk, to be the first to tell some woman she was a widow. They'd show this cowgirl the difference between writing her hayseed term paper on *Paradise Lost* and writing a real story.

Meg hated the hazing, but she had learned from her mother that anything a man thought he could or should do, a woman could do, and should if she thought it might get her anywhere without compromising her character. She had started out running errands for the "boys" who worked the beats and wrote the stories on clattering black typewriters, chewing up their stogies, sneaking bottles of bootleg rye whiskey out of their bottom desk drawers. She learned to smoke cigarettes and hold her liquor when they began to ask her along to prowl their favorite after-hours speakeasies.

Did they hit on her? Did she have a special friend? A lover? Who did she know, besides reporters?

An editor gave her a big break writing obituaries, then another, reporting a story about a man who had hung upside down from the arm of a telephone pole for fifty-two hours, as a publicity stunt. Against her own best judgment, Meg wrote the story as if it were a thrilling escapade, when she knew it was only a pathetic, ultimately pointless bid for someone to notice. She wrote about how the man had lost his job, how his children begged him to do something big, how his wife took care of him during his ordeal by hauling up a basket of cookies on a rope. She climbed the pole and interviewed him personally. The story got Meg an assignment as a beat reporter.

Sally knew the poem Meg had written about the episode, full of tired color and irony, which had made its first public appearance in *Rocks and Rage*.

The city desk editor would try, from time to time, to get her to take on a woman's job at the paper. Write an advice column, he urged. Society notes, he offered. How about recipes? Meg replied that she was as good a news-hawk as any goddamn man, thank you very much.

Sally would look among the boxes for a photo of Meg as a *World* reporter. She imagined her with a cigarette dangling from her lips as she furiously tapped out the latest tale of murder, of the busting of a bootlegging ring or the apprehension of a notorious, heiress-bilking bigamist.

The editors of the *World* loved, more than anything else, publicity. A hard-nosed, fearless news-hen was a novelty they could exploit. Especially a good-looking blond who wore slim, short dresses and bobbed hair like a mannequin. After a while, they began to put her on stories in which she was, herself, the news peg. A photographer went along to take pictures of her. Flying in a blimp wearing goggles, a leather helmet, a silk scarf. Trying out the new and dangerous sport of water-skiing in a jaunty bathing suit. Jazz-dancing in white satin, in the arms of a screen idol, at the Cotton Club in Harlem.

Later, she would recall this strange, complicated scene in the smoky poem, "Ellington."

But Meg didn't want to be the spectacle. And she didn't want to write fluff. So she looked for another job. The *Toronto Star* was looking for a Paris correspondent. A couple of years before, that had been Ernest Hemingway's beat. Now it would be Meg's.

Paris. She was there for twelve years. She'd arrived in 1929, stayed through hard times, modern madness, political strife, explosive art and thought and sensory richness and heady, sometimes scary café conversation all the way to the time when the Nazis marched into the city, cheered on by the cowardly, the despicable, and, perhaps, the confused. For nearly twelve years, she'd written about artists and novelists and critics, about turbulent European politics and breathtaking locales, first for the *Star*, and then for Reuters News Service. Meg watched, appalled, as Germany moved ever more ruthlessly on its neighbors, as one country after another fell. Heard, and reported, rumors of unthinkable atrocities and plans for horrors even more unimaginable.

And finally, the surrender of France. The bad and the opportunistic bowed the Fascists down the Champs-Élysées, through the Arc de Triomphe, while the rest of France hid or raged, plotted insurrection, or, more commonly, wore its confusion and fear and ambivalence with a blank face. Meg had left.

Eleven years of volatile, full, exhilarating, terrifying life. And what had she said about it? The official biography said nothing more.

So on to the interview with Edna:

EDNA: Tell me about Paris.

MEG: It was an interesting place to be. . . . *(pause)* . . . I met some interesting people.

EDNA: Who?

MEG: Artists . . . musicians . . . mountain climbers . . . revolutionaries. Bankers. The artists and the musicians were usually more interesting than the revolutionaries. For that matter, some of the bankers were more interesting than some of the revolutionaries.

EDNA: Which artists?

MEG: Some of the famous ones. Picasso. Braque. Gertrude's people. I preferred less self-importantly avante-garde stuff. Giselle Blum was a very good friend of mine.

EDNA: Blum?

MEG: Yes. A painter, portraits mostly. I met her through her brother, Paul Blum. He was a banker who wrote pieces for the *Economist*. I met him climbing in the Alps. A fascinating man. He played the viola. They came from a very wealthy, old, established French Jewish family. They lived in a beautiful house in the Faubourg St. Honore. Every Tuesday they hosted a musical evening. Such music! String quartets, brass choirs, solo pianists. They printed up programs on rag paper—I kept them all. You'd listen to this heavenly music, and afterward they would open up the doors into the dining room for a champagne supper. I'd never imagined such things existed.

EDNA: What happened to Giselle Blum?

MEG: The Nazis sent her family to the camps. Paul was killed in the Resistance. It was a great tragedy. There were so many great tragedies.

EDNA: Did you know the tragedy was coming when you left?

MEG: Yes. And no. The Blums were liberals; they had many radical friends. Men who fought in the Spanish war, who warned of what was coming. Men whose families had nothing. They'd come to the Tuesdays looking gaunt and shadowy, chain-smoking black cigarettes, with their eyes closed all through the concerts. And when supper was served, they ate as if they'd never stop starving. I remember one very young man who asked if they'd mind if he took a package of food home, and Paul was so ashamed that he packed up everything on the spot and had it delivered to the boy's family.

  They said the fascists would spread hell all over the world, and we all agreed that was so. But I was comfortable. Most of us were. The Blums had everything, had seen anti-Semitism come and go in France over the years. It was impossible to believe the Nazis would actually do what they said they intended.

EDNA: You left in 1940—were you expelled?

MEG: No. I could have stayed, but I had to come back to Wyoming. Two days before the Germans came into Paris, I received a cable that my mother was very ill. Two days after they took the city, I was on a train for Le Havre, to take a ship back to the States. As an American, I was free to go; they couldn't keep me there. Perhaps I should have stayed and joined the Resistance, but I didn't. I came home.

EDNA: Would you tell me more about the time you spent in France?

MEG: Perhaps another time.

  There was no other time. And now the longest part of her life, half a century back in her home state, seemed to take up so very little space in her official story.

Meg had spent the remainder of the interview relating the trials of her return to Wyoming. The long hours spent nursing her terribly frail mother, the quarrels with her rich and increasingly cantankerous and conservative father, who was certain that Jewish bankers were driving the world to ruin. Mac had joined Lindbergh's America Firsters. He had always admired Charles Lindbergh. He also believed that Roosevelt declared war on the Axis because he was secretly Jewish. Gert had always been a tempering influence on Mac, but she died in 1942 and he kept getting worse.

Meg needed to get away from Mac, but she found that all the time she had been away, she had missed her own mountains more than she had understood. Reuters was eager to have her back, but she didn't want to leave Wyoming. What kind of work could she do?

The University of Wyoming was, like many wartime businesses, in the grip of a manpower shortage. Women, there as elsewhere, filled in. Meg found a job teaching composition and creative writing. But unlike the millions of women who got laid off when the Johnnies came marching home, Meg managed to hang onto her job by making herself a fixture in the English department. She would teach four generations of Wyoming kids how to write a clear sentence, how to construct an expository essay, how to use poetic devices in prose writing, how to imagine different points of view. Her tactics included sarcasm, intimidation, and lavish use of a red pen. As she told Edna, she "discouraged the odious and encouraged the possible."

And so it had gone, for almost fifty years. Despite the ups and downs of staggeringly small-time university politics, she taught, trekked the Rocky

Mountains, quietly wrote poetry. She fished for trout, planted gardens, invested in land around Jackson Hole and Aspen, took vacations in warm places. In 1964 she hired Maude Stark to put her life in order, and it stayed in order until her death. She inherited a sizeable sum after her father died in 1966, and she became, finally, almost a part of the landscape. She never married.

The oral history interview revealed a little bit more.

As Meg had told Edna, by the 1960s, a new generation of degree-wielding academics took over most faculty positions. In their eyes, Meg appeared as a remnant of a simple time when college professors hadn't really been qualified for their jobs. One young upstart historian named Byron Bosworth, railing in the faculty senate about "standards," tried to get her fired.

That bastard Boz. At least, Sally thought, you had to give him credit for consistency.

The prodigal daughter returned home to fifty years of more or less placid life in the high country, occasionally venturing to go public with a poem or two so good that editors must have clamored for more. A couple of little press volumes of her work. Then, after she died, the torrent of brilliance, *Rocks and Rage*.

And all that money. What was it all about? Sally looked up, saw the four sets of deft hands on black and white keys, shut her eyes, and covered her face with her own hands. She would open the boxes; she would see.

11

The Dinner Party

Edna McCaffrey was a great fan of the artist Judy Chicago, who had turned women's history into the monumental art installation, "The Dinner Party." Edna knew she could never create great works of art, but she figured that at least she could damn well make dinner. To her, every dinner party was a performance piece. The right mix of guests was the crucial ingredient. She had been somewhat annoyed (no—truly pissed) when Tom had said to her that Saturday morning, "Oh yeah—I met this guy playing basketball, very cool guy, invited him for dinner tonight, hope that's okay with you." This *guy*. What was he thinking?

But then one of her guests had called to cancel, and "this guy" turned out to be Dr. Josiah Green, a new geology professor she'd met briefly during his interview trip to campus last winter. Intelligent smile, decent manners, good credentials, and the science types acted like he was going to bring in big bucks. He was good-looking, a ponytailed post-hippie about Sally's age—maybe they'd hit it off. Edna was hardheaded mostly, but she wasn't above a little matchmaking.

* * *

Hawk Green had spent the day moving into his new Eighth Street house. He wouldn't actually own it until next month sometime, when all the paperwork cleared, but the sellers were happy enough to have him pay on their mortgage until then. Saturday morning, Sheila Czerny had handed him a key and a bottle of cold duck. When he opened the refrigerator to deposit the bottle of sweet bubbly stuff, he found a sixpack of Budweiser with a note that said, LET 'ER BUCK—NATTIE. In spite of himself, he grinned.

It didn't take him long to unpack what he had. He stuck his ghetto-blaster out the kitchen window and snapped in a Jerry Jeff Walker tape. Now, in the late afternoon sun, he sat in his backyard in a folding lawn chair that had lived in his truck for years, drinking a beer and looking at the Snowies. He appreciated having a dinner invitation that night. Considered whether he could take the cold duck as his contribution, and decided against it. Tom Youngblood was married to Edna McCaffrey, his new dean. Hawk had met her last winter, and she'd impressed him as not the cold duck type. He wondered if Laramie had become a place where you could get a bottle of wine that didn't have a screw cap.

The sight of the Snowies did him good. Soon he would be showing geology students places he'd loved a long time, explaining why rocks were mysterious and beautiful. The mountains gleamed silver-blue and cool across the plains. Jerry Jeff sang about how it was when the world felt just right, and Hawk thought he knew exactly what ol' Jerry Jeff meant.

Sally also had a six-pack of Budweiser in her refrigerator, and when she finished work for the day she went downstairs and got herself a beer. Then she filled Meg's big tub and took a bath long enough to read fifty pages of a mystery novel. Still warm and damp, she put on her robe and walked around the house in the afternoon light, feeling empty but peaceful. She decided she needed to hear some music. She stuck one of those mixed-up tapes into the deck and hit play. Jerry Jeff Walker in mid-song, something about a feeling he couldn't explain. Anticipation so strong, it was almost like being in a moment you were waiting for.

What the hell should she wear to this Edna thing? She didn't know who would be there. Should she go for the tight jeans and blazer look? Nice shirt and tailored pants? The pretty summer dress thing? Who would care anyway?

She stood in the big closet of Meg's elegant bedroom, wishing she were Ginger Rogers in pink silk and marabou, not Sally Alder in slightly moist white waffle-weave cotton. A sleeveless scoop-necked rayon dress, little yellow and white flowers on a black background, fitted on top, longish swirling skirt, called out to her from its hanger: better to err on the side of knocking their eyes out. Black wedgie sandals. Dangly gold earrings and red lipstick, good with her short, wavy, dark hair. Probably wasted on a bunch of pontificating middle-aged academics, but at least the cooking would be killer.

Tom Youngblood knew his way around a grill, so Edna could trust him with the lamb chops. Maude's squashes had joined some Japanese eggplants in a ratatouille. A creamy potato gratin was starting to bubble in the oven. Edna had goat cheese and roquefort and olives and baguettes she'd baked herself, and wonderful fresh lettuce and spinach from a friend's garden. Amazingly, you could now get some decent wines, right here in Laramie. Edna took a sip of a tolerable California merlot and placed a couple of marigolds and a sprig of rosemary on the cheese plate.

The doorbell rang. It was 7:05, and here was Sally. Incredible that anyone who had lived in LA would be on time for dinner. In Laramie, people had been known to arrive ten minutes early. The other company, a professor from the English department and his wife, an architect, were coming up the walk behind Sally, carrying a huge bouquet of flowers from their garden. Only Joe Green was missing. Edna hoped he wasn't the kind who came very late, or forgot dinner invitations altogether. Single men could be so irresponsible. So could some married men, she thought, still a little irritated with Tom.

The house was the way Edna loved it, full of gold light, jazz piano music, wonderful smells. They went into the living room for cocktail hour. Tom was bustling around getting everyone drinks. Sally asked for a glass of the merlot. The doorbell rang again, and Tom went to answer. Sally was about to take the first sip of her wine when Tom walked back into the room, followed by Professor Green, carrying a bottle of chardonnay. Edna saw Sally set down the long-stemmed glass without spilling a drop.

"Uh, Tom," Sally said, after he made introductions, "I've changed my mind. You wouldn't happen to have any bourbon, would you?"

"That sounds good to me," said Professor Josiah Hawkins Green, for some reason amused. "I could use a splash of Jim Beam."

They'd both known the moment was coming. They just hadn't known it would be so soon. (Soon? How many decades was soon?) When he'd walked in and seen her, Hawk had a fleeting urge to turn and run out the door. He'd walked away before, a dozen times or more, in the nearly three years they'd been crazy for each other. The last time, he'd run, and he hadn't come back.

But after seventeen years, he'd had plenty of time to reflect on the bitterness. He'd worked it over pretty thoroughly after Mary Langham had sent him the clipping from the *Boomerang*. Sally Alder wasn't the last woman in his life, but maybe she had been the one who got to him most. Whose betrayal had been bad enough, but not the worst maybe. Might have hurt the most. Whatever. They'd probably have to talk, sometime.

Just now, he realized, ironically pleased, the sight of her turned him on. Goddamn, she looked fine, a little thinner and bonier and harder, more weathered, but still round in the breast and hips and ass. Wearing that sexy dress, holding her back straight, working on not gulping her drink, figuring out how much to look at him, trying, he could tell, not to yell or even to stare. She was a yeller and a starer, but she'd clearly worked at getting it under control. He sat back, tasted his whiskey, let the conversation flow around him and glanced sideways at her, from time to time, conjuring up a challenge, a tease, a diversion.

Sally tuned out the conversation, hearing only, for the moment, McCoy Tyner on the stereo, like a soundtrack for a movie scene. The burning memory of the last time they'd seen each other walked through her mind. Hawk had been prospecting in the Mojave that winter. She was going to fly down to meet him in Tucson at spring break, and they were going to drive down into Mexico, to the desert and the beach. Things between them were strained, with him living on the road and her spending so much time in bars, drinking for a living and singing torch songs to horny cowhands and drillers and drifters and college boys.

As sometimes happened, he'd gotten laid off that February. She was always after him to spend more time with her, to make some kind of commitment. He must have decided to surprise her by driving up to Laramie and spending the month there, then heading south with her. Hawk had a key to her apartment. It was snowing, blowing, bone-chilling when he let himself in about midnight. Walked straight into her bedroom without even taking off his coat and found her sitting up, big-eyed, clutching a quilt around her naked body. Sam Branch was sitting right next to her, apparently just as naked but a lot more composed. "Well, Hawk," Sam had said, with that asshole grin, "out of work again?"

Hawk had uttered not a word, just turned right around. She hadn't said anything either: What could she say?

But that was a teenager's lifetime ago. Now here sat Hawk, lean and long-haired and long-legged and seamed in the face and perfectly gorgeously older, eating fancy French olives, evidently willing to be in the same room with her. Hawk—a.k.a "Joe"—hadn't let on to anyone else that he knew her. Edna couldn't possibly have known that this Joe Green was Sally's old Hawk. In fact, he'd said nothing at all. Typical. Everyone else made chitchat while Sally thought about what might come out when she finally opened her own mouth.

Look at him, lounging there on Edna's velvet couch, acting like he wasn't giving her the eye. She had expected their first encounter to be hideous, or at the very least, awkward and brief. Seeing him come through the doorway had made her think for a second that she ought to get the hell out, but that thought had passed as soon as it came. Much to her amazement, she was panting inwardly at the nearness of him. It made her want to rise, make some excuse. Drag him the five blocks to her bedroom and rip his clothes off. Obviously that wasn't an option. She spared him a glance and her heart rate about doubled. *What's your game, baby?*

"So you're new to Laramie, Joe?" asked the English professor, trying to include Hawk in the conversation.

"Well, I've just joined the University," Hawk answered, taking a small sip, measuring his choices and licking his lips. "But I've . . . spent time here before."

"Really, Joe?" Sally cooed, sensing the play. "Me, too."

"Yeah, Joe told me he'd prospected for uranium in this country in the seventies," Tom put in, spreading cheese on bread. He was playing the host now, while Edna fussed in the kitchen.

"I did. Had some prospects around Rawlins and Saratoga, did a lot of work in the Sierra Madre out of Encampment. Came to Laramie for fun, sometimes, on the weekends."

Sally squirmed a little in her chair.

"So you lived here back then, too, Sally?" Tom asked, clueless.

"Yeah, I moved here in 1977. I just drove east on 80 from Berkeley. I spent a few years gigging around playing music in the bars, then went back to school to study history." She rolled a little Jim Beam around in her mouth. "I had some good times." She gave Hawk the big brown eyes, all innocence.

The architect joined in. "Good times? You've got to be kidding. We moved here from Cambridge in eighty-five for *his* job. I was unemployed, bored, miserable, and freezing—God, I thought I'd gone straight to hell!" she exclaimed, swallowing some merlot. "Laramie's idea of a foreign movie was anything starring Arnold Schwarzenegger. But finally I managed to get a couple of commissions restoring commercial properties downtown, and now I'm mostly doing historic building restoration. I've been working a lot with Delice Langham—we've been talking about doing an application for the Dunwoodie house. She tells me you're old friends, Sally."

"Yeah, Delice and I raised a lot of hell together," Sally said, chuckling, "but now that we're so old, we'll probably have to stick to heck."

"Oh, I don't know about that, Sally," Hawk interjected cordially, his face bland. "You don't look like the heck type to me."

They had another drink, and the architect talked about downtown Laramie. All eight blocks of it. A lot of great buildings were being reconditioned and refurbished and recycled. Delice had been a dynamo getting places on the National Register. Rumor had it her cousin Burt was going to be opening up some kind of fancy California-style restaurant in one of the town's oldest buildings, an airy corner spot on Ivinson Avenue with a mint-condition stenciled tin ceiling. They all agreed it was no competition for the Wrangler, though Hasta la Pasta! might have some problems. Then they all agreed that Hasta la Pasta! already did.

Tom had gone to tend the grill, and Edna went to put the finishing touches on the rest of the dinner as he came in the back door, into the kitchen.

"Hey," he said, putting the platter of sizzling lamb chops down on a counter and giving her a squeeze. "I'm sorry about the surprise dinner guest. But it looks like Joe and Sally are hitting it off, huh?"

He was sweet, warm, and extremely attractive, but was it possible that Tom was a typical blockhead male when it came to catching somebody else's sexual drift? "Hitting it off? Are you kidding? The way they're smirking at each other and making little remarks, you'd think they'd spent the day road-testing Meg Dunwoodie's mattress. Jesus, Tom." She took the potatoes out of the oven. "The temperature in the living room went up ten degrees when he walked in."

"You're having a hot flash, honey, sit down," he said, fanning her with a dish towel and earning a poke in the ribs. "But now that you mention it, I wonder . . . do you think maybe they had something going way back when? He was in Laramie when she was doing the bar thing, right? So who was she zoomin' in those days?"

"Very delicately put," Edna retorted. "The thing is, I only knew her in her on-campus feminist banshee mode. We hung out a fair amount, but I had kids, and she was still singing with bands. For a while she had some boyfriend with a funny nickname who lived on the road and camped out in her apartment now and then, but he kind of disappeared. Then she swore off men in general, and sex with men in particular, and she got into that early-eighties, women-are-better-than-men, sisterhood-is-beautiful thing."

"Classic symptoms of one variant of 1970s sex over-dose," said Tom, crossing his arms and lowering his head, squinting his green eyes at her. "I know all the signs."

"I bet you do," Edna told him. "It's a good thing that in your case, the toxic effects wore off and the treatments could be resumed."

Dinner was well lit, well lubricated, and delicious. The conversation was mostly about the future of the University, which was bleak. As newcomers, Sally and Hawk weren't obliged to do much more than murmur sounds of concern, which was just fine with them, because they were very glad to eat and drink and bask in each others' pheromone fields. According to the English professor, the legislature was contemplating abolishing tenure, establishing sixty virtual branch campuses in cyberspace, closing the library, and doubling the athletic budget, all with the enthusiastic backing of the trustees.

"Poetry as we know it would cease to exist," he moaned. "Speaking of poetry," said the professor, finishing off his last sip of Hawk's chardonnay and pouring a glass of the fumé Sally had brought, "how's the Dunwoodie biography coming?"

Sally considered her answer. She'd expected somebody to ask, but had been happy enough to let the conversation wallow in the usual academic quagmire of self-pity and dark forecasts, while she tried to figure out how to take Hawk home with her. "Coming? I've just gotten started. Not much to report at this point, but I'm excited about the prospects." Time to deflect further inquiry. "Did you know Meg?" she asked the professor.

"I knew who she was, of course. By my time she was long retired, but she kept an office in the department. She'd come in from time to time, shuffle papers around, talk to a student or two. It shocked the hell out of everyone when one of her poems showed up in *The New Yorker*—when was it? Nineteen seventy-six?"

"I'd have to check," Sally said.

"Yeah, I think it was seventy-six—it was 'Homecoming'— the one where the Prodigal Son is named Cowboy Joe and plays college football."

"I *loved* that poem," the architect said, chortling. "She rhymed 'Home on the Range' with 'Red Grange'! She sure didn't have any use for American pieties."

"But some of her poetry celebrates Americans, or some Americans anyway. Like 'Sanctuary,' the one about the outlaw Arizona nuns who helped Guatemalan refugees get away from the death squads," Hawk put in unexpectedly.

The English professor gaped at him, and rather rudely asked, "So you're an expert on poetry as well as uranium, Joe?"

Hawk considered. "I guess I can tell a good poet from a bad one. Meg Dunwoodie was a good one. She wrote with a kind of clarity that made everybody think that they already knew what she knew." The professor raised an eyebrow, and Hawk shrugged. "Long ago I was an English major at Yale. I happen to have a weakness for good poetry. I'm a damn fool for *The Faerie Queene.*"

Tom was loving this. As a high school teacher married to a famous scholar, he was familiar with the superior attitude snooty college professors adopted toward those they considered lower on the intellectual food chain. "Maybe we should change the name of our city basketball team to 'The Faerie Queenes,'" he told Hawk. "There are quite a few team members who enjoy poetry."

"I bet we could get away with some cheap fouls." Hawk beamed. "A name like that could really intimidate our opponents."

"You guys aren't working up to some grand homophobic punchline, are you?" Edna warned.

"Naw, sweetie, we're just talking epic poetry." Tom

smiled at her, and turned to the English professor. "In what you might call layman's terms, of course."

"I have no objection to laymen," Sally added, gazing at Hawk, "as long as they know the difference between 'lie' and 'lay.'"

"As a former English major," Hawk told her, with a clear look that had some kind of edge to it, "I've made it a point to practice good grammar."

She was a dolt. She was a complete, unadulterated idiot. That dumb bit about "lie" and "lay." It had to have reminded him of a time when Sally Alder hadn't been that clear on the distinction. That was the chardonnay talking.

The allusion, of course, hadn't escaped Hawk. But in the interest of getting her out of that appealing dress, he decided to let it pass.

When Edna stifled a yawn, Sally decided it was time to split. "I'd better get going," she said. "I've been thinking about climbing Medicine Bow Peak tomorrow, and I want to try to get at least an hour of sleep. Fantastic dinner, Ed and Tom."

"Yeah, I'd better get going, too. School starts this week and I have to get my act together," said Hawk. Hugs, thanks, promises of future lunches and dinners were offered all around. Hawk followed Sally out the door, and Edna and Tom exchanged a meaningful glance.

12

Something Old, Something New

Something vibrated between them, twanging like a steel string. Hawk jammed his hands in the pockets of his jeans, realized he was holding his breath. Sally exhaled at the same moment. When she turned left at the sidewalk, he turned left, too. They walked three blocks without a word.

"Walk you home?" he asked her.

"Sure, *Joe*." She gave the name a good twist of sarcasm. "Go ahead. I mean, if it's on your way." She was near exploding.

He laughed at her. "Actually, it's out of my way. I'm just being courteous."

"Kind of you," she said primly, and then cracked up and gave him a shove that almost sent him sprawling. "Fuck you, Hawk!"

"At your service, Sally." Cackling, he got his footing by putting an arm around her shoulder and pulling her to him. "Any time in particular?"

She thought of several responses, but decided that the best was to throw her arms around him and give him a kiss so complete and so long overdue that it would have compounded kiss-interest, sort of like a checked-out library book. But he was way ahead of her. By the time she figured out what to do, he was halfway down her throat and halfway up her leg and they were struggling to unlock Meg Dunwoodie's front door while still keeping two hands on each other.

Evidently, you could teach an old Hawk new tricks. Long ago, when he'd been a graduate student in Arizona, he'd met a home-wrecking redheaded paleontologist who'd told him she was conducting an experiment to find out all the beneficial uses to which the human mouth could be put. She had asked if he would care to participate in her fieldwork, and he had generously agreed, in the interest of science.

The paleontologist had moved on to other projects, and Hawk, being a genial and curious creature with a large cerebral cortex, had sought to apply the field experience in other contexts. He reasoned that if the mouth could be so flexible a tool, it was worth wondering about the other parts of the body. More than a dozen years of fruitful research ensued.

All this had happened in the many years since he'd been with Sally. Long ago, they had been hot as hell for each other, but they had been, after all, young. Young people tended to be desperate and impatient about sex, even though they usually had more time and energy for it than their elders. Tonight, Hawk and Sally had both time and energy and the benefit of years of hands-on experience. They each fancied that they might be in for pleasant surprises.

"Hmmmm," she said, as he demonstrated several combined hand-mouth techniques, rubbing his body along hers as she tried to get her key in the lock, "I don't remember you doing *that* before."

"I don't recall taking a vow of celibacy," he explained, bending down to try another mouth thing between her shoulder blades. He could feel the goose bumps rise under his tongue.

She was trembling and breathless and could not get the damn door open, and all she wanted to do was turn around and have at him.

"Let me get that door," he said, wrapping her up in his arms and putting his hands over hers to turn the key in the lock. "If I have to leave it to you, we'll end up fucking our brains out on Meg Dunwoodie's doorstep."

They stumbled inside. Neither noticed the dark green 1969 Pontiac Catalina parked across the street, or the bald guy sitting in the driver's seat, smoking, doing nothing in particular. As they crashed, tangled, into the hallway, the dark car drove away.

So the bitch had a boyfriend. Some kind of candy-ass hippie. Disgusting.

Shane had watched her go out earlier, all dolled up. When she was out of sight, he'd done a little business with her Mustang and then gone down to the Torch to have a couple drinks. Had come back just in time to see her and that guy come down the street and start going at each other. Too bad they got the door unlocked. He could have gotten off on watching them do it on the lawn.

Fuck her. He looked again at the soiled *Boomerang* clipping in his lap, rage building. Fucking bitch got what was his. Well, he'd put a little scare into her, at least. Maybe something more. He threw his half-smoked cigarette into the street and headed on back to the Torch Tavern.

Sally and Hawk made it as far as the bottom of the stairs, but they had to stop and kiss for a long time. Her legs got so shaky that he was forced to support her by putting his hands under her bottom. When she returned the favor and kept on kissing, he knew it was time to find a place to lie down. They hauled each other up the steps, so mixed into each other's bodies that the past and the future and even the present fell away. Sally pulled him into the bedroom, down on the bed. He fell on top of her, and they pressed into each other, dress and jeans and shirt like steam over all that bone and flesh.

Sally was dizzy and aching, but she couldn't help . . . asking. She had always thought she was a feckless hedonist, and she had surely done her share of indefensible things, but it had turned out that she believed in, felt somehow obliged to, moral reckoning. He was sucking her fingers and squeezing her thigh, and she was just about ready to beg him to take her clothes off. She was, of course, a moron for risking this moment of wonderful searing desire, but she couldn't help herself any more than she could help pulling his shirttail out and running her hands up his back as she pulled her lips away, got a breath, and said, "Hawk. I just have to know."

Deprived for the moment of her mouth, he switched to her neck. Found the crease of her collarbone with the edges of his teeth. Moving on down.

"I mean it, Hawk," she said weakly, now *really* wanting her dress *gone.* "Listen to me a minute."

He raised his head and looked her in the eye. He was still wearing his glasses, but his eyes were glazed. "What?" he asked hoarsely, rubbing his palms over her ribs, over her hipbones. "What could you possibly need to know right now?"

It sounded incomprehensibly silly, she realized, and stunningly masochistic. "I need to know if you forgive me."

His hands stopped what they were doing, for a fraction of a second. The glazed look of lust gave way to something more serious. He was not accustomed to earnest talk at such moments, and he was certainly not prepared to have this particular discussion. They did, after all, have some things to say. "Come on," he said, hoping the conversation could be postponed.

"No." Then she kissed him very carefully, caressing the muscles of his back, grinding up with her hips, wanting him to know that she hadn't entirely forgotten what they happened to be doing. "Tell me."

She felt so good. Hawk kept holding on to her, kissed her hair. He had spent way too much time figuring out that you might want to hold on to what felt good. "I don't know, exactly. I knew you were back. I knew I'd see you. I didn't think that when I did, my first reaction would be to jump your bones. But it was. And the second, and the third. That must mean something." His hands moved higher under her skirt.

"What does it mean?" she asked, shivering, holding him tight.

"It means we were young, and made dumb mistakes. We're older now, and I really have to get you naked. We'll have lots of time to talk. Lots to talk about. We can talk over breakfast. Now can you shut up and take your clothes off? I want to see your old lady underwear," he said, licking at her ear, his fingers tracing up and down the backs of her legs, inside her thighs.

She rolled over him and sat up, straddling him. Her skirt was bunched up between her legs, between the two of them. She rose on her knees and tugged it free. Then she pulled her dress over her head. Lord have mercy, this old lady was wearing black lace underwear, and her body, all in all, was holding up nicely. The blood drained out of most of his extremities.

"Now you do something for me, Jody," she said, unbuttoning his shirt. She took off his glasses, put them on the bedside table, because she wanted to see his beautiful, dark brown eyes. She pulled the elastic out of his ponytail, because she wanted to feel his soft, dark hair trailing all over her body. She leaned down and pressed into him and kissed him a good one, then took off his shirt while he unsnapped her bra, peeled it away, made her breasts ache with his hard palms and long fingers and sensitive thumbs. His hands full of her, he was wound tight with longing to be inside her, and it hurt exquisitely to slow the desire.

"You're bustin' your britches." She laughed.

"Been bustin' 'em all night," he replied. "Could have been really embarrassing."

She went to work on the buttons of his jeans, aroused to see that he evidently still believed underwear to be unnecessary. He relieved her of her own and oh, she was slippery and soft and warm. Dragging his pants off him, she climbed on top of him again, her mind flooding into her body, wanting the flavor of him, and whispered, "Show me something old and something new."

He showed her.

They probably got more than one hour of sleep. More like three, but not all at one time. They kept dozing and fondling and tasting each other awake for one more drowsy, delicious, increasingly languorous, finally nearly comatose entertainment. They screwed each other silly and sore. Neither had had sex like that in years, and they were delighted and exhausted as the dawn broke, and they lay in each other's arms. Sally had her head on Hawk's firm, warm chest, and the sound of his heartbeat and the first birdsong of the day made her pulse thump, but she was too beat to do anything but smile and lapse into unconsciousness.

Later, he woke first. He could hardly believe where he was, who he was with. One part of his mind told him he was the biggest fool in the world, that he couldn't trust her, that he was begging for the kind of danger he hadn't put himself in for a long time. A smart man would put on his pants and walk out the door and stay gone.

Another part of him asked what he was willing to risk, just to wake up holding her sweet body. It wasn't as if it was a chore to make conversation with her, either. They had always had plenty to say to each other. In so many ways, they had delighted each other. It was barely possible that twenty years before, they'd both run into the best thing that would ever happen to either of them, but they hadn't known enough to know it. They were different people now, but maybe there was still something there that was better than anything else that might ever happen.

Maybe it was time they found out. Or maybe he was a complete sucker. He kept his options open.

13

Up a Slippery Slope

He was starving. He rolled her over. "Wake up, love. Do you want . . . "

"Oh, honey," she murmured, her face against his neck. "I think I'd split in half."

"No. Later, I mean. Er, what I mean is, do you want breakfast?"

"That'd be good." She sighed, trying to go back to sleep. "I've got coffee. Some great banana bread."

"No eggs?"

"Huh?"

"No potatoes? Bacon?"

"Nope."

"Make you a deal. You get up and make some coffee and I'll run to the store and come back and cook you breakfast."

"Most important meal of the day," she mumbled, an old inside joke from when Hawk had been trying to found a cult of breakfast as a miracle diet. "Take my car. Keys on the dresser."

He hadn't noticed the car. Very cherry '64 Mus-TANG. He tried to act like it was no big deal, but it was a sweet machine. Somebody had restored this baby to a fine hum, and he appreciated Sally ever the more for having put it in his hands. Brakes were pulling a little, though. She probably ought to get it into the shop.

At the Albertson's checkout, he ran into Delice, who was buying donuts. The Langhams were famous in Laramie for their love of donuts. It was known that Delice liked cream-filled, Jerry Jeff liked chocolate frosted, Mary liked jelly, Josh liked plain, Dwayne liked crullers, Nattie pretended not to eat them, but considered glazed donuts a diet variety of the species. Dickie adored every kind of donut, as was apparent from his burgeoning gut. Hawk noticed that Delice had bought some of that overpriced fat-free Entenmann's blueberry squiggle coffee cake. Maybe she was trying to reform her brother. Hawk's own cart was obviously full of more breakfast than one skinny man was liable to eat.

"Hey Hawk," Delice said, "what's shakin'?"

"Not much," he said, looking at her stuff on the conveyor belt. "Lotta donuts."

"Health food brunch at Dickie and Mary's," she explained. "Looks like you're still trying to start that breakfast cult," she remarked, eying his eggs and bacon and juice and potatoes and tortillas and a bottle of tabasco sauce.

"I tell you, Delice, it's scientifically proven that if you eat a good breakfast every morning, you burn more calories all day because it puts the system to work. I call it the Eat Bacon and Grow Thin Diet."

"I know, Hawk. You've been flogging the bacon a long time." She smiled sweetly. "So how the hell are you?"

"Can't complain," he said, trying to suppress a shit-eating grin.

But Delice had her radar on. "Seen Sally?" she asked.

"You'd better pay the lady, Dee," he stalled. "Or they'll arrest you for shoplifting."

"You'd better lose the grin, Hawk," she countered, collecting her change, picking up her bag, and clearly logging the conversation for discussion as soon as she got to Dickie and Mary's. "Or they'll arrest you for something else."

"Damn," said Delice as she walked to her car. She and Mary had a bet going on the Sally–Hawk reunion. Delice had bet on a replay of the Cold War. Mary, however, had bet on something like the expression on his face now. Dickie's wife, of course, understood that time made some things easier. "I'm out twenty bucks," Delice snarled, tossing the bag of donuts on the seat, climbing in, and putting the key in the ignition. And then she began to chuckle.

Hawk paid, got the stuff, walked out to the Mustang and got in. Delice was just pulling her Explorer out of the parking lot, and she gave him a wave and a shit-eating grin of her own. He bet that before the day was out, Sally's phone would be ringing, and Delice would be trying to find some casual way of finding out whether history was repeating itself. As the Mustang's engine thrummed alive, he could almost hear the gears of the Laramie rumor mill grinding into action.

Sally said that she still wanted to climb the Peak, especially once she had such a good breakfast in her. Hawk decided he wanted to go along. She was wearing hiking shorts, and he thought it would be fun to walk behind her and watch her legs work on the steep spots.

And he knew they needed time, in a pretty place, on the first day of their next thing. They had demonstrated adequately that they were still attracted to each other. They still had a hell of a lot of past to account for and considerable present to feel out. To be honest, they didn't really know each other any more. Long ago, she'd been terrific, and put him through hell, and vindicated his notion that ultimately, you couldn't trust anyone. He wished they could get by on sex and breakfast.

They packed up the banana bread, apples, cheese, and

water. They kept touching each other and smiling. Sally
let Hawk drive. He was grateful. Hawk was a skilled and
careful driver, and she was a maniac who had terrorized
him every time he'd been her unfortunate passenger. They
stopped off at his house to get boots and clothes. She told
him what a pretty house it was. For the first time, it struck
him as odd that he had no furniture whatsoever.

They gassed up at the Diamond Shamrock, went inside
to pay and buy candy and Coca-Cola, and ran into
Dwayne Langham, who was picking up a box of Little
Debbie cakes and a quart of milk to take to that brunch at
Dickie's. He might have gotten rich as a banker, but
Dwayne still thought like a musician. That rumor mill was
going to be cranking full steam by tomorrow.

As they headed out into the Centennial valley, Hawk
and Sally held hands. He kissed her fingers. She pointed
out antelope grazing. The Mustang's engine kept missing:
it wasn't tuned to the altitude. He said he could adjust her
carburetor, if she wanted. She smiled and told him he already had. Told her no, seriously, maybe he'd take the car
in to a mechanic and get the carburetor looked at and have
the brakes adjusted. He was not at all happy with her
brakes.

They slowed down through Centennial, past the Old
Corral, where Sally had once made the ill-advised decision to agree to a request for "Ode to Billy Joe," a song
Hawk termed "a real room-clearer." As they rolled
through town and up the grade, Sally took a breath and
said, "Technically, I never lied to you."

"Technicality," he declared. "I never asked."

"You should have," she told him.

"I know," he answered.

After a minute, she said, "If you'd asked, it might have
been different. I wondered sometimes, lots of times, when
you were gone, if you really cared."

A minute more. "I did," he said.

"I know," she answered.

Two heartbeats. "You should have known then," he said very quietly. "I told you I loved you."

"Yeah, you did. It stayed with me a month maybe, and then I started wondering again. It wasn't the first time somebody told me he loved me, and I was inclined to take the words for what they were generally worth. It took me a while to realize that those words were hard for you to say, and by then it was way too late."

Hawk drove on, waiting for more.

There was more. "You left me alone a lot," she said. "I was pretty needy in those days, Hawk."

He nodded. "I didn't understand what that meant. Didn't know what I was supposed to do." And he knew, of course, that he hadn't tried all that hard to figure it out. Wasn't love supposed to *solve* problems?

"You were supposed to get the idea and settle down and move in with me."

"It wasn't an option, then." He took a curve a little too wide, but fortunately there was no oncoming traffic.

"Oh," was all she said.

Hawk thought a bit, then took a breath of his own. "I have one main question. You always said Sam Branch was a slimeball. Why in hell would you go to bed with him?"

"He was a slimeball," Sally said. "He undoubtedly still is. I made an error in judgment. I think the three major variables were loneliness, tequila, and a high degree of persistence on his part."

Three major variables. She really was cut out to be a college professor. Now a tougher question. "Did you happen to repeat that error?" he inquired, keeping his hands carefully steady on the wheel as the road wound up the mountain. He tossed a glance her way, as if to say: Moral reckoning, Sally. What's the point in lying?

"Actually, I did." The car swerved slightly, but not dangerously. "Look at it this way, Hawk. After you walked out, the loneliness wasn't exactly going to go away. For that matter, neither was the tequila."

The memories had dulled over time, but now they were sharp as knives. Still, he was a long way from the torment he'd endured then. "I didn't want to talk to you. I told everyone that they were not, under any circumstances, to tell you where I was. Sometimes I thought I should just drive back to Laramie and shoot Branch or shoot you or shoot you both, or at least have a big screaming scene. But after a few weeks it didn't matter anyway, because I decided I had to look for a job as far away from you as possible, and I got hired to log well data in Argentina."

"So you were gone and I was lower than whale snot," Sally continued. "And then there was the fact that Branch-water had a bunch more gigs around the state that winter, and there's nothing lonelier or more conducive to the tequila solution than a winter weekend at some puke-hole in Newcastle, Wyoming, playing 'Jaded Lover' to snow-bound coal miners, then laying up at some godforsaken motel with the radiator banging and the lights from the cars on the main drag and the motel sign glaring in your window all night long. You can only watch so much cable TV. Only smoke so many joints. Do you have any idea what it's like to live on Tombstone pizzas?"

He gave her a narrow sidelong glance, watching the road. "And Sam continued to be persistent," she said.

Sam Branch was the human version of a Tombstone pizza, as far as Hawk could tell. This whole thing had really pissed him off, from time to time, for seventeen years, and it was at this moment freshly infuriating. But Hawk had, after all, just spent an extremely memorable night in her bed, conducting a field trial on Professor Marvin Gaye's theory of Sexual Healing. He was determined to get to the other side of something painful that had happened so long ago that he had put it in the context of worse things that had come before, and after. He reminded himself that this was pretty much old news, and he had no plans or obligations for the future. He was willing to listen.

She seemed relieved to see his willingness, and so told him the rest of the story. "It ended very definitively. I was sick of his games and his ego, and I'd had it with the road and the band. I was really involved with women's studies at the U by then, and I decided that I had to get out from under the sexist crap in my life. I had this inkling Sam might be treating me sort of badly. At the time he was fucking half the women in Laramie and using my phone to make long-distance dope deals. How clueless was I?" Hawk declined to offer an opinion.

"I was still gigging with Penny Moss sometimes, and he hated her. He told me one night while we were packing up at the Gallery that if I wanted to play with some dyke, that was fine with him, but he didn't want people thinking that Branchwater's chick singer was a lesbian. I told him I had lots better things to do than drive seven hours to Buffalo to sing the same goddamn songs and watch a bunch of brain-dead rednecks get commode-huggin' drunk. He told me to fuck myself, because I was probably already doing that anyway, and I was fired. He went out to put his guitar in his truck, and I just went out and got in my truck and chased him down Grand Avenue, trying to run him down."

"You might have had a few," Hawk offered, vastly enjoying the mental image.

"I might at that." She grinned faintly. She had taken her hand out of his and was now sitting with both hands in her lap, looking out the window. Now she reached for him again, a question aching in her eyes.

"All right," he said. "It's okay." That was the best he could do.

She closed her eyes, for a long moment, opened them, gazed at him. "I look at you now, and all I can think about is how much I want to make love with you." She almost smiled, but her eyes were too bright.

"No fair appealing to my libido, Sal," he joshed.

"And I'd like to know why in hell not," she retorted, sliding her fingers up his leg.

This made it hard for him to assess the costs and benefits of giving her another chance. "Okay. Say we use last night as Day One. It wouldn't be a bad thing to use some of it as a kind of template." He thought a minute. "If we do this thing again, there have to be rules," he told her. "No tequila. It evidently shuts off the flow of blood to your brain. And if Branch starts hitting on you again, I break his fucking neck."

She took a breath. "I guess I ought to tell you that I ran into him at that stupid Hasta la Pasta! place at lunch Friday, and he's already started hitting on me." Hawk stared hard at her. She gripped his quadriceps muscle, on the high side. "He must be suffering from amnesia. It's the only thing that can explain it. Or maybe it's just blinding ego. Anyway, he's anything but tempting, believe me. He's a frigging *Realtor*. He's a *Republican*. He's probably in the Aryan Nation. Hey—if you want me to, I can try to run him over again. He made me want to throw up the lunch I hadn't managed to get down. And I have a confession."

"Another one?" Hawk asked, apprehensive.

"The whole time he was coming on to me, I was thinking of you. The food and the service and the atmosphere at Hasta la Pepto were so bad, all I could think about was how much fun it would be . . . to hear you trash the place." He laughed. "I missed you. I've missed you badly, on and off, for seventeen years."

"I've thought of you from time to time, too," he considered with a wry look. "Especially when I was confronted with a truly terrible meal."

They had reached their destination. They pulled off the road, into the parking lot at the Peak trailhead. They were off on a tangent about one of their long-ago favorite topics of conversation, horrible food they'd eaten in interesting places. But as they got daypacks out of the backseat, putting on sweaters and windbreakers against the high mountain chill, tightening up the laces of their boots, she asked, in a low voice, "What about the loneliness, Hawk? I mean, it's not a constant thing. I've gotten to where I need a fair amount of time by myself. I've discovered that I need the solitude so that I have time to think. But if I let you back into my life, you're gonna make me lonesome when you go."

This was a woman he had once, he had to admit, loved. He'd found her in bed with Sam Branch and driven straight south to Colorado Springs, where he'd put his fist through the single grimy window of his room in the Super 8. The cuts had taken months to heal. He could hardly believe that he was almost thinking about falling in love with her again. And now she was telling him that she'd betrayed him more than once. Was he that big a sap?

But she was someone older and new, too now, someone intriguing. A distinguished professor. He preferred women his own age, and in his very eccentric opinion, she probably qualified as a worthy companion and a babe in the first degree. She had also lit him up all night long.

On the other hand, she was a guilt-stricken, vulnerable, complicated, fully adult woman. As far as he knew, she had lately lived alone a lot. So had he. He liked it. It wouldn't be easy to adjust to having someone else asking questions and making demands.

He would have to take it one moment at a time. Hawk decided that wasn't a problem. He was older enough, and wiser enough, to realize that this was a moment for a really good kiss. He gave Sally one, and then put on a daypack and cinched the straps.

She tightened up her own pack and narrowed her eyes at him, awaiting an answer in words. On that late August Sunday, as far as he knew, he wasn't going anywhere except up Medicine Bow Peak with Sally Alder. They'd go up it, and when they came back down, they might get some dinner and then, assuming she was as interested as he expected to be, they might want to go back to bed. Sex wasn't a cure for loneliness, but it was a pretty good placebo. "Let's walk," he said.

The first half mile was gentle. They loosened up their legs and chatted about their new jobs. Sally had caused the University of Wyoming as much embarrassment as anything else during her brief affiliation two decades before. She had gotten drunk and abusive at parties for visiting scholars, had endlessly mocked the pomposity of the ivory tower, had insulted members of the faculty on many occasions.

Hawk said, "It really is amazing they'd let you back in the state."

"It really is," Sally agreed, gasping as they passed the cold shores of Lookout Lake and headed up the loose gray quartzite scree of the switchbacks. They walked on a careful path through fragile meadows dotted with tiny pale phlox, amid stands of spruce and fir krumholtz, scrubby trees flattened by wind. Willow bogs grew level with the krumholtz, providing a home for obstinate late-summer mosquitos.

Hawk had been a boomer, a hitchhiker on the state's mineral wealth at a time when deals created a lot of work for lots of people, most of them horribly maladjusted. He'd been, in the words of an immortal bumper sticker, OILFIELD TRASH, AND PROUD OF IT. What in the hell had happened since the time he was walking up and down the obscure slopes of the Sierra Madre, cashing a paycheck, hoping to find radioactivity? He had loved the stingy, breathtaking country as much as anyone who had ever known it on foot. But what had he done to merit coming back as a college professor?

He told the story as they hauled from switchback to switchback, pausing to take in each spectacle. Glaciers had scooped out immense bowls of whitened rock and ice. The gnarled things that grew out of snowmelt and thin soil spoke mutely with the stubbornness of Darwinian victors in the cold, scant air.

Wyoming's Medicine Bow Peak, in the little-heralded Snowy Range, towered a couple of paces more than twelve thousand feet above sea level. Getting to the top and back was half a day's work. It was a mountain to climb for the views, not for the wilderness champ points. If you wanted coolness awards in the world of climbing mountains, nothing counted except bourgeois Fourteeners in Colorado. The good news was that the spandex crowd tended, to a surprising degree, to leave Wyoming alone.

Hawk and Sally had climbed the Medicine Bow Peak together three times, many years before. She had snapshots in albums, of the two of them with a changing crew of sunburned friends, hair flowing, toasting each other at the top with—could you believe it?—cans of Old Milwaukee. But elapsed time, and the sense of rediscovery of the place and each other, and the putting of one foot in front of another made the walk once again something to be registered, savored, paid attention to. The air kept getting thinner and colder, paler gray and icier like the unreliable rocks under their feet. Even in late August, there were still ovular fields of crusty, wet, rust-streaked snow curving along the cirques. Their boots got soaked and their feet got cold, so they hiked a little harder. Both of them were breathing hard and happy to rest from time to time.

And Hawk had much to tell. How he'd come back from Argentina and decided he might as well go back to school. He'd wanted to study rocks that might make money. "Emphasis," he added, "on 'might.'" He'd worked in the gold and silver country in the Rockies and the Sierra Nevada, and in the high Andes, and in remote parts of Brazil. He had looked, too, for diamonds. His father had taken him in on some gigs in South Africa and Zimbabwe.

"My dissertation was, as geologists say, an advanced piece of arm-waving," Hawk admitted as they leaned panting against freezing boulders, swigging from water bottles, breaking off pieces of a Hershey bar and feeding them to each other. "But it attracted some attention among people with money."

And so he'd worked in wild, hard, compelling places, running field crews up tough woody slopes and down cliffs and into valleys and canyons on foot and in clanking trucks and by helicopter. He'd made a name as an independent, to say the least, consultant, but he'd also kept his hand in, publishing in the scholarly journals. He'd lost and made money betting on the rocks he found.

By the time he'd told this much, they were on the last, high, steep scramble to the top, over slick rocks and slippery snow. They stopped talking. Neither was willing to concede the rigor of this part of the climb, and they were saving their air to breathe. Arms and legs working, they made the summit. And then they looked around.

A small part of Wyoming spread out immense and cold and magnificent before them, swooped endlessly and pitilessly down to high, faraway valleys. They drank more water, ate the cheese and fruit and the banana bread, gaped amazed. They both knew what it was to blow good chances, and they both felt, for the moment, immensely grateful for tastes of good fortune. What in the hell had they ever done that life could be so good to them?

Part Two

Part Two

14

With the Truckers and the Kickers

Over twelve years of sobriety, Dickie Langham had fallen off the wagon only twice. The first time was six months after he'd started cleaning up his act. The second time was seven years ago. And now, for the first really itchy time in seven years, he was sorely tempted to get himself a bottle of Cuervo and call up a friend.

He'd made a fire in the fireplace, and he got up to throw on another log. It popped and hissed. It was way after midnight; he didn't even know how late. Mary had gone with Josh to a state band competition in Powell. They'd called to say they were snowed in at a motel in Thermopolis. Ashley had an apartment with two other UW students, so who knew where the hell she was. Brit lived at home, but she was working. He was staring out through his living room window at snow falling in the night, thick and bright and soft in black velvet darkness. Jimmy Buffett was dreaming of Havana on Dickie's stereo, and Dickie was remembering tropical beaches, big scores, and pretending he didn't have any responsibilities. God, just this once.

Jesus help me.

Jesus, as usual, appeared to be hard of hearing.

Dickie zipped the cellophane off his third pack of Marlboros in twenty-four hours. Struck a "strike-anywhere" match against the brick facing on his fireplace. Filled his lungs up with smoke, let it out, reached for the giant plastic "Diamond Shamrock Fill-er-Up" coffee mug on the end table next to him and took another strong swig.

People on the high plains got real squirrelly the week before Thanksgiving. They knew there'd be a snowstorm that would shut down the roads relatives would try to travel, strand thousands in the Denver airport en route to turkey dinners and family feuds, generally fuck up everyone's plans and leave the world so damned silent and beautiful into the bargain that you felt guilty for resenting the inconvenience. This storm had come a little ahead of schedule, starting on the Friday morning before the holiday weekend. Usually the Thanksgiving blizzard waited until Wednesday night, to have the best chance of screwing the greatest number. Nonetheless, it had generated plenty of action for the newly elected but not yet installed sheriff of Albany County. Cars sliding off the roads, damned fool drivers trying to bullshit their way onto roads the highway patrol had closed, people with gunked-up chimneys setting their houses on fire, housebound husbands drinking themselves into mean-ass stupid brutes when their football teams lost.

And the second incident in a month at the Dunwoodie place.

The first had come Halloween weekend. Sally often parked her Mustang in the garage, but on that particularly risky night, for some reason, she'd stupidly left it in the driveway. The next morning, all the windows were broken and a swastika had been spray-painted on the hood. She'd been pissed as hell of course, and ranted and raved and all that. But ultimately, she'd chalked it up to Halloween pranksters (that's what ten years in LA would do for you) and called the insurance company. Had said that after she got it fixed, she'd go on down to John Elway Toyota (the

Broncos were 11–2, heading for immortality once again) and get herself a Land Cruiser and garage the Mustang.

When they had an informal Wrangler's Club meeting on the following Monday morning, Dickie had explained that Laramie was the kind of town where you could easily find out who was likely to be into swastikas, and he thought he might look into it. Delice had added that she could think of a couple of possible suspects. Sally assured him that she didn't feel like hassling the matter (more blasé LA-type ennui) and insisted that her insurance was covering the damages. Delice had given Dickie a "let's talk later" look and told Sally where to get her windows fixed and who did a good paint job. It occurred to both Dickie and Delice to ask Josh and Jerry Jeff whether they might know about any notorious Halloween mischief.

A couple of days later, Dickie had run into Hawk at the Diamond Shamrock. He happened to mention the incident, and Hawk said he'd see that Sally used her garage. Then Hawk had looked thoughtful for a moment, and finally he'd said, "Actually, Dickie, I took her car down to Mike the mechanic to get the carburetor and the brakes adjusted a couple months ago. When I went to pick it up, Mike told me it was a good thing the brakes were pulling, because otherwise he'd never have found out that a brake line in the right rear wheel was about to snap. Said it looked like it had been filed."

"You might have mentioned that to me, Hawk," said Dickie.

"I would have, if I'd believed it. But at the time, I didn't even tell Sally. I didn't have any reason to think anybody would do such a thing. Now, I guess I do."

"Anything else you haven't said?" Dickie asked him.

"Not that I can think of. If anything occurs to me, I'll give you a call," Hawk said gravely. "There's no reason to worry Sally about this, is there?"

Dickie chuckled. "The less we worry her, the easier it will be for all of us."

That afternoon, the second thing had happened. The Dunwoodie house was empty. Sally and Hawk had taken off that morning, Friday, in Hawk's truck, hoping to beat the storm and get a long way toward Tucson to visit Hawk's folks for Thanksgiving. About two o'clock, Maude Stark had come by to get the mail and check on things. As Maude told the story, she'd come in the front door, heard noises in the basement, and gone immediately back out to her truck to get the deer rifle she kept in her gun rack.

She'd opened the front door as quietly as she could and tiptoed to the basement stairs. She could hear the sound of her own breathing. It seemed to her she could hear somebody else breathing, too.

"Beggin' your pardon, but what in God's name did you think you were doing, Miss Stark?" Dickie had asked her.

"I thought I was going down into the basement to shoot a prowler, Sheriff," she said reasonably. "I was scared, but I was madder than I was scared. And you can call me Maude," she finished.

Turned out she was right about at least one thing. Somebody was indeed hiding in the basement. But it wasn't clear whether mad or scared had the upper hand with Maude at the moment when the intruder came rushing up the stairs and socked her hard enough in the head to flatten her. According to Maude, who was spending the night in the Ivinson Memorial Hospital, the assailant had then hit her several more times, in the head, stomach, and chest, thrown her on the floor and stomped on her back. He'd pulled her up by her hair, gotten her in a choke hold and punched her, and told her she was "lucky he didn't fucking kill her." In the process, she reported, she'd only gotten in one good lick on him, smashing the end of the rifle stock against his left ankle so hard that the gun had broken. That was probably a good thing, she observed, because he would certainly have shot her if he could have.

The sheriff, she added, should look for a man who was limping.

She'd tried to get up and run after the culprit. She was a large, strong, determined, and by that time undilutedly furious woman, but the guy had a big head start, and to tell the truth, he'd hurt her pretty badly. By the time she dragged herself to the door and staggered out into Eleventh Street, bloody, dizzy, enraged, there was nobody in sight.

At least she'd had enough sense to go immediately to a neighbor's and call the police. Dickie had taken the call himself, then sent for the ambulance.

The intruder had broken a basement window and crawled in. Dickie wondered, as Jimmy Buffett gave way to Hoyt Axton singing about dreaming of love in prison, if this particular criminal had a fondness for the sound of things shattering. The man had beaten up Maude and busted windows; he might like to break other things, too. Like brakes. Dickie's shoulder ached (physical violence always reminded him of that long-ago unpleasantness with the bad guys from Boulder), and he rubbed it. He could imagine the hot-cold peppery taste of just one shot of Cuervo Gold, slipping down his gullet. But if he did that, he'd need a little something to keep him alert enough to think this thing through . . .

Still deaf there, Jesus?

He went into the kitchen, cigarette dangling from his lips. Stuck his mug in the microwave. Pushed HIGH.

Pulled the cup out and drank deeply, and thought about making another pot.

Meg Dunwoodie's basement was a hideous mess. According to Maude, the boxes that held many of Meg's papers had been haphazardly organized, to say the least, and Sally had spent the best part of the fall going through the materials, making inventories, arranging things into more or less rational piles. She'd told Maude that she'd decided not to start by reading anything carefully, but instead to begin with identifying and sorting the papers by time, place, and subject matter. She'd left things in precarious, but organized, piles on the floor. Now there was paper scattered everywhere, crumpled and wrinkled and jumbled. Dickie did not like to think about how Sally would react when she got a load of that basement.

Dickie had no idea what the guy had been looking for, or whether he'd found it. The mad disarray of papers bespoke frustration. Sniffing the air, he'd smelled something burnt, and rooted around until he found a cigarette butt ground out hard in the middle of what looked like a typescript of a poem on watermarked vellum paper. Dickie read a few lines, realized he hadn't seen that arrangement of words before, and found himself furious at the thought that some scumbag had put out a fucking butt on an unpublished Margaret Dunwoodie poem. He stepped on the anger and bagged the butt and the typescript for evidence. He smiled grimly and enjoyed the thought that this bastard hadn't reckoned on dealing with a cop who loved poetry.

Maude was going to be okay. Her face would be a mess, and she'd hurt all over for a couple of days, and she'd have trouble swallowing for a week or so, but nothing was broken. She was also the kind of woman who could be a help or a nuisance to the police, and she was plainly pissed off. He let his deputy work methodically through the crime scene while he accompanied Maude to the hospital, and put a little energy into convincing her that her best course lay in trusting the police to see about justice. He wasn't convinced he'd been successful. Her bruised and spattered mouth reminded him of Clint Eastwood when she thanked him politely and told him she was sure they'd "get the prowler and find out what was going on, one way or another."

Just what he needed: a six-foot Social Security vigilante. And who the hell knew how Mustang Sally was likely to react (he recalled the night she'd tried to run over Sam Branch). He knew he ought to be around when she first saw the wreckage in that basement, but he wasn't looking forward to the experience.

Fact was, he'd been keeping half an eye on the Dunwoodie place for quite a while, and had stepped the pace up to a full eye after Josh had told him about the chrome-dome in the land shark. And Dickie knew who it was. The guy was no rocket scientist—he'd just sat there in front of the house, three or four times a week, assuming nobody would notice. Josh got the license plate numbers early in September. County five Wyoming plates. Nineteen sixty-nine Pontiac Catalina, registered to one Shane Parker, age twenty-four, at an address just south of Albany, Wyoming.

Shane had a sheet. Busted for pot in 1988. A couple of charges—no convictions—on B & E. Passing bad checks. Carrying a concealed weapon. Possession and distribution of methamphetamine, convicted in 1995, served six months in Rawlins, then conviction overturned on appeal, on a technicality.

But there were things Dickie knew that didn't show up on his record. Such as that Shane qualified as Laramie's closest thing to a skinhead. That he had been seen around town with strangers who shared his grooming habits and presumably his loathesome politics. That people whispered about guns and dope and neo-Nazi stuff. And that, according to that fountain of local history Delice Langham, Shane Parker was the great-great-grandson of Wilton Shepherd Parker, who'd been the brother of Gertrude Parker Dunwoodie, Meg's mother. When he'd asked Maude about it, she'd admitted that yes, she'd recognized her assailant as a no-good distant cousin of Meg's and a bad neighbor of her own.

Dickie'd gone out to Albany looking for Shane Parker, but nobody was home when Dickie knocked on the door of the decaying ranch house. There were tire tracks in the snow in the turnaround at the end of the driveway, so somebody had been home recently. Judging from the treads, the tires were regular car tires and pretty bald—more than likely Shane's Pontiac. There were bootprints, too, one deeper than the other: The driver was limping. But the falling snow was fast burying those tracks and really coming down by then, and Dickie had to get back to town or face the possibility of being stuck in Albany for a couple of days. He banged on the door one more time, then got in the cruiser and headed back. He was disappointed at not getting to talk to Shane Parker.

Maude hadn't been able to say if anything was missing from Meg's basement, and since they didn't know where Sally was—somewhere on the road, maybe snowbound, maybe not—Dickie couldn't ask her. But he had a kind of bad feeling about what was shaping up. And Dickie Langham had learned to trust bad feelings, the kind that froze your lungs and sent electrical impulses into your bowels and down your legs. He'd learned a lot about that kind of shock while he was on the run. Doing law enforcement in Albany County, Wyoming, wasn't usually very scary or thrilling, but he'd certainly encountered that freezing crackling a time or two. He'd learned to associate it with something evil—a screaming man, a terrified child, a woman with blank eyes. He knew that for all his long history of sinfulness, he wasn't a bad guy. What he hadn't learned, evidently, was how to cope with even a hint of evil without wanting to get wasted.

He looked at the revoltingly full, smoldering ashtray next to him. Went ahead and lit another cigarette anyway. He poked the fire, wished to hell Mary were home. Stared out the window some more. All at once, outside his window, snowflakes danced in the beams of headlights. He heard the quiet scrunch of tires packing down deep falling snow, the sound of a car door. 2:15 A.M. It might or might not help, but Brit was home. He felt a rush of relief, or maybe even happiness.

He knew she'd be in a toxic mood. Who wouldn't be, if they'd just worked a double shift at Foster's Country Corner, one of Laramie's two very busy truck stops, on a night when they'd closed down I–80 going west and would close it eastbound before the night was over and half the truck drivers in the country had braved black ice and ground blizzards only to fetch up in Laramie when they were headed for turkey and pumpkin pie?

"Fifteen fucking dollars," Brit snarled, tracking snow on the carpet, tossing off her hat and gloves, draping her jacket on the stair rail. She threw her tips down on the coffee table and slammed into the kitchen to pour herself a glass of white zinfandel from the wine-in-a-box Mary kept in the fridge. "The kitchen said they turned a Number Four Breakfast every three minutes. The problem was, we were taking like ten orders a minute. Daddy, I would testify in court that I personally served two hundred heart-attack specials between seven and two. Those goddamn truckers must've been saving their change for the juke box. They played 'Margaritaville' at least sixty times." Dickie was glad he'd put on Les McCann and Eddie Harris before she'd gotten home—jazz was so much more credible than oldies.

"That does suck," he agreed supportively. "Look, I know it's what you always dreamed of doing, but maybe it's time to give up your lifelong ambition of a career as a truck-stop waitress and settle for the barren existence of a soul-impaired but extremely wealthy finance capitalist."

Brit snorted. She enjoyed the fact that her dad, who looked for all the world to see like Baby Huey in a khaki shirt and a holster, was a witty guy. "The civilians were even worse. At least the truckers know enough to tank up and go back to their sleeping cabs and get drunk and watch Letterman. The *families* expect you to, like, substitute extra turkey for bacon on their club sandwiches, run down to some jogger's supply store in Boulder to find them their fat-free mayonnaise, and make them a reservation at a motel with free continental breakfasts." She glugged down the glass of wine and went back for more.

Dickie wasn't at all tempted to join her—pink wine was beyond even his addict's craving. Besides, he realized, his problem had been lonesomeness as much as anything else. He lifted his mug and for the first time in hours, tasted the coffee. It tasted terrible, but that was okay with him—he'd never made a decent cup of coffee in his life. She returned and flopped down in the brown plaid easy chair across from him. He wanted her to talk more. "So who were your absolute worst customers of the night?"

"That's way too easy," said Brit, leaning forward, setting down her wine and taking off the thick glasses she wore to work, rubbing the lenses on the skirt of her dumpy uniform to clean off droplets of melting snow. "About eight-thirty, there was a little scuffle at the diesel pump. These trucks had come in that looked like part of a US Army convoy, but weren't. Seems like some guys had pumped thirty gallons into this big camo rig and the pump didn't shut off, so the diesel was, like, gushing out all over the ground.

"The guys with the trucks were, like, very scary—there were like a dozen of them, shaved bald and jarhead haircuts, really pumped up, really buff, and all squinty-eyed mean. A couple pretty tattooed up. It wasn't the army— the gas guys said the truck doors probably had some kind of logo painted on them, but they'd covered the doors with canvas. This real big ugly one got *really* mad about the problem with the pump. He went into the booth and grabbed the attendant out and, like, got all yelling about how he wasn't going to pay for spilled gas. The attendant went out and tried to make them pay, and they started doggin' him big-time."

"Not smart," Dickie said. His rule had always been when in doubt, give up or run. He'd changed the rule somewhat lately, but he wasn't all that sure he'd been wrong before.

"No, not smart. One of the camo guys punched his face in. He's in Ivinson Memorial."

Dickie made a mental note to drop in on the hapless gas station attendant and get what information he could on the mysterious military convoy, when he went to the hospital in the morning to visit Maude.

"Why didn't you call me?" Dickie asked.

"Mr. Howitz said he didn't want 'police involvement.' Here was one of his employees with his nose gushing out blood and the manager gets all exercised about how we weren't 'servicing the customer,'" Brit said with disgust, taking a big hit of the white zin. She *hated* the manager at Foster's. "'The customer's always right!'" she mimicked savagely. "Anyway, he said we had to give the whole sick-ass Oklahoma City–bombing batch of them a free dinner, in the interest of customer relations. So we end up feeding these scumbags steak dinners, all in my station, and they order all kinds of extras and desserts and all this shit they think of while they're slopping ketchup all over their porterhouses, and when one of their fearless leaders gets up to go, you know what he tells me?" she asked, clenching her teeth.

"I can't imagine," he admitted.

"No, you can't," she said, tiring suddenly as she drank her wine and watched him light a cigarette. "Dad, these dickheads ordered like three hundred dollars' worth of food and didn't leave me *one dime*. This one guy told me I was lucky they were comping the meal, because truly free people despised tipping, and he usually calculated the tab by figuring the cost of the meal and taking off the tax, because, he said, 'Free people don't pay for welfare chiselers who hold society back.' I should consider myself tipped because he wouldn't make me pay the tax, and furthermore, because it would make me struggle harder to prove my fitness to survive.'"

"Jeez," Dickie said. He'd seen some lousy tippers, starting with most cops, but this was a new and goofy one. "Your thoughts?"

"I thought about ripping his lungs out, miserable pig," she said, "but I figured I'd lose my job." She got up and poked the fire.

"That's my girl," Dickie said, moving to the fireplace and putting on one more log. "You could be a finance capitalist yet." Give it to Brit: She had a good feeling for the despicable. Dickie'd known his share over the years, knew they'd carved out a cavernous niche since the '80s, knew they found places to den up in wide, scarcely patrolled country. There were doubtless plenty of people in his own county who would piously quote the Constitution on the necessity of meeting potential government tyranny with a "well-regulated militia." But Dickie had seen neighborhood thugs before. Anyone who couldn't spot them was either one of them or likely to be useless later on, Dickie thought, feeling more than a little paranoid. Hell, he was the sheriff. He got to decide what was worth worrying about and what to heave.

Definitely worth worrying about. And it made him want to heave.

It was after three, and time to get to bed. Tomorrow he'd pay a courtesy call at Ivinson Memorial, then chain up the county's Blazer and go out in the snow looking for Shane Parker.

15

The Stay-at-home Soldiers

It was snowing a foot an hour, and they'd closed I–80 west of Laramie. Bobby Helwigsen had left Danny Crease to tip the waitress and sent Arthur Stopes off to get some motel rooms while he went to the pay phone at Foster's Country Corner. He could have used his cellular telephone (he was an oil and gas lawyer in Casper, and the firm had insisted he have one) but he never used it when he was out on maneuvers with the Unknown Soldiers. He assumed that the computer geek at Whipple, Hipple & Abernathy must have been ordered to wire everybody's phones to be able to listen in, to make sure all the employees were doing things that were billable but minimally actionable. He knew W, H & A, like all law firms, didn't give a gopher's ass for attorney-client privilege or any other kind of confidentiality when it came to billing employee hours and covering their pin-striped butts.

Number One answered on the first ring. "Where are you?" he whispered.

"Is somebody there?" Bobby whispered back.

"My grandchildren are watching *The Lion King* in the den," said Number One.

"I love *The Lion King*," said Bobby.

"Report, Number Two," Number One whispered impatiently.

"We're in Laramie, it's snowing, and I sent Arthur to find some motel rooms," Bobby reported. "As soon as I hang up I'll take Danny and Dirtbag and go debrief Shane."

"Use numbers," hissed Number One, a reactionary millionaire Teton County rancher named Elroy Foote, who had recently decided they needed more anonymity in the militia he was bankrolling.

"I can't keep the goddamn numbers straight," said Bobby.

"No profanity," warned Elroy. "The Unknown Soldiers stand for God and Freedom."

"Whatever," said Bobby, who had signed up chiefly in the hopes of getting a reasonable quantity of Elroy's money, and hated it when Elroy talked in capital letters. "Anyway, they've shut down the interstate, so we can't get to, uh, where we're going tonight anyway. Shane, er," he racked his memory, "Number Sixteen carried out his first mission today, but we don't have any idea what he's got, so we have to go find out."

"I don't like the motel-in-Laramie idea at all," Elroy said in a flat voice Bobby was supposed to find menacing. "Somebody's bound to notice the trucks and wonder what you're up to. You could divert to Little America."

"Right. Like every speed-freak trucker in the world not to mention the Wyoming Highway Patrol wouldn't notice our trucks, and besides, by the time we could get there, if they haven't by some miracle shut down the interstate east of here, there won't be a motel room left this side of Nebraska."

Bobby wasn't all that tickled about it himself. He hated being seen in public with the Unknown Soldiers. He could always count on one or more of them for some kind of outburst. There'd been plenty tonight, that completely unnecessary business with Dirtbag at the gas pump, and

Danny looking like he was about to wig out on the waitress. Bobby had kept his hat and sunglasses on, his eyes
on his plate, and his mouth shut except when he was shoveling in steak and potatoes. He was not all that eager to be
made as a member of Elroy's goon patrol. After four
nights of freezing his ass off in a tent in the Laramie
Range, just so Elroy's boys could say they were tough
enough to defend Wyoming from invaders who had the
bad sense to attack during the winter, he'd a hell of a lot
rather have been hammering down for Casper, a good
hunk of a bottle of scotch, and his own bed.

Elroy said nothing for a moment, and Bobby could
hear "Circle of Life" faintly in the background. He
hummed along in his head, knowing Elroy would give his
order quickly because he thought every telephone call
over two minutes long was recorded by the FBI.

"Go debrief Number Sixteen and then call me from the
motel. For God and Freedom!" he whispered fiercely and
hung up.

Bobby shook his head. Sometimes he wondered how
he'd gotten into this Unknown Soldiers idiocy. He was
not a right-wing antigovernment conservative or a big-
government liberal or anything else for that matter. Privately, he described his politics as "acquisitive." Less than
a year ago, he'd been down in Cheyenne during the legislative session, schmoozing and drinking and moaning
about the crushing burden of state tax and regulatory laws.
Bobby had been working out of state for the past few
years, but had come back to Casper to take the job with W,
H & A, and he was trying to make connections.

One of the senior partners had introduced him to Elroy,
an old Harvard buddy and a very important client of the
firm. "Young Helwigsen," whispered the partner, "suck up
to Mr. Foote from Teton County. He has more money than
God and less sense than your average hunting dog."

Bobby Helwigsen was six-foot-three, two hundred
pounds of Nautilus-perfect muscle, blessed with sincere-

looking blue eyes and a winning smile. He looked just like the kind of guy Elroy Foote imagined must be an icon of patriot virtue, like Ollie North, really, only bigger and more handsome.

Several Johnnie Walkers into the evening, after working the Harvard connection right into the ground, Bobby had figured out that Foote was a wacko. This made him very optimistic that a savvy guy like himself could lighten the old man's wallet. Within a month, Foote was insisting that Bobby handle all his legal affairs, and within two, Bobby was also handling some things that might not have quite met everyone's prosaic definition of legal. Being an Unknown Soldier was stupid, but at least it was billable.

Through Elroy, Bobby met some guys who had gotten no closer to Harvard than the college pennants on the walls of the weight room at Elroy's ranch—or in one case, the federal penitentiary at Attica, New York. Elroy was backing a secret militia operation that called itself the Unknown Soldiers, or U.S., as Elroy called them in fond informal moments. They were dedicated to defending the cause of freedom, religion, and Elroy's expansive property rights, as far as Bobby could tell. Most of the Unknown Soldiers were intellectually challenged good ol' boys and mentally rearranged Vietnam vets who thought for various reasons (too many wilderness areas, too many missile silos, the advent of bad cappuccino at the local Diamond Shamrock) that foreigners and the federal government were engaged in a secret plot to take over Wyoming. Bobby figured that if he had to at some point excuse himself from the U.S. and enter the witness protection program, they would be way too dumb or insane to find him once he was established as a Cuban émigré corporate lawyer in a posh seaside suburb of Miami.

Some of the others, however, gave one pause.

Number Three, a.k.a. Arthur Stopes, looked like a small-town schoolteacher, which was what he had evidently been, in a small Powder River Basin town, until

God had spoken to him. God told Arthur that he should give up his position as a minor bishop in the Church of Jesus Christ of Latter-day Saints, which was, in case Arthur hadn't noticed, being taken over by liberals who thought blacks could be saved. Even those who still claimed to cling to true religion had gone nuts for money and basketball. The next Revelation, God told Arthur, would come directly to Arthur, somewhere on a mountaintop in the state, but only after Wyoming had been liberated. Shortly after this, Arthur had been having lunch at the Burger King in Casper when he'd happened to see a tabloid Elroy Foote was publishing, featuring some of Elroy's impassioned writing about black helicopters and U.S. Forest Service employees and other threats to Wyoming. Elroy could come close to orgasm while denouncing the horrors of the federal government, even though, as Bobby knew well, he'd made his hideous fortune gravy-training government contracts and sucking up every federal subsidy in the West for the last forty years.

Sitting in that Burger King, eating a Whopper, wiping a splotch of ketchup off the now-precious tabloid, Arthur Stopes told Bobby, he had been so moved that he'd driven straight to Teton County to find the author, who had instantly recruited him for his militia. Arthur was a skinny, pale-haired, goose-necked man with very thick glasses. He looked harmless until you got close enough to see his eyes. He had been Number Two until Elroy found Bobby, so Bobby flattered Arthur and tried not to get too close.

Then there was Howard "Dirtbag" Robideaux, who had played on the defensive line of the Dallas Cowboys during an era in which being a lineman described what you put up your nose as much as who you disabled on Sunday afternoon. Dirtbag had done some of both, on and off the field, and had managed to get himself sentenced to three years in prison for several errors in judgment. There he had learned all about race from some Aryan Brothers who referred to him fondly as "Soap Boy." Dirtbag was not the brightest of the Unknown Soldiers, but he could bench press a car and would do anything his superiors told him was necessary to beat back the encroaching power of (fill in hate term for ethnic group here). Even though he had been recruited early, he was automatically moved down in the numerical order every time somebody new joined up. Nobody wanted Dirtbag Robideaux thinking he was in charge of anyone else. He was currently Number Seventeen.

Danny Crease, Number Four, was the one who had found Dirtbag back when they'd pledged him for Phi Beta Aryan. Although Danny had once been as big an opportunist as Bobby, his incarceration had transformed him into a devout neo-Nazi. He would have started the Fourth Reich in Colorado, where he'd grown up, but there were already too many Jews and homosexuals and Mexicans there. He required a rugged, potentially viciously Darwinist white man's country like Wyoming as his heartland. All the other Unknown Soldiers knew what Danny believed, but they weren't all that worried about it. Gleefully, they had told Bobby all about a little act of ethnic cleansing the previous summer, when two illegal aliens in a Ford Fiesta had blown a tire on the Snowy Range Road. When Danny and the others got through making their point about Wyoming being for Americans only, there wasn't much left of the wetbacks. Too bad, huh?

Bobby knew that Danny had a brief history in Wyoming that predated his current affiliation with the Unknown Soldiers. Danny had told him the story to pass the time while they were shivering in the hills. Danny had once been a leg-breaker for a Boulder dope distributor. Many years ago, Danny and his fellow enforcers had driven up to Laramie to collect a debt owed their boss, and the chiseling bastard who owed them the money had skipped out and left them squeezed into an orange plastic booth in a pretentious restaurant. The boss had held the four of them responsible, and since the chickenshit bastard owed fifty grand, they each had to come up with $12,500. The Laramie guy hadn't been the first or last chiseler to stiff Danny, but he was the only one currently alive.

Danny considered himself a thorough man. Therefore, even as he was working to purify the nation for the white race, he was awaiting the chance to capture, torture, and murder a white, Anglo-Saxon protestant Wyoming native whom Danny referred to as "a scum-sucking born-again law-abider." Danny intended to collect, and soon. He figured that with sixteen years' interest compounded daily, that amounted to pretty much the price of the guy's life, to be paid one fingernail at a time.

Bobby didn't take Danny's vendetta very seriously, but at the same time, the Harvard lawyer didn't much care for the Colorado cutthroat. Bobby was somewhat worried that he'd have to shoot Danny in the back before things got too far. The good news was that absolutely no one except Elroy would miss Danny, and Bobby knew he could handle Elroy.

Their current operation, Bobby knew, was the product of chance. A couple of the Unknown Soldiers had been drinking at the Torch Tavern in Laramie one Saturday night last August. They had run into Shane Parker, a local skinhead who was pounding down Seven-and-Sevens and raging about how he'd been denied his inheritance. He'd shown them a clipping from the *Daily Boomerang* about some broad who'd gotten some bogus job at the university, and they hadn't paid much attention to Shane until he started yelling about how there were millions involved, and for some reason, the money really belonged to him. An old lady named Meg Dunwoodie had died and left a bundle, and Shane was her closest living relative. Old Meg's father, who'd after all been the bastard who'd *made* all that money in the first place, would surely have wanted Shane to have it, because if Mac Dunwoodie had believed in one thing, it was that Wyoming ought to be a white man's country, of the white man, by the white man, for the white man. Shane's own great-granddaddy, Shep Parker, Jr., was a cousin of Meg Dunwoodie's and had been in the Klan with Mac Dunwoodie back in the '20s.

Instead, the money was being wasted on charity, and some of it was going to a Jew whore who would get what she deserved before it was all over.

Shane moaned that he'd never have the money to hire a lawyer to get his inheritance away from the fucking university. But everybody knew there was a fortune in Krugerrands and who-knew-what-else buried on old Mac's Woody D ranch in the Sierra Madre. If they could just get into Meg's house and have a look around, they would probably find a map or some kind of clue to where Mac's treasure was hidden. He'd been watching the house, keeping track of this Sally Alder bitch, and even, he said, snickering, fixing her wagon.

The boys told Bobby about Shane and his problem when they passed through Casper on their way to Elroy's ranch. They were hot to help out a fellow American, but Bobby thought it was typical U.S. nuttiness. He thought the likelihood of somebody leaving a treasure map (or the treasure for that matter) lying around an empty house, waiting for a stranger to move in and start snooping around, was about the same as the chance of the Unknown Soldiers ever doing anything except wasting a lot of Elroy's money on trucks, fatigues, camping gear, and automatic weapons. Elroy, however, liked the idea of looking for the white man's treasure and it turned out that his own grandfather had been in the Klan with Mac and Shep. So Elroy had a personal and nostalgic interest in the matter.

At Elroy's urging, Bobby decided to check out the Dunwoodie story with Sam Branch, a real estate developer rumored to be next in line for the university's board of trustees. He'd met Branch last year in Cheyenne during the annual bribe-the-legislature fest, and instantly recognized a kindred mercenary spirit. Branch would know, if anyone did, what was up. Bobby could hang on a little longer, at any rate. Elroy was clearly slipping and when he truly lost it and they had to have him declared incompetent, Bobby Helwigsen intended to be holding Elroy's power of attorney.

Danny had gone to Laramie and returned to Teton County with Shane Parker, now known as Number Sixteen. Elroy had decided that Shane was to continue keeping the Dunwoodie house under U.S. surveillance, as the first step in an operation that would liberate Mac's treasure. The Alder woman was a nuisance, of course, and a Jew. Shane assured his superiors that he would get her out of the way long enough to get into the house. He'd already done a couple of little things to try to get her attention: leaving a dead cat in her yard, messing with her brakes while she was out. He figured he could intimidate her by busting her car windows and giving her the swastika treatment, but she turned out to be too jaded to be scared.

The Unknown Soldiers were undaunted. Their ultimate goal, they agreed, was to restore Shane's rightful inheritance as a white man, which he would then of course hand over to the Unknown Soldiers.

Shane had reported that he'd seen Alder and the boyfriend pack up and drive off that morning, and he was going to break in, steal whatever looked promising, and rendezvous with Bobby that evening to report and join the convoy. Sending the rest of the Unknown Soldiers off to find Arthur and the motel, Bobby, Danny, and Dirtbag got into one of the trucks and drove to a deserted trailer in a mobile home park in West Laramie.

There were no lights on or any other sign that anyone was inside, but when they opened the door they found Shane shivering on the freezing floor, smoking, surrounded by ground-out cigarette butts. He looked up sneering, doing a terrible job of covering up the fact that he was scared to death. Looking at Danny and Dirtbag, Bobby could understand the reaction.

* * *

Shane knew he'd blown it. He'd only been in the house half an hour, scattering papers and having very little idea of what he was looking at or for, when the old lady showed up. He waded in panic from pile to pile, stuffing things into his pockets. After running up the stairs and taking care of the housekeeper (his ankle was killing him— she was *big*) he had hightailed it for home.

Now the cops would start hanging around the Dunwoodie place. He also knew that Elroy Foote would be disappointed, Bobby Helwigsen would be disgusted, and Danny Crease would be displeased. He wondered how far out of Wyoming he could get and figured he could go home, pick up whatever stuff he needed and get halfway to California or Texas before they came looking for him.

But Shane was Wyoming-born and bred and he knew a Thanksgiving blizzard coming on when he saw one. The tires on the Pontiac were so bad he barely made it home. Besides, he still wanted that treasure. He knew now, after getting a look at all the shit in that basement, that finding clues in there was beyond his capabilities. Still, that didn't mean the key wasn't there, or that he and his patriot buddies couldn't find it. He had a couple of things from the papers, including a letter from old Mac himself, a letter from somebody else in Wyoming, and a postcard from Capetown, South Africa to "Darling Greta" signed by somebody named Ernst. The U.S. was just going to need some professional help, and he figured he knew who to call.

Six years earlier, during his spectacularly unsuccessful freshman year at the University of Wyoming, Shane had received a passing grade in only one class, ancient history. The course had been taught by Professor Byron Bosworth, a man Shane considered the one non-phony bastard in the whole university if not the universe. Bosworth adored the Spartans and loved the Caesars, and he had been such an inspiration that at the end of the term, when Shane dropped out and sold his books back to the bookstore, he returned to steal the ancient history text.

The Unknown Soldiers were, Shane wanted to believe, the nucleus of the world's next great army. But there wasn't a man among them who could have made sense out of those stacks of papers, or could even have an idea of how to use what Shane had managed to steal as a beginning. They needed the advice of a trained professional. They needed a historian. He felt sure he could talk to Dr. Boz, as he liked to be called, and get some help.

Now here came three of the Unknown Soldiers, crowding around him, expecting some answers. He lit a fresh cigarette off the butt of the one he was smoking, looked up at them, and calmly said, "We need a historian."

"Why not get a fuckin' ballet dancer while we're at it?" Danny snarled, reaching down and slapping Shane hard across the face, nearly making him swallow his cigarette.

Bobby stepped in to prevent the conversation from deteriorating instantly into a beating. "At ease, Number Four," he snapped, glaring at Danny and flexing his muscles. "Number Sixteen has obviously failed miserably in his mission. He will explain at once, and then I will decide what to do about his failure. Number Seventeen, you will stand ready for orders."

Dirtbag smiled, not a pretty sight.

Bobby had managed, amazingly, to keep Danny from going berserk and killing Shane and possibly old Number Two himself. Dirtbag appeared to be content to await instructions to harm somebody. Bobby exhaled. "Stand at attention, Number Sixteen," Bobby barked. "And report."

16

Second Coming, High-Rent Rendezvous

While Dickie fretted and coped, and the Unknown Soldiers contemplated the prospect of bringing in a consulting historian, Sally and Hawk were on the road. That morning she had locked the doors of Meg Dunwoodie's house, a Laramie milestone. They had thought they'd beat the blizzard by leaving Friday, but by the time they left, around eight A.M., it was already snowing in the pass over route 287, packing down around LaPorte, gray and miserable in Broomfield, bumper-to-bumper from the Mousetrap to the Denver Tech Center. They were in Hawk's truck, and he was driving. He kept saying things like, "It'll be better as soon as we get out of this godawful traffic." But the traffic continued horrible all the way to the Douglas County line. "Denver goes on forever," he said with a heavy sigh.

"I've got a theory," Sally said, pouring coffee into the cup-top of her thermos, taking a sip, and handing the cup to Hawk. "My theory is that the city's sold its soul to the devil so that the Broncos win the Superbowl this year. And in return, Denver will be turned into traffic hell for eternity."

"And then, as extra punishment, the team will be sold

and moved to San Antonio," Hawk agreed. "And John El-way will be elected governor on the Republican ticket."

For some reason, the line of cars suddenly started moving, and an Isuzu Trooper in front of them got so excited that it lurched forward, fishtailed, and slammed into a Toyota Camry, which in turn whacked a BMW.

"Shit," said Hawk. "The snow's really coming down now. Let's get out of here." He swerved over onto the shoulder, took the exit at County Line, and headed south on the first road west of the freeway. "We'll cruise south a while and then go back to I–25 when the traffic's lighter."

The mounting snow made the going slow. Hawk got out and locked the hubs and put the truck in four-wheel drive. The naked sprawl of endless Denver could have been unbearable in its ugliness, and they told each other as much. It was precisely the kind of time they might get frustrated and annoyed and start picking at each other. They'd been getting along great, for the most part, in this second coming of their romance. But there had of course been testy times. After all, they were crotchety and middle-aged and used to making their own rules.

Hawk was squinting hard through a thick windshield. Sally, not wanting to bug him, looked in his glovebox for tapes and found three: *Workingman's Dead*, a Merle Haggard greatest hits compilation, and the Allman Brothers' *Eat a Peach*. She put in *Workingman's*, and sat with her thoughts about the things she'd started finding in Meg's basement.

As it turned out, the key she'd gotten from Ezra Sonnen-schein hadn't opened the office closet, and when she'd called his office to ask him about it, he was off on a safari in the Kalahari or someplace. She'd thought seriously about breaking into the closet, but she hadn't yet worked up the guts to tell Maude she wanted to do it, and she didn't feel right about taking a hammer to the lock without asking permission. Sally had found herself fighting a complicated internal war between curiosity, manners, and patience. Patience had never been her long suit, so she substituted method.

She'd started in the basement, resolving to get through every box there, then go to work upstairs. She hadn't really read things yet, had just made piles and lists. She'd quickly given up on the reams of financial stuff, old bank statements and stock dividend reports and letters from brokers and tax crap. It was a hideous mess. Deal with it later.

There was a lot of the kind of plain junk files teachers collect over the years—faded and yellowed mimeos of assignments, papers students hadn't ever picked up, defunct memos from deceased administrators. There were a dozen boxes of those things. Just contemplating having to go through those damned boring files page by page made Sally decide to charge this trip south to her Dunwoodie Foundation travel account—she'd think of a reason later.

Slightly more interesting, and rather heartening when you thought about it, there were literally hundreds of letters from grateful students, most of them formulaic, in the nature of thank-you notes. But occasionally there was something eloquent. Sally had collected a few of those from her own students, but the sheer volume of those unsolicited testimonials made her think Meg must have been something special as a teacher. One note in particular had caught her eye, a letter signed by a boy who had become a famous man writing spare stories about the high plains. "You were hard and fair," he wrote. "Thanks for not being nice to me."

Then there were the cards and letters from friends and family, which tended toward the genres of "Having a wonderful time in Miami," "Cousin Emilia is recovering from the gout," "Come see us in Jackson," and "Looking forward to our visit to Wyoming next July." She wondered wryly, watching the heavy windshield wipers labor back and forth, if she'd find any letters from devoted pals who were looking forward to their visit to Wyoming next February.

Sally had also made piles of travel brochures, souvenirs, random train tickets, itineraries and triptychs, hotel receipts, and restaurant menus. She'd found printed programs from the musical evenings Meg had talked about in the interview with Edna. There were lots of fragile old maps, which she hadn't bothered to unfold. Meg had done quite a bit of traveling when she was living in Paris, much of it to the Alps in France, Italy, and Switzerland, to the Pyrenees in France and Spain. It seemed she'd found plenty of occasions to get back to the mountains. Sally hoped there would be photographs.

Like most reporters, Meg had kept scrapbooks of her clippings. Sally expected to spend lots of time trying to envision Meg as a witness to, perhaps a participant in, the big events people like to call history. The scrapbooks would be invaluable.

Most exciting of all, Sally had begun to find typescripts and handwritten drafts of poems she was certain had never been published. When she'd found the first one, she'd spent an hour reading, puzzling, savoring, and admiring. When she'd found ten more, she'd read them through without trying to work out the meaning. When she'd come across another thirty, she'd glanced over them and stacked them up for later careful study. Eventually, she would have to consult with somebody who knew something about poetry. But at least, she thought in her philistine way, a cache of new Dunwoodie poems was bound to make waves on the literary scene, not to mention pumping up the market value of the biography.

It had felt like a good idea to make a separate pile of stuff Meg collected during her European years. There were notes from her mother and many letters from her father. A few glances told Sally that Gert Dunwoodie's letters had consisted mostly of funny anecdotes, encouragement about Meg's writing, and concern about the dangers of the political situation in Europe. Mac's letters were something different, long on denunciations of the New Deal in general and FDR in particular. Even somebody determined not to read those letters of Mac Dunwoodie's had to notice those pointed references to Jewish bankers and international conspiracies. As a historian, Sally was grimly looking forward to taking a closer look at those loaded letters from the father to the daughter.

Other letters were from Wyoming friends like the Professors McIntyre and White, and from assorted Paris connections, including the artist Giselle Blum and her brother Paul. Meg also had a few regular correspondents in other places. There had been dozens from a man who, from the stamps and postmarks, lived in Berlin but traveled all over hell and gone. His name was Ernst Malthus.

Sally had found those letters early Thursday evening. On a roll, making piles, sorting things, she got to the box with the Malthus correspondence. She had been slouching in the basement since eight that morning. Her back hurt, but her mind was utterly focused. She was dying to wade into Malthus's letters—any man who wrote that often had to be a lover. It was plausible that a lover didn't matter, but in Sally's expert opinion, the ones who wrote letters did.

On the morning she'd opened the Malthus box, something jogged her memory. She went back to the stack of programs from the musical evenings in Paris. Yes. There was his name, Ernst Malthus. He'd been listed as piano soloist on a program in June, 1929.

His hands in the Giselle Blum drawings? Was his the "brush of the key" between memory and hope? The questions flew through her head. Night was coming on, but Sally'd had no more intention of breaking for dinner than she'd managed to take time for breakfast or lunch.

Maude, however, had other ideas. Maude had figured out that sometimes when she was working, Sally wouldn't get around to eating unless somebody dragged her off and fed her. Sally was in the process of putting the letters and postcards from Malthus in chronological order according to the date on the postmark, when Maude arrived and insisted that Sally stop at once and have something to eat. For the first time that day, Sally noticed that she was feeling a little light-headed, so she got up and went upstairs and let Maude stuff her with pot roast and mashed potatoes. Then Hawk showed up, coincidentally in time for dinner, wanting to know if she was all packed. She hadn't even started, which made him grumpy.

"We need to get an early start and it's already eight o'clock," he'd pointed out. He generally liked to be in bed by nine. This was one of the things that bugged her. When she felt like working, she didn't like to be told it was time for bed or anything else, great sex notwithstanding. Middle-aged Sally was ready to sacrifice the likelihood of bodily pleasure for the possibility of an intellectually fruitful couple of hours. Who the hell would ever have believed *that*? Feeling slightly embarrassed, she'd put off returning to the basement and gone ahead to bed with him. The sex might have even been worth it.

The interruption, Sally thought, was probably all for the best anyway. Once she'd gotten started on this new and fascinating thread, her plan to sort the whole mess first would be shot to hell. And more to the point, if she'd gotten going, she wouldn't have wanted to quit working and go on vacation. Now she had a break and knew that when she got back, she'd pick up the work at a great place, with plenty of momentum.

"Hey, Mustang," Hawk broke into her musing. "What are you thinking about?"

She realized then that he had only heard *Workingman's Dead* maybe fifteen hundred times, and he probably needed some entertaining at this point, threading his way along snowy back roads toward I–25. And she was thinking about whether she preferred sex or work. Not something he needed to hear. "Aw, I was just kind of making a list of the stuff I piled up in Meg's basement. I found some letters I'd really like to go through right away, but I'm wondering if I ought to stick with my original plan of opening all the boxes just to see what-all's there."

Hawk raised an eyebrow. "Fascinating question."

"Yeah, I guess it's always gripping to hear somebody talk about their homework."

Hawk didn't push her. As he knew, she was supposed to keep quiet about her research, and he was a man who didn't believe in making anybody talk about anything. He drove on in silence. But after a while, he must have decided he needed the sound of her voice to drown out the monotonous shushing of the windshield wipers. "I suppose there are advantages and disadvantages to stopping in the middle of the piles to take on something in particular, or going through all the boxes before focusing on anything. Or, you could just heave everything into the middle of the room and pull papers out at random."

"It'd probably make as much sense," she admitted. "There's no logic either way."

"You must have some idea of what in there is likely to be interesting," he said, spotting a sign for the interstate and carefully turning left, his tires slipping a little.

"Oh yeah, definitely," she said, thinking about the poems, about what might be love letters from Ernst Malthus, about all the letters from Mac, the Paris friends, the bits and pieces from so many trips. And she even thought idly about Edna's story about the legend of buried treasure, but so far she hadn't found anything that looked like a topo map of the Sierra Madre with a pirate's cross marking the spot. "At this point, I'm not far enough along to have my head around it."

Hawk steered the truck up the on-ramp to the interstate. "Well, why don't you try to think of something to keep me amused while I work on sledding this thing on down to Tucson."

So to pass the time in a friendly way, they decided to

play a game called, "What I'm Going to Do to You When We Get to a Motel." There were a number of subthemes in the game, including what kind of motel, where it would be, what kind of room they needed, in what order and how to deal with the clothes they were wearing, how a bathtub and a shower might become useful equipment, how fortunate it was that they had a bottle of whiskey. They moved on to a question and answer format, to wit:

Sally: "I realize that in these weather and driving conditions it would be inadvisable for me to remove my shirt, but if I did, would you find it a distraction?"

Hawk: "It would certainly be a distraction. Indeed, it's a little bit disconcerting contemplating the prospect. Maybe you could just sneak your shirt up a little bit for a second or two and flash just a little bit of skin, so it would be only a little distracting and not actually inspire me to drive off the road."

This sort of conversation kept him in a variable but enjoyable and not too distracting state of alertness from Colorado Springs to Pueblo. He looked so cute, his ponytail half pulled out, concentrating on the road with his hands tight on the wheel, that it had her wondering aloud if it would be worth the likelihood of a fatal accident if she put her head in his lap. Signifyin' woman, that Sally.

They should have made Pueblo by lunchtime, but instead, dusk was coming on. More and more they were quiet. Hawk listened to the AM radio, hoping for reliable weather reports. The blizzard let up some in south Colorado, but the news wasn't good—this was a huge, wet storm, stretching all the way back to the Sierra Nevada, which was only getting a running start on dumping a hell of a lot of snow on everything north of Albuquerque. They pulled off the interstate at a Pancake Inn in Pueblo, debated whether to push on over more coffee and onion rings that had evidently been fried in motor oil. This place made the Wrangler look like Chez Panisse. "We could get a room and start out real early tomorrow and still make Tucson by late tomorrow night," Sally tried lamely.

"I'd rather keep going as long as we can," Hawk said, taking off his glasses and rubbing his eyes and hoping to put a dent in his fatigue with the lousy coffee. "Depending on how much it snows tonight, we could end up stuck wherever we stop for a couple of days."

Man, he had good brown eyes. Big and dark and deep, and his eyelashes were longer than any girl's she'd ever known. It was a lucky thing he was so nearsighted and wore those John Lennon spectacles. Otherwise, she'd be beating off the competition with a two-by-four. "In that case," said Sally, "I vote for Santa Fe. At least there'll be good coffee and hot chile."

"And an amusing California chardonnay, if it comes to that," Hawk sneered lightly at her as he put his glasses back on. "Next best thing to being in Santa Monica."

"I wouldn't turn it down," Sally admitted.

Sally was driving as they fought whiteouts between Raton and Glorieta. She was actually a much better driver in rotten weather, which made her careful. It was dark but bright with swirling snow. They'd decided that what they really wanted was a motel room with a hot tub, and they figured Santa Fe was the only town between Denver and Tucson that would be full enough of bicoastals to have the amenities. Their necks and backs ached and their eyes burned from staring into the dappled blackness. Sally's insides felt like poisoned rocks from bad coffee and worse food.

And then suddenly, sometime around ten o'clock, a hole opened up in the storm. They drove through a ground blizzard into a clear place where a huge, spotlit billboard reared up in front of them advertising the Legacy of Conquest Inn on Cerillos Road, an establishment claiming to be "New Mexico's most authentic hostelry," boasting "in-room movies, Jacuzzis, and HBO."

"Conquest my ass," said Sally.

"My pleasure," said Hawk, giving her thigh a little squeeze as she navigated her way off the freeway, down the icy artery, and into the motel parking lot. "But I think they're really thinking about conquering our credit cards."

He was, of course, right. A room with a Jacuzzi at the Legacy of Conquest set them back $185. Hawk was liable to get stubborn and decide that he'd rather stomp out in disgust and sleep in the back of the truck. So Sally slapped her Visa on the counter and said, "It's on the Dunwoodie Foundation research and travel fund. We're conducting an experiment on the rigors of winter travel in the intermountain West. Very historically significant."

He gave her a look, but said nothing until they were heading out to the car to pick up their bags. "For a hundred and eighty-five bucks, I expect a blow job along with the room."

"For my hundred and eighty-five bucks, I reckon that one's on you," she said haughtily, giving him a good pinch on the ass.

They were both bone tired, but the room conquered them immediately. It was somebody's idea of what authentic New Mexico looked like if you added reliable hot and cold running water, a gorgeous bathroom with a sunken tiled bathtub big enough for a YMCA, a Sony Trinitron TV, a bed you could park a truck in—either direction—more pillows than a slumber party, a well-stocked fridge and wet bar, and a kiva fireplace, fire all laid out, close by a balcony loaded with more piñon logs than most authentic New Mexicans would see in three seasons of salvage woodcutting.

Sally went to the bathroom. Hawk listened to his joints snap and pop as he stretched his muscles and rubbed a few of the dozen places he ached. His head was still filled with the white noise of the road, but the sense of having found sanctuary was starting to sink in a little and loosen some of the knots. He lit the fire, turned off the lights, put some ice in a couple of glasses and poured them each three fingers of Jim Beam. "Now about you taking off that top," he said, turning around to find her standing there in a long clinging ivory silk nightgown that left exactly enough to his imagination.

He handed her a glass, and she took a hard swig, tossing her head back and letting the bourbon burn down her throat. She was letting her hair grow out, and it swung back with her head, catching a gleam of firelight. He stroked the back of his fingers down the path the bourbon had taken, down warm skin to graze the silk that fell low between her breasts. He took another swallow. "Where'd you get this thing? It looks like something out of an old movie."

During a rummage in Meg's attic, Sally had found trunks full of such things, shimmery romantic garments from a long time ago, carefully packed in tissue paper and quilted satin bags and boxes. She had decided that no one would mind her borrowing just one nightgown for a perfect snowy evening.

Hawk moved his hand a little to the left and closed it over one of those breasts he'd admired all these years. She sighed and shuddered and stretched. He teased the nipple a little with his thumb, and it poked hard against the silk. He put his drink down and closed his mouth over the place his thumb had been. Their original plan had been to get a drink and then soak in the big tub for a while, but they were both old and young enough to change plans.

Hawk was a man who ran hot. Sleeping next to him was like snuggling up to a furnace. She wanted to feel the heat of his skin, and thought briefly about ripping his shirt off, but she didn't want to give him ideas about what he might do to Meg's nightgown. So she settled for sending her mouth down after every button she unbuttoned, wished she could just take a big bite out of his nice hard chest. Instead, he pulled her tight against him, moving body to body with his hands stroking her all up and down, and she took his face in her hands and kissed and kissed him. He pulled back and very gently kissed her closed eyes and the corner of her mouth and several places on her neck. He really had become an amazing kisser. Then he pulled down the strap of her gown and bit her on the shoulder, and she went so goddamned crazy she didn't remember anything very precisely after that except the sound of silk ripping and two people gasping and getting hotter and sweatier and slicker and saltier and coming and coming until he begged her to go over one more time, just one more, baby, one, *more*.

Later on, in the big bathtub, they had another drink and examined with slightly painful amusement the rug burns on their knees, backs, and behinds. This led, after a while, to some very slow, lazy foreplay and a slippery underwater encore. Rosy, happy and tuckered out, they stoked up the fire and looked out the window and figured they were likely to be snowbound in Santa Fe for another day anyhow. Sally allowed as how at forty-five they were entitled to at least one high-rent rendezvous and they should chalk it up to that. Hawk was way too tired and satisfied to argue. They got into the big bed and were asleep almost before they had both feet under the covers, curled up against each other, while outside the snow fell and fell and fell.

17

Jumping Cholla

Thanksgiving had come and gone by the time Dickie
tracked Sally down at Crawford and Maria's trailer in
Jumping Cholla, Arizona. There hadn't been any telephone listing for a Crawford Green anywhere in or around
Tucson, a fact that had held Dickie up until Tuesday,
when Delice remembered that Hawk's father was married
to a woman named Maria Mendoza. Maria had a cellular
phone number and an address listed simply as "Jumping
Cholla." Jumping Cholla was not even close to being a
town, but was instead a loose clutter of double-wides,
domes, yurts, and other bizarre structures scattered
among the spiny flora and fauna of the Tortolita Mountains. The motley inhabitants, who avoided all contact
with each other and humans in general, had incorporated
themselves as a "town" in defense against the gobbling
sprawl of Tucson.

The cellphone was usually turned off. Crawford considered telephones to be tools of the devil, and Maria used
hers only for essential purposes. But being less misan-
thropic, more obligated, and more practical than her husband, she did have voice mail. That was how they'd gotten

the message from Hawk and Sally that they were delayed in Santa Fe and might not arrive until Monday.

Sally was a little nervous about the whole thing. She had met Hawk's father and stepmother eighteen years ago, when they'd passed through Laramie on a summer driving vacation once when Hawk was around. They'd come over to Sally's apartment, barbecued steaks, and hit it off splendidly. She'd thought then, as she did now, that if Hawk looked like that in twenty-five years, whip-thin and white-haired and intense, she'd still be thinking about changing his oil every ten minutes or so. She and Hawk had gone to meet them a couple of weeks later for a camping trip on Battle Mountain in the Sierra Madre. That weekend, listening to Crawford talk, seeing in his eyes all he'd had and all he'd lost, and watching the way he watched and touched Maria, she'd learned why Hawk described Crawford as a near-tragic genius. Hawk's father had run away, brokenhearted when his wife died, leaving a three-year-old son in the care of austere Yankee grandparents. He'd made and lost more fortunes as a mining geologist than Hawk liked to think about, through a combination of scientific brilliance and financial innocence. Hawk spent his childhood in Hamden, Connecticut, with a grandmother who was determined to have him uphold the family name despite his failure of a father, the father who sent him interesting postcards from exotic places when he wasn't too far away or too drunk or too ashamed to write.

The best thing that had ever happened to Crawford was Maria Mendoza, a ninth-generation Sonoran and a graduate in economics from the University of Arizona. Maria had saved Crawford from his own abundant self-destructive tendencies. He'd fetched up in Tucson in 1962, working for Phelps Dodge in a job he hated but couldn't afford to quit. He'd given up on love and hope when Maria walked into the bar where he was working on a mortal dose of tequila. She'd seen something in him not apparent to the naked eye (she was already an accomplished amateur astronomer), and taken him home with her. It was still a mystery why a highly intelligent, ambitious, beautiful, and evidently sane woman would have saddled herself with a thirty-five-year-old wreck, but her instincts proved to be excellent.

It turned out that Crawford was a drunkard because he was horribly unhappy, not because he was biochemically destined. Make him happy and he cleaned up pretty good, though he never got to where he felt like hanging around civilization again. Maria brought home a regular paycheck, and meanwhile got him back to where he was willing to resort to the telephone now and again, and call up a few old contacts who were delighted to pay him to go somewhere extremely remote to look at rocks. Most of the time, Maria supported him by working as an office manager at a Tucson bank. At night they sat on the front porch of their trailer, far out of town amid the ocotillo and the cholla and the saguaros, drinking wine and looking at the clear sky through an excellent amateur telescope. Maria still hoped to discover a new star.

Crawford had asked Maria to marry him in 1964, and she had agreed on one condition: that they bring little Jody out to live with them. Without calling ahead, they jumped in Maria's Oldsmobile 88 and drove out to Hamden to get him. Hawk, at twelve, had long since given up praying that the day would come when his father would want him back, and when they pulled up in front of the house, he didn't recognize Crawford. "That's your father," said his furious grandmother, "and that's his new wife, the one with the foreign-sounding name."

Grandmama had drilled manners into him, so he stuck out his hand and said, "How do you do, sir?" Maria had started to cry and hugged him so hard and warm it very nearly hugged all the hurt out of him. She promised she'd never let him go. Forever after, he idolized her. But it didn't make him any more willing to trust people in general.

Maria and Crawford knew all about Sally's betrayal of the older Jody, and Sally worried that they wouldn't be real excited about welcoming her back. But they did. Crawford, of all people, knew that nobody was perfect. Maria whispered to her, as Sally helped wash up after a wonderful dinner of *camarones al mojo de ajo*, that Jody looked skinny but pretty happy. Sally experienced the bliss of mercy, and relaxed.

She loved Arizona. Maria and Crawford took them on long fascinating walks in the low hot mountains, in the Sonoran desert staggeringly lush with things that stung and bit and pricked. They drank wine and looked through the telescope and had a Thanksgiving dinner that couldn't be beat. They were all having such a good time that Maria didn't even check her messages again until Friday.

Surprisingly, Sally didn't totally freak Friday morning when she heard about the break-in. She was much more worried about Maude than she was about the burglary attempt. The young Sally Alder would have given way instantly to hollering and tears, but this older one just poured a cup of coffee, took it and the cellphone out onto the porch, and got to work dealing with the situation. Dickie assured Sally that Maude was recovering faster than anyone expected, and that the hardest part was keeping her quiet. The cops had done their best not to wreck the basement further, but it was pretty bad anyway. When Sally got back and got ready to straighten things up, Dickie would be wanting a full account of anything that seemed to have particularly drawn the intruder's attention, and anything that might be missing.

That was the one thing that almost set her off. Her voice rose as she told Dickie that she had promised not to divulge what she found until the book was done, and in her mind, that included telling the police. Dickie said that he could easily get a subpoena for everything in the basement if he needed to, and decided to start cluing her in on some things. "I already know that there are some original manuscripts of unpublished poems down there, Mustang," he said. "The bastard put out a cigarette on one of 'em."

"A fucking smoker," Sally muttered. "Figures."

Maude had ID'd the prime suspect, Dickie said, a skinhead moron named Shane Parker, who happened to be a distant relative of Meg's. He hadn't been seen since the break-in, though they'd found his car in West Laramie. Dickie was still trying to track him down, although he couldn't give the matter his full time since the snowstorm had stranded some unattractive people in Laramie and had brought out the usual nasty behavior in the locals.

Dickie did not explain, just yet, that he had reason to believe that Parker had been staking out her house for some time, with clear intent to do harm. There was that story about a filed brake line on the Mustang that Hawk had told Dickie. Knowing about that, and with this break-in, Hawk would probably put two and two together, and he might well tell her what he knew.

And Dickie would have to tell her about the mutilated cat. "You'd better come on home, Sal," Dickie told Sally. "I'll fill you in on everything we've been able to piece together then."

Then Sally called Maude, who insisted that she was just fine, was furious that she hadn't been able to shoot the son of a bitch, and was having a burglar alarm installed. Sally told her that she and Hawk would start for home a day early, and Maude said it wasn't necessary. "I've been staying here since I got out of the hospital," she said. "I bought a new Winchester. If he comes again I'll be ready." Sally explained that she didn't find the idea of Maude sitting in her house with a loaded rifle, waiting for a skinhead, all that reassuring. Maude told her that she'd seen and done worse in her time, and left it at that.

Her third phone call went to Edna McCaffrey, to tell her that the Dunwoodie Foundation ought to be notified about the burglary attempt. Edna had already heard, and had called Ezra Sonnenschein, who was still out of the country. She had also called around and finally found Egan Crain, the archivist, who was having Thanksgiving at his Uncle Malcolm's ranch. Egan had immediately started demanding that Meg's papers be removed from the house and sent to the archive. Edna had persuaded him to put off thinking or doing anything, at least until everybody was back in Laramie after the holiday. She reminded Egan that nothing could actually be done until the Foundation was notified through Sonnenschein. Sally asked Edna for the phone number at the Crain ranch, so she could call and mollify Egan herself.

Before she could dial, Maria's cellphone rang. It was Delice, who said that she was generally concerned about everything that had happened, including the prospect that whoever had broken in and bashed Maude might return and do real and permanent harm not only to the occupants, but to the house. Sally remained calm, but her patience was wearing thin. "Don't worry, Dee," she said. "It's good to have the house be a notorious crime scene. You can put that on your application for the Historic Register." Delice apologized for sounding mercenary, and said that really she was worried about Sally. Sally admitted that she was a little worried, too.

Two calls later, she'd had it with the phone and was itching to get on the road. While she'd talked, Hawk had fixed bacon and eggs and hash browns for everyone, eaten breakfast and drunk coffee, loaded all the stuff from the Tuff Shed into the back of the pickup, packed his bag, and had started making turkey sandwiches for the drive. He'd run crews on many a road and knew how to keep the operation moving when the hitches set in. She finished talking to Ezra Sonnenschein's answering machine and went into the trailer's guest bedroom to pack her clothes. Now that she was no longer collecting information, reassuring upset friends, or dealing with future possibilities, the impact of what had happened hit her. That was when the tears came. When Hawk found her, she was sobbing into a Neville Brothers T-shirt.

For a long while, he just held on to her and rubbed her back and kissed her hair and let her cry. Then he gave her his handkerchief. Hawk kept his possessions spare and useful, but he always had a clean handkerchief. "Don't talk now," he said. "I know it's awful, but this demands some thinking. And it'll give us something to talk about on the drive."

"I sh-shouldn't t-talk about it at ah-all," she hiccupped. "That was the d-deal."

"The deal's off. The rules change when it gets dangerous to stick to them. Somebody wants something out of that house, and you've got to figure out what that something is. I'll help you figure, if you want. That doesn't mean you should go around blabbing about everything you've found to everyone you know. But hell, Sal, you're going to have to give Dickie the rundown at the very least."

"Thanks a lot!" she snapped. "I'm too sure I'd go around spilling my guts to everyone I know just because some dickhead busted into my house and beat up my housekeeper. I mean, that happens all the time in LA—shit, you practically can't rent a house without signing something that says you agree to be robbed once a month."

"No offense, honey, but there was a time when you would have been runnin' your mouth about something like this. You weren't exactly known for your stoic demeanor." He gave her a grin so quizzical she had to snuffle up a smile in return. He was, of course, correct.

"All right, all right. But you do acknowledge that I've grown up," she said, folding the T-shirt and zipping up her bag.

"I do," said Hawk. He was being pulled further into Sally Alder's grown-up world, a more complicated world than he'd bargained for. "Now get moving so we can get out of here."

As so often happens, the back side of a Rocky Mountain blizzard brought warm weather and dazzling blue sky. Hawk did most of the driving, and Sally did most of the talking. As they wound north through canyons and mountains, then sped east a while on I–40, she told him everything she knew about Meg Dunwoodie's life, her house, her papers. He listened mostly, asked a rare question here or there, and his questions helped her get things clear in her own mind, see things anew. He was a wonderful thinking partner.

By the time they made Albuquerque, they were dragging. It was almost ten. They checked into a La Quinta Inn that looked relatively new. They took showers, got into bed, and then they hashed and rehashed everything. First, what kinds of things did burglars generally want? Jewelry, electronics, stock certificates, cash. Sally assumed Meg had had jewelry, but if there was any in the house, it was in that locked office closet upstairs. The same went for stock certificates and cash, and the television and stereo were also in the office. Anyone who had cased the house and looked for such things would, if they had half a brain, have stayed in the office and tried to break into the closet. Instead, this thief had spent his time in the basement, riffling through papers.

That could mean any number of things. The poetry manuscripts were, Sally believed, the most valuable things in the house, and probably worth stealing. Insanely, however, this burglar had so little interest in those that he'd put out a cigarette in the middle of a poem. So clearly, he was looking for something else. What?

There was an obvious answer. They worked over Edna's story about the legend of Mac Dunwoodie's treasure. Maybe somebody was, idiotically, hoping to find a map to a hidden fortune in Krugerrands or something. You know: six miles from Encampment, turn left at the lightning-struck tree, X marks the spot.

"But if I were somebody with a map to buried treasure, I sure would put it away carefully in a locked closet, not in a pile of randomly thrown-together boxes of every old kind of junk in the world," said Hawk.

"Yeah, of course you would," Sally replied, wondering once again how soon she could get into the closet herself. "And I'm sure the thought would occur to any half-wit who'd been upstairs. So he didn't get that far. He broke in through the basement, stayed there messing with things, was interrupted by Maude, did a number on her and took off."

"So why would he hang around in the basement long enough to dig through stuff? Judging from what Dickie told you, he must have been there a while anyway, tearing through one pile and another. Why wouldn't he have given the house a once-over first?"

"Well, presumably he had some reason to think that what he wanted was in the basement," she said.

"And presumably," Hawk said very quietly, "he thought he had plenty of time."

A chill ran down her back. "But why would he think that? I mean, I'm there all the time. For the last two months, I've been practically living in the basement day and night."

Hawk answered, his mouth hardening. "He knew you were gone. He'd seen us drive off. He figured the basement was the place to start because he knows you've been hanging out down there." Sally just stared at him.

Hawk knew now what he hadn't known when he'd taken her car to Mike the mechanic back in August, when he'd dismissed the possibility that somebody would have deliberately tried to mess up her brakes. He knew more than he'd known when her car had been vandalized, again, at Halloween. He gathered her close, tipped her face up to his, looked her solemnly in the eye and said, "He's been watching you, love."

18

Huck and Tom for the '90s

"Well, isn't this an interesting development," Sam Branch said quietly to himself on the Tuesday morning following Thanksgiving, popping a Pepcid AC and reaching for his cashmere sport coat and his cellphone. He swung out of his spacious office in a strip mall on east Grand, told his secretary that he'd be having lunch at Hasta la Pasta!, and got into his Range Rover. He ran his hand lovingly over the leather seats, thought how life had been very, very good to him. But life was good because he was smart. A case could be made that he was lucky to be alive at all.

Only a couple of years after Dickie Langham had disappeared, Sam had made the decision to avoid any possibility of a similar fate and get out of the dope business. All through his four years at the University, and then for some time to come, he'd been Laramie's most successful main man. But it was high time, as they said, to consider other lines of endeavor. He'd saved plenty of the money he'd made selling sinsemilla to high school kids and cocaine to those who appeared old enough to vote (he had some ethics, he liked to think), and he put his profits directly into a no-brainer real estate deal that had made so much money, so fast, that he wondered how it could possibly be legal. Turned out that not only was it legal, it was only barely taxable, thanks to the legislative effectiveness of the real estate lobby, all the way up to Congress.

Sam had always known he had a head for money, but for some time he'd had to conceal his genius for fear of being sent to prison. So he'd fashioned a persona as a sleepy-eyed, loose-living country western front-man and gigged his way around the West while putting together a very lucrative and entirely unlawful "medical practice," as he'd liked to call it. It had been a good life—loaded a lot, more sex than you could imagine (and very nearly as much as he would have desired), plenty of time to go fishing when he felt like it. On contemplative days, he'd thought of himself as a kind of late-'70s Huck Finn.

But he'd been on the sunny side of shady for years and years, and he was, as the century neared an end, a major figure in the Wyoming business world, a rising star in the National Association of Realtors, and a serious player in the state Republican party. What kept his sordid past from catching up with him and ruining him was the fact that a surprising number of influential people had been regular customers back in those more tolerant, less efficient times.

Minutes earlier, Sam's office phone had rung.

"Hey there," said a hearty voice. "This is Bobby Helwigsen. We met at the legislature in Cheyenne, remember?"

Sam remembered. Helwigsen had impressed him as precisely the sort of sharp, cynical operator who might be of immense use at a future time. At thirty-three, Sam saw Bobby as a guy who wore tailored suits and had never done anything but go to school, work out at the gym, and hold a high-paying job. Probably figured he had all the angles. At thirty-three, Sam hadn't even finished throwing up yet. Now, nearing fifty, Sam was pretty sure he had some angles little Bobby was still seeing as straight lines.

"Listen," Bobby said. "I'm down in Laramie and I'd

love to take you to lunch, chat about this and that. Any chance you're free now?"

Sam had heard that Bobby was doing a lot of work lately for Elroy Foote, one of the richest and least balanced men in Wyoming. Bobby hadn't been too specific about what he wanted to talk to Sam about, but Sam figured it was worth enduring a miserable couple of hours at the mercy of Hasta la Pasta! to find out.

The Unknown Soldiers had left Laramie early in the morning on the Saturday before Thanksgiving. Most had headed home—to Cheyenne and Rock Springs, Douglas and Riverton, small towns and little ranches scattered across the state, where they awaited their next mobilization. Bobby badly wanted to go back to Casper, but he decided he'd better accompany Arthur Stopes, Danny Crease, and Dirtbag Robideaux, who were taking Shane Parker to Elroy Foote's place, Freedom Ranch. Once Shane told them he'd blown the burglary, they'd known it wouldn't be long before the cops would be after him. There weren't that many skinheads in Laramie, and Maude had gotten a good look at him. He'd been hanging around the place a lot, and somebody might have noticed. He needed to disappear until they figured out what to do next.

Danny, predictably, wanted to kill Shane instantly. Arthur and Bobby admitted that Shane had become a liability, but they argued against executing him (as Arthur put it) because they thought they might need him later, once they'd figured out what to do. Danny grudgingly conceded that they were right, but privately told himself that if they didn't come up with a plan quickly, he might be tempted to cut his own losses by killing them all and letting God sort them out.

Elroy had been very disturbed at the news that the break-in had failed, and seemed at a complete loss to know what to do next. They all retired to private quarters

Saturday night, frustrated and, in several cases, somewhat deranged. Bobby had managed to buy himself a bottle of scotch when they'd stopped for gas, and he worked it down steadily while he tried to come up with a way to turn what was looking like a big mistake into something with potential. He looked at the tattered *Boomerang* clipping he'd taken from Shane, unable to figure how he'd gotten mixed up in this ridiculously low-percentage Dunwoodie mess. "I'm a goddamn lawyer," he'd cried aloud after knocking off several inches of Johnny Walker, then reminded himself to shut up or he'd have Dirtbag or somebody coming to find out what was up. "I don't even give a shit about Mac Dunwoodie's treasure, the white man's right to rule Wyoming, or, for that matter, Elroy's property rights," he continued, muttering to himself. "All I care about, as I've reminded myself all along, is my bottom line. What am I doing with this crazy bunch of bozos?"

It was almost too easy.

He was a lawyer. He sued people and got paid for it. Whether he won or lost, he billed hours, and by now, he was practically writing checks on Elroy's accounts. One of the first things he'd done when he'd started handling Elroy's affairs was to set up a nonprofit, nonpartisan foundation, the Foote Freedom Foundation (FFF), which was mainly devoted to paying Bobby's legal fees. What he needed was somebody for Elroy to sue, and some reason to sue them. He looked again at the clipping, thought about the weird way that Dunwoodie endowment seemed to work. Maybe old Meg had not quite been in her right mind when she'd written her will. If so, then it was worth keeping Shane alive awhile in case Bobby had to use him as plaintiff and rightful heir in a challenge to the will.

He wondered, too, if the University had any business taking that money, with all those strings attached. And apron strings at that. Hell, the old lady had practically ordered them from the grave to burn every bra in Laramie. Some chick she'd personally handpicked was getting paid to pretend women had ever done anything. It was sort of like reverse discrimination. Perhaps there might be some people at the University itself who would consider a bequest so full of conditions and stipulations and women's liberation to be a violation of academic freedom. Naturally, Bobby didn't care one bit about academic freedom, but there must be people who did. Talk radio was very popular in Wyoming.

He thought about Shane's description of his idol, Dr. Bosworth, and looked again at the clipping. The history department did not appear to have profited by the bequest; perhaps there were bruised feelings. And surely he could convince Elroy to bankroll a lawsuit that was supposedly about freedom, even if it was academic. Bobby would of course make some money, but it was also a good idea to convince Elroy that this was a better strategy for shaking loose more information about the Dunwoodie fortune than trying to break into that house or, Shane's *brilliant* plan, kidnapping a historian and forcing him to do research. By morning, he'd mapped the whole thing out.

"I hate this plan," said Danny Crease. "We're going to end up offing people anyway."

"I like it," said Elroy, who was the one who really counted.

"I'll go along with it," said Arthur. "Perhaps it will bring me closer to revelation."

Bobby shivered.

The other Unknown Soldiers, Dirtbag blessedly included, wouldn't have to be involved at all. Most would remain at home, on call, and Dirtbag would be detailed to assure that Shane remained quietly out of the way, at the ranch.

So right after the Thanksgiving weekend, Bobby and Arthur drove down to Laramie. They went to the history department claiming to represent a group of alumni worried that the Dunwoodie gift violated academic freedom.

(There was some truth to that; Bobby had partied his way through UW law school.) They made an offer, on behalf of the concerned alumni, to seek legal counsel in the matter, and to think about bringing suit on behalf of similarly concerned faculty members.

They didn't even have to sell Bosworth—he'd already thought about taking legal action, but said that on his salary he couldn't have afforded to hire a lawyer. "Money," Bobby told him, "is not a problem." And it had been that simple. They would round up a group of aggrieved faculty, who would file suit to challenge the bequest. Bobby would handle the legal end, and a generous, concerned donor would provide the cash. Bosworth asked who that donor might be and Bobby explained that he'd be paid by the Foote Freedom Foundation, a nonprofit, nonpartisan group whose politics he described as "libertarian." Bobby's next move was to line up political support and think about the best way to threaten the University into believing somebody really planned to sue. (He didn't. He mostly intended to bill. But if he had to sue, he could do that, too.)

He was still on the clock. All was right with the world.

"Beefcake alert," said one waitress to another as they poured water into spotty glasses at Hasta la Pasta! Bobby Helwigsen, looking coolly corporate in a white shirt, blue tie, and dark Brooks Brothers suit, had just walked in, found Sam Branch sitting at his usual table in the bar, and gone over to join him. "Two at once."

"If the other one's like Sam Branch, you'd better watch your ass, girl," said the other waitress, a veteran.

As they shook hands, Bobby and Sam loaded all the manly sincerity they could into their twinkling blue eyes and firm grips. Bobby, impressive in his suit, had three inches on Sam, but Sam, in blue jeans, a denim shirt and an expensive sport coat, had been ruggedly charming longer. Bobby was sporting the kind of jarhead haircut you didn't usually see on lawyers, and Sam noticed. Sam's gold-and-silver hair was curling over his shirt collar, evidently not a liability for rancho deluxe Realtors, but something that caught Bobby's eye. Sam had already ordered a Heineken, and Bobby asked for the same. Bobby was from a generation that had never learned to drink at lunch, but when you were trying to get something out of a guy, you ordered one of whatever he was having.

The waitress brought his beer right back, bending over both of them to lay menus on the streaky, not quite clean table. She stood a little too close to Bobby as she announced the specials (both men knew enough not to bother listening) and hung around a little too attentively waiting for them to order. Bobby had no more illusions about Wyoming haute cuisine than Sam did. They both ordered the Hasta la Pasta! version of a grilled ham and cheese sandwich. By the time she left, they'd both moved silently beyond opening cordialities into the wary dance of business.

"So what brings you to Laramie?" Sam asked, putting Bobby immediately in the position of being the one answering questions, and putting himself immediately in the position of the one who gathers, but doesn't give out, information.

"Oh, I've got some depositions in Cheyenne tomorrow, and I thought I'd stop here on the way and do a thing or two at the University," Bobby said blandly, taking a sip from the Heineken bottle and wiping the foam off his lips with the back of his hand, seeking a casual effect that was ruined when the bottle foamed up and overflowed onto the table. He dabbed ineffectually at the spreading pool of beer with a tiny bar napkin, and the waitress came running with a towel. In her enthusiasm, she swept most of the spilled beer into his lap.

Sam chuckled briefly at this little calamity, but said

nothing and tried to look sympathetic while the wiping up was going on and the waitress brought a complimentary second beer. ("Our fault entirely, sir," she simpered, getting no response.) Sam waited for Bobby to speak.

"So how's life treating you, Sam? Going over to the legislature in January?"

"I might," Sam allowed, "if there's something worth going for."

"Always some interesting tax stuff on the agenda," said Bobby.

"Tax stuff is never interesting, but it's always on the agenda," said Sam.

Sam could have kept this up all day, but Bobby'd had enough sparkling repartee. "I hear the governor plans to appoint you to the trustees," he said.

"You hear lots of things in Wyoming," said Sam. "It's a state full of ears."

"Be a great thing for the University, Sam," Bobby offered warmly, "guy with good solid politics and good business sense."

"What the hell do you care?" Sam asked, sick of the hearty two-guys thing and delighted at catching Bobby completely off guard.

Bobby wondered how he ought to play this. The political zealot: Make a lot of pious noise about concerned alumni and aggrieved faculty and academic freedom and the reputation of the university? The political operator: Talk about the money, and get right down to horse-trading? Bobby didn't know Sam well enough to know for sure what would work, but he suspected that the zealot routine would be as transparent to Sam as it would be to Bobby himself if somebody like him tried it. Or to his own self be true, be a lawyer, by God, and answer a question with a question.

"What do you think about this Dunwoodie Chair thing?"

Sam looked surprised at that one. He'd given the Dun-woodie Chair thing relatively little thought. As the whole town knew, Sally Alder's ass (which Sam considered still enticing) was sitting in it. He knew that there was a lot of money involved, but Sam didn't really care how the University got or spent its money as long as the basketball team won and they didn't raise property taxes. "I don't," he said shortly. "Why do you ask?"

"Well," Bobby drawled, "a lot of people are asking questions about it. Of course, there've been gifts like this that other universities felt they had to turn down on the grounds that they violated academic freedom. Yale had that Bass Professor fiasco a few years back, where they turned down millions for a chair teaching the goddamned classics of western civilization, on the grounds that it usurped curriculum decisions that properly belonged to the faculty. United Parcel Service tried to endow a chair in occupational medicine at the University of Washington, but the university turned it down when the bequest named the guy who was to be appointed to the chair, and it turned out he'd done a lot of research that proved that workers' back problems were caused by family stress, not on-the-job stuff like lifting four-hundred-pound packages. And it isn't just conservatives who've been getting the shaft. Yale turned down money from that gay agitator, Larry Kramer, to endow a chair in gay and lesbian studies. I mean, this is a hot topic!" he exclaimed, flinging his arms out and nearly upending the waitress, who'd arrived with half-done sandwiches that had unfortunately been exposed to a grill upon which a twice-thawed filet-o-fish had recently been deposited.

Sam could smell his sandwich without taking a bite; he settled for the limp but non-fishy fries. "Hot topic," he said, shaking his head.

Bobby had tasted his own sandwich and was obviously disgusted but clearly not surprised. He was working at getting ketchup out of a Heinz bottle that had recently been refilled with industrial-grade condiment.

Sam squinted steely-eyed at Bobby. "I'm trying to figure out why I should give a rat's ass."

Now Branch was gaming him, and it pissed Bobby off. Branch was worth a bundle, Bobby'd heard, but he was not in the same financial universe as Elroy Foote. "The rat's ass you give," he told Sam sharply, shoving his odious lunch aside, "may be your own."

Sam smiled. He could learn to like this guy. "Exactly how?" he asked, unwrapping and lighting a thin cigar.

Bobby was all lawyer now, on home court. "As of this morning, the ball is already rolling on a challenge to the Dunwoodie bequest, on the grounds that various aspects of the management of the gift violate principles of academic freedom, compromising the integrity and standing of the University. An associate and I met with a professor in the history department, and he's been talking with a group of faculty on whose behalf the suit will be filed. I'll be handling the case, and I just thought you might like to know what's going on from the get-go, so that you have time to plan your response when you're asked where you stand."

"Who'd you talk to, Bobby? The Boz?" Sam had of course known Bosworth a long time—the man's second, or was it third, ex-wife used to buy grams from him. Every time the Boz showed up in a bar where Branchwater happened to be playing, Sally Alder had said, "Oh goodie. Here comes the *blancmange*." Sally said looking at Byron Bosworth always reminded her of that episode of the Monty Python show where the *blancmanges*—white jiggly Jell-O puddings from outer space—turn all the tennis players into Scotsmen because Scotsmen are notoriously bad tennis players and the *blancmanges* want to win Wimbledon. The man was shaped like a soft, lumpy, glutinous pyramid, pale beige from head to toe.

"Professor Bosworth is a party to the suit. But as I understand it, there's been considerable discussion among the faculty about the bequest."

Sam smoked, thought. "I'm sure there has. But this still doesn't tell me why I might find any reason to get on board on this, which is what I presume you're trying to get me to do."

"I'm not trying to get you to do anything," Bobby lied carefully. "But you might also be interested in knowing that, in addition to the fact that Whipple, Hipple and Abernathy will be representing the plaintiffs, the legal expenses will be paid by the Foote Freedom Foundation."

Deep pockets. Elroy Foote owned companies worth more than the state of Wyoming. Several. For that matter, he owned companies worth more than most states, and many countries. If Foote wanted to pursue this matter, not only could he pay lawyers until everyone involved was broke, busted, disgusted, or dead, but he could also pay for a publicity campaign that would saturate Wyoming like a sponge full of piss. The question was, *why*. As everyone knew, Elroy Foote was a Harvard man.

"Why in the name of God does Elroy Foote give his own very wealthy rat's ass about a piddling five-million-dollar gift to a university he didn't even go to?" Sam asked.

"Let's just say he chooses to see this matter as an assault on the only public university in his home state, by the forces of repressive political correctness. Mr. Foote doesn't mind putting his money where he thinks it can do some political good," Bobby tossed out, looking like a man baiting a hook.

"Oh, he doesn't?" Sam said, carefully grinding out his cigar stub in an ashtray that might never have actually been washed. He looked up and met Bobby's earnest, calumnious eyes with a gaze equally frank and dishonest. "Well now. That's an admirable trait in a man."

19

Good Answers

The winter snowpack had come early to the streets of
Laramie. Down on Old Ivinson Avenue, the muffled
crunching of tires and the curses of pedestrians slipping
and falling on icy sidewalks vied with the blare of endless repetitive Christmas music. Right after Thanksgiving, the Merchants' Association had decided to inspire
holiday shoppers by putting up loudspeakers on stan-
chions and blasting everyone with a taped selection of
spending-friendly, non-sectarian music. You could not
therefore avoid Brenda Lee singing "Rockin' Around the
Christmas Tree," Jose Feliciano's ever-popular "Feliz
Navidad," and of course Bill Haley's always enjoyable
"Jingle Bell Rock." By the second week in December,
employees in the bars and boutiques were ready to shoot
out the speakers.

On the corner of Second and Ivinson, the workers who
were gutting and remodeling the future home of Burt
Langham's Yippie I O Cafe took a page out of the U.S.
Army's psychological warfare book, so successful in
Panama when they captured Manuel Noriega, and blasted
heavy metal music right back. On days when the wind

blew out of the west, which was most days, you could hear the racket six blocks away at the Wrangler. Delice finally got sick of it and called the mayor, who got the city council to pass an emergency antinoise ordinance covering Christmas music. Peace restored, Delice could go back to running her restaurant, pretending not to be running the future Yippie I O (while meeting with Burt and John-Boy and the architect and the contractor and suppliers almost every day) and worrying, when she had time, about Sally Alder and the Dunwoodie House. By now, she'd become so accustomed to thinking of Sally's temporary residence as a historic site that she was mentally capitalizing "House."

Sally herself was not a bit distracted by the Ivinson Avenue war between Megadeth and Brenda Lee. The moment she laid eyes on the mess in the basement, she'd given up on any illusion that this was a typical history project. Unlike anything else she'd ever worked on, and unlike 99 percent of historical enterprises, somebody really cared about this one. Cared enough to bust into a locked, usually occupied domicile, beat up a big woman, ruin precious manuscripts. To Hawk's mild amazement (though he was getting used to the idea that Sally had achieved a measure of self-control), she didn't even stop to have hysterics. She walked through the ragged heaps of paper with Dickie, assuring him that there was no way she could tell if anything had been taken, if she ever could, until she'd gotten things straightened up. Dickie, reasonably, understood that she was right and there was no point pressuring her. They agreed, however, that it had begun to seem that there was some unknown urgency to what she was doing.

Dickie'd had no luck finding Shane Parker. Nobody had seen him since before Thanksgiving. But then, as everyone he asked about Parker was inclined to say, "Shane is kind of a loner." Dickie assumed that Shane was hiding out until things cooled off, but he had no idea where to start looking. For that matter, he had no clear idea as to Shane's motivation. Looking for stuff to fence to buy dope? A Parker family feud? A skinhead harassing a Jewish feminist from California in a town where both skinheads and California Jewish feminists were scarcer than surfboards? Maybe hoping to find that map to buried treasure? From what his daughters had told him about the former Laramie High School loser, Shane was dumb enough to pull something like this for nothing more than the hell of it. Dumb and obviously violent. Bad combo. Next time he showed up, Dickie wanted to be ready.

Egan Crain was lobbying hard to have all Meg's papers immediately moved to the Archive. He'd been haranguing Edna McCaffrey about it every day, and she could see his point. She'd mentioned to Sally that it might not be a bad idea, given the fact that whoever was interested in the papers obviously didn't mind assaulting people. Edna was pragmatic, as usual. The papers should be kept safe, and there was of course the matter of the University's liability in case of mishaps. She was also genuinely scared for Sally. Egan insisted that he understood the restrictions placed on the bequest, and would leave strict instructions that no one at the Archive but Sally was to have access to the papers until she was finished with them. Sally knew that there were excellent reasons to let them move the papers.

But Maude was against it. They talked about it over coffee and fresh cranberry scones in Meg's warm, well-insulated kitchen. "Nobody asked me," she said, as if that had ever stopped Maude from offering an opinion, "but I think Meg's stuff ought to stay here. I reckon Egan means well, and he may think he can keep people away, but he doesn't sleep at the Archive. And he can't be everywhere at once. The story about Mac's treasure, stupid as it is, is common knowledge by now." That was putting it mildly. When the *Boomerang* ran its story on the break-in, the reporter managed to include virtually the entire rumor about the alleged subterranean cache, including the alleged Krugerrands, really playing up the mystery of—what else?—"the Treasure of the Sierra Madre." Sheesh.

Maude was far from done. "The Archive is a big building, and even if they put the papers in a locked room, there are plenty of people in and out of that building every day. You can't be there all the time to control access, Sally," she continued. "Do you think Egan himself would be able to resist the impulse to take a little peek?"

And of course, Maude had her own take on Shane Parker. "I've known him since he was a miserable snot-nosed brat," she said. "You have to understand, Sally—I grew up in Laramie. And for as long as I've been alive, everyone's been saying there are two kinds of Parkers: the ones who leave, and the ones who are too shiftless to go anywhere. The family started ranching in this country in the eighteen-eighties, and a fair number of them made a go of it. But by the Depression, the smart ones started looking for something more profitable to do, and the throwbacks just kind of squatted on the land until they lost most of it. Shane comes from a long line of good-for-nothings who think the world did them wrong. The one thing none of them ever had was guts. He screwed up, and he won't be back." She devoutly hoped.

Maude made Sally feel like the two incidents were the work of a bungling malcontent who would be too chicken-shit to try anything else. This was very reassuring. Sally had decided Egan was more or less honest, but she also figured he was human, and susceptible to temptation. And, goddamn it, this was *her* project, her responsibility. She put the question to Hawk, who weighed the pros and cons carefully, summed up the pluses and minuses efficiently, sympathized with her predicament satisfactorily, and declined to offer an opinion one way or the other, absolutely. It was her call.

And so in the end, Sally said she thought the papers ought to stay put. She reminded Egan and Edna that any change in the execution of the bequest had to be approved by the Dunwoodie Foundation, which meant getting the okay from Ezra Sonnenschein. Sonnenschein had finally called his secretary from a luxury encampment somewhere on the Elephant River in South Africa. Over a very scratchy transatlantic telephone connection, he'd said that he'd seen literally thousands of gemsboks and kudus and was heading out of the Kalahari by Range Rover within the week. He had plans to visit three more game parks, and would be in Capetown by the middle of the month. He would be returning to the U.S. around the first of the year (this news made Sally grind her teeth, awaiting the closet key), and as far as he was concerned, there was no rush about moving the papers. A will was a will, and shouldn't be violated frivolously. He had known Maude Stark for nearly forty years, and he had great confidence in her judgment (and would put her up against anybody of any sex or size when properly warned and riled). He was, however, insisting that his own Colorado security experts check out the system Maude was installing at the house, and make recommendations for anything else they thought necessary. Sonnenschein assumed that the Wyoming idea of an alarm system was a handgun and a large ugly dog.

Dickie really wished they'd move the damn papers, but with Sally and the formidable Maude dead against it, and the Foundation's representative withholding consent, there was nothing he could do. He would make sure patrol cars drove by at frequent, irregular intervals. He might drop in now and again himself. He'd had his fill of Entenmann's fat-free coffee cakes and was ready to test-drive all those goodies Maude was supposed to be such a genius at baking.

The matter of the location of the papers settled for the time being, Sally set to work with a vengeance. The Coloradans arrived and wired every potential point of entry, installed panic buttons by the doors, put in a new telephone system, and even pruned Meg's trees and shrubs, but Maude balked at the thought of bars on the windows, and Sally backed her. Meanwhile, Sally barricaded herself amid chaos with the intent of making order.

The time had come for plodding, for precision, for method. She was feeling guilty at having nearly succumbed to the temptation to leave the job of cataloguing half-done, and digging right into the juicy stuff she was sure she'd find in the Ernst Malthus correspondence. Not to mention the idea of breaking into the closet—Maude had surely had enough of break-ins for a while.

She'd given herself a stern lecture about discipline, damn it. She was an experienced professional with an endowed chair, and Meg Dunwoodie deserved careful treatment. Before she gave herself permission to pick and choose what she'd work with, Sally needed to get the whole crazy collection of stuff in reasonable shape. Sigh.

This time through, she had an idea of the categories under which she could classify papers, and decided to make files instead of piles. She set up a phalanx of empty boxes along one wall. Having asked Egan to supply her with fifty archive boxes, a thousand archive-grade, acid-free folders, ten boxes of labels, and six dozen boxes of plastic paper clips—a request he found reassuring in a small way—she made labels to be clipped to each document, letter, poem, or souvenir. Each labeled artifact would go in an appropriate file, which would go in a designated box. There would be boxes for folders dealing with Meg's early childhood, her years in high school in Laramie, her time as a student at UW. Boxes for her time in New York and her years in Paris, with folders arranged both chronologically and topically. Boxes for the many years back in Wyoming, again filed topically and chronologically. Correspondence would be filed by year, except for the people who had written to her a lot, in which case it would be filed by the name of the writer (Dunwoodie, MacGregor;

McIntyre, Clara F.; Malthus, Ernst, for example). Those files would be put in boxes set aside for correspondence. If any file or set of files got too complicated or cumbersome, she could relabel, reclassify, subdivide. It would be the system that worked for her, and if the Archive didn't like it, well, they could take off all the labels and start over.

It was a good plan—systematic and flexible. She was willing to work twelve-hour days as long as it took to get it done. And she put in a number of such days, slogging and slaving away, before she emerged from the basement feeling as if she'd spent a year in solitary confinement. An hour and a half later she was sitting at the bar at the Wrangler with a Budweiser, staring glassy-eyed at Hawk and listening blankly to a band called, honestly enough, Hat Act. The band was playing a tepid cover of "All My Exes Live in Texas."

"I can't keep up with it, Hawk," she whined exhaustedly. "It's too much. In ten years at UCLA I was known for having the messiest desk in the history department. I had memos buried on it so deep and for so long that they became historical artifacts before I threw them away. Now I've become the world's highest paid file clerk. And I suck at it. I'm okay with the labeling—it gives me a chance to take a quick look at the papers, and I'm getting a real good picture of Meg's life as I go along. But the filing, the fucking *filing*!"

Hearing her yell, Delice came over from the other end of the bar to see what was up. Delice put up a shot glass and poured her a Wild Turkey, on the house. Delice was fairly beat herself, having spent the entire day shuttling back and forth between the future Yippie I O (where they were having problems with a city inspector who wondered if the historic building in which the restaurant was to be housed was going to burn down if it was wired and plumbed and bricked and hooked up for all the fancy kitchen crap Burt wanted to put in—a wood-burning pizza oven?), dragging Jerry Jeff out of the principal's office, where he'd been sent for staring into space in math class (the teacher was obviously having a lousy day, too), and dealing with an actual (but small, and not too odiferous) grease fire at the Wrangler. While she was at it, she poured herself a shot of the Bird.

At that moment, Brittany Langham walked in and sat down next to Sally. She looked even worse than everybody else (in the case of Hawk, that wasn't hard; he looked fine). She ordered a glass of white zin and bummed a cigarette off the bartender.

"I thought you quit," Delice nagged.

"I quit quitting," Brit snarled. "I got fired tonight."

"Fired?" Delice hollered. "Since when does Foster's fire anybody? I thought you had to barf on the floor or slug a customer to get canned there."

Brit drew hard on the cigarette, took a sip of wine, and looked down. "Well, there's at least one other alternative," she admitted.

"And that would be?" Sally asked, becoming interested.

"When you've just gotten stiffed by, like, your third table of the night, and your feet are killing you, and you think it's the absolute most demeaning and tedious job in the entire world, and Mr. Howitz, the manager, starts hissing at you for, like, the millionth time that you're not 'servicing the customer,' you have finally had enough, and you yell, 'You want me to suck *what*?'"

Sally and Hawk and Delice nodded thoughtfully. Delice took a sip of whiskey, cocked her head, pursed her lips, considered, and said, "Yep. I'd fire you for that." She poured Brit more wine.

"On the other hand," Sally put in, "I would be surprised to hear you ask her to service a customer."

"We are not that kind of establishment," Delice announced solemnly.

"And all these years I'd kept hoping," Hawk lamented.

"I suppose now you'll be reduced to doing something more in line with your abilities, like running the Pentagon or the ACLU," Delice said.

"Brit is very capable," Sally explained to Hawk, "but what she's said to be best at is underachieving."

Brit grunted something unintelligible.

"Well, I sure could use some help around here," Delice began.

"Ohhhhh no," Brit interrupted. "I've told you a million times, Aunt Delice, I have no intention of being the next Langham woman to run the Wrangler. I've slung my last chicken-fried steak," she vowed.

"Not waitressing. I wouldn't want you cussing out the clientele. I mean, I could use somebody in the office, getting me organized, working on the books, that kind of thing. Things seem to be getting kind of hectic and complicated around here," said Delice, and then realizing she didn't want to give away too much control, added, "just part-time, of course."

"Are you good at getting people organized, Brittany?" Hawk asked.

"Let's put it this way," Delice answered for her niece. "All those years Dickie was, er, indisposed, this little girl ran that household like a sergeant major. I'd go over there and find her sitting in Mary's kitchen making out daily and weekly schedules, grocery lists, and chore charts for everybody from Mary to Josh. If it was Thursday, you knew that Ashley was supposed to do the laundry, Josh had to take out the trash, Brit had to make breakfast and pack everybody's lunch, and Mary had to pick up Kentucky Fried Chicken on the way home from work. Or whatever. It was all on a chart on the wall. They made spaghetti or stew or chili every Sunday, depending on what was on special at the grocery store, because Brit comparison-shopped the Wednesday ads."

Brit blushed. "It was no big deal. After Mom gave up on vegetarianism, it got a lot easier."

"So let me ask you something else, Brittany," Hawk said, evidently pursuing some thread of his own. "How are you at keeping secrets?"

"Omigod!" Delice goggled, grabbing her head and jangling her jewelry. "One time when she was at Laramie High, Brit and Ashley sneaked out at night, and when they were climbing up the porch to get back in their bedroom the window, Brit fell. She'd broken a bone in her foot, but she was so worried about what Mary would do to her that she didn't tell her for three weeks!"

Hawk nodded. "How are you with secrets that don't involve physical pain?"

Brit looked at him scornfully. "Depends on whether it's, like, a serious secret or a stupid one."

"Good answer." He smiled.

Sally was beginning to see what he was driving at. She had been obsessive about protecting her own exclusive right to look at those papers, but she did, she admitted, need help. She continued foolishly to believe, against forty-five years of experience, that sometimes you ought to take a risk and trust someone. And, she admitted, she could see a little of her own smart-ass, at-loose-ends younger self in Brittany Langham. Professor Clara McIntyre would have wanted it that way; for some reason, she was sure Meg Dunwoodie would have wanted it, too. She hoped to hell Maude would approve, but she had the feeling that would be okay as well.

"You know, Brit," she said, "I am in dire need of somebody to help me work on those papers in Meg Dunwoodie's basement. Somebody extremely well-organized, smart, totally honest, not full of crap, and absolutely able to keep a secret until I tell them it's okay to talk. Somebody who'd be willing to do endless shit-work filing in a boring basement, drink as much excellent coffee as necessary, and work for, oh, let's say ten dollars an hour. And you'll have to quit smoking again."

"It's a dirty job," Hawk picked up, "but somebody has to do it."

"Or otherwise," Sally said, moaning, "I'm liable to go completely insane."

Brit had, of course, heard the treasure rumors, as well as the legend that the Dunwoodie house was haunted. She didn't buy any of it. But she was looking for something to do while she figured out what it was she wanted to do next. She had a long-ago memory of being a toddler and being taken to Washington Park on a summer evening to hear Sally and some other woman sing beautiful harmonies. The sound of their voices had enchanted her, and had stuck in her mind, though she had no idea what songs they'd sung. "I could think about it," she allowed.

"Of course," Delice added, "the vow of silence would be suspended when it came to your devoted auntie."

Brit and Sally exchanged a look. "Crammit, Auntie," said Brit.

"Good answer," said Sally, vastly relieved.

20

Night and Day

December's days grew short and dark, and Sally sank further into her subterranean journey into Meg Dunwoodie's world. But for all the dusky chill outside, the gray watery light that slipped in through the barred basement windows, the banging of the furnace going on and off, Sally had begun to imagine herself in a universe full of color and light, excitement and danger.

Hiring Brittany Langham had turned out to be the best leap of faith she'd ever made. Brit was a wizard. She'd come to work at eight Monday morning, taken one look at the boxes, the files, and the loose papers, and realized that what Sally thought of as crackerjack order was about as tidy and efficient as your average fraternity house. She'd seen instantly a way to streamline and refine the whole system, and within two days had wrapped her head around pretty much everything Sally had done so far. The two of them had worked out a plan of attack—Sally would look each document over first, make a few classifying notes on a Post-it, and then leave the cataloging and record-keeping and filing to Brit. Within a week, they'd gone through half the basement. Naturally, they'd found nothing that vaguely resembled the famous treasure map, so that at least was a relief. While Brit took meticulous care putting the whole collection in order, Sally was ready to dig deep.

Had she been a methodical gentlewoman and scholar, she would have approached Meg's life chronologically— the way it happened. You weren't supposed to assume that anything in history *had* to happen. You shouldn't pluck out any incident of a life that unfolded in the accidental and bumpy domain of time, and treat it as crucial or, God forbid, destined. Conversely, she could pay attention to the present, and start out by trying to find out what she could about Mac Dunwoodie's inconvenient and probably nonexistent treasure. That would surely be a reasonable, practical course, given the publicity. Any sensible person would surely want to find out why this Shane Parker was willing to get violent about what was in those papers. But Sally knew by now that she was not methodical, practical, or reasonable by nature. Neither had she ever fancied herself a gentlewoman. She did claim to be a scholar, but she had always gotten to the point of sitting down to write history books by playing hunches and going with her gut. And her gut said: Paris.

So while Brit worked the collection, Sally began to go slowly through the material that dealt with the years between 1928 and 1940, when Margaret Dunwoodie had worked as a foreign correspondent headquartered in Paris. She'd held two jobs, working first for the *Toronto Star,* then for Reuters. The clipping books were incredible. Meg covered everything from the cabaret scene to the Spanish Civil War. She'd been in Munich for Jesse Owens's great victory, in Barcelona when it was a workers' city. She'd covered bicycle races and political rallies, had written vividly about art exhibits on the Left Bank and climbing trips to the Swiss Alps.

Sally was thrilled that Meg had bothered to save some telegrams from her editors, detailing not only some of her assignments, but also suggesting something of how she felt about them. The editor who dispatched her to London to cover the abdication of King Edward VIII in 1936 had wired: Go immediately to London for Duke and Wally STOP Don't care if you think FLUFF STOP. A 1936 telegram, sent to Munich, read, "Brilliant stuff STOP BE CAREFUL STOP."

Sally opened a photo album, and was mesmerized. Here was a picture of Meg in a sharp tailored suit and snappy fedora, drinking an aperitif at a sidewalk café with a beautiful dark-haired woman and a dark, handsome man. The women were laughing; the man was looking at Meg with a small, serious smile. And here was the picture Sally knew she'd find: Meg at the typewriter, cigarette dangling, fingers flying. Another, a head-and-shoulders shot that had clearly taken her unawares, sitting exhausted in a chair, her head thrown back, eyes closed, her throat achingly exposed. Then Meg in an evening gown and fur wrap, standing outside a theater with a group of elegantly dressed men and women. The dark-haired man and woman were there, and was that Cole Porter? All the men, except the one who might be the famous composer, were staring frankly at Meg. She had been a stunning young woman.

As Sally turned the pages, she realized that more and more of the pictures had been taken outdoors, in breathtaking settings. Meg, in trousers, sitting in a glade by a stream, drinking out of a tin mug. Sweatered and knickered on skis amid enormous glacial mountains. Rosy-cheeked and grinning ear to ear in a mountain meadow. Sally turned another page.

And there he was.

She knew it the minute she saw him, standing then and forever in that same high meadow. Hatless, sleeves rolled up above his elbows, sinewy arms, a rucksack stretched across his broad shoulders. He stood at a slight angle to the camera, loose-limbed and relaxed, with his hands on his hips. But his eyes took the lens straight on. There was so much intelligence, intensity, and sensitivity in those eyes that Sally was nearly knocked flat, even now, how old would he be now? He was looking at whoever took the picture with the kind of quiet joy Sally associated with the discovery of love. Jesus.

As if to confirm her assumption, the next shot was the two of them together. They were a matched pair. Meg was tall, but he was taller. She was strong, and so was he. Her hair, long and wavy, was pulled back in a ponytail. His, straight and combed back, was as blond as hers. Sally could not, of course, tell the color of his eyes from a black-and-white photograph, but they made Meg's blue ones look dark. Blue, or light green, and very clear. Sally's lungs felt tight. In this picture, they stood close together, looking at each other as if they were alone in the world.

Sally leafed through the rest of the album in a wonder-struck daze. There were dozens of photos of Meg and the man, in Paris and out—at restaurants and nightclubs, at prizefights and the racetrack, fishing, hiking, skiing, looking through binoculars. Squatting to examine rocks. One page of pictures that really stopped her. Hands on a piano keyboard, in different positions. And then the photographer pulled back to reveal the beautiful man, eyes closed, laying passionate fingers on the instrument.

This had to be Ernst Malthus. Brush of the key.

The hell with method.

Saying nothing to Brit, who was slogging through Meg's unbelievably disorderly financial papers (now *those* were fascinating!), Sally went to the correspondence files and dug out the folders labeled MALTHUS, ERNST. The letters, notes, postcards, and telegrams were in chronological order, dating from 1929 to 1939. There was a short formal note on the top of the stack, dated June 23, 1929, which began,

Dear Miss Dunwoodie,

*Thank you for your kind words at the Blums' Tues-
day last. I had thought it the greatest delight of my
life when Cole asked me to play his song, but now
know other delights may be greater still. I hope you
will permit me the pleasure of your company at dinner this Friday evening.*

Yours sincerely, Ernst Malthus

Cole? Play his song? Sally went to the file labeled
BLUM—MUSICAL EVENINGS and found the program she'd
seen before, for a Tuesday night in June, 1929. The
printed card announced solo piano selections by Brahms,
Chopin, Satie. Just below the last, Meg had written in
ink, PORTER, 'NIGHT AND DAY.' The featured artist was
Malthus.

He had written frequently but by no means exclusively
from Berlin, where, it seemed, he lived and worked. He
travelled quite a bit—to France and the Low Countries, to
Switzerland and England, and sometimes to South Africa.
He said he thought it ironic that he'd become a geologist
out of love for wild, remote places, and had ended up in
the diamond trade, in the filthy provinces of cities and
mines. (Mmm, Sally thought. Where had she heard that
before?) He would, he wrote, have to take such beauty as
he could find, and in her he always found it. Sally thought
of Crawford Green looking at Maria, of the way Hawk
looked at her, sometimes, when he thought she wasn't
noticing. She stared briefly into middle space, then shifted
her eyes back to the Malthus file.

Meg had not stayed "Dear Miss Dunwoodie" for long.
Soon she was "My dear Margaret." By 1931, she was
"Darling Greta." And even "My own." He wrote about all
kinds of things in clear, vivid, graceful Euro-English.
Places and people and music; what he'd been reading and
thinking; what a river looked like, how it had been made.

And he wrote about his yearning. Sally felt like a voyeur, kept reading.

There were love letters such as she had never seen. The man wrote about touching his lover's body as if he were composing music, the pitch, the pressure, the tone, the timbre. Ernst had seen a story of Meg's in the *Times of London,* a review for Reuters of a retrospective exhibition of plant photographs by Karl Blossveldt: He wondered if she thought all modern art must necessarily concern itself with the tension and intimacy between nature and machines, or whether aesthetic beauty was enough? The photographs, he conceded, were beautiful, and they reminded him of his Greta—prickly, finely textured, stark and irresistable. They made his fingers tingle. He wrote to her in Spain, from Paris, to say that the weather was wretched and so was he, there, without her. In a letter from a fishing camp in the Pyrenees, he explained how sitting by a fast-running brook reminded him of the way he could make her breath catch somewhere near her heart. He dipped his hand in the water and felt himself inside her.

Sally was undone, captivated by his eloquence and his sexiness and his intellectual range and his desire. His remarkable body, his fascinating face. His hands. But there was a dissonant note in his spellbinding melodies. If you could judge from his letters, his pictures, his music, he was a man to admire, maybe adore. But he was a German, a man of some influence, coming and going as he pleased, in and out of Nazi Germany. And of the many things he wrote so clearly and knowingly about, politics was conspicuously absent. He obviously followed her work, often commented on stories he'd found interesting, challenged her analyses, suggested ideas for new pieces. But he never, ever mentioned the serious stories she'd done—the profile of the Spanish Republican soldier, the interview with the British fascist Nancy Mitford, the report on anti-Semitic violence in France. If they spoke of such things, they didn't commit their thoughts to paper.

Still, how could he write anything revealing or personal from Germany? Sally sorted the letters again, by postmark, and realized that he didn't. Although he'd written often from Berlin and Dresden, he'd sent chiefly postcards, jottings about concerts and scientific lectures and parties, about remarkable gemstones he'd come across in the course of business. Things the Gestapo wouldn't find too fascinating. He'd sent the love letters from other places. It was a perilous game.

Music and science and the diamond trade, at least internationally, were still domains in which a good Aryan boy like Ernst was liable to find himself in the company of Jews. Paul Blum was a banker with international connections; Giselle Blum was a painter with a growing reputation. It looked, in fact, like Ernst was almost flaunting his relations with the Blums—the letters from places outside Germany conveyed warm greetings to his good friend Paul, and to *chere* Giselle. By the early thirties, Sally knew, German Jews had begun to leave the Fatherland. Some had established themselves in Paris, undoubtedly circulated in Meg Dunwoodie's set. Meg was herself an American who made no secret of her friendships or her left political leanings. The Nazis kept very close tabs on German citizens' contacts with foreigners, and Ernst Malthus made no secret of his cosmopolitan connections. The Gestapo must have been watching him very closely, probably Meg, too.

Meg, too.

What the hell was Meg up to?

She put the Malthus correspondence back in chronological order. After 1937, Ernst appeared to have been spending less and less time in Germany. More and more in Paris and Antwerp, London and Capetown. After August, 1939, there were no more letters.

Who was Ernst Malthus? Why did the Nazis give him so much room?

No more letters. After *those* letters. Meg had lived on,

more than half a century after those letters. Had gone back to Wyoming, never married, taught school, been angry and brilliant, written poetry. Sally had a million questions, and hardly any answers.

But she couldn't help zeroing in on one pivotal moment among years of moments. Ernst Malthus's letters to Meg Dunwoodie had stopped, as far as she knew now, in 1939, before the invasion of Poland, before the fall of France. Before Europe exploded. But it did explode. What the hell had happened to him?

Sally didn't even hear Brit leave at five. The file in her lap held everything they'd found that Ernst Malthus had written to Meg Dunwoodie, and Sally read it again, slowly. Looked at the photographs, again and again. His eyes. She couldn't have explained why she found them so compelling, and wouldn't. It seemed a shameful secret somehow, like something that would hurt Hawk if she told him. She took a step back from herself, into the historian part of her. The historian, the competent adult spoke to the sentimental self that sat on the floor of Meg Dunwoodie's basement, half in love with Ernst Malthus. "You're right," said the grown-up Sally to the quivering sap. "This is a hell of a story. There's something there. Something critical to Meg's life. You need to understand. Watch yourself."

She pulled out the files labeled BLUM, GISELLE—CORRESPONDENCE and BLUM, PAUL—CORRESPONDENCE. Aside from short notes observing the proprieties (thanks, invitations), Giselle's file consisted almost entirely of letters, in French (shit!), sent from a seaside villa in Nice to Meg in Paris, every summer between 1929 and 1940. Of course Giselle would have no reason to write when they were both in Paris, and Sally assumed Meg's assignments to other places usually happened on such short notice, and lasted a short enough time, that none but the most devoted correspondents would write.

Sally's rotten French wasn't going to get her through these letters tonight, she realized. But they might give her a few glimpses of Giselle's life. Exhausted, Sally slogged her way through a few, understanding only fragments, looking for impressions. Giselle wrote about her painting, happy when it was going well, despondent when she couldn't get what she saw on paper or canvas. Various Blums *("cousine F——," "mon chère frere," "ma tante Y——")* came and went; obviously, it was the Blum summer place. There was always some family crisis, the particulars of which were, at the moment, lost on Sally. Sometimes Giselle illustrated her letters with sketches of the people she wrote about, and the drawings of the relatives, for the most part, reminded Sally of Daumier's caricatures.

Giselle invariably referred to people by their initials, followed by dashes. *"P—— ici,"* she'd write, or *"E—— ecrit qu'il veut visiter la semaine prochaine."* And there was someone she referred to as "M————" who appeared frequently, but evidently not frequently enough for Giselle. *"Jours heureux!"* she wrote, *"M—— arrive samedi."* Sometimes P——, E——, and M———— were there together, Sally noticed. Paul, surely. Ernst? Who was M——?

A man. In a letter from July, 1936, there was a sketch of the three, captioned *"P——, E——, and M—— à la plage."* Three young men in bathing gear, playing in the waves, their bodies and faces captured in spare lines. The dark man from the photograph in the café, squinting at the artist, head tilted to one side. Paul. Another man Sally had seen in other photos, slender, tall, light-eyed, smoking a cigarette even as he stood in the waves. M——. And Ernst, unmistakable, grinning, splashing the others. *"Viens ici,"* Giselle had written in that letter. *"Viens."* You must come here. Come.

Did Meg go to Nice? Sally had no idea. She was incapable of thought. By eight, she had been at it for twelve hours. The fatigue and the French made the letters swim before her eyes. She was midway through Giselle's letters, missing most of what the woman had written, couldn't go any further. She could start again tomorrow.

They were all dead.

Sally ate canned soup, fixed a huge cup of orange spice tea. Thought about calling Hawk, but he was grading term papers, and she didn't want to bug him. Thought about calling Edna or Delice, but didn't feel like conversation. Thought about turning on the TV, listening to music, reading some crappy novel. But she couldn't concentrate. Her guitar stood in the corner of Meg's living room, next to the Christmas tree. She and Hawk and Edna and Tom had skied up into the Snowies, dragging sleds, to cut trees the previous weekend. Sally's tree was small and full and decorated with tiny white lights, a few shiny glass balls from the "Seasonal" aisle at the Safeway, and a dozen ornaments she'd picked up at a semi-okay local craft fair at the Ivinson Community Center.

It felt good to tune a guitar.

The Christmas she'd been in the seventh grade, the Byrds had released "Turn, Turn, Turn." That had become her only real Christmas anthem. She remembered sitting for hours in the den with no lights on except the colored bulbs on the heavily festooned Christmas tree (great Jews, those Alders!), looking at the tree and listening to the song, over and over. The music had turned something over in her that winter. She was never the same.

Something else was turning over in her, now. She dragged a dining room chair over by her own small, hopeful tree, put on fingerpicks, touched the strings, began to sing. Sang the songs she'd loved so long, Byrds' arrangements of Seeger and Dylan, some early pretty Neil Young stuff, meditative Joni Mitchell and Stephen Stills. Didn't want to sing her own songs, face herself, just now. Wanted the comfort of the company of other singers and song-writers.

When she found herself singing Emmylou Harris's "Boulder to Birmingham," she knew she was going to cry, but didn't want to stop. It was a great song about surviving what you'd loved and regretted most. Everybody's life broke in half somehow—her own, Hawk's. Maybe Meg's. Maybe Ernst's. Who the hell knew who else's? Whoever lives, survives. It was like being in an earthquake, and having the ground open up under you, and suddenly find-ing yourself at the bottom of a rip in the planet. And climbing out. And finding the world you'd known only hours or minutes or seconds before utterly different.

Meg and Ernst and Giselle and Paul, the man called M——, to see such lives in the shadow of death, shook her to the bone. Death in the midst of love and life, so hor-rifyingly everywhere. Death could kill even love. And Meg had survived.

Death leered at Sally, murdered a cat, cut a brake line, scrawled a swastika, scattered papers. Viciously attacked Maude. It could have been her. The chasm had opened up, and the past spilled into the present. Maybe the future. Sally choked her way through the rest of the song, then put her head down and wept.

After nineteen term papers, Hawk had had it. He eyed his dirty coffee cup, grimacing. Got up from his desk and stretched. Looked around and thought he'd made his house pretty homey, for him. He'd bought the bed. And a dresser and bedside table. A reading light. In the living room he'd put a chair, a television, a desk with a lamp. His books were on the shelves. He'd moved his box of camp cooking stuff into drawers in his kitchen. Cozy.

But it was ten at night, and he had barely moved from his desk all day. He was restless, felt like a walk. He put on a down jacket, stuffed the legs of his jeans into felt-lined rubber boots, headed out the door into the silent town, hands jammed deep in the pockets of his coat. He was determined to maintain his independence, much as he was enjoying spending time with Sally. Still, he ended up, as he'd known he would, standing in front of her house. The house was dark except for the little white lights on her Christmas tree.

He rang the doorbell.

After a moment, her voice came, weak and shaky, on the other side of the door. "Who's there?"

"It's me," he said.

She opened the door with one hand, was holding her guitar in the other. Her chin was trembling and there were tears running down her face. He stepped inside, shut the door. Took the guitar, leaned it against the wall. Put his arms around her and stood there holding her for a long, long time.

Part Three

21

Blue-Eyed Devils

Christmas came and New Year's went. The weather continued snowy and blowy. One morning Sally woke up hot and guilty in the midst of an extremely kinetic erotic dream. Her waking mind could recall only that the dream had moved from place to place (her car, an empty apartment in some faceless city, a park, other places she couldn't remember). The sex had been remarkable. The partner had been a morphing man whose identities included both individuals she had, er, known, and unidentifiable but familiar-seeming strangers. It seemed they/he had blue eyes.

The dream memory came to her in a flash, as such things do, at the same instant that she realized that it was Saturday and she was wrapped tightly around a deeply sleeping Hawk Green. That was where the guilt came in. One of the shape-shifter's morphs had certainly been Sam Branch. She had seen Sam various times in the months since she'd been back in Laramie, and had played music with him and Dwayne and the Millionaires on several occasions. Sam had aged pretty well, but Sally hadn't been the least bit attracted to him, no matter what kind of moves he tried out. She was, after all, a professional historian trained to keep the past, well, past, and the past they shared could be plausibly described as vile. As for the present, he was clearly still scruple-impaired.

But she'd been jamming fairly regularly with the band, and tonight they had a gig, a party Sam and Dwayne had given for five years, which they called the Millionaires' Ball. Everybody including Delice admitted that this was the party of the year. Sam had told Sally to dress sexy. She loved to dress up for parties, but the idea that he might think she was doing it for him kind of spoiled things.

The hell with it. A dream was a dream, and you could giggle about it and forget it. Look at it this way—there had been a number of morphs in her dream man/men, and Sam Branch was hardly the strangest one. It seemed Ernst Malthus (whose eyes may have been blue, or green, or the color of the sea off the Côte d'Azur) had made an appearance and that was truly ill, all things considered. But then so, she admitted with a sigh, was Sally. Her subconscious mind leaned so heavily toward history that she had once actually dreamed she was doing it with Thomas Jefferson.

Well. Management not responsible for the behavior of the subconscious mind. But very much responsible for choices and actions. You didn't have to do everything you thought about doing. That was, she grinned to herself, the difference between Jimmy Carter and Bill Clinton.

On the other hand, some things you thought about were definitely worth acting on immediately. She was still pleasantly warmed up, and lying next to a very real, nicely shaped man who had come to her in her hour of darkness, stayed with her through the holidays, and was giving no sign of looking for the exit. She shifted a little and kissed him on the ear. Hawk said, "Mmmphh." She stroked his chest, moved her hand down his hip, caressed his thigh. Hawk muttered, "Huh?"

"This is your wake-up call," she whispered, rolling him

on his back. Even though he appeared to be still mostly asleep, he smiled when she crawled on top of him.

Ride, Sally, ride.

By nine they were at the gym, Hawk for a Saturday morning basketball game, Sally to run like a laboratory rat on a treadmill and to pump various machines. Then they went to work. Hawk went home to write a grant proposal. Sally had decided to take a break from the basement. She'd finally worked up to telling Maude she'd really like to see what was in the closet, but Maude had put her off. She didn't have a key, she said, and they might as well wait until Ezra was back from Africa. He was due any day.

Maude was jerking her around, Sally thought, but there was nothing she could do about it. All the boiling impatience of her forty-five erratic years wouldn't get her in that closet without the key, a locksmith, or a crowbar. The key was promised, any day. So she decided that she'd go to the library to see what she could find out about Europe in the 1930s, about people with names like Dunwoodie, Blum, and Malthus.

What she learned didn't particularly surprise her. For those who had money (and as far as she could tell, that included virtually all the people she was most interested in), the continent was, well, a moveable feast. Meg's scrapbooks had testified to the fact that a woman with the right job and the right attitude could go almost anywhere. How much easier still it would have been for a man like Ernst Malthus to move around, welcome wherever he went.

Clearly, throughout the '30s, the Nazis were already making their plans, already watching and plotting. But they were not, by any means, all making the same plans. Some drew up designs for crematoria; others were plotting to kill their Führer. And it was clear that lots of Germans, still dazed at what they were permitting to happen, were hoping hard that they wouldn't be forced into having to take a stand.

She found a few references to Giselle Blum, and one reproduction of a painting in a catalogue for a 1985 exhibit at a museum in Amsterdam, featuring painters of the Holocaust. The picture, titled *"En repose"* and dated 1938, was recognizably a portrait of that lean man, M——, sitting in a chair, reading a book. Blue eyes. She stared hard at the picture, knowing that the man reminded her of someone but unable to place him. He looked a little like Daniel Ellsberg, but that wasn't it.

According to the painter's biography, Giselle Blum had been murdered at Auschwitz, on the day she arrived at the death camp. It was common practice, the catalogue explained, for the Nazis to take male Jewish deportees off to work them to death, and to kill Jewish women quickly. Sally's eyes narrowed with fury and grief. But she knew how it had been. In the eyes of serious Nazis, there was absolutely no reason to let Jewish women live; they were no more or less than incubators for more nasty Jews.

On this first foray into the library, she pulled a bunch of books about Nazi Germany off the shelf, but found no reference to an Ernst Malthus. The only Malthus mentioned at all was someone named Rainer Malthus, a young army officer attached to the staff of General Ludwig Beck. When Beck resigned from the army in 1938 in protest against the invasion of Czechoslovakia, Rainer Malthus also quit the army, becoming Beck's secretary. Beck was soon among the leaders of a group of German officers, aristocrats, and diplomats looking for a way to overthrow Hitler. The group began to refer to itself as the Kreisau Circle because they met often at Kreisau, the Silesian estate of Helmut von Moltke, another central figure. But they had another name, given to them by the agents of Himmler's secret police, who infiltrated their innermost ranks. To the Nazis who watched them, the resistance was known as the *Schwarzekappelle*. Black Orchestra.

Beck became a ringleader in the botched plot to assassinate Hitler in 1944, and Malthus, as his aide, had faced the same firing squad as his commander when the scheme failed. Was Rainer Malthus related to Ernst? Why did he end up in the assassination plot? Obviously she'd need to do more research, but maybe not on this guy. Ernst was her quarry. Still, she wanted to know more. The UW library didn't have any books specifically on the Kreisau Circle, but she had found some citations on the German Resistance. She filled out slips for interlibrary loan, left them at the loan desk. She probably could have found the information she wanted by surfing the Web, posting queries on the Internet, but she had never quite trusted the safety of cyberspace, especially for stuff about Nazi history. Who knew what evil lurked behind the bytes and bits of machines?

On the other extreme from sending a message in a bottle out on the Web waves, there was the personal approach. Whenever Sally had found herself digging into stuff that was outside her field, she'd known that she could always ask a colleague for some pointers. On many occasions, she started out by consulting friends, and had saved who the hell knew how much time by listening to people who knew the subject. There were one or two people at UCLA she could call.

And there was, of course, a simpler option. She could start by finding out what Maude knew about the Blums and Ernst Malthus and anybody else Meg had known during her years in Paris. Yes, it was definitely getting to be time to start asking Maude questions.

Sally hit the library catalogue one more time, then went back to the stacks to get books on international banking in interwar Europe. She hoped, but did not expect, to find some mention of the banker, Paul Blum. His name didn't appear, but she got a pretty good picture of a very screwed-up situation, a shell game so huge and complicated that nobody had yet sorted it all out. By the end of the day, she had a picture of bankers as pivot players in a very dangerous and tangled network involving national loyalties and cosmopolitan sensibilities, profit motives and patriotism, love of big stakes, and fear of heavy consequences. She'd always thought bankers were sober, conservative types, but in Europe during and between the wars, the job of making and taking loans, tracking money and storing capital was so political and volatile, so riddled with big scores and big mistakes, that the term "risky business" acquired scary new dimensions. Top it off with the fact that lots of these guys were Jewish, doomed if they opted to keep playing instead of running, and you had a gut-churning situation.

On her way to check books out, she glanced through a window and saw the sun sinking lower in the sky. She dumped the books on a desk, went in search of a couple of volumes on the history and business of diamonds. Maybe she'd find Ernst there. Added them to her pile, and headed for the circulation desk.

She needed time for a long bubble bath before getting dressed to go out. She had managed to talk Hawk into going to the Millionaire's Ball only by reminding him that she would be wearing the kind of dress that would give people ideas, and she preferred to hear those ideas from him. He'd protested that the only party featuring Sam Branch that he had any desire to attend was a funeral, but then she'd offered to try the dress on for him. "Trying on clothes isn't exactly a guy thing, Sally," he'd grumbled, pouring himself a cup of coffee. Then she'd come into the kitchen with the dress on. Blue velvet, form-fitting and slit to the knee, buttoning all the way up the front. Or down, depending on the situation. His expression didn't change. "What time do I pick you up?" he asked.

Sally was not the only one who cleaned up pretty good. Hawk arrived at eight, carrying his down coat and wearing a black Armani suit, black shirt, black tie. "Close your mouth, Mustang, you look like an idiot," he said sweetly, sidling in.

Sally reclaimed the lower half of her jaw. "God!" she finally exploded. "Since when do you dress like that?"

"Well, ah, honey," he began, blushing slightly, "you remember I told you that I had a little run of good luck working in Peru for this exploration outfit out of Houston?" She nodded. He cleared his throat. "See, I had this Brazilian girlfriend who'd grown up with quite a little bit of money, and she used to say that nothing got her hotter than drinking a couple of martinis at Cafe Annie at lunch, then spending the afternoon shopping at Saks and Neiman Marcus. Usually I let her do her own shopping and just met her back at the Ritz in time for an afternoon nap, but she got me to go along once on the grounds that I needed some clothes that would make a really good impression and that she wasn't wearing any underwear that day."

"Trying on clothes isn't exactly a guy thing," she mocked.

Hawk shrugged.

"Too much information," Sally said.

"Right," Hawk agreed, and grinned. "You don't look so bad yourself."

The party was in the alleged ballroom at the Holiday Inn. You couldn't say all that much for the decor, which consisted of a linoleum floor and some beige drapes on the big windows. But the bar was well stocked and fully open, and much to Sally's amazement, there was food. She had never been at a party given by any member of Branchwater at which actual solid food had been available. And what food! Clearly Dwayne, always a devotee of the Little Debbie school of catering, had let Nattie take charge, and she had had the bright idea to hire cousin Burt and John-Boy and tell them money was only slightly an object. To Sally, the buffet table looked like the mirage a dazed and starving Californian would hallucinate when marooned in the culinary desert of Wyoming.

Guests were only beginning to arrive, and Sally went straight to the stage to get ready for the sound check.

Hawk went to the bar, requested a Budweiser, and sauntered over to talk to Dickie, who was pounding sushi and washing it down with Coca-Cola. The sheriff looked the part in a dark brown western-cut suit and brand-new Stetson hat.

"Glad to see you got the night off, Dick," Hawk greeted him. "Are you sure the criminals will be able to get along without you?"

"If there's one thing I know," Dickie replied, "it's criminals. And if you consider the fact that this party is being given by a banker and a Realtor, you're led to the obvious conclusion that the most corrupt assholes in Laramie will be here tonight. Perfect place for a peace officer, wouldn't you say?" he asked, cramming another piece of rainbow roll into his mouth. Casually, he glanced at Sam Branch, who was tuning his guitar and surreptitiously eying Sally's butt as she bent over to adjust the volume on the vocal monitors. "Good thing most of them are mostly reformed."

"Present company included," Hawk observed.

"That's so," Dickie agreed genially.

By nine, the band, decked out in tuxedos with the exception, of course, of Sally, was ready to start. The ballroom was filling up with people who were, Dickie noted, "dressed to impress." Quite a few of them had been around when the original Branchwater had plied its raunchy blend of country, rock, and soul. For years on end, they'd paid money to buy watered drinks and listen to Sam and Dwayne play, and they had been glad to hear that Mustang Sally was back in the saddle. When the Millionaires opened up with "Wild Night," the dance floor filled immediately.

Sally hadn't had a real gig in years, and she was fully in hillbilly heaven. She'd missed the sweet harmonies, the driving rhythms, the soaring solos. And she'd missed the crowds dancing and stomping and yelling for more. When she was onstage, she forgot about all the angling and wriggling that went on in a bar or at a party. She didn't have to worry who was checking who out, who had some kind of agenda or grudge, who was falling in or out of love, who was thinking about picking a fight with whom. On stage, she was Emmylou and Linda and Bonnie and Patsy and Loretta and Tammy and Etta and Aretha. She was above it all.

As a longtime bar owner, Delice watched the crowd with keener eyes. There could, of course, be fights, but there was always plenty of subtler and probably more dangerous stuff going on. On occasions like this, Delice considered herself a twentieth-century Miss Kitty, and dressed the part in tight-fitting crimson lace and dangling antique gold earrings. She danced a couple of fast dances with Hawk, then went to get herself a whiskey and sat at a table, taking in the action. She made a quick scan of Langhams. Dickie and Mary were going nuts to Sally's best Queen of Soul version of "Chain of Fools." Like Dickie, Mary had put on a few pounds over the years, and like many women her age, she covered up the extra with flowing draperies, in this case, chiffon cascades in a blushing shade of peach. She looked like a big happy dessert.

Josh and Jerry Jeff, in sport coats and bolo ties, were assaulting the buffet table; imagine them going for raw fish like that! Delice made a mental note for the Yippie I O menu. Nattie was standing against a wall in her Cruella DeVille outfit—black and white and some kind of feathers. Scowling. Delice could tell that she was bored with Dwayne again and was probably getting ready to try to have another affair. Maybe this time they'd actually get rid of her.

Brittany looked fabulous. Her dress was silver, short, and bare, perfect with her white-blond hair and creamy skin, looking deceptively fragile. Delice figured some fool would fall for it, and Brit would, as usual, break his fucking heart. The probable victim appeared to have signed on for the night. Brit was sitting at a table in the corner, talking to somebody Delice didn't know, a big, buff guy in a tux. Or rather, the guy was talking, and Brit appeared to be bored but listening. He had big blue eyes and a winning smile, which he was really turning on at just that moment in a way that made Delice nervous. She might just have to get herself a refill and see how old Brit was doing.

For Bobby Helwigsen this was a huge chance to observe and interact with a number of Laramie people, some of whom he might shortly be suing. Sam Branch had graciously extended an invitation to his bash, and Bobby had eagerly accepted on the grounds that he wanted at least to have a look at the horrible Sally Alder, symbol of Feminazism, usurper of the Dunwoodie millions. He also wanted to check out Sheriff Dickie Langham, who was evidently continuing to question people regarding the whereabouts of Shane Parker. Bobby had gotten out his old Harvard debutante ball tuxedo (still fit!), rented a room at the Holiday Inn so he wouldn't have to drive, and climbed into a Johnnie Walker. He could get up in the morning and enjoy his hangover with a bad cup of coffee and the Sunday morning *Boomerang,* in which he would find a story about the threat of a faculty group lawsuit against the University's acceptance of the Dunwoodie money.

Bobby liked to think of himself as a completely rational, greedy man, but even he had his failings. And one of them had walked right past him ten minutes ago, on her way to the bar. He liked them young, blond, pale, skinny, and sulky, and she fit the bill. As an active member of the Harvard Alumni Club of Wyoming, he was at least aware of every straight-A student who had managed to get out of the state in the last ten years, and—Praise the Lord—he'd never laid eyes on her transcript.

Advantage: Helwigsen.

She ordered pink wine.

Game and set. His serve.

Bobby approached the bar, gulped the last of his first Johnnie, and received a refill. He managed to brush against Brit, and she gave him half a glance. He wasn't somebody she knew. She'd already sidestepped passes from three geezers her father's age who had known her before she was toilet-trained, and had been studiously avoiding a guy she'd slept with once, in an uncharacteristic fit of stupidity, two years before. The guy in the tux was big, extremely good-looking, and smiling at her in a friendly way. Tux-man looked like the kind who might stand around for hours talking about himself, but at least it would be someone she could pretend to be interested in while Mr. Fit-of-Stupidity tried to catch her eye. She smiled back.

Bobby introduced himself to her and steered her to a table. She identified herself as just "Brit," no last name. He didn't care if her last name was Manson with legs like that. She was supposed to be impressed that he was an oil and gas lawyer from Casper, and a friend of Sam's, but Brit did not appear visibly overwhelmed. He tried a different gambit, one he'd used to excellent effect on a couple of occasions. He asked her about herself.

There was something about his voice, his posture, the shape of his body, that told Brit she had seen him somewhere before, but she couldn't remember where. Until she figured it out, she wasn't volunteering much information. She drank a little wine, told him she'd graduated from the University last May and was working part-time at present. He asked if she was from Laramie, and she said, "Yeah." She wasn't working at being a conversationalist, but that didn't seem to bother him in the least. He went back to talking about himself a while until the band played "San Antonio Rose," and he asked her to dance.

This guy Bobby had some moves, Brit had to give him that. But he'd acted like she ought to think it was so great that he knew both Dwayne and Sam, through business and

politics. Big whoop. Brit had cast her first vote for the
presidency for Ralph Nader. She hated even Dwayne's
milky middly Republicanism, but put up with him because he was her uncle and a nice guy. Sam Branch was
another story, not just because she despised his pandering
to right-wing assholes and split-leveling every pretty
place he got his hands on, but most importantly, because it
was common knowledge that he'd been boinking her Aunt
Nattie, not to mention half the women of Laramie, for
years. Sam had goggled a big leer at Brit when she walked
in tonight. Really, the man was in a class by himself.

It was unfortunate, she thought as Bobby spun her in
an intricate, graceful western swing pattern, that a guy
who could look and dance that good was probably a fan of
Pat Buchanan. Oh well, she didn't have to do anything but
dance with him tonight, and that was turning out to be not
all that bad. They stayed on the dance floor until the band
took a break, then went to the bar.

Delice caught up with them there, introduced herself to
Bobby. Now he understood that Brit was Dwayne's niece,
and more importantly, Sheriff Dickie's daughter. Bobby
failed to notice that Delice had seen the way his eyes
shifted ever so slightly when he heard Dickie's name mentioned.

Delice suddenly realized who this Bobby looked like.
The fact that it was Oliver North only made her more suspicious.

Soon Brit and Bobby were sitting at a table, joined by
Dickie and Mary, Dwayne, and Dwayne's wife, Nattie,
who was looking at Bobby as if he were a perfectly
cooked steak. The conversation was all about the party—
how great the music was, how inspired cousin Burt's
catering. Bobby was putting considerable effort into not
letting Nattie make eye contact.

Her dad, Brit noted, had gone into his sheriff routine.
He was teetotaling, as always, but was acting even more
laid back than usual, and not all that obviously bright. He

did this when he wanted people to think he was a hick cop who didn't see much action beyond drunk driving and lost dogs. Was that for Bobby's benefit? Dickie was so over-protective when it came to guys who were hitting on her.

And obviously, Bobby was interested. He was cruising on several ounces of decent scotch, doubtless contemplating whether it might be worth trying to get Brit to go to bed with him. She had barely spoken to him. She made a habit of not bothering to talk to men who were trying to get into her undergarments. But she was dancing with him, so why wouldn't he think she'd be up for a little horizontal boogie?

Maybe she would. Sometime. But she was not going to rush into anything that might make her wake up in the morning, having designated somebody Mr. Fit-of-Stupidity, Jr.

When Sally Alder came over to the Langham table to say howdy, Bobby Helwigsen got his first close-up look at the woman he was being paid to get rid of.

Sally was flushed and high on performance adrenalin, working on a Jim Beam and hanging onto a man who looked, to the uninitiated, like nothing more than a skinny hippie in a black suit. If this was the formidable holder of the Dunwoodie Endowed Chair in Women's History, thought Bobby, he was John Wayne. What the hell was a flesh-eating vampire feminist doing in a skin-tight fondle-me dress, belting out "Feelin' Single, Seein' Double"? She laughed her head off at something the sheriff said, rubbed against the hippie, laughed some more at a rude remark by Delice. Bobby sized Sally up in a phrase: more tits than backbone.

If she didn't fold at the first threat of legal unpleasantness, he bet he could get her out of town quick with a cheap payoff. If Elroy wanted to keep paying him to take Shane's challenge to the old lady's will, he didn't mind billing a few thousand more hours. He only wished he could dispose of Danny Crease and Dirtbag Robideaux as easily as he'd get rid of Sally Alder.

Delice and Dickie had both watched the Casper lawyer dancing with Brit, and wondered now why he was so evidently interested in Sally. They exchanged a look, then cut their eyes at Hawk. His posture was relaxed, a pleasant smile on his face, and behind his glasses, his own eyes were genially blank. Whatever this Bobby Helwigsen was up to, Delice mused, not much of it was getting past Hawk.

"Break's over!" crowed Sam Branch, swaggering over to the table, waving an arm at Dwayne, grabbing Sally by the hand, and pulling her away from Hawk. "Glad to see you met my friend Bobby, Sal. You guys have a lot in common." Everyone wondered why he said that, but he let it lie there. "But that's enough fun for now. Time for all good little chick singers to get back to work."

Hawk blinked, once.

"If I were a good little chick singer, Sam," Sally smiled, removing her hand from his, "I probably wouldn't succumb to the urge to tell you that your fly is open. And since I'm in a rare mood, I'll give it a pass this time." She turned to Hawk, gave him a strong kiss. "Don't mind Sam, honey," she told him. "He's been this way ever since the lobotomy."

Late into the evening, Hawk and Dickie stood by the ravaged buffet, sampling petit-fours, listening to Sally singing the line, "You're no good" about a thousand times.

"Great lyrics," said Dickie.

"Unpredictable," assented Hawk.

"So who's that asshole dancing with my daughter?" Dickie asked him, warily eying the by-now very sweaty Bobby, who had taken off his coat, rolled up his sleeves, and loosened his tie. Brit still managed to look cool, but she'd been dancing with Bobby all night. "You know anything about him?"

"Never laid eyes on him before tonight. I guess he's some big Casper lawyer Republican pal of Branch's, which is about all I need to know," Hawk observed, deciding against a second petit-four and starting on his last Budweiser.

"Looks just like Ollie North," Dickie noted. Hawk nodded.

"I find it rather interesting," Dickie said, daintily picking out a small chocolate eclair and swallowing it whole, "that even as it's apparent that he's hitting on my little Brittany, he's quite obviously watching your girlfriend's every move."

"My girlfriend?" asked Hawk, very intent on peeling the label off his beer bottle.

"Give it up, Hawk," said Dickie, sending a small cream puff after the eclair. "For all your 'lonesome fugitive' routine, you've been hanging with Sally pretty steady these past few months."

Hawk crumpled up the shreds of wet beer bottle label. "I'm enjoying her company," he said.

Dickie wiped his mouth with a cocktail napkin that had MILLIONAIRES' BALL embossed on it in gold letters. "Gee," he told Hawk, "that sounds like a major declaration of love coming from you." Hawk said nothing, so Dickie shifted the subject. "What was that crap Sam was slinging about this Bobby and Sally having a lot in common?"

"I've got no idea," said Hawk. "Sally told me she asked Sam about it, but he said it was just a joke. Weird joke."

"I confess I've never appreciated Sam's sense of humor," Dickie agreed.

Hawk raised an eyebrow, shifted his gaze to the bandstand. Sam had moved over from his own mike to sing harmony into Sally's, their heads close together. "The scum-sucker has been leching after her all night." He sneered a little. Sam had been giving Sally the intense gaze every time they sang harmony on a love song, touching her a lot more than absolutely necessary. "I may have to shoot him yet."

"Which scum-sucker?" asked Dickie, watching Bobby dancing closer to Brit than he found comfortable. "The lawyer or the Realtor?"

"All of 'em," said Hawk. "I may have to rid the world of them. Or at least the county."

"As an officer of the law, I didn't hear that," Dickie remarked.

"In self-defense, of course," Hawk amended.

"Still deaf as a post," Dickie said.

"And as a law-abiding civilian," Hawk returned, "I will avow my ignorance in the event that any particular scum-sucker comes to a bad end not of my own making, due to his evil and ignorant attempt to take advantage of beautiful daughters of local officials."

Dickie pursed his lips, thought. "But in the event that local officials find themselves in a position to have use for information regarding any or all scum-suckers, I do hope you'll keep us in mind."

"I do my duty," said Hawk, grinning widely and clapping as Sally finished off the song and avoided a hug from Sam. "And should any information come to light regarding the reasons for the Casper lawyer's untoward interest in the person you've referred to as my girlfriend, I would appreciate your assistance."

Bobby had his hand in the middle of Brit's back now, moving in circles, slowly south. Dickie looked at them, then looked at Hawk. The sheriff's eyes had gone cold. "This ain't Casper," he said. "And in my town, I always render assistance."

22

Take It or Leave It

Late Sunday morning, the snow was falling thick and piling up. Sally woke up alone. Hawk had made a date with Tom Youngblood to go cross-country skiing, and they'd agreed to leave at eight o'clock. She vaguely remembered being kissed goodbye, but he'd gone quickly and quietly, as was his custom. They'd made an agreement: They were to come and go in each other's lives, as they pleased. Sometimes it made her feel panicky in a way she found embarrassing.

Her head felt snowed in. They'd played until one in the morning. She wasn't used to staying up that late any more, much less sitting around until two drinking nightcaps and doing post mortems on the gig. But then again, back when she'd done this sort of thing on a regular basis nobody had set her phone ringing before noon, let alone at—she looked at the alarm clock—8:55 A.M.

"Sally," breathed Edna McCaffrey.

"Edna," Sally managed to breathe back.

"Have you seen the *Boomerang*?"

"Rumor-bang?" mumbled Sally through the echo of a last Jim Beam.

"Wake up!" Edna ordered. "Get out of bed, get a cup of coffee, and get the damn paper. We're being sued."

"Sued?" asked Sally, beginning to notice the daggers stabbing into her skull, and not liking that old-time feeling. "Why?"

"Some of our concerned colleagues evidently think we're a threat to academic freedom," Edna snarled. "Do you want me to read you the story?"

"No. No. I'm waking up now," Sally said, stumbling out of bed, swaying a little as her head swam. "Give me half an hour, Ed. I'm going to take a shower, make some coffee. I'll read the paper and call you back."

"Take six Advils," Edna advised, recognizing Sally's disorientation for what it was. "And get something in your stomach."

"Yeah. Yeah. Right," Sally muttered, realizing that her body had a stomach, not all that enjoyable a realization. "Call you back," she managed, lunging to hang up the phone, lurching to the sink, splashing water on her face, looking in the mirror, and daring her dripping, ugly-looking self to beat this swirling, brain-splitting hangover senseless and get on with what was sure to be an infuriating day.

Edna, being a humane sort of person, gave Sally a good half-hour to wake it and shake it and focus her eyes. Patiently waited another ten coffee-making minutes, and even gave her an extra two minutes to read the story in the newspaper a first time, for herself. But that was it. She was just getting ready to dial again when her phone rang.

"Bosworth," said Sally.

"Obviously," said Edna. "He's quoted. 'Public universities must maintain their independence from political and other pressure, and faculties must have the right to enforce their professional standards in hiring and curriculum. This bequest violates our most sacred canons, subjecting us to the dictates of political correctness.'"

"First time anybody's ever tried to claim the Boz had any kind of cannon," Sally observed, but Edna wasn't in a laughing mood.

"'Independence from political and other pressure,'" Edna sneered. "I don't recall him complaining every time some mining company gave the geology department a bunch of money to go tear up the national forests. Or that nice grant from the Cattlemen's Association to research the environmental hazards generated by endangered species. But this time, he's worried. The son of a bitch has managed to stir up at least a few of the no-neck nean-derthals around here. Can't figure out how many, or who, but that won't be that hard. If this suit is actually filed, they'll be named as plaintiffs."

Rage had cleared Sally's mind the moment she poured her first cup of coffee and unfolded the paper. Her stom-ach responded gratefully to a bagel and cream cheese. This new unpleasantness should have made her want to go back to bed and pull the covers over her head. But she had become in mid-life one of those people who love crises. The more screwed-up things got, the sharper her focus, the firmer her resolve. "Okay, so they'll have to come out and play. What I want to know is, who's paying the lawyers? UW faculty? What are they doing—selling plasma to pay legal fees? Where's the money coming from, and who's representing them?" She drank more cof-fee, looked again at the article.

"All it says here is that they're represented by a Casper law firm," Edna read at the other end of the line. "Typical. The fools in Casper probably think they can get the Uni-versity to move up there if they make things annoying enough here."

"A Casper law firm? Hey—I met a lawyer from Casper at the party last night. Wonder if he'd know what's going on. He was drooling all over Brit—bet she could get some information out of him."

"Let me do some digging first. I'm going to call that

horse's ass Bosworth and ask him what he wants the University to do about having gotten a big old pile of free money. By the time I'm done with him, we'll know a lot more." Edna was, after all, a skilled interviewer, but Sally figured Byron Bosworth knew enough to keep his mouth shut around people he was suing.

"Okay. I'm going to call Ezra Sonnenschein's office and tell them we need him up here for a meeting the minute he gets back from Africa. He'll need to be involved."

"Yeah," said Edna, "and so will Egan Crain. We need a unified strategy."

It occurred to Sally, at that moment, that she was only one of the many parties involved in this particular little brouhaha. First, there were the aggrieved plaintiffs, who undoubtedly had a variety of reasons for joining the suit (ranging, she assumed, from the understandable to the sociopathic). Then there was the University, which encompassed a whole lot of people who would have many different ideas about whether or not to cave in to pressure or hang onto the money and the Dunwoodie Chair and the Center. And of course, the archives, which was dying to get its hands on Meg's stuff, one way or another. And the trustees of the Dunwoodie Foundation, whoever they were. Maude Stark, whose stubbornness, at least, was beyond question, would insist on having a say.

As for her own self, Sally was measuring her options. The best, of course, would be for the lawsuit to go away, the money to stay put, and her plan to write and teach in Laramie to hold up. But Meg Dunwoodie's story had gotten a sharp hook into her, and she ached to tell it. The ache was turning into a determination to write the book, endowed chair or no endowed chair. She'd told herself she wasn't letting a vicious skinhead keep her from doing it— could she really be afraid of a bunch of peevish college professors? If the university decided to punt on the bequest, she could always go back to LA, but she fully intended to persuade Sonnenschein that she should continue with the biography.

Of course, there had turned out to be unexpected reasons to stay in Laramie, one of which had left a black Armani suit hanging in her closet. No promises, though—at least they agreed about that, right?

"Where are you on this, Edna?" Sally asked.

"Pissed as hell and spoiling for a fight."

"You, or the University?"

"Me, for one. The president, for another—I talked to him. He has a very hard time contemplating giving back five million dollars. And once I talk to the University counsel, I'll have a better idea how they might think about fighting this idiocy."

"Thanks," Sally said, pouring more coffee, drinking, scalding her mouth. "I mean it."

"Call Sonnenschein," Edna replied shortly. "Let's get this thing in gear."

For two weeks, everyone played phone tag, fended off the press, milked, dismissed, and occasionally confirmed rumors, gathered information, and played more phone tag. But by a Tuesday afternoon in late January, they were sitting around the conference table in Edna's office: two members of the board of trustees; Dean Edna; the vice president for academic affairs (a handsome, blow-dried economist with a hands-off attitude; he was representing the president, but Edna assumed he'd give them ten minutes, then plead "another meeting"); the University counsel (a short-haired woman in a no-nonsense suit and turquoise blue silk shirt with a bow at the neck); Egan Crain; and Sally. They were waiting for Ezra Sonnenschein, and for Maude, whom Sonnenschein thought ought to be present. The lawyer and the housekeeper arrived together, ten minutes late but unruffled, and took seats. Sonnenschein accepted a cup of the desk-temperature coffee everyone else appeared to be drinking. Maude declined.

Edna convened the meeting. "Good of all of you to be here. Thanks especially to you, Mr. Sonnenschein, for traveling up here from Denver. You're all here because each of you is in some way involved with the Dunwoodie Foundation bequest to the University to establish the Dunwoodie Chair and Center for Women's History, and to donate the Dunwoodie papers to the Archive. I want to start out by asking the University counsel to bring us up to date on the legal situation. For those of you who don't know her, this is Virginia Minor."

"As you all know," Minor began, "a group of faculty has threatened to file a class action suit alleging that the terms of the Dunwoodie bequest and the execution of those terms constitute violations of academic freedom. On those grounds, the plaintiffs will ask that the University be compelled either to refuse the gift and terminate all arrangements stemming from the bequest, or to renegotiate the terms of the arrangement with the foundation in accordance with nationally standard academic practices regarding hiring, acceptance of donations, archiving of document collections, and execution of the terms of the bequest. I am informed by counsel that his clients are willing to drop the suit, if the University agrees to renegotiate terms as stated."

"Which means what in English?" Maude asked.

"Which means," said the University's lawyer, "that they haven't filed yet, but they will. Unless we either give back the money and fire Professor Alder immediately, or we simply void Professor Alder's contract, and try to talk the Foundation into doing an open search for the Chair, to be conducted under the authority of the history department, and relinquishing control over the monies, the Dunwoodie papers, and the biography project, in favor of management by a joint committee representing the University, the archives, and of course, the history department."

"So with one alternative, the University loses the bequest. With the other, Byron Bosworth comes in as a main player," said Sally.

"And either way," Maude told Sally, "you get canned."

"Hey," said Sally, "if the University and the Foundation want to cave in and let the Boz pick the next Dunwoodie Professor, I would be willing to be a candidate. I'm sure my chances of being hired would be excellent." General laughter.

"I understand," said Sonnenschein amiably, "that the faculty group bringing suit includes a number of members of the department of history."

"Indeed," Edna told him, eyes glittering, "but not exclusively. There are, as far as we know now, approximately twenty plaintiffs."

"Not bad," Sonnenschein observed. "I would imagine that in any university in the country, you could manage to find twenty people willing to file a lawsuit alleging that the sun rises in the west."

Sally suppressed a giggle. She hadn't had much contact with Ezra Sonnenschein, but she liked the hell out of the guy. He fit her definition of suave. He was slim, tall, and graceful, with salt-and-pepper hair and blue eyes she'd have described as both friendly and piercing. She'd never seen him dressed in anything except perfectly tailored suits he probably bought in London. He carried the air of always knowing things nobody else knew, but not making a big deal about it. She felt that he was on her side, and the feeling comforted her immensely.

"These plaintiffs are more the flat-earth crowd," Maude noted.

"In this great free country of ours," pronounced Sally, "even flat-earthers have their day in court."

The vice president announced that he had to rush off to another meeting, shook hands all around, said he knew that they'd work something out, and exited. Edna had been wrong. Seven minutes flat, from the time Sonnenschein and Maude walked in. The trustees exchanged a "what do we pay him the big bucks for?" look.

"I'd just like to say a word or two about the Dunwoodie Collection," Egan interjected in the wake of the VP's departure.

Everyone looked at him.

He thrust out what he called a chin, and took the plunge. "As representative of the archives, I must inform you that we hold it to be in our interests to preserve harmony among those we consider our constituencies. At the same time, we also wish to retain our rights to the Dunwoodie papers. We would not be averse to participating in some sort of cooperative arrangement, including the one proposed by the plaintiffs. A lawsuit would of course be appallingly costly and time-consuming." He looked around the table. "I'm sure we can come to some accomodation with these chaps."

"Neville Chamberlain speaks," muttered Maude.

"We understand your position," Edna told Egan, carefully taking the edge out of her voice, "but we haven't yet discussed the University's position with regard to the proposed lawsuit, so it seems to me premature to be planning how to cooperate with the plaintiffs."

Egan looked sick, but said no more.

"Who's representing the plaintiffs?" asked Sonnenschein.

"A Casper law firm, Whipple, Hipple and Abernathy."

Sonnenschein thought a moment. "Why W, H and A? I thought they were an oil and gas firm. Some railroad and insurance and tax business. Right-of-center Republicans. Hardly the kind of attorneys who take on the civil liberties claims of penurious college professors."

"Well, this *is* a shot from the right," Sally said.

"More to the point," said one of the trustees, a lawyer himself, "it's five million bucks."

"Right," Sonnenschein conceded, "but there are conservative law firms in the Rockies that usually handle this sort of thing. Mountain States Legal Foundation is the most famous, but there are plenty of others, and I've never heard that Whipple, Hipple was doing that sort of litigation. Who's the lead attorney on the case?"

Minor looked at her notes. "A fellow named Bobby Helwigsen."

Sally's eyes narrowed.

"I haven't actually met him," Minor continued, "but according to what I've been able to learn, he's a specialist in tax and estate litigation. He just came back to Wyoming last year, but he's handling some of the biggest money in the state."

"A guy like that doesn't come cheap—who's paying his tab?" the lawyer trustee asked, making a note on a yellow pad.

"The plaintiffs aren't saying, but we're trying to find out," Minor replied.

"That's fine," Sally put in, "but what do we do now?"

Maude looked at Sally, around the table. Nobody quite knew why Maude was at the meeting, but when she wanted to speak, no one was prepared to tell her to shut up.

"You're the Dunwoodie Professor, Sally," she said quietly. "You're the one who was hired to set up the Center, write Meg's biography, teach women's history at the U. These guys want to get rid of you. If you say you don't feel like fighting, you can always go back to UCLA and chalk this all up to foolishness. You can save the University a lot of time, money, and trouble if you bail out, and you don't really lose anything by it. So Boz and the boys win a round—big deal. They're not the only ones who think they have a right to Meg's money. You can save yourself a hell of a lot of problems if you just give up. What do you want to do?"

"At the moment," Sally answered, with fierce and surprising calm, "I want more than anything else to write about Meg Dunwoodie's life. I've found some puzzles I can't leave until they're solved. This is going to sound crazy—maybe you have to be a historian to understand. But I'm beginning to feel Meg's somehow watching me. I don't understand who or what it is that wants to stop me, why some shirttail cousin of Meg's vandalized my car, broke into my house, *Meg's* house, and beat you up. That makes me furious. I can't imagine who's willing to spend big money paying lawyers to get me out of here, but that kind of ticks me off, too.

"To be honest, this *is* all a little daunting. But I'm damned good and sure I'm the right person for the job. If you all think it's expedient to try to compromise with these guys, I'll tell you I'm sorry you feel that way. Byron Bosworth and his group have absolutely no interest in seeing Meg Dunwoodie's story told at all, much less told with care and compassion and critical judgment. I do. I'd like to fight them, and I'm not afraid. I'm fully prepared to stand up to anybody who wants to prevent me from writing that story." It was a brave speech; she hoped she meant it.

Maude had heard what she wanted to hear. She and Sonnenschein exchanged a glance, and he began, "As designated representative of the Dunwoodie Foundation, I would like to introduce to you the chairwoman of the Dunwoodie Foundation, Maude Stark." Maude inclined her head. Nobody had known, of course, but neither was anybody all that surprised. "The Foundation consists entirely of Maude and me," Sonnenschein continued, surprising them a little more. "The chairwoman will now outline to you, the representatives of the University, the Foundation's terms," he finished, turning to Maude.

"Take it or leave it," said Maude.

"Beg pardon?" said Minor, who'd picked up a fountain pen, all ready to write copious notes on her own yellow pad.

"Take it or leave it," Maude repeated. "The University

can either take the bequest, including the terms that Sally continue as Dunwoodie Professor, that the papers remain in the Dunwoodie house so that Sally can go on with her work uninterrupted and unimpeded"—here she glared briefly at Egan, who shrank a little. "The management of all monies and other assets continues as it has, jointly administered by the Foundation, the Archive, the College of Arts and Sciences, and the Center Director"—Sally inclined her own head—"all that. No changes. No negotiations. If they don't like it, too bad. If the University doesn't like it, well then, we'll just take back the money, cut the University out of the deal and start paying Sally directly for the biography."

"And I would be willing to represent Professor Alder in the event that she chooses to bring action against the University for breach of contract," Sonnenschein added smoothly.

Nobody spoke. Egan looked much sicker. Minor stared at her yellow pad, drew little flowers with her expensive fountain pen. Edna frowned, thinking hard. Sonnenschein smiled faintly.

"Wait a minute." Sally broke the silence. She couldn't imagine suing the University. She must be a lousy American. Her thoughts were elsewhere. "I'm not sure I like the idea of writing the in-house biography, Maude. Suppose I write something you won't like? I don't want you or anybody else deciding they have the right to censor or suppress this book."

Sonnenschein answered for Maude. "Sally, nobody knows better than Maude and me that Meg Dunwoodie wasn't anybody's angel. She was a complicated, magnificent woman, who doubtless did some terrible things you'll have to tell the world about. But Maude assures me we can trust you to be truthful, and fair, and to care about her, and to be stubborn enough to write a damned good book. And that's what we've agreed we want."

I will not cry, Sally told herself.

The trustees whispered to one another. One handed Edna a cellphone, and she punched in the president's number. After a rapid conversation, she handed the phone back to the trustee, and said, "The president wants to go for it."

The counsel looked at the determined dean, at the archivist, who was ghost-pale, at the trustees, faces full of care, at the Dunwoodie Professor, whose lips were pressed so tightly together they were white around the edges. "Having reviewed precedents, I can tell you they run both ways. Most challenges to bequests to universities never get beyond the stage of bad publicity and hurt feelings. But when they do end up in court, it's anybody's guess which way they'll go. I am perfectly willing to fight this one, if that's what you all decide."

Egan knew his own choices: Margaret Dunwoodie's papers eventually, versus no papers. Money for other projects, versus no money. "Righto," he said. "No bloody choice about it, so might as well be in for a pound as a penny."

"And as for the pennies," Sonnenschein offered, "my office would be pleased to assist with the litigation, on behalf of the Foundation. We see no reason why the University should have to incur substantial legal fees," he added.

"That seems fair enough," said the lawyer trustee, figuring, what the hell, they were sued or screwed either way. This way seemed cheaper. The other trustee nodded.

Sonnenschein handed Minor his card after writing his home telephone number on the back. "Call me. Sorry to cut this short, but I've got a lot to do." He rose, signaling that the meeting was over. Edna crossed to him to shake his hand. Egan slapped him weakly on the back on his way out.

Sally gave Maude a hug, held out her hand to Sonnenschein, who surprised her once again by putting an arm around her shoulders and squeezing. But surprised or not, she wanted some explanations. "Maude, Mr. Sonnenschein, I think you two ought to come back to the house with me," she told them. "I want to ask you some questions."

"I guess we want to give you some answers," Maude allowed.

"Glad to hear it," said Sally. "And Mr. Sonnenschein, I hope you brought your keys."

"Call me Ezra," said the Denver lawyer, squeezing again.

23

Little Eddie

"So, evidently," Sally told Maude and Ezra as they walked the four snowpacked blocks to Meg's house, "I've passed some kind of initiation test."

Sonnenschein navigated the icy sidewalk with ease, despite his slippery city shoes. "We wanted to see how much this project meant to you. If you'd run at the first sign of trouble, you wouldn't have been the person to write Meg Dunwoodie's story. We know some things that her biographer would have a hard time finding out if we didn't say anything. We've reached the point where we needed to know if we can trust you."

"How do you know you can?" Sally asked, clomping along in her Sorels, her breath nearly freezing in her lungs.

"Judgment call," said Maude. "Mine. Ezra goes along with what I want."

"Why?" Sally asked.

"I'll tell you when we get home. We'll talk, then we'll open the closet," Maude announced, wrapping her arms around herself and putting her head into the frigid wind.

* * *

Maude insisted on making coffee. They were sitting in the kitchen now, and she was taking her time getting started. Finally, Sally was fit to bust. "Come on, Maude, damn it!" she said through clenched teeth. "Spill it."

"All right," said Maude, taking a deep breath. "You know Meg came back to Wyoming from Europe in 1940, right?"

"Right. Her mother was sick. She was needed at home. At least that's the story she told."

"Yeah. Well, Gert was sick, that's true. She had cancer. Took her two years to die, and Mac didn't make it any easier. He was a man who thought the best way to deal with problems was to get good and mad and stay that way. Made those last years of Gert's life hell, raging around the house, yelling at Meg, and no help at all."

"Why was he yelling at Meg? I know people get mad at death, but did something in particular piss him off?"

Ezra cleared his throat. "Ahem. That would be me."

Sally looked at him, skeptical. "You? How old are you, Ezra?"

"He'll be sixty this year," Maude answered for him.

Sally did the math: he'd been born in 1938. "What did you have to do with it? You were—what?—two years old."

"Not quite two, actually," he answered. "My birthday's in September."

"What's your point, Ezra?" Sally asked, running out of patience.

"Well, you see, when Meg came back, she wasn't alone," he explained. "Do you know who Ernst Malthus was?"

"Yes," Sally said, a million amazed questions dawning at once.

"Well," Sonnenschein continued, taking a bracing sip of coffee. "He was with her. And so was I. We, ah, traveled from Paris to Laramie via New York, Chicago, and Denver. As a family."

Sally looked hard at him. Was Ezra Sonnenschein their child? Ernst and Meg had both been blond, rosy, hearty, Nordic. Sonnenschein's hair was going silver from black, his skin olive, his body slim and elegant. If she was any judge, he had the looks to go with the Jewish name. "What were you doing with them?" she asked.

"They were saving my life," he answered simply. "My parents understood that the Nazis were going to do horrible things to the Jews who fell into their hands. My father was in the Resistance, and my mother was worried about her parents. They felt they couldn't leave, but they wanted to get me out. Ernst and Meg agreed to take me to the United States."

"Do you know the name Marc Sonnenschein?" Maude asked her.

"No," Sally replied. But she did know an initial. "M——. The third man on the Riviera. The friend of Ernst Malthus and Paul Blum. And Giselle."

"Giselle," said Ezra, "was my mother. She and my father were married in 1937, but her paintings were beginning to be known, so she never changed her name. Meg Dunwoodie was her dearest friend in the world, and she asked her to take me out of France. My father's family was Alsatian, from Strasbourg. They were financiers who did a lot of business in diamonds. He and Ernst and Paul Blum were very close. Ernst said he could help. And they did it.

"The first thing in my life I remember was being put on the train at the Gare du Nord in Paris. My mother was holding me and crying. She was wearing a suit with a fox collar. I can still remember the way the fur smelled, and the little heads and paws of the fox pelts dangling. My father was walking down the platform, talking to a bearded man. Meg was bossing a porter who was putting the bags on the train. There was smoke and steam everywhere.

"Finally Meg said it was time to go, and my mother put me down. She knelt down and took my hands and told me,

'Ezra, you have to go away for a while. And for now, I want you to do what I tell you. Until Papa and I can come and get you, you are to call this man'—the bearded one— 'and Aunt Meg Mama and Papa. They'll call you Eddie. Can you remember that? It's very important.'"

"Eddie?" Sally asked, incredulous. Ezra Sonnenschein was not an Eddie, but at two he might have passed for one, in a pinch. This had definitely been a pinch.

"Eddie Martin. Ernst had arranged forged passports and papers for all of us. He was heavily disguised, had dyed his hair, affected a beard. We were an American family named Martin—Ernest, Margaret, and little Eddie. Residents of Cincinnati, Ohio, the town in which I had supposedly been born. Fortunately, I was young enough that when the customs agents asked me my name and age at Le Havre and again in New York, I didn't have to say anything. All I had to do was look frightened, which wasn't hard."

"You must have been terrified," Sally managed.

"More than you can possibly imagine," Ezra agreed. "But my mother had told me I'd be safe with them, and that she and my father would come to get me just as soon as they could." He raised the cup to his lips, took a small sip. "I kept on believing her for a long time, even though I never saw her again." He lowered the cup, left his hand on the saucer. Maude put her own hand over his.

"So they brought you to Wyoming?"

Maude took up the tale. "Yeah. Can you imagine— Paris to Wyoming in six weeks? Meg had to go home, and Ernst couldn't stay. She was terrified somebody on board the ship would recognize her or Ernst, but they didn't know what else to do. It was just luck that nobody knew them, and they got away with it.

"Meg figured she could find somebody to look after Ezra until Giselle and Marc could get away. What she hadn't counted on was her father's reaction."

Sally thought about it a minute. "I can imagine. A conservative Wyoming rancher finds that his daughter has come home from gay Paree with a man she's not married to and a small child of uncertain parentage. I assume he wasn't pleased."

"Well, I can't say what he thought of Ernst," Ezra replied, "but I do remember him screaming at Meg in English words I didn't know, but which I understood were angry, and directed toward me. It was clear he wouldn't have me in his sight. Both Meg and Ernst tried to reason with him, but he made us leave immediately."

"Where did you go?" Sally asked. It was an amazingly clear memory from such an early age, but then it wasn't exactly falling off a tricycle. She bet therapy had brought a lot of it back. She ached for the traumatized toddler, the rejected prodigal daughter, and the man who had pulled some very long, doubtless tangled strings to get them to what was supposed to be safe harbor.

Maude answered. "Meg had bought a car in Denver, and they'd driven up to the Woody D from there. They drove over to Laramie, and stayed with Meg's old professors, Miss McIntyre and Miss White. They had to find a place for the little boy, and fast. Meg was hoping that she might be able to persuade one or other of her Parker cousins to take him, but a lot of the Parkers had left Wyoming, and the ones left in Albany weren't one bit interested in taking in somebody's refugee kid. Very nice people," she observed.

"So—who?" Sally wanted to know.

Again, Maude provided the answer. "My mother used to take in washing, and she used to do laundry for Miss McIntyre and Miss White. Meg and Ernst and little Eddie had been at their house a couple of days, racking their brains, when she came over to pick up the wash. I went with her. Eddie was sitting on their kitchen floor. I was eight years old and I really wanted a baby brother. I found a set of tin measuring spoons and gave them to him to play with. You really liked those spoons," she recalled, looking fondly at Ezra. He returned the look. "So my mom asked who he was, and Meg told her, and she said she'd be glad to give the poor kid a home until his parents could come for him, whenever that might be."

"You had a nice mom," Sally told her.

"Yeah, I did," Maude agreed. "A nice dad, too. He was a veterinarian, used to having banged up critters around. Mom brought Eddie home and we all loved him from the start."

"That was an amazing offer," Sally exclaimed.

"It was. But Ernst kept telling everybody that he was sure that Eddie's parents would be coming to get him soon, and that he would do everything in his power to help them. We had no idea what that meant—for all we knew, he was a businessman from Cincinnati, who happened to be a friend of Meg's from Paris. She didn't tell us who he really was until much later."

Sally wondered what kinds of powers Ernst had had. Evidently they extended to doctored passports and disguises. What else? "How long did Ernst stay in Wyoming?"

"He took Meg back to the ranch, and I don't know how long he was there. Not long, I think. We saw him one more time, in the summer of 1943, wearing the same disguise."

"He stayed in the U.S.?" Sally wondered.

Maude shrugged. "According to Meg, he traveled around throughout the war. New York, London, Zurich, Capetown, South Africa. And Berlin and Paris. He was a diamond trader, and as far as we know, he stayed in business. From time to time, he sent Meg money for Giselle and Marc's son. My parents put it in a bank account, in Ezra's real name."

"Malthus was a German citizen, right?" Sally asked.

Ezra nodded.

"How did he manage to travel so freely in enemy territory?"

Ezra and Maude looked at each other, and he answered. "We wish we knew. There's no doubt he was involved in intelligence work. He kept in contact with the French Resistance through my father. It appears he did some work for the Resistance, laundering money, that kind of thing. Perhaps other things. Ernst had friends in high Nazi places. His brother was one, but it turned out that his brother Rainer wasn't as loyal a follower of the Führer as he should have been."

"Rainer Malthus, of the *Schwartzkappelle,*" Sally said.

"The same," Ezra answered, pleased that she'd gotten that far in her research. "Executed when the assassination plot failed."

"So Ernst was in the Resistance?" Sally inquired, romantically hopeful.

Another look passed between Maude and Ezra. "It's not clear. That's one thing we're hoping you might help us find out. Certainly he was funneling money and weapons to my father's cell. But he may also have been working in some capacity for the Fascists, or for their sympathizers in other countries. Or he might have been an agent for the Communists. We just haven't got him figured out yet." Ezra shook his head sadly.

"He saved your life," Sally told him, as if that settled the matter.

"He wasn't a monster," Maude replied. "What else he was or wasn't, we aren't quite sure."

Sally expected to do quite a bit of work finding out. The first thing she'd do was file a Freedom of Information Act request for any government files on Ernst Malthus, and for that matter, on Meg Dunwoodie. "Did Meg come to visit you much?" Sally asked Ezra.

"During the first couple of years, Meg came whenever she could, but she had to be at the Woody D and take care of her mother, and for that matter, her father. Gert took a long, hard time dying, and it was clearly tough on Meg," Maude remembered. "Every time she'd come to see us, she looked skinnier and tireder, and by the time the end finally came, she was worn down to bones and nothing. They buried Gert on the ranch, and it wasn't a week later that Meg showed up in Laramie with a couple of suitcases, looking for a place to live and a job."

Sally considered. "So then you saw a lot of her."

"She thought of herself as my aunt," Ezra said. "She loved me. So did Ma and Pa Stark and Maude. Meg wasn't exactly close with her own family, and the Starks kind of adopted her as a cousin."

"So you grew up in Laramie?" Sally asked, incredulous. Laramie did not add up to Ezra Sonnenschein's kind of suave.

"I lived there until 1948. That was when my father came for me."

Postwar Europe took some time sorting itself out. Marc Sonnenschein had managed to evade the Nazis through five horrid years. He'd lost countless friends and loved ones, including his parents, all his siblings, the wife he adored. It took a long time for him to reclaim what was left of his life before the deluge, to reassemble his profession, scrape together what he could of his property, and make his place in a new society. With all he'd sacrificed and all that had been taken from him, he lived for years on the promise that his son was safe and well cared for, somewhere in the wilderness of America.

Ten-year-old Ezra, known to his Laramie pals as Fast Eddie, loved Stan Musial of the St. Louis Cardinals, the novels of Edgar Rice Burroughs, and the Rocky Mountains. He was known around town as "that war orphan the Starks took in," and considered a success story. If he was a little quiet and intense, a little too studious, he was also a wiry ball of energy, a base-stealing, power-hitting Little League phenom. Doc Stark said he wouldn't be surprised if the kid made it to the bigs.

Then Marc Sonnenschein showed up.

Ezra was overwhelmed. The life he'd come to think of as natural was the one he was expected to leave without a thought. Paris to Laramie, eight years before, had been terrifying. But the prospect of Laramie to Paris, now, seemed nothing short of devastating. A thin, hollow-cheeked foreigner had come to claim him. Marc looked at Ezra as if he were seeing a ghost. Later Ezra realized that he must have thought he was, seeing his own eyes looking back at him in the childish rendition of his dead wife's face. And the child knew himself as Eddie. It startled him when Marc called him Ezra, with the accent on the second syllable.

Father and son: strangers. And his father's arrival made the fact of his mother's tragic death inescapable.

Marc had a house in Paris, a partnership in an international financial house. He was resuming his position as a man of wealth and influence. Paul Blum, seeing disaster coming in the late thirties, had put all the family's holdings in Swiss banks. Ezra, at the age of ten, was a very wealthy little boy.

"A hell of a lot for a kid to handle, I thought," Maude told Sally. Maude had been determined to do something to make things easier on her little brother, so she went to Meg to ask her to find some way.

Auntie Meg made the whole thing possible. She convinced Marc not to take Ezra away immediately, but instead to spend a month in Wyoming getting to know the boy's world, know what he was taking him away from, think about what he was taking him to. That month made all the difference. They made Marc welcome in Wyoming, and he ended up loving the people and the scenery (it was, after all, summer). By the time Ezra packed his baseball glove and his Tarzan books, they had all forged ties that would span the Atlantic and last half a century and more. Ezra promised he'd come back and live in the Rockies when he grew up, and to Maude's great amazement, he did.

Ezra had stayed with his father in Paris, attended the

Sorbonne. Bilingual, bicultural, he always planned to return to the United States, and he wrote often to the Starks
and to Meg. He convinced Marc that it would be a good
thing for him to attend law school at Columbia. Upon
graduation, he joined a top New York law firm and specialized in international corporate law. He shuttled back
and forth between Manhattan and Paris, lived the life of a
high-powered cosmopolitan. But he always took his summer vacations in the Rockies, and made a point of visiting
Laramie every year.

"My father died in 1970," he said. "And I realized that
there wasn't anything holding me in New York. I'd gotten
married a couple of times, but I turned out not to be very
good at marriage."

"That made two of us," Maude commented, assuring
Sally, "we can talk about that later."

"So, to get to the end of this rather tedious story," Ezra
resumed, "I moved to Denver in 1972, set up my own
firm, and have never regretted the change. I have a cabin
in the Snowies, a place in Jackson that was, actually, a gift
from Meg, and I'm where, it appears, through no fault of
my own, I belong."

"Now about you . . ." Sally said, rounding on Maude.

"It's past five," Maude announced, and suddenly they
were all aware that the sky outside was dark and the
kitchen was dim. "What do you say we move into the living room and have a drink?"

They drank from crystal old-fashioned glasses the size of
a baby's head. Ezra had a dry martini. Maude had a Gibson. Sally had a Jim Beam. They turned on the silk-shaded
silver lamps in Meg Dunwoodie's living room, sank into
chair and couch cushions. Sally contemplated a Tiffany
cigarette lighter and Lalique ashtray and wished she could
smoke something, anything.

Instead, she went after Maude. "About you," she began
pointedly.

Revelations clearly were in the offing, but Maude hadn't worn nerves on the outside for years. She narrowed her eyes, took a sip of her drink, and said, "Meg saved my life."

"A familiar story by now," Sally replied, meeting Maude's glare.

"What the hell do you know about anything?" Maude returned. "Why don't you shut up and listen?"

"I'm sorry," Sally said, ashamed to have made Maude cuss.

Maude nodded, let her off the hook. "I graduated from UW in 1953." The year Sally was born. "I hadn't exactly been the queen of the prom. I chased off every boy who wanted to date me, never had time for 'em. Most of 'em were perfect boneheads anyway." Score another point for Maude's clear-sightedness. "I started out as a secretary, and worked my way up into management. By 1960, I got offered a job running the commissary over at F.E. Warren Air Force Base in Cheyenne. I was making good money. The military is full of idiots, but the ones who aren't, well, they keep things interesting."

Sally waited.

"One of the interesting ones was Captain James Tolliver. He was a pilot. We got to be friends. Eventually I started going out with him. We ended up getting married in 1963," Maude recited, reducing what was undoubtedly a really complicated and interesting story to its barest bones, but Sally was willing to put the details off for another time.

Maude took a big swallow of her Gibson. "Jimmy shipped out to Vietnam in September of 1964, just after the Tonkin Gulf incident. Was one of the first in there flying bombing runs over the country. On his first run, in October, he was shot down and killed." Her face was ghostly. "And I was pregnant."

Ezra stared into his drink. Sally looked at Maude, then

at the floor. The wind shrieked against the big windows, rattled the casings, blew wisps of freezing cold between the cracks.

"Jim's pension was pathetic. My salary wasn't much better. I was thirty-one years old after all, and had never imagined myself as a mother, let alone a single mother. I couldn't see how I could raise a baby on my own. I thought I had two choices: kill myself, or get an abortion," Maude declared quietly.

Sally looked up, met Maude's eyes. "I can't imagine how you'd go about finding out how to get an abortion in Wyoming in 1964."

"You can't. Neither could I. And I knew my parents would be appalled. So I asked Meg."

"Why did you think you could trust her?" Sally asked.

"Meg once told me," Ezra put in, "that she didn't give a damn about families or religion or country or any of that other pious crap. She had one rule, and that was that you always had to help out the people who proved you could trust them."

"So how had you proved yourself, Maude?" Sally asked.

Maude couldn't find breath to answer.

"By begging her parents to take me. They would have done it anyway, but the way Meg told the story, Maude was the one who had the idea and insisted they do it," Ezra said softly.

They listened to the wind howl.

"So," Maude resumed at length, "I told Meg, and she made the arrangements, and drove me down to Denver, stayed with me, brought me back and made me stay with her until I felt okay. By that time, I didn't feel like going back to my job at the base, and it was clear she needed somebody to take charge of her house. It's actually kind of funny," Maude said, sipping her drink and managing a small smile. "She kept insisting on making me cups of tea, but by the first afternoon I was there I was washing the teacups because she apparently didn't comprehend the concept of doing dishes."

"So you've been here ever since?" Sally asked.

Maude nodded. "There's plenty of time for ever since. I think we should go upstairs and have a look in the closet."

Ezra handed Sally the key. She unlocked the door, opened it. It was, in some ways, a typical household storage closet for valuables. Shelves held objects in flannel bags, which Sally assumed were silver serving pieces. She opened one, pulled out a heavy cream pitcher, put it back on the shelf.

There was jewelry, too. A large box held a multitude of small velvet boxes. Earrings, bracelets, rings, necklaces. Gold, pearls, precious stones. Platinum. Plenty of diamonds. Lovely things, but nothing out of the ordinary for a wealthy woman who had lived nearly a century. "I can't believe this stuff isn't in a vault," Sally said.

"This is Wyoming," Maude replied, "Remember? But you're right. I should take it all down to the bank and get a safe deposit box." She put the jewelry back in the box, closed it, and turned it over. Then she slid a section of the bottom sideways, revealing a satin-lined secret compartment that held a velvet pouch. Sally opened the pouch, and pulled out six carefully folded pieces of paper. Each held a glittering gemstone. The stones were enormous, each cut a different way. Three were deep yellow, one was pale blue, another deep blue, and the last was rosy pink. She put them back in the bag, speechless.

"They were here when she died," Ezra explained. "We don't have any idea how she got them, or what they might mean. Neither of us knows much about gems, but we're pretty sure they're diamonds. I meant to take them with me when I went to South Africa, see if I could learn something about them, but then, well, I just didn't find the time to get up here to pick them up before I left."

"Whatever the hell they are, they're gorgeous. I bet they came from Ernst, the diamond trader. A gift." She handed the pouch to Maude.

"Maybe," Ezra answered. "I don't know how you'd find out."

"I might know somebody who could help. Could you hold off taking them to the bank for a couple of days? If you don't mind, I'd like to show them to Hawk." Maude glared, Ezra looked concerned. "I'm sorry, but I broke the confidentiality agreement. I didn't want to make a big deal about it, but having somebody spray-paint swastikas on my car spooked the hell out of me. Then, after the break-in I had to talk to somebody. Brit Langham has seen the papers, of course, and I've been bouncing thoughts off Hawk since Thanksgiving. Brit's the kind of kid who'd keep a secret under torture, and I've known Hawk a long, long time. He won't tell anybody anything, and as it happens, he knows something about diamonds."

"What do you think, Maude?" Ezra asked. "Who's this Hawk?"

Maude considered. What she knew of Hawk Green was pretty much limited to a couple of conversations when he'd showed up at dinnertime. He'd been friendly enough, funny, dry. He impressed her as a man who kept his mouth shut. She searched Sally's face, found not a trace of silliness, and nodded, handing the pouch back.

Sally looked around. In one corner of the closet stood a stack of large cardboard portfolios and canvases on stretchers. She opened one portfolio, carefully slid out an ink and watercolor portrait of Paul Blum, deep in concentration, working at a desk. "Are all these Giselle Blum's paintings?" she asked.

"All," Maude said. "Eight watercolors, four oils, various subjects. Meg never framed them, for whatever reason. We haven't figured out yet what we want to do with them."

"Shouldn't you have them?" Sally asked Ezra.

"These were Meg's," he replied. "Over the years, she gave me thirty of my mother's pieces. These paintings are a collection that belongs with the bequest. How and where to display it is still a question. We could give them to the University Art Museum, of course. But if we decide eventually to turn this house into a museum, perhaps they belong here."

Sally could see the point. She looked at the portrait of the artist's brother, was humbled by the drawing technique, the subtle color, the depth of feeling conveyed in simple strokes. She very carefully placed the painting back in its portfolio.

Another shelf held five manuscript boxes. Sally opened one. The top sheet read, "Rays of Doubt." Paging through, she realized that she held in her hand the manuscript for a collection of poems never published. She'd seen drafts of many of the poems in the basement papers, but evidently Meg had taken care to put them together precisely as she wished. The other boxes held similarly arranged collections, varying in length from a few pieces to a hundred pages.

Sally looked up at Maude. "You knew these were here," she said.

"Of course," Maude answered. "Meg wasn't as brainlessly disorganized as people thought. She just couldn't throw anything away."

"If you don't mind telling me," Sally said, ignoring a passing urge to grab Maude by the throat, "what has been the point of having me flogging all that trash in the basement, looking for literary treasures?"

"The poems aren't all dated, or rather, some of the drafts downstairs are dated, whereas some of the versions here aren't. There's historical work to be done figuring out when they were written and why she put them together the ways she did," Ezra replied.

Again, they made sense. Sally looked around at all the treasures. "Well," she said, "I guess all that's missing is the Krugerrands, huh?"

Maude and Ezra looked at each other. "We know the rumors, of course," Ezra began, "but Meg never, ever made a single reference to her father's supposed buried fortune."

"If you want to know the truth," said Maude, "after Mac died, she never even mentioned his name again."

24

Shane's Luck

Shane was sick of these freaks. He hadn't joined up with
the Unknown Soldiers to be kept a prisoner in a freezing
cabin on some asshole zillionaire's ranch. He'd had to lay
low awhile, until the cops gave up on the break-in and got
back to running speed traps. Well, he'd been holed up in
East Bumfuck for months now. He'd smoked up all his
pot, gotten bored enough to pierce his own eyebrow, and
had been giving some thought to doing his tongue. Dirtbag, who almost never let Shane out of his sight, had begun to make suggestive remarks about prison and to look
at Shane in a way he didn't appreciate. He had started to
doubt whether the Unknown Soldiers gave a flying fuck
whether he got his inheritance or not, started to wonder if
they might, well, you know, be *using* him. By now, he figured, Sheriff Dickhead would have forgotten all about a
little B&E in which nothing had been stolen except some
scraps of paper, long lost. It was time to blow this puke-
hole.

He put on his crusty jeans, his jackboots, and his
leather jacket and tossed a glance at Dirtbag, who was
snoring in his bunk. The animal slept like a corpse on any
given night, but on this one, Shane had made extra sure,

dumping the contents of six capsules of phenobarbitol (stolen from Foote's wife) in Dirtbag's pork 'n' beans. It was a dose that could have sedated a steer, which Shane figured was about right.

Shane had sixty-one dollars, a .40 caliber Ruger automatic he'd stolen from Foote's gun room, three ammo clips, and a plastic Evian bottle full of vodka. He waded out into the snow, headed for the garage. The U.S. vehicles were parked far out of sight of the house in a converted stock shed, but Shane didn't want to attract attention by driving around in a camouflage humvee anyway. The ranch house garage held the vehicles used by the family: a couple of ATVs, two snowmobiles, a battered Dodge pickup, a fully loaded Jeep Cherokee, a Volvo station wagon, and Foote's personal ride, a vintage navy blue Mercedes. He settled on the last. Shane expected to have to disable the alarm and hot-wire the sucker, but found, somewhat to his disgust, that the zillionaire's paranoia did not appear to extend to worrying about his car. This was Wyoming, after all, not to mention Foote's ranch being a secured piece of private property bigger than some Arab countries. Foote's car was unlocked. The keys were in the ignition.

Shane got behind the wheel, sneering at the ease with which he was making his escape, and pressed the garage door opener. As the door slid up, he turned the key. The big German engine throbbed to life. He rolled down the driveway past the electronic eye that opened the ranch gate.

As he reached for the Evian bottle, he laughed out loud. If he felt like it, he could go to Casper and have a chat with Helwigsen about contesting old Meg's crazy will. Or maybe he'd go home to Albany, get some of his stuff, and head on down the road. Or maybe he'd knock over a liquor store somewhere, and head south. It would be cool at least to stop off in West Laramie and score some dope. So he decided to head for Laramie and then figure it out. He was a free man.

He didn't think the U.S. would come after him. Why the hell should they? They had nothing to gain by keeping him around, and some reason to hope he disappeared and couldn't be connected with them. He took a big swig of vodka, turned on the radio, which was tuned to right-wing all-night talk radio. He put the bottle between his legs, draped an arm over the steering wheel and leaned back to enjoy the ride.

By mid-February, Wyoming roads display an array of potholes, snowdrifts, black ice patches, and assorted hazards rarely achieved elsewhere. Even the most skilled and alert drivers are known to run afoul of one thing or another. Heading up over Togwotee Pass, through Dubois, Crowheart, and Lander, Shane's luck held up pretty well, considering that he'd gotten on the outside of a pint and a half of Smirnoff's. Route 287 was pretty much clear and dry, with only an occasional slick spot. Eventually, however, he found one. He nodded off heading into Muddy Gap. His tires skidded north and his luck headed south.

Shane considered himself a rebel and an outlaw, but he was from the generation that had imbibed the idea of buckling up along with mother's milk. The seatbelt had prevented him from hurtling through the windshield when the car spun off the road at sixty miles per hour. He woke with a wrenching start as the Mercedes plowed into a snowdrift and stuck fast. The steering wheel was covered with blood, as was he, and he realized he'd knocked out a couple of teeth. His chest was badly bruised, his neck had been jerked hard sideways, and his head felt like somebody had hit it with a brick, but nothing else seemed broken. For a while, he couldn't tell how long, he just sat in the car, bleeding and seeing stars and breathing hard. When his remaining teeth started to chatter, he realized he was shivering. He found a box of Kleenex in the car and shoved a wad into his mouth to stanch the blood.

He thought about lighting a cigarette, speculated

briefly about whether the car might explode, and figured, what the fuck. As a kid, the first drug he'd ever bought was a bottle of Tylenol, purchased at the Safeway shortly after the landmark product-tampering incident in Chicago where some loony had poisoned a bunch of capsules with cyanide. Back then, he'd liked the idea that his number might come up any time he popped a headache pill (even though he'd doubted it would). When he flicked his lighter and wasn't blown to bits, he decided he might as well try to start the car.

By daybreak, he'd used up nearly all his gas running the heater and wondered what the hell to do next, a million miles from fuckin' anywhere. Just then, his luck rolled over again. A long-bed Ford F–250 with a king cab, big-hip fenders and double rear tires, made for hauling stock trailers, appeared over the horizon. Shane put on the emergency flashers and grabbed the Ruger. He sat very quietly as the truck moved closer, slowed, and pulled up at the place where the Mercedes had left the road. A tall, bowlegged young cowboy in a well-worn Stetson and a sheepskin coat walked over to the Mercedes to see what had happened and if anybody needed help. When the cowboy opened the driver's door, Shane shot him in the leg, blowing a huge hole in the kid's thigh. The kid staggered back and blood sprayed all over the snow, just before he fell into a drift.

Shane got out, threw up, spat hard, walked to the truck, and helped himself to the bills in the cowboy's wallet. Amazing. This was the second time that night that he'd happened on a vehicle with the keys in the ignition, just when he needed to go somewhere.

The cowboy's luck was obviously not great that morning, but it could have been decidedly worse. Falling in snow minimized trauma to the wound, and the cold slowed the bleeding. Not half an hour after Shane Parker had shot him, taken his money and his truck, and left him bloody and unconscious in a snowdrift, a police car drove up. Officers P.W. "PeeWee" Corkett and Curtis Kates of the Wyoming Department of Criminal Investigations, on their way home from working the night shift, saw the Mercedes and pulled over. If they'd been half an hour later, the victim would have been dead. Shane had left the kid's driver's license in his wallet, so while Kates administered first aid, Corkett radioed in the cowboy's name and address, ran the Mercedes's plates, and explained that they were heading for the hospital in Casper with a gunshot victim who was also suffering from hypothermia. The assailant, Corkett reported, appeared to have driven off in a long-bed truck with double rear tires, and they called for officers to secure the scene, and a lab team to be sent.

An hour later, law enforcement around the state received word that there had been a grand theft auto and shooting on U.S. Highway 287 in the vicinity of Muddy Gap. The nineteen-year-old victim, one Jed Barnes, was in serious but stable condition in Casper. All officers should be on the lookout for a silver-gray Ford F-250 long-bed king cab pickup with double rear tires, Wyoming plates #6–2985, registered to the victim's father, Jethro C. Barnes, at a rural route address outside Sinclair. The assailant, who had abandoned a vehicle registered to an Elroy Foote of Freedom Ranch, Wyoming, was presumed to be armed and dangerous.

Shane was at that moment hurtling east along I–80, hell-bent for Laramie at eighty-five miles an hour. Kates and Corkett were starting the paperwork and making phone calls from the DCI office in Casper, and they were not looking forward to dealing with the owner of the Mercedes, who was fairly well known in the state for acting as if the huge ranch he owned was an independent country.

Shane's luck was holding. Two Wyoming Highway Patrol officers who were, by this time, supposed to be taking their shifts on the stretch of the interstate between Rawlins and Laramie, happened to be tanking up on warmed-over but free eggs and sausages and hash browns and coffee at the Country Kitchen in Rawlins when the pickup had sped onto the interstate entrance ramp. The officers were discussing college basketball and never saw a thing.

Dickie Langham was at home, taking a shower, when the call came into his office. The Albany County dispatcher radioed for two units to go out to watch the interstate. Lamentably, the county's Chevy Blazer was at home with a deputy who lived twenty miles north of Laramie in Bosler, where the temperature was only just pushing above zero. When the deputy turned the key, the engine gave a couple of labored coughs and died. It took him forty-five minutes to get the truck running. By the time he was on his way into town, Shane Parker was exiting Interstate 80, entering West Laramie.

He got to West Laramie in a curious state of exhausted frenzy, and headed straight for the house of Sherry, his methedrine dealer. Shane really needed a big hit of crystal. He knocked on the door and she answered, wearing a dirty tank top, smelling of stale cigarettes and sweat, hair matted, dark circles under her eyes, looking far better than Shane did.

"What the fuck do you want, you bastard? Where'd you get the truck?" she asked, eying the big rig parked out front, noticing the Wyoming plates that began with the number 6, meaning Carbon County. "You owe me a hundred bucks."

"Shut up, Sherry," he said, pushing her out of the way and walking into her filthy house. "I got money." He'd found $270 in the cowboy's wallet. "I got what I owe you, and another hundred. Gimme meth and some weed."

"Get outa my house, asshole," she said, wiping her nose with the back of her hand. "You get nothin'. The fuckin' pigs put out the word a couple months ago—they're lookin' for you. We don't need no trouble."

He walked over to her, grabbed her by a bruised and pockmarked arm, and put his face right in hers. "You gonna give me what I want, or should I just take it, bitch?"

She snarled at him, yanking her arm away, and said, "Okay, but lemme see the money, and then you get outa here fast."

Shane pulled out a wad of bills, peeled off five twenties and two fifties. He could easily beat the shit out of her and take the drugs, but he didn't want to risk dealing with Terry, her old man, who ran the meth lab in a series of ever-changing locations, and whom Shane had once seen eat a live cockroach. Terry kept pit bulls that were well known in West Laramie. He appeared not to be home but might come in any minute.

Sherry nodded, went into another room and returned with a baggie of marijuana and a small plastic envelope half full of white powder.

"Gimme some works," he said, licking his lips, and she brought him a piece of flexible rubber hose, a torch, a spoon, an eyedropper, a syringe, a cup of water, and a stoppered bottle of bleach. Shane cleaned out the needle with the bleach, cooked, tied off, fixed. The speed roared up his arm and straight to his heart, blasting into his brain like a sonic boom.

At that moment, Sherry's boyfriend walked in and gave Shane the same look he'd given the unfortunate cockroach. "Get the fuck outa here," said Terry.

"Yeah, get the fuck out, Shane," Sherry snarled. "And don't come back."

Shane went out to the truck, heart hammering, screamingly high. He was seized by the urge to take the Ruger back in and blow them both away. But the memory of the cowboy's jeans exploding in a wet red bloom had him dry-heaving by the side of the truck. He'd never before even seen anybody shot, much less shot somebody himself. He'd shot the kid with Foote's gun, left Foote's car sitting there. The realization that he had fucked himself *big* this time slammed into him like another hit of meth.

He could hear Terry's dogs barking. Wild-eyed, he jumped into the truck, rammed the keys into the ignition and peeled out of there, heading out of town on Highway 230, on his way home. He had no idea where else to go.

The phone at Freedom Ranch rang at 8:17 A.M. Officer P.W. Corkett of the Department of Criminal Investigations wanted to know if Mr. Elroy Foote was aware that a Mercedes registered to him was sitting in a snowdrift in Muddy Gap, and that whoever had been driving it appeared to have shot somebody with a large-caliber pistol and then driven off in the victim's truck. Elroy said that he'd been home all night and wasn't aware that his car was anywhere except his garage, but that there were a number of people on the property who had access to the many ranch vehicles. He would check it out and call Corkett back. Corkett said, politely but firmly, to do that as soon as possible, and added that he would be driving up to Freedom Ranch the next morning to talk with Mr. Foote in person.

Elroy went first to the gun room and noted the Ruger's absence (one of his favorite handguns, dang it!) and then to the garage. It might be that one of his regular cowboys had gotten drunk and a little out of hand. Then again, it might be one of the Unknown Soldiers, several of whom were staying on the place. In any case, there had been an inexcusable breach of security. It was bad enough that his gun and car had been stolen, but the telephone call from a Wyoming state policeman was beyond tolerating. The idea that state cops would insist on entering his personal domain, and that he probably had to permit them access, reminded him once again why he was dedicating himself to fighting government oppression. A crime, after all, had been committed against *him*! It ought to be Elroy Foote himself who administered punishment. But they'd taken away that right. When it came right down to it, though, Elroy just did not like having to deal with government lackeys, especially low-level ones.

Danny Crease was in the ranch house kitchen drinking coffee and reading *Soldier of Fortune*, about to be served pancakes and bacon by Elroy's dim but suitably reactionary wife. Elroy told him about the thefts and the shooting, and sent him to the bunkhouses to see who was missing. He went straight to Shane and Dirtbag's cabin, where there was of course no sign of the former, and the latter was still sleeping heavily, making a sound like a wrecking ball working on an old Vegas casino. Danny smacked him hard. Dirtbag snorted twice and turned over, curling up in his bunk like a kitten. Drugged.

"It was Shane," said Danny, annoyed to find upon returning that Arthur Stopes had joined Elroy at the table and had taken Danny's place and was tucking into his breakfast. Mrs. Foote, who didn't like scenes, gave Danny another plate and went upstairs to take a Valium.

"How did he get out?" Arthur wondered.

"He must have slipped Dirtbag an elephant trank. Bastard's still zoned out."

"So what do we do?" asked Elroy, excusing both the use of personal names and the profanity in this time of crisis.

"What have they got? Your car. If they find a bullet, they can potentially identify your gun, provided they also find the gun. Crimes were committed with your property. *Stolen* property," Arthur explained.

Danny stuffed a piece of bacon in his mouth, chewed hard, took a scalding sip of boiled coffee. "Figure they also have Shane's prints off the car, which they can match since he has a sheet. They make him as their only suspect within a few hours. If they find him and take him, he's liable to talk to cut a deal. You think a couple of state cops showing up today is bad—we'll have the FBI crawling all over this place in a week."

Elroy did not at all like the idea of the FBI invading his private property, let alone finding out what he had stashed up at Freedom Ranch. He could, of course, see that the various convicted felons currently on the place scattered before the police arrived. And it was not in all cases illegal for private citizens to possess the kinds of armaments he had managed to purchase from various offshore entrepreneurs. But he knew that it was frowned upon. He admired militia heroes like Randy Weaver, but considered himself too rich for martyrdom, or even bad publicity. "So we have to try to find Parker before they do," he acknowledged, mentally excommunicating Shane from the U.S. with the mere mention of his actual last name.

"Give me your plane, Mr. Foote. I want to fly down to Laramie and see if I can't pick up a trail. If I can get to him before the cops find him, I'll shut him up for good," Danny said, looking scary.

"But in the meantime, Number One," Arthur cut in, "it's important that you make some explanation to the police. They'll call back any minute. Perhaps you might say that one of the men you hired on a temporary basis, say, to help pull cattle out of snowdrifts, is missing."

"Not bad, Arthur." Danny smiled nastily. "Give them Shane's description and a fictitious name, phony social security number, all that. Obviously, he fed you a line, then ripped you off. It'll keep them busy until I can get to the little pencil-dick. We should have taken him down when he screwed up the Dunwoodie job."

Arthur nodded sadly. "We must do what we can to rectify the mistake, even as we construct a position that enables us to restore security."

"What the hell does that mean, Art?" Danny sneered.

"It means we step on it. And it means"—Elroy fixed a steely stare on Danny—"that when you carry out the sentence, you must under no circumstances leave witnesses or evidence that might implicate the Unknown Soldiers or in any way jeopardize our mission."

"With all due respect, Mr. Foote," Danny said, choosing bluntness, "we're up to our ass in implications. But if it makes you feel better, I promise not to waste him when anyone's watching."

"See that you don't. I'll call the state police back. You," he said, indicating Danny, "call my pilot and have him gas up the plane. Call a leasing outfit in Laramie and make sure they have a car waiting at the airport. Then, get a couple of men and wake up Number Seventeen to take him to the stockade for discipline. As soon as I'm done talking to the police"—Elroy nearly spat on the last word—"I'll call Number Two in Casper and brief him. I want him here before the police arrive. Now let's go!"

Shane was shaking hard by the time he got to to his place south of Albany, the mouse-infested, dilapidated dwelling that was all that remained of a once-thriving Parker family ranch. Halfway down the muddy, rutted driveway, the truck high-centered and stalled out. Somebody'd torn up the road since he'd driven the Pontiac in and out at Thanksgiving. Shane didn't feel like trying to get unstuck, so he trudged the rest of the way to the house. The front door creaked on its hinges, but thankfully didn't fall off as it had once before when he'd returned after a long absence. He was way too wired to have the patience to fix it, terminally too tired to have the strength, and it was maybe eight degrees above zero outside, tops.

His tongue felt as if it had been Velcroed to the roof of his mouth. He went to the kitchen, still piled with his dirty dishes from months ago, and found a glass. But when he turned on the tap, nothing happened. His pipes were frozen solid.

Now thirst was really getting hold of him. He'd have to melt snow. He found a saucepan, went outside, filled it with snow, and came back in to turn on the burner on the stove. Nothing again. Hadn't paid his propane bill since September. No gas.

Panic struck. His heart was pounding his chest so hard he wondered crazily if it would break his ribs. That meth had really done a number on him: He needed something to take the edge off it. Shane had once had a girlfriend who'd left a bottle of Librium in his bathroom. He considered it a "chick drug," but this was an emergency. He went in the bathroom, carrying the saucepan, found the pills, ate five, and washed them down with a handful of snow. He was still shaking so hard his teeth hurt.

At least there was nice dry wood stacked next to the fireplace. He laid some logs on the grate. Grinding out the last of the speed rush, he rummaged through cobwebby cupboards until he found an ancient copy of *Reader's Digest*. He ripped it up ferociously, crumpled a bunch of pages, shoved them under the logs, and found his lighter. Amazingly, it occurred to him to open the flue before he flicked the Bic on the paper.

To his enormous relief, the fire roared to life at once, shooting up flames high into the chimney with a great whoosh. The room warmed right up, and Shane fell gratefully onto a couch that most people would have declined to touch without rubber gloves. The Libriums kicked in, his head spun hard twice, and he sank into unconsciousness. High in the chimney, which hadn't been cleaned in twenty years, the residues of a thousand dirty fires began to smolder, and the mortar between the bricks began to crumble. Sparks shot out high above the chimney top, showering fireproof asphalt shingles, except in the places where the shingles had fallen off the aging roof, exposing tar paper and even bare timbers. The chimney was going off like a roman candle as Shane lay senseless below, and some of the sparks caught on wood and paper and began to blaze. The Parker place was known for its great privacy. No one passed by to notice as the fire licked its way down from the roof to the studs, roared down walls, engulfed the house.

At eight A.M., when Sheriff Dickie Langham arrived at his office in the Albany County Courthouse and heard the news of the incident in Muddy Gap, he gave himself a good cussing out about not getting officers into position in time to have a chance to head off the suspect. The bad guy might very well be speeding along one of the roads in his jurisdiction, or holed up somewhere in his county, or, God forbid, committing another senseless crime upon some undeserving citizen. Dickie drank a cup of coffee, ate three donuts, smoked two Marlboros and put in a call to PeeWee Corkett, the investigating officer from the DCI. PeeWee had been an instructor at the law enforcement academy when Dickie was there, and he recalled PeeWee telling a memorable joke involving a can of BBs mistakenly poured into a blueberry pie. Dickie laughed in spite of himself.

"Glad to hear from you," PeeWee told Dickie. "We've got a lab team taking prints off the Mercedes. They'll run the prints through the FBI computers and maybe come up with a match by the end of the day, if we're lucky. It's a bitch of a case in more ways than one. The car belongs to a rich shithead named Elroy Foote, who's claiming it was stolen by some drifter he'd hired recently, along with a Ruger automatic. Foote gave me the guy's name and social security number, but when we traced the number it turned out to be a phony.

"*Then*," PeeWee continued, exasperated, "I got a call from some asshole lawyer in Casper who claimed to be Foote's 'representative.' What's this with a guy having a representative? Must have too much money and not enough brains to pour piss out of a boot. Anyhow, this representative told me how much he appreciated the state's effort to retrieve Mr. Foote's stolen property, and how he hopes this whole affair will be handled with minimal invasion of Mr. Foote's privacy."

Dickie was sympathetic. "A representative talking about privacy? You're gonna be wadin' through it on this one, PeeWee."

"Tell me about it," PeeWee said. "I explained to the lawyer that we'd do what we can to protect Mr. Foote's property *and* his privacy, but it was likely that a felony had been committed with a weapon registered to Mr. Foote, and a nineteen-year-old kid was seriously injured, and the perpetrator was still at large."

"Was he impressed?" Dickie asked.

"No, but we're gonna go impress him. My partner and I are on our way up to Teton County to Foote's ranch. We'll scope things out and talk to Foote. I'm sure this Helwigsen fella, the representative, will be up there by the time we make it."

Dickie cradled the phone between his ear and his shoulder, taking notes. "Well, we'll keep a lookout for your bad guy, PeeWee," he said, wondering how in hell he'd do that. "What was that lawyer's name again?"

"Helwigsen," said PeeWee, taking a puff off a Marlboro of his own and chasing it with a bite of a congealing Egg McMuffin. "Robert Helwigsen. Name ring a bell?" he asked.

Of course. "Yeah, it does. Let me make some calls. I'll let you know if we come up with anything."

"Likewise," said PeeWee.

Danny Crease arrived at Brees Field in Laramie not much after noon and instructed Foote's pilot to wait at the airport until he returned. A car rented to Freedom Ranch was, of course, waiting for him. He drove down route 130 to the intersection with 230, headed southwest. One of the Unknown Soldiers had been to Shane's place once (getting high, he didn't admit) so Danny knew where to go.

Two miles from the turnoff to the dirt road that led to the Parker place, Danny saw the smoke. Even with the windows closed and the heater on, he smelled it. He turned into a torn-up mud driveway he didn't really want to take a rental car down, just in time to see the roof fall in, sparks and flame exploding all around. A ranch pickup with county 6 plates was mired some ways from what had once been a house but was now a roaring blaze. Danny parked his rental car, got out, and thought he smelled roasting meat. He couldn't be sure it was Shane—hell, for all he knew it could be a dog or an antelope—but then again, the fire had to have started somehow. If the asshole had burned himself up alive, it just saved Danny the trouble of killing him. Sparks were falling on the trees around the cabin, hissing out on wet, snowy branches. Given the amount of smoke, fire trucks would show up eventually, and Danny didn't want to be around when they did.

Danny got back in the car, heading for the airport, then realized that he might as well take his time. In fact, he decided he'd grab a motel and stay the night. There was no reason for him to be at Elroy's place when the state troopers showed up. Why not drive around Laramie, do a little reconnaissance? He still meant to exact payment of the debt Dickie Langham owed him. Maybe he'd stop for lunch at Foster's Country Corner where, he knew from experience, the customer was always right. On his way back into town, a Laramie fire engine screamed by, siren blaring, headed the other way. It was followed by an Albany County sheriff's car, lights flashing. Danny drove on, grinning.

25

Putting Out Fires

Bobby had just finished a grueling duel with the Butt-Blaster when his cellular telephone chirped. He liked to get to the gym early and be pumped up and gleaming with sweat by the time the babes walked by the strength-training area, on the way to the sunrise step aerobics class. He'd met some interesting women that way. Well, maybe not interesting, but you could count on their knowing exactly what percentage of body fat they were carrying, and it was always within the acceptable range.

It was Elroy calling, and for once he was showing the kind of real discretion the cellphone required. "There's been a robbery at my ranch," he explained in a flat voice. "A vehicle and a weapon have been taken. A temporary employee is missing, and so is the gun. The car was found by the state police in a remote location, where someone was apparently shot. Two Department of Criminal Investigations officers are coming to Freedom Ranch tomorrow to investigate, and I want you to be here when they arrive. I am, of course, eager that my privacy and my property rights be respected to the greatest extent, and I would prefer to minimize my own personal involvement in the mat-

ter. As my legal representative, it will be your job to remind the police of those rights."

"Let me check my calendar, see what I can rearrange,
and I'll get back to you."

"I *am* your calendar, boy," Elroy said. Bobby had to admit that with what he'd been billing the Foote account, Elroy had a point.

"Right. I'm sure I can clear my schedule," Bobby continued, sweat dripping off his face and onto his phone.
"I'll charter a plane and fly to Jackson. Have someone
meet me."

"Affirmative," said Elroy, slipping dangerously into
U.S. jargon. "Get here as soon as you can so I can brief
you."

"Of course," Bobby soothed, wiping off the phone with
a towel and trying to calm Elroy's fraying nerves. "Why
don't you give me the name and number of the officer you
talked to, and I'll call and let him know he'll be dealing
with me."

Elroy did so, then told Bobby, "Plan to be here a couple
of days. We have several matters to discuss."

"At your service, sir," Bobby answered, trying to mask
irritation with obsequiousness. They signed off and he sat
staring at the phone in his hand.

He could just imagine what had happened. Some goddamn ranch hand had gone on a toot, grabbed a truck and
snagged one of the countless guns Elroy owned, probably
gotten into a tussle with somebody he picked up in a bar,
and now a couple of traffic cops were about to violate Elroy's sacred property rights. It probably wasn't any of the
half-dozen Unknown Soldiers who were staying at the
ranch. Most of them were either too straight or too far
gone to imagine stealing from Elroy. The only Soldiers
there who were capable of such a thing were Danny
Crease, who was far too calculating, and Shane Parker,
who had Dirtbag sitting on him, probably literally by this
time. Well, Elroy paid Bobby plenty for the privilege of

having him sweat the small stuff, so he'd spend some more Foote money rushing to the rescue.

So much for the hot Friday night Bobby had planned. He finally had a date with Brittany Langham. Bobby had managed to get her pager number, and he'd called a dozen times since The Millionaires' Ball, but she'd only called back twice. The first time, the day after it had become public knowledge that he was handling the lawsuit against the Dunwoodie bequest, she'd told him she didn't have time to see him. He asked her if she was shining him on because of her father being friends with Sally Alder. She said no, she didn't give a damn about that, she was just pretty busy. The second time she'd called back she was friendlier, for her. What she said was, if he kept calling her, she'd probably break down and go out with him just to get him to stop bugging her. He'd said he'd come down to Laramie and take her out to dinner and dancing. She'd said, "Okay," and he'd pounced on it.

He'd thought that by now the Dunwoodie thing would be over, that the University would cave in at the first hint of bad publicity, or that the Foundation officers might be flexible. At the very least, he believed Sally Alder would decide that spending winter in Laramie wasn't so much fun that it was worth the hassle of battling her fellow professors for the right to hang around and freeze. If any one of those things had happened, Bosworth and his fellow plaintiffs would get what they wanted, Elroy would think he'd knocked out one more radical sniper's nest in Wyoming, and Bobby would have made some nice change for basically no work. To his amazement, they'd all stood firm. The University counsel had called him up and rejected the deal he'd outlined, explaining that the Foundation officers had no interest in altering provisions of a valid will, and that the University intended to accept the Foundation's offer.

According to the *Boomerang,* Foundation lawyer Ezra Sonnenschein said that, "These were the terms Meg Dunwoodie explicitly outlined to me, and we see no legal or ethical alternative to fulfilling the letter and the spirit of her most generous bequest to the university. The Foundation trustees are particularly eager that work already under way, including the cataloguing of the Dunwoodie papers and research on the biography, be completed in a professional and timely fashion by Professor Alder."

Sally Alder told the *Boomerang*, "Anyone who wants to get me out of the Dunwoodie Chair had better blow up a bomb under it." Bobby hated to think that there were a few people among his personal acquaintances who could easily be induced to do so.

He *really* didn't feel like pursuing the matter further. In fact, he'd called Bosworth and advised him to abandon the lawsuit. Couldn't a really motivated group of petty, spiteful professors make Sally Alder's life in Laramie so miserable that she'd just go away? Bosworth was offended at the idea of dropping the suit. He kept Bobby on the phone for half an hour of very expensive billable time (on Elroy's nickel, of course), pontificating about the principle of the thing. By the time Bobby got off the phone with Bosworth, he was sick enough of pompous academics that he'd called Elroy and told him he was wasting his money on the UW matter. Then he got another half hour of blab about Elroy's daddy and his friends Shep Parker and Mac Dunwoodie, more drivel about the principle of the thing, and for good measure, a lecture on the universities as battlegrounds for hearts and minds. Bobby was a lawyer through and through, but even he reached a point where he began to wonder why he'd chosen a career that required spending so much time listening to assholes.

So he still had the lawsuit, which he was pretty sure wasn't worth pursuing (he, for one, didn't give even a tick's ass where the University of Wyoming got its money, so long as the least amount of it possible came out of his own pocket). And now he had this ranch hand business.

He tried to be optimistic. Maybe it would distract Elroy from his paramilitary adventures for a while.

Bobby called Brit's pager, selected the message option and left word that something very important had come up, and he had to break their date. Then he closed up his phone, put it in his gym bag, slung the towel around his neck, and reminded himself that no matter how much he had to put up with now, the payoff could eventually be astronomical. Lots of people got paid a whole lot less to listen to assholes; waitresses and cops, for example. He thought briefly about calling the DCI, but then looked up to find Miss Casper Hardbody standing over him, smiling slightly. "Are you done with the Butt-Blaster?" she asked sweetly.

Bobby wiped off the machine with his towel and smiled back, flicking a glance at her iron butt. "Blast away," he replied warmly. He could call the cops from the car.

Delice Langham was using her charm on Steve Baca, Laramie's new fire chief, as he hassled her about the permit for her newly constructed brick pizza oven. She had so intimidated the regular fire inspector that Baca had decided he'd go and take her on himself. He didn't half mind, being new in town, recently divorced, and susceptible to tight jeans, black hair, and the jangle of silver jewelry.

"I'm not just nit-picking here, Miss Langham," Chief Baca said, stroking his handsome mustache and looking sweetly serious. "This is a hundred-year-old, heavily timbered building. You have just installed something called a 'wood-burning oven.' Does that strike you as a potential problem?"

Delice had a weakness for firemen, who were always in great shape and always had cute mustaches. She considered Steve Baca a very promising prospect, but she wasn't going to let him win this one. "My chef and manager assure me that every penny-ante tourist town in the West has a hundred-year-old building with an upscale restaurant in it, and every single one of those places has a brick oven. This building's mostly brick anyhow. For heaven's sake, chief," she added demurely, closing in on her best argument, "do you know what kind of business was in this building in 1883?"

"No ma'am," said Baca, "but I bet you do."

"I looked it up in the city directory for that year," Delice told him, inspecting her nails with a small smug smile, then raising her eyes to Baca's. "Swensen's Blacksmith's Shop and Stable. Open fires, hot coals, dry straw, nervous horses, and the nearest running water at a pump a half-block away. If Swensen's hot horseshoes couldn't burn this place down, do you think a designer pizza can?"

Baca gave her a wry look, shaking his head. "I'll have to give it some thought."

Delice was just about to suggest that he call her by her first name, and do his thinking over dinner at her house some night, when the radio on his belt screeched. Two engines had been dispatched to a house fire south of Albany. Baca radioed back to ask for directions, received them, excused himself and ran out to his truck.

"Damnation!" exclaimed Delice, the minute Baca was out of earshot. She recognized the location. The old Parker place, a ranch she'd been thinking about as a potential historic site. The house was falling down, but could be stabilized, even reconstructed. It had the potential to be a fantastic example of late nineteenth-century ranch culture. Delice was well aware that Meg Dunwoodie's mother had grown up on the Albany ranch, and she'd half-hoped to persuade Sally to get the Dunwoodie Foundation to buy the place and have it restored.

Despite what she had been saying not three minutes before, Delice knew precisely how fast a fire could scream through an old building. The Parker ranch house could have been burning for a while before anyone noticed and called it in, and it could very well be beyond saving. Still, she thought, even destruction was history in the making. She pulled out the cellphone that Burt had insisted she get, punched in Sally's number. Sally answered on the second ring. "I'm coming to get you," she said. "We're going to watch a fire."

By the time Delice and Sally got to Albany, the blaze was pretty much out. There was a pickup truck stuck halfway down the road, and the fire engines had had to crash through brush to get around it. Firefighters had pumped water from a tank truck onto what was left of the house, and were now searching the smoldering, blackened ruin that had once been the Parker ranch for any sign of human remains. Dickie Langham and a deputy were banging in stakes and stringing crime scene tape around an area that clearly included the pickup. Delice and Sally parked and got out of Delice's Explorer just in time to hear Steve Baca yell to Dickie, "Call the coroner's office and have them get a van out here. We found something."

Dickie had just hung up his own cellphone, after informing PeeWee Corkett that they'd found the Barnes truck. He'd secured the scene and called in the state crime lab, but he'd be willing to bet that the prints they'd found on the Mercedes belonged to one Shane Parker, the repeat offender at whose residence the truck had been parked. The residence in question was now history, Dickie told PeeWee, and so, possibly, was Parker. According to the fire chief, Steve Baca, it looked like the fire had started in the chimney. Half the people in Wyoming who burned wood were unaware that they had to get their chimneys swept on a regular basis, with the result that chimney fires were a common cause of property loss, injury, and death in the state. Obviously, though, somebody had started a fire in the fireplace, and it was logical to assume that it was Parker himself.

PeeWee, sitting in his office in Casper, thanked Dickie

for the information. "At least someone around here is interested in figuring out this mess."

"What do you mean?" asked Dickie.

"I just got a call from my commander," PeeWee began, obviously annoyed by interference from his superiors. "He told me that he'd had a call from somebody from the governor's office, who'd heard that we were going up to Freedom Ranch to investigate a crime, and he warned me to be careful to respect Mr. Foote's privacy. He reminded me that it was my job to see that Mr. Foote wasn't doubly victimized, first by the robbery and then by the police. Sounds like that damn lawyer called in some favors."

Helwigsen again. Dickie really wanted to talk to Sam Branch. And to Brit. "Somebody put the squeeze on," said Dickie. "Have fun."

"Laugh a minute," PeeWee said. "Does it strike you that this Foote is playing it pretty defensive for a crime victim?"

"Well what do you expect from a reclusive billionaire?" Dickie asked him.

PeeWee laughed. "Yeah, you're right. He's probably got his own private dungeon out back for people who tangle with him."

"Later," Dickie signed off, catching sight of Delice and Sally. "What the hell are you girls doing here?" Dickie asked Delice.

"The Historic Preservation Commission has been thinking about doing a site application for this place for the National Register. I just happened to be talking to Chief Baca when the call came in about the fire. I thought Sally would want to come along to see the last days of Meg Dunwoodie's mother's house, if you really want to know. We won't get in your way," she added, backing off a little.

He turned to Sally. "Do you happen to know that the person living here now is Shane Parker, the guy we think broke into your house?"

Both women gaped at him, for different reasons. Delice knew Shane Parker was living there, but Sally didn't. Sally knew he was the only suspect in the break-in, but didn't know he lived in Gert's old house.

"Is that his pickup?" Delice asked brazenly, knowing very well that she was poaching on police business.

Dickie just gave her a look. The smoke had made his eyes smart and given him a headache, and a medium-bad morning looked like it might be turning into a genuinely trying afternoon. Somewhere in all this, Helwigsen, the lawyer who was chasing his daughter and suing the University, was involved. The last thing he needed was the assistance of two women he considered among the nosiest people on the planet, and now, to make matters worse, a silver Suburban was bumping to a halt down the dirt road. Maude Stark got out.

"I saw the smoke from my place," she explained, "and thought I'd come investigate. History repeats itself."

Dickie, Delice, and Sally looked at her. "What are you talking about?" Sally asked, shivering in her down jacket. She was looking at the bare branches of the neglected lilac bushes that surrounded the ranch yard, thinking how Gert Dunwoodie, as a young bride, had shaken the snow off the blossoms.

"Guess you didn't know that Mac Dunwoodie's house at the Woody D burned, too, in 1966," Maude said. "Old Mac was a careless smoker to the end. They said he had a heart attack and left a cigarette burning," she told them. "Started a fire and burned the place right down to the ground. Wasn't enough left of him to bury," she finished, watching the firefighters inspecting the smoking rubble.

"So Meg didn't give him a funeral?" Sally found herself asking.

"Meg wasn't much of a one for funerals," Maude said, avoiding Sally's eyes.

26

Everybody Was Frustrated

Officer P.W. Corkett was frustrated. He and Officer Curtis Kates drove all the way to Teton County, six and a half hours in light snow, to take a look at Elroy Foote's place and talk to him. Mrs. Foote had served them coffee, but Mr. Foote was not feeling all that hospitable. Helwigsen, the lawyer, was already there, clearly determined to limit Foote's liability for anything that Shane Parker might have done with Foote's car or his gun. Foote, followed closely by Helwigsen, took them into the room from which the Ruger had been taken. As a peace officer, Pee-Wee hated the thought that anybody in Wyoming possessed such a huge private arsenal, especially when Kates felt compelled to point out that he'd seen lots of bigger gun collections, growing up in Wyoming and all.

Foote said he'd hired the man the police had identified as Shane Parker the same way he'd hired lots of temporary ranch hands, paying minimum wage and room and board for work not expected to last more than a couple of weeks. He'd never had any trouble before, praise the Lord: This was the first time. This guy had evidently drugged his bunkmate's dinner, waited until he was fully knocked out, taken the Ruger and the Mercedes and hightailed it out of there while the whole ranch slept.

As they inspected the garage, Kates took photographs and Corkett asked questions. The officers were mildly surprised to hear that the keys had been in the car, but Foote explained that on his property, it had been, and would continue to be, a matter of principle with him to feel secure in his possessions. Foote talked like that. He went on and on, paying no attention when Corkett wondered aloud how it had been possible for Parker to open the main gate, which was ten feet tall, topped with razor wire, and clearly built for heavy security. The keypad next to the entrance suggested that you had to punch in a code to get in or out.

Helwigsen put his arm around Corkett's shoulders (PeeWee *hated* it when guys tried to soften you up by cuddling—what were they thinking?) and drew him aside. "This is a little embarrassing," he confided, "but actually, the Mercedes and one other vehicle are equipped with automatic bypass signals, because Mrs. Foote drives them, and she has a hard time remembering the combination. The electronic sensor recognizes the vehicle and opens the gate." He smiled sympathetically. "Parker couldn't have known, of course—he just got lucky."

"It's not very lucky to be burned up alive," PeeWee commented sourly, but Bobby was hustling him along, asking if he wanted to see Shane's bunkhouse.

Dirtbag was nowhere in sight, having been sent, along with the other Unknown Soldiers and any regular cowboys who happened to have been previously convicted of crimes, to remote parts of the ranch. When Corkett asked where Parker's roommate was, Foote could honestly say he didn't know precisely, but that some cattle had gotten loose the day before and he'd been sent out to fix fences. The roommate's name, said Foote, was Howard Robb, which was close enough to Robideaux that Foote could remember it. Bobby had advised Elroy to tell as much of the truth as possible, since most people, even sane ones, had a hard time maintaining a consistent lie.

The bunkhouse was a disgusting mess, reeking of cigarette smoke and dirty laundry, but nothing suggested to Corkett and Kates that it was anything more than the temporary abode of a couple of run-of-the-mill lowlifes. Bobby had taken the trouble to remove the right-wing literature but had left the porno magazines, and had hauled off anything he thought might have Dirtbag's fingerprints on it. Corkett and Kates took more pictures, bagged a beer bottle full of cigarette butts to dust for fingerprints, and picked through the piles of laundry, going through shirt and pants pockets. Kates felt something in the back pocket of a really nasty old pair of fatigues, and reluctantly inserted his hand in the pocket. He pulled out an old postcard from somebody named Ernst to somebody called Greta. Bobby's heart lurched when he realized that he'd seen the postcard before, in a trailer in West Laramie. But then he reminded himself that the police had nothing to tie anybody but Shane to the burglary at the Dunwoodie house. He'd already worked out a strategy: Once they had Shane on the break-in, he and Elroy would profess surprise at Shane's involvement with the Dunwoodie matter. He would gently suggest to the police that the demented and desperate Parker must have imagined somehow that Margaret Dunwoodie's controversial legacy gave a twisted criminal like himself and a public-spirited influential citizen like Elroy Foote some common ground.

"Find something interesting?" Bobby asked Kates, whom he judged to be the softer of the two because Kates, being born-again, said "amen" every time Foote said "praise the Lord."

Kates gave him the cop-stare. "Everything is interesting, Mr. Helwigsen," he replied coldly.

The roads were freezing up when they left, and after a slippery ride over Togwotee Pass, with gusting crosswinds nearly blowing the cruiser off the road, PeeWee and Curtis had decided to spend the night in Dubois. They were accustomed to long hours driving questionable roads, but they knew when to call it a day. They got a motel room, sent out for a pizza, and discussed the day's events. They agreed that Foote definitely had something to hide, but they weren't sure whether what he was hiding had anything to do with the theft and shooting. They couldn't see any reason why Elroy Foote would have somebody steal and wreck his own car and shoot somebody with his gun. They wanted to bring in Parker's roommate and ask him some questions, but they had no evidence of any involvement by anybody else. By the time they got to Casper the next day, there was another message from the commander reminding them to wrap up this no-brainer of a case, and telling them there was no need to further trouble that public-spirited influential citizen, Mr. Elroy Foote.

The postcard, Corkett learned from Dickie Langham, confirmed the suspicion that Shane Parker had committed the November break-in. But that didn't tell them anything they didn't really know. They still had no motive for the theft or the shooting. Something about this smelled as bad as Shane Parker's bunkhouse, and all too often, Corkett got to thinking about Jed Barnes, the young cowboy in Muddy Gap. It bothered the hell out of him.

Dickie Langham sucked more poison gas out of a cancer stick and reflected on two weeks of fruitless police work. They'd been unable to identify the human remains from the Albany fire using dental records, so they had to go the much slower route. That meant sending what was left of the person everyone was sure was Shane Parker to the FBI lab for DNA testing. The Department of Criminal Investigations had matched the fingerprints in the Mercedes, along with some prints found on a beer bottle, with Shane's, and they'd taken blood samples from the car to send to the FBI lab. Dickie had the Barnes truck at the Parker house, with Parker's prints all over it and blood they'd also sampled and sent to the FBI lab. In a couple of months, Dickie was sure, they'd have DNA matches all around, incontrovertible scientific proof that the person who'd stolen the car and shot the kid, and the one who'd died in the fire were one and the same. The image of O.J. Simpson riding on a golf cart across velvety green grass flitted through his mind, but he had no reason to assume that Helwigsen would pull a Johnnie Cochran on this one.

The postcard the troopers had found in Parker's pants tied him conclusively to the Dunwoodie burglary, which was on some level reassuring. The break-in had been such a rookie job that Dickie felt reasonably sure it was Shane's idea, and probably wouldn't be repeated. Shane Parker, he assumed, had committed a series of crimes, which had now been solved, with the perpetrator no longer in a position to ride on a golf cart. Once the FBI lab finished the testing and sent him the results, however many months from now that might be, he would close the books on some ugly stuff. He ought to feel like he was doing his job.

But there were dots Dickie couldn't connect. Why had Shane Parker broken into Margaret Dunwoodie's house and stolen a postcard? Where had he gone after the burglary? When and why had he ended up at the ranch of the guy who was dumping a hell of a lot of money suing the University over the Dunwoodie bequest? PeeWee Corkett thought Elroy Foote and Bobby Helwigsen were covering something up. What was it?

To answer those questions, he'd started with Shane's "friends," who included some of the most dishonest, most odious losers he'd encountered in nearly half a century of mixed living. Mostly he and his deputies got the same answers they'd gotten when they'd questioned them the first time around. Hadn't seen Parker in months, didn't know a fucking thing, so leave them the fuck alone or they'd scream police harassment. Dickie did turn up one nice piece of evidence when he'd gone to talk to a really fun couple, Terry the meth dealer and his junkie girlfriend Sherry. They said they'd kicked Shane out when he'd come to their place to borrow money the day of the shooting and the fire. He'd been driving a big F–250 with the County 6 plates. "You owe me, Langham," Terry had yelled over the sound of barking dogs as Dickie walked back out to his car. Yeah, right. If they could ever actually manage to find Terry's lab, he'd get what was coming to him. The first thing they'd do was get rid of those murderous pit bulls.

Having worked the Shane connection dry, Dickie went to work from the other end, with Elroy Foote. That meant, he knew, starting with Bobby Helwigsen, whom he'd last seen groping Brittany at The Millionaires' Ball. He needed to have a chat with Sam Branch.

Dickie drove to Branch's office out on Grand on a particularly hideous afternoon, the kind of winter day when it got dark around two o'clock. He fought to open the cruiser door against a fifty mile per hour wind and walked into Branch Homes on the Range unannounced. The receptionist sent him right into Branch's office, where Sam was sitting behind a desk made from a gigantic slab of granite and in front of a paneled wall on which about a thousand plaques were hung, testaments to Sam's prowess at bulldozing the prairie, spewing out cardboard developments, and selling people houses they couldn't quite afford. Ah well, even back when they'd been in the same lucrative business, Dickie had never had the flair for profit that Sam possessed.

"Sheriff," said Sam, leaning back in his seat.

"Realtor," said Dickie, closing the door behind him.

"Looking to move up to a home more befitting your recent rise in the law enforcement racket?" Sam inquired blandly.

"With what the county pays me," Dickie answered,

"I'm lucky I don't have to live in my squad car." Sam snorted. "Sorry, Sam, but I'm here on my business, not yours. Tell me about your buddy Robert Helwigsen."

Sam didn't really need any defense, but he believed in a good offense. "What's he done to attract your attention, besides hang all over Brit at my party?"

Dickie considered the question, got out a cigarette, lit it. "Actually, he did first attract my attention at your party, when you mentioned that he and Sally Alder had a lot in common. And then the next thing you know, he turns out to be suing the University to get her fired. I figure you might have had a little inside information."

"I wasn't aware that it was a crime to sue the University," Sam countered.

"'Course not," Dickie answered genially, "and that's what makes this country so great. You can sue anybody you want for any reason including that they just piss you off. And I have no reason to suspect that Helwigsen has committed a crime of any kind, but his name just kind of keeps coming up. So I need to know what you know about Helwigsen's connection with a Mr. Elroy Foote."

Since that revolting but interesting lunch at Hasta la Pasta! Sam hadn't seen or heard much from Bobby Helwigsen. He'd let Bobby know that, much as he hoped Mr. Foote might help him out in the event he got around to running for office, he wasn't committing himself to supporting the Dunwoodie lawsuit until he got a handle on the public reaction. Amazingly, the Dunwoodie Foundation and the University had stood firm. The public, not so amazingly, didn't really seem interested one way or the other. Anybody hoping to end up on the board of trustees would be crazy to die on this particular hill, even if Sally Alder had once tried to run him over and continued to be a pain in the ass. There had been rumors in Cheyenne during the legislative session that Elroy Foote, always one Crayola short of a box, might have finally gone off into the Wonderful World of Color. When Sam had seen

Bobby at the Hitching Post and asked him how things were going, the lawyer just smiled and changed the subject to the tax code.

It was frustrating for Sam to think that he couldn't come up with a way to grab some of Foote's money without owing him something he might not want to pay. But it looked like that was the case, so he decided to more or less level with Dickie. "Yeah. Well, Helwigsen carries a lot of water for Foote," he said. "Scuttlebutt is that he's been handling pretty much all of Foote's legal business, which is a significant chunk of change. Young Bobby's a very shrewd little Harvard boy with an eye to the main chance, and Foote's money is what you might consider a very main chance. The suit against the University is flea shit compared to the rest of it."

"So why bother with flea shit?" Dickie asked.

"Price you pay for really big shit," Sam answered. "Something the old man wants him to do, so he's gotta do it. He took me to lunch, told me all about it, gave me this stupid line about the University being the battleground for the hearts and minds of our children. But to tell you the truth, Dickie," Sam looked right at the sheriff, narrowing his eyes, "I didn't buy it. Oh, I have no doubt that Elroy Foote thinks it's worth a million or so to try to get some bitch who makes a hundred K a year fired from her stupid job. He probably thinks he's making a stand for the American way. Everybody in Wyoming knows that Foote's a freaking kook who gives a lot of money to what we like to call 'social conservative' causes these days. But frankly, Dickie, I think Bobby Helwigsen couldn't give a good goddamn about social conservatism, or the Dunwoodie Foundation, or anything that doesn't figure into his bank account. He's a mercenary bastard, that Bobby," Sam said, obviously hoping to get rid of Dickie and get back to making money that day. "I'd watch him with your daughter if I were you."

The last remark had the desired effect. Saying nothing,

Dickie got up and left. He walked out to his car, wrestled the wind for the car door and won a narrow victory, nearly decapitating himself in the process. He sat for a minute, gritting his teeth, then drove over to the Dunwoodie house, where he found Sally buried among books about the anti-Nazi resistance in Germany, and Brit working through a stack of what looked like bank statements, typing notes into a computer. He asked if he could borrow Sally's assistant for an hour, getting a distracted wave from the boss, who didn't even look up from her books. Brit got into the cruiser and they drove down to El Conquistador, where Dickie ordered an afternoon snack of a large combo plate and a Coke and Brit asked for coffee.

He dipped a chip in the flaming salsa, ate it, beat around the bush. "So how's the work going?"

"Fine," she said. Dickie did actually seem to have some interest in Meg Dunwoodie's life, but he wasn't spending taxpayers' time to talk about history or poetry with her, as Brit was aware. "Sally's onto some interesting stuff, and she's given me a couple of projects she considers too tedious to be worth her time. Okay by me, as long as she keeps paying." Brit shrugged, taking a swig of coffee and bumming a forbidden cigarette from her father. "What's on your mind, Daddy?"

"You seeing anybody in particular these days?" Another shrug—she could drive Dickie crazier with shrugging than any human being he'd ever met.

"Nobody particular," she said. "Why?"

Dickie stared at her, trying to work up a subtle way to ask her, and failing. "What about that Casper lawyer friend of Sam Branch's?"

Brit did not like this line of questioning from her father. She had a plan of her own for helping out Sally Alder while getting a couple of steak dinners out of a cute sleazebag she intended, eventually, to stomp upon. She'd vowed to *get* him after their night on the dance floor, when she'd found out that he was the lawyer suing to get Sally fired. Bobby had no idea that Brit was involved with Sally in any other way than her parents' friendship, a pretty meaningless thing. Brit had told Sally he'd called her, and that she was going to go out with him to see what she could learn. Sally had been against it at first, but Brit insisted that there was absolutely no risk involved, and Sally finally gave in.

Brit had almost been out to dinner and dancing with Bobby once, but he'd had to break the date. They'd talked on the phone some. He had never bothered asking about her work. She was sure he thought she was extremely dumb, a great cover. If she asked the right kinds of questions, she thought he'd let slip some piece of information Sally could use against the lawsuit, some night while he was bragging about how great he was. Brit found it frustrating that her dad might stick his nose in and screw up everything. "I might go out with him, Dad. No big deal," she said smoothly. "He's good for a filet mignon and a bottle of wine. Got some moves on the dance floor."

Dickie could tell that she was up to something. "You know he's the one handling the Dunwoodie lawsuit, honey," he said, searching her face. "Don't you feel a little strange going out with the enemy?" She shrugged again, goddamn it. "Does Sally know?"

"Yeah, she knows. She says that since there are only, like, eleven good-looking, reasonably intelligent single men in Wyoming anyway, she understands why going out with him is better than picking up morons at the Wrangler. She gave me a can of Mace and told me if he tries anything I should Mace his ass."

Dickie laughed. "That sounds like Sally." His food came, and he dug in. "Gotta say I really wish you wouldn't see this guy," he said through a big mouthful of enchilada ranchera. "I can't believe you'd actually go out with a Republican. Next thing you know, you'll be blaming all the problems of the world on welfare mothers and subscribing to the *Wall Street Journal*. If I had my way, the next time he calls, you'd tell him your dad won't let you go out with him."

Her dad was way too interested in this, Brit realized, much to her frustration. She figured that if he'd just leave her alone, she might be able to make her plan work. But Dickie wouldn't, and it pissed her off. "I wasn't aware I'd asked your permission, Dad. I'm not fifteen anymore," she sulked, snagging a tortilla chip and dunking it into his refried beans. "Why don't you, like, just put him in jail and get it over with?"

The more Sally read, the less it seemed she knew about Meg Dunwoodie and Ernst Malthus. She was learning a lot about the Germans who fought Nazi domination in various ways. There were cells of resistance among the Communists, and certain groups in the churches, as well as in the army and civil service. A number of influential men in and around the famous Kreisau Circle had evidently managed to travel to other countries throughout the war, that is, until the failed assassination attempt of July 20, 1944, when virtually all of them were tortured and executed. Rainer Malthus, who turned up in virtually every account of the conspiracy, had been a military man who was considered an expert in foreign policy, and he'd been one of those who showed up in places like Stockholm and London, making contact with British and American intelligence agents. The problem was that anti-Nazi Germans who stayed in the Fatherland, holding important government jobs or military posts or positions in business, could never quite convince potential foreign allies that they weren't double agents. No matter how passionately they insisted that they were determined to bring Hitler down, and no matter how much the Allies wanted to encourage the German fifth column, the British, especially, remained suspicious.

You couldn't entirely blame the Allies for leaving the Black Orchestra to its tragic fate. History was full of plots, counterplots, deep undercover agents, and opportunists playing both ends against the middle. The more she read about the people who had lived through Europe's hell, the more she understood that their choices were unbelievably complicated. Sure, there were plenty of people of all kinds who signed on to the Nazi program and cheered it to the end, but they weren't always easy to distinguish from the ones who informed on their neighbors because they didn't want the next midnight knock on the door to be at their house. There were people who spent most of the war as "good Germans" who committed isolated heroic acts of sabotage or mercy.

Ernst Malthus was a diamond trader, a Christian in a business dominated by Jews. He was rich and very well connected. He was a moving target. The Gestapo had certainly been watching him, but had left him alone at least enough to permit him to send money to a Jewish refugee in America. He'd even *been* to America in the middle of the war, according to Maude. Had the Gestapo been using him? Had he been using them for purposes of his own? Had he been hooked up with the American OSS, the agency that eventually became the CIA? What had happened to Ernst after 1943 was a mystery, and Sally was hoping to hell that the government records she'd requested through the Freedom of Information Act would provide some answers. But the government's responses to FOIA requests were maddeningly slow and capricious. It could take anywhere from months to years to get the stuff, and there was of course no telling what records there might be. Ezra had said he'd put in a word with some of his friends in Washington to see if they couldn't speed things up.

Then there was the matter of the diamonds. Hawk had made it clear to her that he planned to be out "in the field," as the geologists said, a lot of the time. This time, he'd been on a field trip in the Mojave for three long weeks, and she'd had to wait all that time to show him the stones they'd found in Meg Dunwoodie's treasure closet. Now he was back at last, and that night they sat in Meg's living room, enjoying a whiskey before dinner. She'd planned to lay out the whole amazing story of Meg Dunwoodie and Ernst Malthus and Ezra Sonnenschein and Maude Stark, then tell him about the closet, then show him the gems, but she decided she couldn't wait. "I've got something to show you," she'd said.

"Does it involve garter belts?" he asked hopefully, looking forward to an end to three frustrating weeks of celibacy, trailing his fingers up her leg.

"No," she answered, half-wishing she'd thought of that, "but it might get you in the mood anyway."

She'd brought out the velvet bag and taken out the little packets of paper, watched him open the complicated folds as if he knew what he was doing. And of course, he did. He'd worked diamond exploration in South America and Africa along with other exotic gigs, she thought, recalling the story about the Brazilian girlfriend in Houston with a grimace.

As the stones fell into his hand, Hawk whistled and took a big swallow of Jim Beam. Sally looked at him expectantly. He looked back. "Where'd you get these?"

"They were in the upstairs closet, along with a bunch of other stuff that should have been in a bank vault long ago. I'll tell you all about it over dinner. What are they?"

"Well," said Hawk, taking another swig, "in my moderately expert opinion, these are diamonds of various cuts and colors."

"That much we figured out," she said. "What else can you tell me about them?"

"I'd estimate the weights at anywhere from ten to thirty carats," he said, "and I'd need a jeweler's loupe to tell you anything about the quality." He held the largest, a yellow oval, up to the light, carefully bracketing it between his thumb and forefinger. "Pretty."

"Can you tell me anything about where they might have come from?"

"Not definitively. Could be lots of places. India, Brazil, Tanzania, and of course South Africa. The pink one," he said, picking up a teardrop-shaped gem, one of the smaller ones, "might have come from Australia. But then again, it's hard to tell, because they've probably been treated."

"Treated?" Sally asked. "What do you mean?"

"Irradiation. You can get a colorless diamond to turn green or blue if you expose it to radiation. If you irradiate some diamonds and then heat them up, you can get yellow or orange or pink. Naturally colored stones are incredibly rare and unbelievably expensive, so most of the colored diamonds you see have been treated. That's probably the case with these—they're pretty big, Mustang. Untreated colored diamonds this size would probably be in a museum, not in a closet in Laramie."

"Could you tell if they'd been treated?" she asked, feeling a little disappointed.

"Sure," he answered, holding a blue square-cut gem up to the light, "with the right equipment. But people who really know diamonds could tell you just by looking at the color. Hell, Crawford could probably tell you exactly where and when they were mined."

"But he's in Arizona. Could anybody around here tell us that? Somebody in the geology department maybe?"

"Sally, the minute you show those things to anybody, the whole world will know they're here. Even if they're treated diamonds and every one of them is seriously flawed, they're worth money—some ignorant rich bimbo like Nattie Langham would pay a fortune just to flash a big fancy rock in the face of the girls at the Realtors' convention in Miami. If by some miracle they're the real thing"—he looked down at the gems glinting in his hand—"they could be worth millions."

"Shit," said Sally.

"Right," said Hawk, clearing his throat and taking a drink of whiskey. "I'd really like to show these to my dad. He'd know what he was looking at, and he's so antisocial, you could be sure he wouldn't blab."

She held out her hand, and he poured the diamonds into her palm. They seemed to tingle on her skin, like freezing fire. They made her shiver. "Could he come up here? I've got to get these things to the bank as soon as possible."

Hawk shook his head. "Not any time soon. He hates cold weather, and you know how hard it is to get him out of Jumping Cholla. He and Maria are planning to come up here for a visit in May. You could get them out of the vault for a day and show them to him then."

"Great," she said, handing him back the diamonds to fold back into the packets and put into the bag. "Another delay. Let's see, this is February. Only four more months of winter, and I can sit around here and listen to the wind howl and wait for the government to process my FOIA request and wait for your father to show up. By June I ought to be completely frigging nuts."

Hawk ignored her raving and looked at the velvet bag in his hand. "You know, Sally, it makes me jittery having these things in the house. If we were in Brazil, I'd put 'em under my pillow and sleep with a loaded gun."

She rose, went to get the Jim Beam bottle, and poured them more whiskey. "So big diamonds make you nervous?" she asked, putting down the bottle, taking the bag from him and tucking it down the front of her V-neck sweater, into her bra. "Maybe just a little edgy?" She sat down and put her legs in his lap. "Kind of off-balance and excitable?" He put down his whiskey and his fingers crept back to garter belt country.

So much for one source of frustration, anyway.

Part Four

27

March Madness

Springtime in the Rockies. Forget those Sierra Club calendar pictures of alpine fields riotous with wildflowers amid snowy peaks and improbably blue skies. Most people in Laramie referred to this particular time of year as "Mud Season." The skiing was sloppy, the roads impassable, and the wind, well. One dark gray day stretched into the next and the next. Going outside for even a minute meant bundling up from head to toe, leaning at a forty-five-degree angle into a headwind, freezing half your face in a crosswind, or flying on a tailwind. Everybody started using the term "cabin fever" and calling their travel agent.

Edna did not believe in driving to her office. She arrived home in the six o'clock darkness that Friday afternoon in late March, nearly defeated by a very long week and the eight-block war with nature. She was ready for a glass of wine, a pleasant dinner with friends. Or at least that was what she told herself. Another part of her wanted to sit in the bathtub for two hours, drink a good bottle of California red, scramble up a couple of eggs, and fall into bed.

Not possible. Company was coming—Sally and Hawk, Virginia Minor, the University lawyer, and Minor's partner, Dr. Helen Singer, Laramie's hilarious orthodontist. Edna got out the osso buco she'd made last night, started it warming gently, and shuffled through the mail on the kitchen counter. Thank God, their plane tickets for Cabo San Lucas had arrived. It hadn't been easy talking Tom into a spring break vacation that would feature lots of lying around instead of daily mortal risk and cardiovascular exertion. She'd had to make all the damn reservations and promise him many margaritas and torrid sex under slowly revolving ceiling fans. She could hear him getting in the shower upstairs, could envision his sweaty gym clothes in a heap on the floor where he always left them following his Friday afternoon basketball game. He redeemed himself every week, however, by making sure to have a bottle of wine breathing when she got home. Ravenswood zinfandel, special ordered from Napa. He'd read her mind.

This was going to be one of those dinner parties that ended up all shoptalk if she wasn't careful. She hadn't seen much of Sally or Virginia Minor in the past few weeks, but the Dunwoodie lawsuit had started gobbling up more and more of everyone's time. Lawyers from both sides had been taking endless depositions and requesting mountains of documents. The Faculty for Academic Freedom, as Bosworth's group called itself, was clearly flirting with the idea of adding a discrimination suit to the mix. FAF (a.k.a. Byron Bosworth) had contacted the University's equal employment opportunity officer, who'd then called Edna and asked her for records indicating that the Dunwoodie Chair hiring procedure had conformed to federal affirmative action guidelines. And of course, it didn't. The Dunwoodie Foundation (i.e., Maude and Ezra) had only one candidate for the Chair, Sally Alder, and that was that. No search, no oversight, no paper trail to fall back on.

And so, ironically, Edna had spent the past couple of weeks, on top of her regular duties as dean, figuring out how to get around affirmative action procedures in defense of feminist scholarship. Sheesh. Loathing herself, she'd called Virginia Minor and told her to see how California's recent abolition of affirmative action (and the push to do the same thing in Texas) might be useful. "Ick," Minor said, and Edna had to agree.

Edna, meanwhile, decided to do a little research of her own. As she well knew, a place like the University of Wyoming hadn't had uniform hiring procedures until, really, the 1980s. When she'd finally been hired for a tenure-track job in 1982, with years of teaching, several books, and an international reputation, the anthropology department's idea of an open search had been to make her compete against the wife of the new basketball coach, a woman who made her own arrowheads. The guys in FAF (a list of the membership revealed that all eighteen members were, coincidentally, white males) had for the most part been hired long before, according to the practices of the old boy network. A department chair would call up one of his buddies from graduate school, ask if he had any students who needed a job, and that was usually that. Edna was willing to bet that most of Boz's pals had never even had to interview for their positions before they signed the contracts that had made them UW's for life.

Edna liked to be sure. She'd gone after their personnel records, found pretty much nothing documenting the hiring procedures on any of them, and then called in the lawyers. By the time Virginia Minor's crew got done interviewing the FAF members about their own experiences going to work for the University, they'd decided not to file an EEO complaint. The University's employment officer, an MBA who thought affirmative action was a bunch of bullshit anyway, was relieved not to have to pursue the matter.

Stuff like this made Edna wonder why she'd been crazy enough to become an administrator. Ick, indeed. Long ago, she'd resolved to focus on the satisfying things in her life. You usually had to put up with a lot of crap to get what you wanted. She poured herself a glass of wine, asked herself the question, "If you could be doing anything at all right now, what would it be?" Standing on a hill in Katmandu? Bodysurfing at Cabo? Soon enough. She took a sip of lovely zinfandel, smiled, then set her glass aside. She didn't have time for a bath, but if she hurried, she could catch Tom in the shower.

Within fifteen minutes of the guests' arrival, Edna, Sally, and Virginia Minor had gone into the kitchen to talk shop, while Tom, Helen Singer, and Hawk sat in the living room shoveling tapénade onto crackers and arguing about who would win the NCAA basketball tournament. Helen, as an orthodontist, felt compelled to defend the idea that the team with the best-fitting mouth guards had an overwhelming advantage, supporting her claims with the kind of detailed description of athletes' oral habits that listeners other than Tom and Hawk might not have found such a screamingly funny accompaniment to tapénade.

This was Sally's first social encounter with Virginia Minor, who arrived, amazingly, in jeans artfully torn out at the knees, a lime green angora sweater, and Doc Martens. Virginia refused the zinfandel in favor of a vodka martini and collapsed onto a stool to watch while Sally washed spinach leaves and Edna got a *poire bruleé* ready to pop in the oven to be done just in time for dessert.

"How in the world do you find the time and energy to cook, Edna?" Virginia asked. "By the time Helen and I get home we barely have the strength to argue about who has to pick up the phone to call Domino's. Last fall she decided we needed more home-cooked meals, and we still have the freezer full of Lean Cuisines. Neither one of us can manage to put the little plastic packets in the boiling water."

"It must be hard work, saving my ass," Sally commented. "After a day of your kind of heavy lifting, I'd settle for a bowl of cornflakes."

"Actually," said Virginia, snagging a slice of pear,

"they're pretty good with water if you can't manage to get to the grocery store to buy milk. Low-fat, too."

"So how's the ass-saving going, Vinnie?" Edna asked.

Virginia shrugged. "We're eating up a lot of staff time researching precedents and talking to people at Yale and the University of Washington. The Yalies haven't been all that much help. What with their problems in the past, Yale doesn't want any part of endowed chairs for the foreseeable future. When donors with big bucks call, the Yale development people try to steer them toward giving the money to the general fund or bankrolling capital improvements. The Washington people are standing by the UPS chair endowment, and they're betting the controversy will pass in a couple of years. Hey, they figure they'll be a wholly owned subsidiary of Microsoft any minute, if they're lucky and their legislature doesn't just abolish higher education."

Sally sipped the excellent wine and looked disgusted. "I've never understood the argument that one person's freedom to do irrelevant research is suppressed if somebody they disagree with gets hired to do their own equally trivial research. Can't we just hit them with the Sly Stone Brief?"

"The Sly Stone Brief?" Edna asked, stirring the tantalizing stuff on the stove.

"Something about different strokes, for different folks," Sally said.

"Sure, we can do that," Virginia answered. "And we can also point out all the places where donors have endowed chairs at public institutions, specifying any old conditions they chose, and nobody made a peep. We can subpoena all kinds of university officials from all over the place, and holders of chairs, to testify to the fact that the positions they hold aren't keeping anybody from doing anything they please. We could even open up our own can of worms and start talking about one or two chairs that have been endowed here, say, by agribiz, with the express purpose of creating government-subsidized labs in which to research the cheapest way to turn an ordinary cow into unimpeded cash flow." Virginia paused and got up to freshen her martini.

"The real problem, of course, is the principle of faculty governance," Virginia explained to Sally, who didn't really need it all explained again but who was listening carefully. "The way you were hired breaks rules that were written to bust up the old boy networks in the first place, and give women and minorities a decent chance. And, of course, the idea that the faculty ought to have established procedures and a regular role in personnel matters is reasonable enough in theory. But in practice it gets a lot stickier when, as is always the case, half the faculty hate the other half's guts. And naturally it's a lot worse when you find out that the other side has somebody like Elroy Foote paying the legal fees. I feel like somebody who keeps a gun around as protection against prowlers, and then gets shot with it when some creep breaks in."

The mention of break-ins twisted something in Sally's stomach. "What about *my* academic freedom?" she complained. "Here I am, working on a biography of Wyoming's most important writer, a project everybody in the state ought to be freaking begging me to get finished and out before a grateful public, and I've had to deal with everything from a homicidal skinhead to a neo-fascist gazillionaire who's willing to bankrupt the University to get me the hell out of town! And I used to think the Boz curling his lip at me was a problem."

"Well, at least it looks like they've backed off the EEO complaint," Edna said, deciding that a little gossip was in order to lighten things up. "I found out today how the Boz was hired." Virginia and Sally looked up at her with interest. "I heard it from that secretary in the provost's office who's been here since the Civil War. You know how academics are always joking that the only way they know where the good jobs will be next year is to read the obituaries in the *New York Times*? Evidently, Bosworth spent about five years hanging around Columbia after he finished his dissertation, getting increasingly desperate because nobody would hire him. At the time, the UW history department had one famous member, a guy named Hilson Hobby-Orson, who'd written like sixty definitive books on the economic history of the Roman Empire.

"One day in the middle of the fall semester of 1964, Hobby-Orson was explaining to his ancient history class how the U.S. was going through its version of the decline and fall of the Roman Empire, and they had better all tell their parents to vote for Goldwater, and he evidently worked himself up to a myocardial infarction and expired before their very eyes. Bosworth saw Hobby-Orson's obit in the *Times,* but instead of waiting for the job to be advertised or even rumored, Boz got on the phone right away, called the history department, and told them he was a postdoc in ancient history at Columbia, and he could be on a plane the next day if they wanted him to take over Hobby-Orson's classes. I mean, the body was still warm. The department chair just said, yeah, okay, whatever. And Boz has been here ever since."

"That's good. That's very very good. And the man wants to question the way I was hired," Sally said, shaking her head.

"They say lawyers are ambulance-chasers," Virginia commented. "First time I ever heard of anybody chasing a hearse."

28

Enjoy Beef Daily

Bobby had definitely been earning his money lately. Not only had he handled the state police expertly at Elroy's place, but it looked as if he'd also headed off the investigation with a few well-placed calls to friends in the governor's office. He'd advised Elroy to order all the Unknown Soldiers to stick close to home for a while, and those who didn't have homes should be dispatched back to whatever hidey-holes or locked wards they'd come from. The one exception was Dirtbag, whom Elroy had decided to keep around as his bodyguard. Bobby wasn't exactly sure where Arthur Stopes and Danny Crease had gone, but after getting to know them, he wasn't missing either one. And he had to admit, he wasn't lamenting the presumed demise of Shane Parker, moron punk. If there had been some way to vaporize every one of the Unknown Soldiers without being held personally responsible, Bobby would cheerfully have used it.

It wasn't like he was sitting around looking for something to keep him busy. The lawsuit against the University was grinding on. He'd handed over most of the research and deposition work to the firm's junior associates and paralegals, but he continued as lead attorney on the case.

He kept hoping the University would lose its nerve as the legal expenses piled up, but so far they were hanging in there.

Tax time was coming, and he spent a lot of time with Elroy's accountants, going over changes in the tax laws to try to figure out how Elroy could not only keep all of his money, but maybe even get the government owing him more. After the last legislative session, the latter was a distinct and pleasing possibility. Maybe next year, Elroy would send him to Washington to lobby Congress and they could really clean up.

Hell, maybe one of these years he'd *run* for Congress.

He didn't mind working long hours, and he even found endless meetings about tax codes pretty interesting. But there was one little thing that disturbed Bobby's current sense of well-being.

Elroy was having a little problem with the IRS.

Sometime in mid-March, Foote had received a letter from the Internal Revenue Service, informing him that the government was planning to conduct an audit of his tax returns for the previous five years. Elroy's reaction was as might have been expected—he was absolutely certain that the feds were plotting to destroy him, and he was ready to declare independence and roll out the troops. It took a lot of cajoling and bombast before Bobby had managed to convince him that when a guy had as much money as Elroy, in as many different businesses and countries, even the most vigilant government bean-counter couldn't find all of it. It just meant that Bobby and the accountants would have to get Elroy's records in order and add meetings with auditors to their schedules.

Elroy had reluctantly given up the idea of revolution and agreed to let the lawyers and the accountants do what he still thought bullets did better. Bobby faced the prospect with mixed feelings. Not that he wanted his biggest client to get into a shooting war with the United States, but he wasn't at all sure, in fact, that the govern-

ment *wasn't* out to entrap Elroy. It was possible that somebody, say, at the Bureau of Alcohol, Tobacco and Firearms
was keeping tabs on the quantity of firepower Elroy was
amassing at what the media would probably call "a remote compound in the rugged Rocky Mountains." Maybe
the ATF had tipped off the IRS that they might want to
look into Foote's returns. If you were Elroy, that chain of
events could certainly be considered a government conspiracy. If you were Bobby, you kept a close eye on
things, billed Elroy promptly and cashed his checks
quickly, and watched carefully so that you wouldn't miss
the moment at which turning state's evidence might be the
prudent thing to do.

In the meantime, he was doing very well on the Brit
front. He'd taken her to dinner at the Holiday Inn in
Laramie and dancing at the Wrangler a couple of times.
Last month he'd been down in Cheyenne and she'd driven
over to meet him at the Hitching Post. He'd poured
enough white zinfandel into her that she'd stayed over and
shared his hotel room, although the details of what had
transpired were a little murky, since he'd decided to drink
the rotten pink stuff himself to keep her company. But
having broken the sex barrier (he presumed), he was expecting to get lucky again tomorrow night. He had to go to
Laramie to meet with Bosworth, and he'd called and
asked her if she wanted to go out. She'd said he could buy
her a steak if he wanted. He'd said he wanted. They agreed
to meet at the Cavalryman at seven. He had booked a
room at the Holiday on the assumption that she'd go back
there with him after enough animal protein and alcohol.

Her face and her body knocked him out. He certainly
wasn't spending time with her for the witty conversation.
He had to do most of the talking when they were together,
and half the time he wondered if she was paying any attention. Whenever he got desperate and asked her what
she was up to lately, she said, "Not much. Filing. Shit-
work." That was okay with him. All in all, he preferred

talking about his own life to hearing about the fascinating world of secretarial labor.

Even when her attention wandered, however, her face fascinated him—the full, sulky lips, the enormous, bored blue eyes. She had a body like a supermodel, and he was damned if he knew how she managed it. Every time they'd been together, she'd packed down a pound of tenderloin and a baked potato loaded with sour cream and butter. Bobby was meticulous about watching what he ate. As far as he was concerned, fat and red meat were occupational hazards of living in Wyoming, and he ate steak only when he was trying to suck up to a client, or he'd been eating Elroy's dehydrated meal packets for a week, or when it appeared that the best available alternatives on the menu came in the form of patties.

Brit had laughed at him when he'd ordered the swordfish at the Hitching Post in Cheyenne, and when his dinner arrived looking like the ominous first scene in a '50s horror movie, he had to admit that she had a point. He hoped that later in the evening he hadn't given her further cause for laughter. If you really wanted to know, he didn't even like steak all that much. Now and then, as a Wyoming native, he felt kind of unpatriotic about not being a red meat fan in a state that posted billboards at its borders that said, "Welcome to Wyoming. The Cowbelles Encourage You to Enjoy Beef Daily." But tomorrow night, he was determined to eat and make love like a man. He'd been living on Power Bars and alfalfa sprouts for three days in anticipation of their carnivorous rendezvous.

Bobby got to the Cavalryman at 6:45 and went to the bar to wait for Brit. He was looking forward to a large Johnnie Walker after a meeting with Bosworth that had seesawed between the tense and the tedious. Bosworth was always trying to get Bobby to meet with the entire FAF group, an idea Bobby found both ridiculous and risky. For one thing, he had no reason to think that listening to eighteen professors pontificate would tell him anything he needed to know about running a lawsuit. Having spent time with Bosworth, he couldn't imagine anything worse than multiplying him by a factor of eighteen. For another, he had no desire to be put in the position of making spontaneous public statements about the case. If, as he hoped, they would eventually drop the suit and get back to earning their pittances, nobody would ever remember that he'd been involved. If, on the other hand, he actually had to try the case, he wanted to do it as a nit-picking attorney and not as the champion of a pack of whining pedants.

Bosworth had a new axe to grind this time. He wanted to know if Sally Alder's "obscene" salary gave them grounds for an equity suit. Bobby knew that Alder's Dunwoodie Chair paycheck, while off the charts for UW professors, was less than a quarter of what he had made for his previous year's work on behalf of Elroy Foote's money. Bobby told Bosworth that there was such a thing as market forces, and in Wyoming, arguing against the market would be like walking into the rotunda of the state capitol and burning an American flag.

The waiter brought his scotch (they poured an honest drink in this place, he was pleased to see), along with the white zin he'd ordered for Brit. Bobby reflected on what an unattractive mound of phlegm he'd drawn for a client on this one. Christ, even Bosworth's wrists were wrapped in flopping flab. He closed his eyes at the thought, and when he opened them, he welcomed the refreshing sight of Brit in a high-rise red leather miniskirt, black tights, and ankle boots that matched what there was of the skirt.

He put his arm around her, pulled her in, kissed her shiny hair. She smelled like Obsession. She looked up at him with an expression on her face halfway between a small smile and a slight sneer, stood on her toes, and laid a kiss on him that had him thinking maybe he'd have the Cattleman's Cut tonight.

* * *

She waited until he was well into his second double-Johnnie, their salads had come, and he was rubbing her thigh under the table before she said, in a voice that couldn't care less, "So how was your day?"

"Nothing too taxing," Bobby replied, feeling flattered that she bothered to inquire. "Had a meeting with the guy from Faculty for Academic Freedom. They're the ones suing your parents' friend," he explained, thinking that she'd been so indifferent when he'd broached the matter before that he needed to remind her about the lawsuit.

"Yeah, I know who they are," Brit said, secretly furious that he thought she was too dumb and out of it to remember. "I went to UW, right?"

"Oh yeah, of course," he said, distracted for the moment by the tactile revelation that she was wearing thigh-high stockings, not tights. "Did you ever have a history professor named Bosworth?"

"Nope. I never took any history classes," she answered truthfully. "I was a poli sci major. But I know who he is. Big beige lump of lard, teaches ancient history. He gave my sister a D last semester. My dad took away her Mobil credit card. Now she runs out of gas like once a week."

"Boy," said Bobby, taking his hand off Brit's leg long enough to pick up his fork and take a bite of his salad, using his other hand to pick up his glass and get back to his scotch. "Bosworth sure doesn't run out of gas. I can't wait until this whole thing is over and I can stop listening to him slime on for hours. But," he added, brightening, "as long as I get paid to listen to him, I'm gonna keep on doing it. I'm a trained professional."

Brit looked up from the roll she was buttering, meeting his smug, laughing eyes through her lashes. Between the scotch and her stockings, she knew, he wasn't fully in charge of his mouth. It occurred to her that the last place she'd seen that satisfied expression on his face was at the Hitching Post. That night, she'd agreed that she'd had too much to drink to drive back to Laramie. To tell the truth, she'd been loaded and horny enough to sleep with him for the hell of it. Approximately twenty minutes later, they'd been in his room. He'd drunkenly thrust off all his clothes, given her the same smile as she'd gone into the bathroom. Then he'd toppled onto the bed naked and was passed out snoring by the the time she opened the bathroom door. She'd spent most of the night curled up on the couch, watching MTV with the sound turned down low and weighing her options. Around five A.M., she'd stripped down to her underwear, crawled into the bed, given him a kiss and told him it had been unforgettable, but she had to get back on the road. He'd grunted and turned over, and she'd left.

Whatever incipient attraction she'd felt toward him had curdled since that wine-soaked night, firing her anew with the resolve to *get* him good. "I still don't understand what this lawsuit's supposed to be about. I mean, like, who gives a damn?"

"College professors specialize in getting completely livid about nothing at all. They all see life as a zero-sum game—if somebody else gets something, there's less for them. That's why they're all liberals. They all think property is theft." Bobby shook his head, forked up the last of his salad and and signaled for a refill on their drinks.

"Well, you can kind of see their point. They make really shitty money. I used to work at Albertson's, and you know what? Nobody shoplifts more groceries than college professors. I once saw an econ professor stick a package of frozen chicken breasts down his pants and walk out with it."

"Maybe he just got off on having frozen breasts in his pants." Bobby giggled.

"Hey," Brit told him, "that guy was, like, a kleptomaniac. He never left the store without hooking at least a stick of beef jerky. You could pretty much count on the fact that after he'd been in the store, you'd have to restock tuna. He used to slip five or six cans at a time up his sleeves."

"Why didn't you turn him in?" Bobby asked.

"I'm too sure," she scoffed. "I was making minimum wage. I didn't care if people walked out of there with Thanksgiving turkeys in their pants."

The waiter arrived with their steaks—a filet mignon, medium rare, with a baked potato for Brit, and a large porterhouse, well done, with fries for Bobby. Nibbling at the spiced apple slice that garnished the plate, Brit said, "So I guess I can see Bosworth's point a little, but what about your boss? Why does some big jillionaire give a damn about this?"

"What you've gotta understand," Bobby explained, lowering his voice, "is that Elroy Foote is a rich fanatic. He thinks people like Sally Alder are shock troops for the New World Order. Once they've established a beachhead at the University, they'll be brainwashing the kids through the Internet or rigging the microwaves in their dorms to broadcast the *Communist Manifesto* every time some sophomore warms up a burrito. Besides, the legal expenses on this suit don't even make a dent in one of Elroy's dividend checks for the year. His money makes so much money, it's incredible. Hey," he waved a hand at a busboy, "can I get some ketchup?"

The busboy looked disgusted at the thought of some fool ruining a fine piece of beef, but brought the ketchup. Bobby stuck his knife in the neck of the bottle to loosen up the contents and dumped red stuff all over his steak dinner.

Brit watched him, with the sudden uneasy feeling of déjà vu. The bite of fork-tender filet mignon in her mouth seemed to take forever to chew. As an experienced waitress, she was an expert on the eating habits of American diners. All kinds of people wrecked their food by drowning it in ketchup, but most people opened the bottle and tried pounding the bottom before they resorted to the knife trick to get the ketchup out. She'd seen somebody go for the knife first only once in the past year. At Foster's Country Corner. One of the asshole camo guys who'd come in and made such a scene, just before Thanksgiving. This one hadn't said a word, had kept his hat and sunglasses on in an apparent effort not to be recognizable, had barely looked up from his food. He'd done the knife thing, poured ketchup on a porterhouse steak, eaten it silently, and then gone over to use the pay phone before the hassle over the bill. She now realized it had been Bobby Helwigsen.

Her mouth was so dry, she had to take a big gulp of water. She would have loved to bolt right out of the Cavalryman, go straight to her parents' house and tell her father she had an idea that Elroy Foote might be behind a militia group that included some of the rudest people she'd ever waited on. But she didn't want Bobby to get suspicious, and besides, it wasn't every day she got a free dinner at the Cavalryman. "So Elroy Foote's got lots left to spend on other ways of saving Wyoming from the commies?" she asked. Brit really hoped Bobby was looped enough not to notice that she'd asked more questions tonight than in their entire previous history.

Bobby laughed, licked ketchup off his lips, and leaned over the table, his face close to hers. "Oh yeah, honey, he's got a million ways to keep fine American girls like you safe from the boys in the black helicopters. But if I told you what they were, I'd have to kill you."

29

A Rough Night and a Draggy Day

Bobby had of course been terribly disappointed when Brit told him she couldn't come back to the Holiday Inn because she had to get up early for one of her temp jobs. She intended never to see him again, but she didn't want him knowing it. When they got to their cars, she gave him a kiss that made her feel like a total whore and told him she'd call him sometime soon. The wind was blowing so hard that even Bobby, half-delirious with lust and Johnnie Walker, didn't drag out the goodbye.

Her parents were up, watching good-looking doctors stick tubes into people lying on gurneys on *ER*. She sat down on the couch, waiting until a commercial came on and her mother got up to go to the bathroom, and then turned to Dickie. "Daddy," she said, "I have a confession."

Dickie braced himself. Pregnant? Joining a religious cult? Piercing something visible? Something *in*visible? "What is it, darlin'?" he asked sweetly.

"You know how much I hate having you butt into my private life?"

"Yeah," he said, taking a drag off a Marlboro.

"And you know how you asked me a couple of weeks

ago if I'd been seeing Bobby Helwigsen, that lawyer from Casper?"

"Yeah," he repeated.

"Well, I've gone out with him a few times. Nothing serious," she added, inwardly relieved that the evening at the Hitching Post had turned out as it had. "I had dinner with him tonight at the Cavalryman. I watched him pour ketchup all over a big beautiful porterhouse steak, and it reminded me of something I thought you might want to know about."

"That fool put ketchup on a Cavalryman steak?" Dickie asked incredulously.

"This goes back a couple months," said Brit. "Remember when I came home the night of the Thanksgiving blizzard . . . "

While Brit was filling Dickie in, Sally and Hawk were standing in Meg Dunwoodie's kitchen, having the first really big fight of their second time around. He'd been planning for months to spend spring break at Big Bend National Park in far southwest Texas, one of the lonesomest, most beautiful places in the United States, camping and hiking around. When he'd asked her weeks ago, Sally had said she wanted to go along, but now, on the day before they were due to leave, she was insisting that she couldn't get away.

"I don't understand," he'd said a little too quietly. "Why can't you go? It's not as if you're teaching and can't miss a class, or working a nine-to-five job where you're on the clock. You can do whatever the hell you feel like doing," he told her.

"I hate this," she retorted. "I hate the way you act like I don't work just because I'm doing research instead of teaching."

"I don't think that," he said, trying to defuse that potential land mine. "I know how hard you're working. That's exactly why I think you need a break. Take a week to get away from the weather and see some pretty country. Clear out your brain. When you come back, you'll have a whole new perspective on Meg Dunwoodie."

"I don't need a new perspective," she insisted stubbornly, even though she suspected he was right. "I need to keep digging. There's some big piece missing. It feels like I'm just about to figure it out, but I've got to keep working. The stuff from the FOIA request could come any time, and I want to be here when it arrives."

"The stuff from the FOIA request might not show up for years," he retorted reasonably, "and even if it does show up, it'll keep. You can ask Maude to sign off on the shipping receipt."

"Maude's gone. She's off on a tropical vacation, remember? You had that long conversation with her about bird-watching in Costa Rica. Told her she'd double her life list. She said she was opposed to ecotourism in principle but not in practice. She booked tickets for a jungle adventure at some research station a hundred miles from San José the day after the fire in Albany. She left yesterday. She won't be back until the end of May."

"Oh, yeah. Well, she really needed the break, and so do you. Come on, Mustang, let's go camping." He took a step closer, put his arms around her.

"Hawk, I can't just drop everything that matters to me and go off with you every time you feel like it." Direct hit; completely unfair. He let go of her and stepped back. She'd really hurt his feelings, and feeling guilty about it made her even more defensive. "I just know there's something missing, something that links the Paris part to the Wyoming part. Something that explains what Ernst Malthus was doing here in 1943, and why Meg never talked about her father after he died, and where those diamonds came from. It's all a jumble now. You've always made a point of coming and going as you please, but I can't just forget about it and go gallivanting off to Texas to commune with nature."

"You used to love to go gallivanting off to commune with nature," he said bitterly. "But now you're turning into a dried-up academic who'd rather sit in a basement and play with her papers than get out and explore. I *thought* you wanted to spend time with me. I've put a lot of time into planning a great trip for us." Clearly, he'd gotten sucked into this relationship a little too far. He had, against all experience and judgment, begun to trust her, to develop expectations. Big mistake. He put on his down jacket and headed for the door. "Sorry you're too busy to have fun. Have a great spring break."

When Brit showed up at nine the next morning, Sally was hunched over a cup of coffee in the kitchen. "You look like ten miles of bad road," Brit told her. "What happened?"

Sally grunted. Brit waited for the explanation.

"Fight with Hawk. Five minutes after he walked out of this house, I had the bright idea of going down to the Wrangler to find Delice and have a couple of beverages. Your aunt's still having trouble getting the Yippie I O to meet the fire codes, and arguing about the damn pizza oven isn't helping her in the campaign to get something going with Steve Baca. So Delice poured herself three fingers of Cuervo Gold. I settled for good old lethal Jimbo. We closed the place down at two," she finished on a moan.

Brit was a fairly good judge of hangovers, and the one Sally was nursing struck her as a medium-range one, more than cotton mouth and a mild headache, but substantially less than the promise of a day worshipping the porcelain god. Sally was gulping her coffee, and even eating a piece of toast. So Brit figured she was in good enough shape to hear the latest. "I had dinner with Bobby at the Cavalry-man last night," Brit began.

"Oh goodie," said Sally savagely. "Did he choke on a piece of prime rib, turn blue, and expire? I certainly hope so," she snarled, tearing into her toast with her teeth.

"No, he's still alive," Brit answered. "But I did watch him pour ketchup all over a porterhouse."

"I didn't think my opinion of him could get any lower," Sally commented. "I bet he even ordered it well done."

Brit let that pass. "Yeah, he's gross. But that's not exactly a satellite news flash. I realized as I was watching him do it that I'd seen him do the same thing before."

"So you continue to see this pig, despite his nasty eating habits, which you've heretofore ignored on the grounds that watching him eat can be of some use to me. Very noble." Sally got up to pour more coffee.

"Hey—have a shitty day yourself. If you don't want to hear what I have to say, why don't you just take your lame attitude and your stupid hangover and your dead poet and shove them . . . "

"Okay, okay, don't yell at me," Sally begged, putting down her cup to go to the sink and splash water on her face. "I'm not feeling very well this morning."

"I can see that," Brit said. "Aunt Delice called my mom this morning and asked if she could go down to the Wrangler and work breakfast for her. Guess she isn't feeling very well either."

"This town is too damn small," Sally muttered, feeling better for having a cold, wet face.

"So what's the deal about Bobby and the ketchup?"

"Just that I saw him do it before I even knew who he was. It was when I was working at the Country Corner, during the Thanksgiving blizzard. I had to wait on this bunch of jerks who were, like, all dressed in fatigues, and some of them were real gonzo specimens. I kept expecting somebody to pull out an Uzi and start mowing down truckers. And Bobby was one of them! I couldn't really see his face, since he kept his hat on and he was wearing mirrored shades, but I watched him unscrew the cap of the bottle, stick a knife in, then turn it upside down and pound on the bottom. He did it again last night! Ask any waitress—you won't find one in a hundred people who do that, let alone two who do it so they can pour crap all over a porterhouse steak!" Brit helped herself to a cup of coffee.

"So he puts ketchup on his steak, and he's in the National Guard or something. So what?"

"Not the National Guard. This wasn't any real military outfit—they had a convoy of trucks with canvas over the doors to cover up the logos. They acted really crazy. I mean, we're talking some kind of militia or something."

Now Sally was puzzled. "Why would a slick lawyer with a giant client and huge ambition join a militia? I mean, everybody knows he's a big wheel Republican, but I think of him more as a screw-the-poor Republican than an Army-of-God Republican. Must be the giant client," said Sally, smiling faintly as she reached the obvious conclusion. "You told your dad about this, right?"

"Right. And in about five minutes, he's going to be calling you up and telling you to keep the hell out of this and let him handle it," Brit predicted.

The phone rang. Brit was five minutes slow. Sally answered it fast. "Hi Dickie," she said, "I hear I've got a militia after me now. What next, Islamic Jihad?"

Dickie told Sally that the best thing she could do about this new business with a possible militia was nothing. He was working the angle and would tell her if he turned up anything she really needed to deal with. In the meantime, however, she should keep her mouth shut on the subject of Elroy Foote, in all situations. Something very unkosher was going on here, but Dickie and other duly designated law enforcement types would handle it. So she should just let them, and not discuss any of this with anybody, especially Delice. All he needed was Delice in this. Jesus. And not Maude or Sonnenschein or Edna McCaffrey either. Next thing he knew, they'd be forming a liberal counter-militia to march on Teton County.

Sally said she'd be glad to let duly appointed authorities take care of things. All she wanted was some peace and quiet and a sudden lightning bolt of insight that would illuminate Meg Dunwoodie's life like a hydrogen bomb blast. That was all that mattered.

She wished she could tell Hawk about this latest wrinkle. He would find a way to make things make sense. She realized, with dismay, that she'd come around to thinking of him as someone she needed to tell everything to, who counted as part of herself rather than another person when she promised to keep a secret. And now she'd hurt him and sent him off to Texas alone. She wasn't at all sure that he'd want to take back up with her when he returned. Hawk did very nicely by himself, as he'd proven over four and a half decades. And so, goddamn it, did she.

Yeah, right. If there was any reason to think that she was a target for some rogue army full of psychos, then she was going to get her chance to show how well she could do on her own. Dickie was on the job, and that was a comfort. But with Maude gone, Delice out of the loop, and Hawk probably actively wishing she were dead, she was pretty exposed. Still, she couldn't just let this go.

Brit's strategy of having dinner with an asshole had worked; they'd learned something they needed to know. Sally could use a version of the same plan. She got the Laramie phone book, looked up a number, and dialed.

Sam Branch had been dumbfounded and instantly suspicious when Sally Alder called his office to ask him to lunch. She acted like she wanted a friendly chat, but obviously it was business. Now that they were middle-aged, everybody did business over lunch. Where had all the flowers gone?

Sam, of course, already had a lunch meeting, but he said he could meet her for a drink after work. They agreed to meet at six at the Buckhorn Bar, down on Ivinson Street, because it would be crowded and noisy enough on a Friday afternoon to make private conversation possible.

Sally was sitting at a table when he arrived. She was drinking club soda and lime, looking like hell. He went to the bar, got a beer, and sat down. "To what do I owe this honor?" he began.

"Oh, I just thought we should talk about a practice schedule for The Millionaires," she said. "We ought to work up some new material for the Yippie I O opening." John-Boy and Burt didn't plan to have live music in their place, but for the opening night party, Delice had insisted they needed a band, and Dwayne's group was the obvious choice.

Practice schedule? Sam was well aware that they could have done that on the phone. "Wednesday nights at Dwayne's, seven to nine," he said. "Next question?"

For a man as full of bullshit as Sam Branch was, he sure knew how to cut through it. Sally got to the point. "You're a friend of Bobby Helwigsen, right?"

"Not precisely. I know him. We do a little business." Sam got out a cigar, lit it, narrowed his eyes over the smoke. "I'm not about to get involved in the Dunwoodie lawsuit, Mustang, just for your information, so don't even ask."

"Come on, Sam. Telling me what kind of guy Helwigsen is won't affect your campaign to get on the board of trustees. You've known me a long time. This is just between us"—she leaned forward—"desperados waiting for a train."

He leaned closer, too, smiled handsomely. "What do I get in return?"

"Not a fucking thing." She smiled back.

That made him laugh. "Good old bitchy Mustang Sally," he said. As they sat there cracking each other up, it amused Sam even more to see Hawk Green and some big skinny guy come into the Buckhorn, looking sweaty and thirsty. They hadn't seen Sally and Sam yet, but they would. She hadn't seen Hawk yet, but she would. Sam had no intention of telling her anything about Bobby Helwigsen, and he planned on getting out of there very shortly, but just for the hell of it, Sam took Sally's hand, started fiddling with her fingers. "OK, sweet pea," he said. "Come a little bit closer."

After a completely miserable night, Hawk had decided in the morning he was in no shape to start driving to Texas. He'd made a big breakfast, futzed around his house, fixed a leaky faucet. Since he was around, he decided he'd go play in the Friday afternoon basketball game. The lack of sleep didn't improve his game. He was slow and sluggish and his shots kept clanking off the rim. His team got creamed.

Tom Youngblood knew love trouble when he saw it— Edna had given him his share of rough nights and draggy days. Joe—er, Hawk—looked like he needed a friend, so Tom asked him if he wanted to go get a beer after the game. Hawk, who had no other plans, said sure. Tom called Edna to tell her he'd be late getting home, and they decided to go to the Buckhorn, where nobody would mind that they needed a shower and they could get a little lost in the smoke and the crush.

They were standing at the bar, getting a couple of Budweisers, when Tom saw Sally, sitting at a table with a guy whose face he couldn't quite see. Hawk had his back to them. Tom thought about telling him she was there, then figured he'd better give Hawk a chance to vent a little before he mentioned that his supposed girlfriend appeared to be holding hands with some big stud in a fancy sportcoat.

"Sorry about the game," Hawk said, tipping back his beer. "Bad night last night."

"You having problems with Sally?"

"We had our first major fight yesterday," Hawk admitted. "She backed out of going to Big Bend with me, said she had too much work. I planned to leave this morning, but I felt too lousy to do the drive. Guess I shouldn't have expected her to come. Probably try to leave tomorrow."

Tom nodded, watching the blond guy lean over to put his hand on Sally's face. He was at the point of deciding whether to tell Hawk that Sally was there, in an apparently compromising situation, or to get him out of there and spare him the sight, when Sally noticed them standing at the bar and saw the disgust on Tom Youngblood's face.

"Thanks a lot, Sam!" she yelled, attracting the attention of five or six drinkers at nearby tables but her voice getting lost in the general hubbub. "I should have known why you were turning on the bogus charm. You *knew* Hawk was over at the bar, you asshole! And you're not gonna tell me jack about Bobby Helwigsen!"

Sam grinned. "That'll teach you to try to run people over," he said. "We're even now."

Before Sam was out of his seat, Sally was over at the bar, flinging herself at Hawk. "You're still here," she cried. "I thought you'd be halfway to west Texas."

Hawk just looked at her, face full of heartbreak. "What are you doing in the Buckhorn, Mustang? I thought you were chained to your basement."

They had a rule. No lies; not even technical truths. "I've been having a drink with Sam Branch." Sally had only seen Hawk's beautiful eyes look like that once before, and it killed her to see it again. She followed his gaze, watched Sam get up, shoot that Realtor finger at them, and walk out the door. "It has to do with work, I swear. I'll tell you all about it, but not here," she said desperately, clinging to him. "I'm sorry about what I said, and about bailing out on you, and a whole lot of other stuff. I need you, Hawk. Will you come home with me and let me explain?"

At forty-five, Hawk Green was capable of contemplating things he hadn't been able to consider at twenty-five, or even thirty-five. Sally, he knew, had done some growing up, too. Hawk looked at Tom, who chose not to offer any opinion. He looked down at Sally, whose eyes were pleading with him. His jaw tightened in a hurt grimace. "I don't know why I should give you the chance," he said.

"Why not? What does it cost you?" she asked reasonably.

It appeared to cost him his dignity. His freedom. His damn fool breaking heart, which he'd sworn would never ever happen again.

Sally was distraught, but she'd learned how to argue after so many years in academia. "Look at it this way, Hawk. If you tell me it's over, we both lose any chance of continuing to have fun together. If you listen to me, the fun might or might not continue, but you'll be able to make an informed choice. I'm not asking you to do any more than hear my side. And this isn't sixteen years ago. I *do* have a defensible side."

Hawk liked a logical argument. It surprised and pleased him that she had developed the capacity to reason in tight places. And his night of thinking he might lose her had not been pleasant.

"You've got me," he said. "I'll listen." He turned to Tom. "You'll excuse us?" he asked.

"Naturally," Tom replied. "I'm due at home anyway. Edna will be needing her merlot by now."

They drove to her house in separate vehicles. A light freezing rain was falling, making the streets slick, but Sally's Mustang was handling like a champ. Hawk had given her new tires for Christmas.

Sally had to concede that some things about him never changed. He would always be the kind of man who didn't mind spending money on a woman, but thought tires were a better present for his sweetheart than diamond earrings. And that character trait in him would always both attract and frustrate her. Hawk would prefer lonely vacations in the back country to trips to New York or San Francisco or Paris. He would be off by himself for weeks and months at a time, even when she wanted him near. He would meet her volcanic eruptions of emotion with a calm rationality that would both soothe and drive her crazy. And yet, this man was a lover who pleased himself by seeing how much pleasure he could give her, who surprised her with his passion and delighted her by occasionally going helplessly wild in her hands. He was a maddeningly true man.

Sally wanted Hawk in her life.

She read him right. As he drove toward Sally's house, it occurred to Hawk that it was about time to get the snow tires off his truck. He really ought to switch them out before he drove to Texas and put all those miles on them. At this rate, it would take him two days to get packed and ready to go. By the time he got to Big Bend, he'd practically have to turn right around and come back. Sally had really messed up his plans.

This was true, of course, on a larger scale. God knew, Hawk hadn't intended to fall back in love with Sally Alder in Laramie. He'd made all his decisions with the expectation that after all that time, they'd find a way to make Laramie big enough for both of them. And he'd known, the instant he saw her again, that he would have to come up with an alternative plan.

She drove him nuts. Nobody made him laugh as much or think as hard, and yet they could be perfectly at ease sitting quietly with each other. They had great sex. But the things they'd never had in common could fill an average lifetime. Sally liked noisy big parties, and Hawk could hardly stand them. Cities made him want to scream. She was a fanatical Bronco fan, and he thought pro football was stupid and violent. He should never have told her about that afternoon in Houston—now she was always nagging him to go shopping.

And Hawk knew that if he had to go one more day thinking he might have to live without her, it'd split him in half. He wanted to be with her, right now. He didn't want to make bigger plans than that.

Sally put the Mustang in the garage and went around to open the front door. Hawk parked the truck and walked up to her. Their arms came around each other and their mouths came together. That was their apology. The explanations could wait.

They just had to have each other. They flew up the stairs and fell hard onto the bed, tangled up in damp coats and gloves. The basketball game had given him a head start on sweat, but by the time they got their clothes off, she had caught up. They were on fire.

He loomed over her, pinning her wrists above her head, and slammed into her with a force she lunged up to return. They bucked and arched and rolled and fell onto the floor, oblivious to everything except besieging each other. She would have teeth marks on her neck. He would have scratches on his back. Panting and begging, they took each other higher and higher, and then, miraculously, began to slow down. On long, slow strokes, he wrapped himself around her, kissed her, asked her to love him. They crashed to earth together.

30

Anomalies

"Well, I guess it's time for me to give up and go through the financial stuff," Sally told Brit one morning in May when brilliant skies and the bright nodding heads of daffodils belied the chill of the tireless wind. She'd been over and over the letters and the poetry, the news clips, the school files, and all the miscellaneous stuff that had captured her fancy. She hated anything that had numbers on it, though she knew numbers could be revealing. She'd saved the stuff she found most tedious for last.

"I've been done with the financial papers for weeks. They're sorted and filed in boxes twenty-five through thirty-one, according to category and document type—bank statements, stocks, bonds, real estate, mineral leases, estate and probate correspondence, tax returns and so on."

"Boy, I bet those tax returns are gripping reading," Sally commented.

Brit, as usual, shrugged. "We've got all her old checkbooks, too, if you want to look at them. I just put them in order and put them in box thirty-one, but the archives will probably throw them away." Brit had long since finished the work Sally had originally hired her to do, but she was still putting in a few mornings a week, often doing again what she'd already done. She was pretty sure Sally kept her around because it made her feel that at least somebody was efficient, which Sally clearly wasn't. She'd set Brit to work this week listing and cataloguing the poetry manuscripts, a job Brit appeared to be enjoying immensely. As she'd told Sally, she lived with her parents, she didn't have a boyfriend, she didn't really have a job, and even this late in May, the weather continued chilly and windy. She might as well read poetry.

Sally watched Brit trying to act as if she wasn't absorbed in the poems. Brit was her father's child, a lover of poetry and intellectual puzzles hiding out in the guise of a Wyoming philistine. Sally approached her own morning task with resignation. She'd called the FOIA office at the State Department and been told only that they "would process her request." They'd also said that if they found anything, they would of course excise any material that might have bearing on current matters of national interest. She asked what that meant, and the person on the phone explained, "That means that if we do find anything we can send to you, don't be surprised if passages are blacked out. If the federal government has had reason to collect information on individuals, it's generally because somebody considered the investigation relevant to national interests."

That conversation had dampened Sally's hope that government records might solve the multiple mysteries of Meg Dunwoodie. She wasn't expecting that the endless tedium of bank printouts, stock statements and IRS forms would open the doors of perception, but she had to look them over, determined to be a thorough professional.

It was mind-numbing work, day after day, but after a while a story emerged. She began with the files on Mac Dunwoodie's estate, and Meg's own. His estate, distributed in 1967, was based on a will he'd updated in 1962. Most of it went to Meg, although Sally noted that he'd earmarked charitable contributions to the American Can-

cer Society (homage to Gert, no doubt), the Committee
for Cuban Liberation (anti-Castro, she assumed) and the
John Birch Society (his favorite). His holdings had ranged
from oil leases all over the west to a uranium mine in
southern Wyoming and had included a diverse portfolio of
blue chip stocks and long-term bonds. He owned large
tracts of property—four cattle ranches in Wyoming, including the Woody D, three more ranch properties in
Montana, and five in Colorado. He had retained the mineral rights on the ranches, and owned mining claims in a
number of other places. His accounts at the Centennial
Bank in Laramie totalled two hundred fifty thousand dollars in cash. His will also listed "coins, jewelry, and miscellaneous household items" bequeathed to his daughter,
Margaret. The total was valued at eight million dollars.

By the time of her death, Meg had more than tripled the
value of her substantial inheritance, acting often on the advice of Ezra Sonnenschein. She'd sold most of the ranches
and invested in sizable parcels of land around Aspen, Vail,
and Jackson Hole. She'd hung on to those holdings until
the offers she was getting from developers were too huge
to pass up. She had a stockbroker who did a nice, conservative job of managing her portfolio. The oil leases and
uranium mine paid off big for a while and then slacked
off, as such things did. At the time of her death, she'd dis-
posed of most of the real estate, retaining only her house
in Laramie, a cabin in Jackson Hole, and a house on
Holmes Beach, near Bradenton, Florida, which she'd purchased in 1975. Sally wondered idly whether the beach
house was still available. Maybe she and Hawk could go
there sometime and have a vacation to make up for the one
to Big Bend that hadn't happened.

It appeared that Meg hadn't been sentimental about
ranching, not so surprising in the author of "Still Life of
Fascists With Herefords." The Woody D was her home,
but she'd even let that go, as a gift to the Nature Conservancy in 1982. What the Nature Conservancy had done

with it then, Sally couldn't tell from Meg's records. Or perhaps Meg had retained enough of an attachment to her home place that she wasn't willing to sell it to guys who'd want to turn every pasture into a ski condo. Then again, as far as Sally knew, no developer had ever seriously suggested that Encampment could be the next Steamboat Springs.

After a week of following the inheritance thread, Sally had done a lot of cross-checking the estate correspondence with the information in the various files. (Did the real estate transactions match up according to date and amount of money changing hands? How'd she do in the stock market between 1967 and 1994? Jeez.) But she soon gave up that game on the ground that Meg's business dealings had seemed straightforward enough. The estate records had turned out to be more revealing than she'd expected. But then, of course, she'd started with the most interesting stuff. It was time to get down to the really, really boring.

The bank statements. Brit had filed them in chronological order, dating all the way back to 1941, when Meg had opened an account at the Centennial Bank. Sally gawked at the fading sheets of ledger paper, hand-typed, all the information computed with an adding machine. Meg had received one every month for more than thirty years. Sometimes there were little handwritten notes clipped to the statements: "Don't forget to come in and get your Great Customer award for 1970, a Proctor Silex Toastmaster!" Those were the days when banking was work, Sally mused.

In 1976, the Centennial Bank went to computerized statements, Sally learned after seven hours of paging through, year by year. This glimpse of the automation of Wyoming gave her a pang of loss, but she brightened when she saw a note stapled to the statement for June congratulating Meg on her thirty-fifth year as a valued customer and reminding her that she hadn't yet picked up her electric can opener. They were holding it at the service desk.

To judge from the amounts in her account, Meg's fortunes had followed a path that Sally would have expected. From 1941 through 1967, her deposits had been meager, the paychecks of an English instructor at a poor state university. Her withdrawals were regular and careful. Nineteen sixty-seven was the year of her windfall, and the Centennial Bank was clearly delighted to participate in the management of all that money. Sally had followed only a few transactions from the last thirty years of Meg Dunwoodie's life, but of the large cash transfers listed, the ones Sally had traced looked like they matched up with business deals documented elsewhere.

Apart from the notes about toasters and can openers, every statement looked like every other one, columns listing deposits and withdrawals, monthly fees, starting and ending balances. Going through them was tortuous work, so mind-numbing that she almost paged right past the one anomaly in the whole stack. Sally had only gotten up to 1982. It was after six o'clock at night. She'd been at it since early morning, and she needed to quit and take a shower because Hawk was coming to take her out to dinner at seven-thirty. Crawford and Maria had come to town, and they were all going out to the Cavalryman. She'd been down to the bank the day before to get out Meg's diamonds to show to Hawk's father.

Maybe it was the thought of her visit to the safety deposit box that made her see it. There, on the August, 1982 statement, was a special entry she hadn't seen before, added on to the fee section at the bottom of the page. A five-hundred-dollar debiting of Meg's checking account, paid for rental of a safety deposit box for twenty years in advance at twenty-five dollars a year.

Sally shook her head to clear it. She didn't remember having come across any mention of a safety deposit box at the Centennial Bank in any of the files. Nothing about it in the will, or the executor's report on provisions for disbursement of Meg's estate, or any other damned place. Maude hadn't mentioned it, and neither had Ezra. Maybe she'd just missed something, but she didn't think so. Meg had put something away and made sure that it could stay put away for twenty years, if need be.

Who the hell rented a safety deposit box paying for twenty years up front? Why? Who else knew?

Excitement growing, she dashed upstairs to call Ezra and found him at home in Denver. "Listen, Ezra," she began breathlessly, "I've just been slogging through all of Meg's Centennial bank statements, and I came across an entry for a safety deposit box rental paid up twenty years in advance, back in 1982. What do you know about it?"

"Safety deposit box?" he asked in a puzzled tone that had Sally all but leaping up and down. "Noooooo, I don't recall her ever having mentioned a safety deposit box. There wasn't anything about it in any of the estate documents. You saw what was in that closet—I was under the impression that she didn't bother putting her valuables in the bank. Typical Wyoming attitude." He laughed. "I wonder if Maude knows anything about it."

"She'll be back finally, on Sunday. I'll ask her then," Sally said, congratulating herself on her patience during the weeks Maude had been gone. "But since she hasn't mentioned it to you either, I bet she doesn't."

"Maybe not. One way or the other, it's an interesting development," said Ezra. "I certainly hope she does, and that she's just forgotten about it. If there is something we don't know about, sitting in a safety deposit box in the bank in Laramie, it would be convenient if Maude happened to have the key," Ezra observed.

"And if she doesn't?" Sally asked.

"Well then, I guess you'll have to look for it," he told her.

* * *

The daffodils were in full bloom, the tulips were beginning to open, and there were pale green buds, and even a few tentative leaves, on the gray branches of the trees. The cleaned-up Sally went to answer the door and was stunned to see that, despite the chill in the evening air, spring had come at last.

The excitement of her discovery sparkled in her eyes, but then so did the knowledge that she had a small fortune in diamonds stowed in the little black silk bag she carried as a going-out-to-dinner purse. She wore a fitted red dress, high heels, and sheer black stockings.

"Are those your high-heeled sneakers?" asked Hawk, looking her over approvingly. He knew she was bringing the diamonds, and diamonds did make him nervous. He had a loaded Smith and Wesson .38 in the glove box of his truck.

She kissed him, smearing her red lipstick all over him. "'Cause we're goin' out tonight," she sang, fishing in her bag for a tissue to wipe her lipstick smile off his face. "Forgot my wig-hat and my boxing gloves."

"Don't think you'll need 'em," said Hawk, who gave her a look that said maybe he should just take her upstairs and see whether all his hints about garter belts were getting through. "Looks like you had a good day in the dungeon."

"Maybe," Sally said, turning to the hall mirror and getting out her lipstick to make repairs. He was making it hard for her, wrapped all around her and working her from both ends, his lips moving down the back of her neck while his hands headed up under her skirt. "Wait 'til you hear."

Hawk had warned his father that Sally had some gems she wanted him to look over, but everyone agreed that they should save that part of the program for later in the evening, when they would all return to Hawk's house. So they all enjoyed a conversation about Crawford and Maria's summer plans along with their beef. Laramie was their second stop on a summer-long North American odyssey. Crawford and Maria had plans to travel up through Wyoming and Montana into Canada, all the way to Alaska, getting home some time in September. They were traveling in a Toyota Land Cruiser packed to the roof with camping and fishing gear and supplies, but Maria confided to Sally that she'd booked some reservations at nice hotels along the way.

"Crawford will complain that staying in hotels is a waste of money when you could be camping, and that you see the country in a different way when you sleep in a tent. But even he gets tired of swatting mosquitos and picking dirt clods out of his dinner."

After two hours of avoiding the subject everyone was plainly ready to discuss, Maria was running out of conversational ploys, Sally was ready to burst, and even the two men, who competed at giving the word *laconic* new meaning, seemed a little jumpy. Once they got back to Hawk's house, Crawford's deliberate preparations had Sally nearly leaping out of her skin. Telling Hawk to open a bottle of wine, Crawford went into the bedroom, where he and Maria were staying, and got his daypack. He took out a rectangular pad, covered in black velvet, a jeweler's loupe, a pair of tweezers, and a small binocular microscope. Taking a seat in Hawk's only chair, he instructed everyone else to make themselves comfortable. Then he motioned to Sally. She got out the velvet pouch and handed it to Crawford. He opened it, unfolded the paper envelopes, and set the diamonds out on the velvet pad, face up. Crawford's face was completely blank.

Then Crawford went to work. He picked up each stone in turn—the large yellow oval, the smaller yellow oval, the yellow marquise, the baguette-cut pale blue, the emerald-cut deep blue, and finally, the rosy pink teardrop. He examined each through the loupe, from every angle, then put it under the microscope and inspected it again from all angles. He took his time, utterly silent, and nobody else talked. For fifty-six minutes, according to the clock over Hawk's desk, Crawford worked. Maria, who had seen similar procedures before and knew how thorough he would be, was reading a romance novel. Hawk, fascinated to watch his father in action, needed no diversion. Sally spent the first half hour of sitting on the floor trying to arrange her legs, and the second half hour practicing meditation techniques she'd learned twenty-five years before during a flirtation with Buddhism.

Finally, he looked up from the microscope and carefully replaced the pink diamond on the velvet pad. His eyes went to Sally, narrowed. "Where'd you get these?" he asked.

"They were in a jewelry box in a locked closet in Meg Dunwoodie's house," she answered, trembling.

Crawford shook his head. "And they've been in the bank since you found them?"

"Yes."

"Take them back there the minute they open up tomorrow morning," he told her.

Everyone waited for him to say more. Finally, Maria spoke up. "For goodness sake, Crawford, tell us about the stones!"

He looked around, found the glass of wine he hadn't touched since he'd started the examination, took a sip, then a gulp. "All right, then. What you're looking at here is a bloody fortune in very rare, naturally colored 'fancy' diamonds. I'd need a spectrophotometer to be absolutely sure," he said, "but the quality of color and the unevenness of the color in each tells me that these weren't irradiated in a nuclear reactor or heated to produce pigmentation. Again, I can't be absolutely certain in the absence of better equipment and gem lab lighting, but I've seen some diamonds in my day, and I think I know what I'm looking at. You can see for yourselves that they are unusually large stones, but unless I miss my call, they're also of a quality that you generally find only in museums, or in the private collections of diamond merchants or the very rich. The only defects in them I can detect are the ones that give them the pretty colors. In other words, finding them in a closet in Laramie is unlikely," he finished, with typical Green understatement.

"Can you say anything about where they might have come from?" Hawk asked.

"I can talk about probability rather than certainty, Jody," Crawford told him. "Now, it's possible that the yellows and blues came from India, where nearly all the diamonds in the world came from before the late-nineteenth century. But it's a good deal more likely that the yellows came from the Cape Province of South Africa, which produced most of the stones of this canary color, between the late-nineteenth and early twentieth centuries. The blues might have come from Minas Gerais in Brazil, but they're large enough that I'd wager they came from one South African mine in particular, the Premier, which began operating in 1902."

"So they all could have been mined and cut before World War Two," Sally observed.

Crawford nodded. "Likely they were." Then he picked up the pink teardrop. "All but this one, probably. This looks to me like stones I saw when I did some work in Australia. They go for about a hundred grand a carat. They came from the Argyle mine, which has produced most of the pink diamonds in the world today. The Argyle started producing in the late 1970s. So this lovely thing, which is probably worth a million bucks now, is the anomaly," he said, putting the glittering rosy stone back on the pad at a slight distance from the other gems.

"What do you mean?" Sally asked.

Crawford considered. "First of all, it couldn't have been acquired before, say, 1978. The others might have been purchased much earlier. But also, these"—he gestured toward the velvet pad—"are magnificent specimens of a particular type and range of color. They look like a collection to me."

"So maybe Meg collected diamonds," Sally said.

"Maybe. But to get your hands on these, you'd have to be right on top of the market. Most gems like these get snapped up by the big diamond merchants themselves."

Sally and Hawk looked at each other. "Meg Dunwoodie had a lover who was a German diamond merchant," she told Crawford.

Hawk's father frowned. "A diamond merchant who stayed in Germany during World War Two?"

"Evidently so," said Hawk. "We've wondered about that."

Crawford took a deep breath. "You do know, don't you, that most diamond merchants in the western hemisphere have been Jews." Everyone nodded, holding their breath. "Of course, some of them were great collectors. According to the stories I've heard, the Nazis stole a number of the world's greatest diamond collections when they murdered the owners in the camps. Nobody knows how many of these kinds of things are still sitting in vaults in Swiss banks. These"—he pointed at the dazzling yellow and blue stones—"might very well have been one of those collections."

"Maybe it belonged to the Blums. Maybe Meg smuggled out their diamonds, along with their child." Maria's eyes widened, and Sally said, "I'll tell you about that later."

Hawk walked over, picked up the pink diamond, held it up and let it catch the light. "What about this one?"

"I can't tell you anything about how that one might have gotten here," Crawford said. "When was it you first got to Laramie, Jody? Nineteen seventy-nine? It probably didn't get here before you did."

31

Freedom Ranch

For the first time, Bobby was really starting to feel that circumstances might have moved beyond his control. He'd just gotten off the phone with Elroy's chief accountant, who indicated that he had some serious questions about the client's tax returns from the early '90s. It turned out that the guy had only just started working for Foote, and he'd simply plugged in the numbers Foote had given him from previous years. Foote's losses, deductions, and allowances had somehow always outpaced his income, even though he was one rich son of a bitch. Nobody had ever bothered to wonder why he never seemed to make any money until the IRS started sniffing around.

Bobby knew that he personally would not remain wealthy if he didn't make money, but he had always figured that the very rich were not like you and me. Now, however, the auditors were asking where all of Elroy's money was going, and rumors of his tax troubles had reached Wall Street. Stocks in Elroy's public holdings had taken a beating, and Elroy was not happy about it. Bobby himself was uneasy with the thought that he had to call Elroy up and ask him some intimate questions. Elroy would insist that Bobby come up to Freedom Ranch for their conversation, instead of talking on the phone, but Bobby had decided that he absolutely wasn't going up there this weekend. The Unknown Soldiers were due to hold their Memorial Day muster, gathering at Foote's ranch before taking off for maneuvers in the Absaroka Range, and Bobby was trying to put a little distance between himself and Elroy's mad militia.

Elroy answered the telephone in a jolly mood. His older daughter and her two children were spending the holiday weekend with him, and he was a doting grandpa. He asked how the lawsuit was going, and Bobby told him it might go to trial by fall. Eventually, Elroy got around to asking Bobby whether he'd handled the tax situation yet, and Bobby had to say, "Well, no, not exactly."

"I don't understand," Foote said coldly. "Why am I paying you so much if you can't solve problems for me?"

"Believe me," Bobby told him, "I'd love to solve this problem for you, but I need a little more information."

"What kind of information?"

"Well, like why your tax returns from 1990 show all kinds of holdings making all kinds of profits, and then by 1996 you were losing money hand over fist. The auditors don't understand how your net worth went into the toilet precisely at the time the economy started getting well. They think you're hiding something."

Elroy began to fulminate about government interference with private property, but Bobby interrupted him. "I'm your attorney, Mr. Foote," he said. "You need to confide in me. Anything you tell me is privileged information, of course."

Elroy seemed to consider the matter. Bobby could hear the theme from *Barney* in the background. Elroy's grandchildren evidently watched a lot of TV. "OK, Helwigsen," he said. "Can't we have this conversation in person?"

Bobby said it was impossible. He and the accountants would be working the whole weekend, trying to figure out a way to deal with the IRS.

"All right. Call me back at this number in twenty minutes. Don't use your cellphone." Elroy gave him a number Bobby had never used, then hung up. Bobby picked up his mail, got himself a cup of coffee, closed the door to his office, read his mail, and dialed the number. Elroy answered, sounding echoey and far away. Bobby asked where he was, but Elroy cut him off, talking fast.

"I'm at a secure place, speaking on a secure line. That's all you need to know. Last year, I learned that the lawyer and the accountant who were handling my affairs had bungled my finances. Too much of the profit from companies in which I held a majority interest was being distributed to stockholders as dividends. I was being deprived of what was rightfully mine," he said with disgust.

Bobby took a sip of coffee. "Well, Elroy, it's pretty common for stockholders to get dividends when they invest their money in a company," he observed.

Elroy didn't like that observation at all. "It may be common, Bobby, but it is far from universal, and I saw it as a way to cheat me out of millions of dollars. Why, my own lawyer and accountant were collecting some of those dividends themselves, and they didn't even see it as a conflict of interest! And to make matters worse, I was paying taxes on far too much of the money I made through the sweat of my brow."

Bobby tried to think whether he had ever seen Elroy do anything more arduous than get into a pickup truck.

"Naturally I was distressed," Elroy continued, "so I decided to take matters into my own hands. I had the lawyer and the accountant set up companies chartered in countries that truly welcome free enterprise, unlike our own, and moved most of my capital out of the publicly traded corporations and out of the United States. Of course, neither the government nor the investment community has caught on to this, and I expect you to see that they remain innocent of my affairs."

Bobby experienced the sudden insight that Elroy was

not nearly as dumb as he seemed, but was surely as crazy. "I'll see what I can do," he tried lamely, and then couldn't help asking, "What happened to that attorney?"

"Poor Walt Flanders. It was terribly unfortunate," said Elroy, sounding not a bit sad. "He and Danny went out one afternoon looking for antelope, and he shot himself with his own gun."

"And the accountant?" Bobby gulped, in something of a trance.

"Another bit of bad luck. Mickey was leaving here after a meeting and his brakes failed in Togwotee Pass."

"Oh," murmured Bobby.

"Yes," Elroy intoned piously. "The Lord works in mysterious ways."

Bobby didn't know about the Lord, but he understood a lot more now about how Elroy Foote worked. "I guess I'd better get cracking," he finished.

"See that you do," Elroy told him. Elroy pressed the disconnect on the speakerphone in the secret bunker he'd had built not far from the ranch house, buried beneath an abandoned barn. Danny Crease sat across from him, cleaning a handgun. "What do you think?" Elroy asked him.

"He's weak. I'd say he's about half a step from going off the reservation," Danny replied, looking up from his task with slitted eyes.

"I've been a patient man, but I'm growing tired of his impertinence and incompetence. I should have known never to trust a lawyer. Take care of him," said Elroy. "Take the plane." And meanwhile, Elroy thought to himself, it was time to go to Code Red.

Bobby spent two hours debating his prospects with himself. He could continue to do everything possible to protect Elroy Foote, a course of action dictated by the strong possibility that if he didn't, Elroy would have him killed. He could go to the bank, withdraw all his money, call his stockbroker, cash in all his investments, buy a plane ticket to Tonga and change his name to Vince. Or he could go to the police, cop a plea on his own relatively minor crimes (giving false information about Shane Parker being probably the worst) and try to stick Elroy Foote where the sun would never again shine on his evil carcass. None of his choices looked too desirable.

In the end, he got in his BMW and drove to the Department of Criminal Investigation. He didn't notice the rental car that had just pulled into his office parking lot as he got into his car, which didn't park but instead followed him to the cop shop. Two officers stood out in front inspecting a crack in the windshield of their car as he pulled up, parked, took a deep breath and got out. The cops said hi, and Bobby returned the greeting. He walked inside. The rental car pulled away.

Officers P.W. Corkett and Curtis Kates were sitting at their desks, working their way down stacks of paper. Corkett appeared surprised to see Bobby. "Officer Corkett," Bobby began, "I'm afraid I haven't been entirely candid with you."

"I'm disappointed to hear that, Mr. Helwigsen," Corkett replied, though he was far from it. He had known for a while, from Dickie Langham, that something was going on up at Freedom Ranch, but he hadn't had a spare minute to look into the matter. "It's never too late to turn over a new leaf. Have a seat." He indicated a chair next to his desk. Kates came over and leaned on the desk, folding his arms. "Where shall we begin?" Corkett asked.

"Uh, I'd like counsel present," said Bobby, realizing that he must be in trouble, because he needed a lawyer.

Danny Crease knew a lot of cuss words, and he used them all. He'd been a minute too late to grab Helwigsen in the parking lot, and the only place he'd had a clear shot at him had been in front of the police station. He wasn't about to kill even a scumbag lawyer with police officers as witnesses. But his self-restraint was slipping. If he didn't watch himself, he'd lose it.

Things, he knew, were about to go wrong in a big way. Danny had worked for Elroy Foote on and off since 1990, and he'd never let one get away before. Both he and Foote had gotten sloppy. Helwigsen knew way too much. Foote would expect him to report soon, and Danny knew Elroy would blame him for failing. He saw no reason to go back to Freedom Ranch. Elroy would be furious, and there was no question that the place would soon be swarming with cops. So Danny drove to the Greyhound station, left the car in the parking lot, and bought a ticket on the first bus out of town. Much as he'd hoped to build a new world starting with Elroy Foote's money and power, it was time to get the hell out of Wyoming. Boarding the express bus to Denver, he reflected that he would have to return soon for one brief encore. His last act in the state would be finishing his personal business with Dickie Langham.

PeeWee Corkett turned off the tape recorder and lit a cigarette. Bobby Helwigsen asked if he could go to the bathroom. Kates took him, while PeeWee listened to Helwigsen's lawyer trying to argue that they shouldn't press charges against his client for giving false information to an officer investigating a felony. PeeWee didn't intend to bargain away that chip until he felt sure that he had Helwigsen's full cooperation on all matters having to do with Shane Parker or Elroy Foote or the Unknown Soldiers. PeeWee was just beginning to get a picture of how many charges they could hang on Elroy Foote and his paramilitary gang.

He called his commander and gave him a summary of what they'd learned from Helwigsen. "We're going to need to call in some help on this. According to the lawyer, there's enough firepower at Freedom Ranch to take over a small country. Foote has helicopters, jeep-mounted rocket launchers. He's even got a tank."

"I know," said the commander. "The FBI and the ATF got wind of some illegal arms purchases a couple of years ago, and they've been keeping an eye on him ever since. I didn't know anything about it until that shooting in Muddy Gap, when I got a call from the FBI agent here in Casper asking if we'd back off our investigation. They've had a guy inside, and they were worried he'd be compromised."

PeeWee fumed. "Leave it to the feds. What the hell do they think they're doing, screwing up my case?"

"Catching a bigger fish," said the commander. "And as of this morning, it looks like something's happening. Their undercover guy reported in this morning. Said the militia was gathering for a routine Memorial Day exercise, when all of a sudden Foote announced that they were on combat status and ordered a lockdown of the place. He and his family have gone into some kind of bunker near the ranch house, with the militiamen setting up defensive positions nearby. SWAT teams are on the way."

"How many of them are in there?" Corkett asked.

"Besides your lawyer friend, apparently only one of the militiamen isn't accounted for, a guy named Danny Crease. Did time in Colorado for assault with a deadly, one manslaughter charge in Boulder County, dropped, a couple of narcotics charges but no convictions. Very not-nice person, and we aren't sure where he's gone. As for who's still in there, maybe a dozen militia types, a handful of cowboys, the undercover FBI guy. And Foote and his wife, daughter, and grandkids."

"Jesus," said PeeWee. "Welcome to Ruby Ridge."

"Tequila, mon amour," Dickie Langham groaned to Pee-Wee Corkett. "Thank Christ it's not my jurisdiction." There was no way they could keep a lid on this. The FBI, the ATF, the Teton County Sheriff's Office, and the DCI were sending officers to Foote's place. Within hours, television crews would be flying into Jackson and Cody, showing up in helicopters, renting every available vehicle, and heading up to cover the Siege of Freedom Ranch. By morning, half of Wyoming's sterling politicians would probably be denouncing the federal government at whose trough they so greedily fed, and declaring Elroy Foote a martyr to states' rights. Dickie hoped there wouldn't be violence. If anything happened to anyone on the ranch, the political posturing would be unbearable.

"Just thought I ought to keep you up to date. Oh yeah, one of the maniacs has gone missing. I'm faxing you the rap sheet on him. Keep a lookout."

"Sure," said Dickie. "Just like we did before, with such great success."

"Don't beat yourself up about that, Dickie. It's not your fault Shane Parker got loose, shot someone and ended up dead," PeeWee soothed.

"Presumed dead," Dickie retorted. "We're still waiting for the forensics. There wasn't all that much left to test."

"If it matters," said PeeWee. "Take some deep breaths. Go get a milkshake. Go make love to your wife. Forget about the tequila," PeeWee advised. He'd also been rather too closely acquainted with Jose Cuervo at one time, though he wouldn't join AA because he hated meetings of any kind. "That fax oughta come through in a minute. Let us know if you run across this guy."

"Right. Thanks, PeeWee," Dickie signed off. The fax machine was beeping. He waited for the transmission to be complete, watched the sheets of paper move through and drop into the tray. And froze as he looked down at the mug shot and criminal record of a man he had hoped never to encounter again. Danny Crease was in Wyoming, was somehow in the middle of as big a mess as Dickie had seen in his law enforcement career, a mess that had reached out and oozed right up on his own daughter and one of his oldest friends. For all Dickie knew, Danny Crease was on his way back to Laramie to collect the debt

Dickie owed him, from so long ago. Dickie bet he was the kind who held grudges.

Almost nobody knew about Elroy's bunker. Today it was much more crowded than he was used to. His wife came in only to clean, and his daughter and her kids hadn't even known it existed until today. Arthur had of course been in there before, but Dirtbag had never had the privilege, and he found it cozy. He and the kids were watching *Rugrats* on satellite TV and eating canned fruit cocktail. Arthur had suggested that Elroy shouldn't subscribe to cable, because the government might have ways of using it to monitor activities on the ranch. Just now, Elroy was wishing he didn't have the satellite either, because the kids' shows were driving him batty. They'd been down there overnight, and the television had been blasting every hour the kids were awake. He grabbed the remote, punched MUTE, and was about to hit the off button and hurl it against the wall when he accidently hit the channel changer button and tuned the set to CNN. A booger in the corner of the screen assured the viewer that what they were seeing was LIVE, as if you couldn't tell by looking at the picture. A blow-dry guy in a camo jacket stood holding his ear and yakking into a hand-held microphone, trying to hear and make himself heard over machine noise and a deafening wind. In the background, Elroy was stunned to see the gates of his own ranch. He turned the sound back on.

"We've just arrived at Freedom Ranch, where federal and local law enforcement agents are on their way to a standoff with a social conservative billionaire and his personal militia. As you can see through the gate"—the correspondent gestured toward the gate—"the militia members, who call themselves the Unknown Soldiers, have set up defensive positions here at the remote compound of entrepreneur Elroy Foote, a man as well known for his devotion to conservative causes as for his immense wealth."

He paused for a moment, cupping his earpiece, as the voice of a studio newscaster cut in with a question. "What kinds of weapons do they have, Drake?"

"From what we can see from here, Roberta, there appear to be machine guns mounted on Jeeps or humvees. All the militia members are carrying automatic rifles and pistols, and several appear also to have hand grenades. Of course, that doesn't tell us what we *can't* see from here." Drake paused again, this time for effect. "Only time will tell."

Elroy roared and lunged for his walkie-talkie, hollering at the Number Five man in the Unknown Soldiers, who was supposed to be securing the perimeter. "What's going on out there, boy?! How come you haven't apprised me of the situation? How many government troops are out there?"

"This is Number Five," came the reply. "Sorry, sir, but the press has just arrived. They came in helicopters and landed about five minutes ago. Kicked up a hell of a lot of dust—we've had our hands full keeping our weapons in firing trim and our butts from blowing away."

"I can see the reporters are there, by heaven!" Elroy screamed. "I'm watching CNN! I asked you how many *troops* are there. How many police, federal agents—you know!"

For a moment, Number Five was silent. Probably trying to estimate the forces arrayed against them. "Um, let's see. Still a lot of dust out there, sir, visibility is poor."

"Just give me a ballpark guess!"

"Okay. Um . . . looks like one squad car, so far, from the Teton County Sheriff's Office. And . . . oh yeah, here comes a truck, maybe a Forest Service pickup. Oh boy!" He was getting excited. "Here come a couple of state police cruisers. Yeah, they're coming in. Looks like at this point, we're talking about eight or ten guys. Oops," he said as two shotgun-wielding officers emerged from one of the cars. "One of 'em's a girl."

"Doesn't exactly sound like a siege," Elroy said, sounding oddly disappointed.

The studio correspondent on CNN appeared to be making the same observation to Drake, the guy in the camo jacket. "Shh," said Elroy, watching the television to find out what was happening.

"That's right, Roberta," Drake said. "Law enforcement teams are only now beginning to mass here at the gate. As you've correctly observed, CNN arrived *before* the police. We'll be here covering this very volatile situation *live* as it develops. Ah—I'm now seeing what looks like a troop transport coming down the road. People are getting out and, yes! It's the FBI SWAT team!" said Drake, sounding as if he was broadcasting the Rose Bowl Parade. "And now here come the ATF sharpshooters!"

"The press got here before the police?" Arthur asked incredulously. "What kind of discipline do they have in those government agencies anyway? Somebody's going to pay for that leak!"

Dirtbag, who'd been extremely disappointed when Elroy had turned off *Rugrats*, asked the obvious question. "So what do we do now?"

The various law enforcement agencies were quickly taking up positions, and somebody was going up to Drake the camo-man and rudely suggesting that he get the hell out of the way. But then the sound of helicopters drowned out all talk. Half a dozen copter pilots jockeyed and jostled for landing spots, and there was very nearly a massive collision. By the time all six had landed, disgorging media people from the major networks and a team of advisers to the governor of Wyoming, the camera crews were all screaming at each other, the governor's men were reaming out the cops, and the law enforcement teams were at each others' throats about who would coordinate the operation.

Arthur turned quietly to Elroy, the gleam of cold metal

in his translucent eyes. "We need to take advantage of this situation, Number One," he said. "Their disarray is our opportunity. I respectfully suggest that you order a unit to engage in diversionary tactics, which will give you and Mrs. Foote and the family time to get to your escape vehicle. Howard and I will escort you, and then return to defend the property."

Elroy nodded. He could see their chance slipping away. The FBI SWAT team was fanning out to quell the riot and get everyone organized. The ATF agents were taking up positions, and only a few reporters were still shoving and shouting. "Calling Unit Patrick Henry, Patrick Henry, do you read me? Over," he screamed into the walkie-talkie.

A voice came back. "We read you, George Washington. Over."

"Create a diversion, immediately. Over."

"Diversion? What kind of diversion? Over."

Elroy gave it some thought. "Blow something up. Over."

Arthur and Mrs. Foote exchanged apprehensive looks.

"George Washington, this is Patrick Henry. What should we blow up? Over."

"I don't give a damn what you blow up!" Elroy said, so panicked that he forgot to say "over." "Just throw a grenade or something!"

"Should we use the rocket launchers? Over."

"Yes! Employ whatever weapons necessary!" Elroy yelled.

Arthur gathered Mrs. Foote, the daughter, and the grandchildren together and indicated to Elroy, who was very red in the face, that he was taking them out of the bunker and heading for the escape vehicle. "Howard," he told Dirtbag, "you bring Mr. Foote along." He snatched up another walkie-talkie, so that he could keep in contact. Hustling the women and picking up the children, Arthur opened the bunker door, led them through the tunnel under the barn and ran several hundred yards to the vehicle that waited with its engines running, a Harrier vertical-takeoff-and-landing aircraft illegally purchased from the French government, which wasn't particular about its arms customers. As they reached the Harrier and climbed in, they heard the men of the Patrick Henry unit debating what to blow up. Some had decided to fire their guns in the air as part of the diversion.

"How about blowing up that abandoned barn over there?" asked one.

They cheered the idea so enthusiastically that they couldn't hear Elroy Foote shrieking at them through the walkie-talkie.

"Take off!" Arthur yelled to the Harrier pilot, a man who'd learned in places like Angola and Nicaragua that when somebody told you to take off, you did.

"Wait!" screamed Mrs. Foote. "I'm afraid of flying!"

But nobody paid any attention to her, because they were by that time hurtling straight up in the air as the barn, and the bunker beneath, exploded with an ear-splitting roar.

Given the chaos erupting in and around Freedom Ranch that Memorial Day, it was a miracle there weren't more casualties. One Unknown Soldier accidentally shot off the left buttock of a fellow militiaman. Several of Elroy's troops, three reporters, and six network sound technicians suffered severe hearing loss from the shock of the explosion. Only three deaths were reported. The millionaire rancher Elroy Foote and his bodyguard, a former professional football player, Howard "Dirtbag" Robideaux, had of course been blown to bits by their own men. Mrs. Henrietta Foote had suffered a massive heart attack at the moment the Harrier took off.

The government forces took advantage of the fact that the Unknown Soldiers appeared so stunned by the explosion that they weren't ready when the leader of the FBI SWAT team sped up to the gate in a Chevy Blazer, punched in the access code, and led a parade of vehicles onto Foote's ranch, leaving behind just enough law enforcement officers to restrain the maddened media and deal with the governor's men, who were all shouting into their cellphones. Within an hour, all the Unknown Soldiers were in custody, the ranch's civilian cowboys were being held for questioning, and the local volunteer fire department had arrived to extinguish the burning remains of the barn and the bunker.

The Harrier landed a hundred yards from where it had taken off, and medics rushed in too late to save Mrs. Foote. They had been alerted to the emergency by the FBI agent who had called himself Arthur Stopes. He had a gun to the pilot's head, and had his hands full with Mrs. Pamela Appley, Elroy Foote's daughter. Her parents, she shrieked, were martyrs to the cause of freedom, and the government, she assured FBI Agent Stopes, would pay.

No doubt she was right.

32

Oral History

Like everybody else in Wyoming, and many people around the country and the world, Sally Alder watched the spectacle of Freedom Ranch on cable television. Edna had called to tell her to turn on CNN. For a while, it was like O.J.'s Bronco chase all over again—the viewers were just watching, and nothing much was happening. The militiamen stood around with their guns, and the police and the media seemed to be taking their places. Then suddenly, Foote's soldiers started firing their weapons and there was this tremendous blast, followed by insanity. Media crews scurried around trying to get good camera angles, law enforcement officers shouted and ran to their vehicles, ambulances came screeching down the road. The CNN correspondent, who'd dived for cover, screamed a steady stream of voice-over, but couldn't quite keep up with the action. Something had clearly been blown up, but nobody knew what. Before anyone could quite figure out what was happening, the cops had somehow opened the gate to Freedom Ranch, and the militiamen appeared to be surrendering without firing a shot. Sally wondered where Bobby Helwigsen was, and found herself hoping he hadn't been there. After all, she'd met him, and Brit had dated him. Most Americans who watched the debacle were shocked, but Sally mixed in a little guilt and a fair amount of wondering what it all meant for her personally.

Bits of the story emerged over the next few days. A private army that styled itself "The Unknown Soldiers," financed by the eccentric Elroy Foote, had been stockpiling weapons and holding training exercises in Wyoming for nearly three years. Nobody was completely certain what they stood for, although there was plenty of sloganeering. Three people had died: Foote, his wife, and a former Dallas Cowboy lineman. Most of the members of the group were in custody, but one was still at large. The FBI had been running undercover surveillance of the group, and Foote's attorney, Robert Helwigsen, had come forward to tip the state police. Bobby was getting a lot of face time on TV, looking serious and sincere and generally acting like a hero.

Sally couldn't manage to be entirely sorry about Freedom Ranch. Wyoming, she thought, might have had a little too much Freedom lately, but things were looking up. She no longer had to worry whether she was being stalked by loonies playing soldier, and the Faculty for Academic Freedom had lost their sugar daddy. Bosworth assured the other FAF members that Foote's foundation would go on even if the founder had gone on beyond, but then Mrs. Pamela Appley, Foote's daughter and the acting chief officer of the Foote Freedom Foundation, announced that she was dropping sponsorship of the suit and reviewing the Foundation's activities. The Boz even tried to get his comrades to put up their own money: yeah, right. One FAF member told the *Boomerang*, "Do I look like I'm walking around with a sign on my back that says KICK ME?" Game over, boys.

At the same time, the demise of the Unknown Soldiers was proving a distraction from what Sally really wanted to do. The newshounds got so desperate for stories that they even started calling her up, trying to flog another story out of the event. The ringing telephone was driving her and Maude and Brit nuts, as they took the house apart, looking for Meg's safety deposit box key.

Sally had called the Centennial Bank and learned that Meg did indeed still have a box in the vault. And yes, said the person who answered the phone, they'd need Meg's key to get access to the contents. Sally knew she could call up Dwayne Langham and ask him if he would lean on somebody to let them into the box, but she didn't want to ask the favor until they'd made a real effort to find the key. So they set to work looking. Maude had come back from Costa Rica, tanned, rested, and on a roll. She knew nothing about the box and had no idea what might be in it. Two days of searching the house brought no results, and they'd resorted to sifting through the papers, looking for obscure clues. They got to where they were Xeroxing the poems and cutting them up to see if anagrams or codes emerged.

Hawk found the three women hard at it one balmy lilac-scented evening, when he'd walked over with a six-pack and some idea of going for a sunset stroll. They were all sitting on the floor of the upstairs office, surrounded by scraps of paper. They looked like a coven in search of a spell. He offered the beers around, popped the top on one, and sat down on the couch to watch them. But he was the kind of person who loved beating everyone at Scrabble, so soon he was sucked into the game. Brit had the poem index she'd made, and was getting ready to take a scissors to it when he grabbed it out of her hand. "Humor me," he said. "You guys have a head start."

He sat paging through it slowly, while the three women snipped and shuffled. Brit's index was arranged alphabetically by key words and concepts in each poem (quite a little feat of literary criticism for a poli sci major, he thought). Key words. Key concepts. Hell, he'd read enough of Meg Dunwoodie's poems to know that she was a real fiend for keys.

He looked through until he found the entry for "keys."

There were listings for poems that spoke about two kinds of keys, the kind that opened doors, and the ones on pianos. He thought a minute.

"You know," he told them, "if there was a piano in this house, I'd look there. Keep the key with the rest of the keys, get it?"

"But there's no piano, so thanks a lot anyway," Brit said.

Sally looked up and was about to say something equally snide, when her eyes lit on the Blum drawings hanging on the wall, just above and behind Hawk's head. In one, the hands were poised above the keyboard. In two more, the pianist had several fingers on keys. In the last, a single finger brushed a single key. The drawings were hung on nails, with picture wire. She jumped up and with shaking hands, carefully took each off the nail, turned it over. *Brush of the key.* And there it was, fastened to the brown paper backing of the last sketch with yellowing Scotch tape.

Sally and Maude went to the Centennial Bank together, into the vault together. Maude signed in, and the bank clerk found the box. Sally and the bank clerk turned keys together. The door swung open, and Maude slid out the metal box. The bank clerk showed them into a private room and left, shutting the door behind her. They opened the lid, and inside were three tape cassettes and a plain white envelope.

The envelope held a note, written in the disciplined but spidery script of advancing age and dated March, 1989. It said, "I don't know who is reading this, but either you've done some fine puzzle-solving, or the bank has kicked me out of the vault for nonpayment of rent. Maude and Ezra, if you're still alive, you have all my love. Sally Alder, if you continue to survive your errant youth and my heirs have honored my wishes and persuaded you to write my story, you will be needing these tapes. I made them seven years ago and put them away. They will explain a lot. Margaret Parker Dunwoodie."

The dead speak. The historian's wish fulfilled.

Sally was stunned. Maude told her, "She was determined that you be the one. That's why Ezra and I have done things the way we have."

"Why?" Sally asked. "What the hell possible reason could she have had? She didn't even know me."

"Do you think the people in Deadwood didn't know Calamity Jane? Come on, Sally, you were a bit notorious in your day. We always went to the summer concerts in Washington Park. We actually went to a few women's studies events, although you probably didn't notice the old lady and her companion hanging out on the fringe. We heard you and Penny Moss singing together on more than one occasion. I recall you joking about how you'd been blacklisted from the bars, so you were forced to stoop to singing in churches."

Sally chuckled. That had been one of her favorite lines.

Maude went on. "Meg knew you were giving them hell in the history department, and the university grapevine pegged you as somebody who'd either end up dead in a ditch at twenty-eight, or grow up and get a handle on all that talent. Half of Laramie was amazed when you published your first book and it did so well. The other half wasn't. Meg was in the 'wasn't' camp."

Her first book had been published in February of 1989. The Sunday *Times* had given it a big write-up. Even the *Boomerang* had reviewed it. "She followed my career?" Sally asked Maude.

"Didn't you notice her copies of your books? She saw some of herself in you. You both loved to write. You both got out of Laramie. Oh, she wasn't hanging out in bars or having sex with reprobates when she was here, but she understood how a girl could get stuck in a tight place."

"But she came back," Sally whispered, her throat very dry.

"She had to come back. And finally, she wasn't sorry. She loved Wyoming. She always understood that nobody is alone in the world, that every person has a chance to make things better or worse for at least *somebody* else.

"Most people make those differences in their kids' lives. For people who don't have kids, there are other choices. Clara McIntyre, Meg's English professor, had changed Meg's life by making it possible for her to leave. Meg had given Ezra and me our chances." Maude swallowed hard. "As she got older, she didn't know whether anyone would ever appreciate her poetry, but she did know she could make a difference with her money. As far as Meg knew, she'd never really made it as a poet, even though she always believed her work was good. She figured that as a musician who never hit the big-time, you'd have some sympathy for that. And that you'd have the heart and the imagination to find other things that mattered about her life.

"She wanted to give you the chance to return here, and to make your own differences. She asked me lots of times in those last years, when you were in Los Angeles and doing so well, whether I thought you'd want to come back. I told her I honestly had no idea. She made me promise we'd ask."

Sally burst out crying.

"I knew you'd do that," said Maude, digging in the back pocket of her jeans and offering a clean bandana.

Sally asked both Maude and Ezra if they wanted to listen to the tapes first, but both declined. "This is your project," Maude said firmly. "We'll listen to them later."

So there she sat, alone at a table in the basement, with her laptop, her cassette player, yellow pads and pens, and the three tapes. Each cassette was numbered. Sally reminded herself that what she was about to listen to was a product of memory, and memory, she knew, could be the

furthest thing from history. But you needed memory anyway. She began with tape number one.

"My name is Margaret Parker Dunwoodie," Meg said
in the same strong, aging voice Sally had heard on Edna's
oral history tapes, "and I am recording this at ten P.M. on
July 21, 1982, in the town of Laramie, Wyoming. I am
making this tape in secret, because it will reveal stories of
crimes committed by people who will never face a court
of law. I am one of those people."

Here, Meg took a long breath. Sally did the same. "My
father was a fascist and a traitor. I am not sure, but it may
be that my lover was his accomplice. I killed them both."

"I've often thought that 1929 was a bad year for everyone
in the world, except me," Meg resumed after a long silence. "That was the year I went to Paris. The year I met
Giselle Blum and Paul Blum and Marc Sonnenschein.
And Ernst Malthus." Her voice broke on the last name.
Meg evidently turned off the recorder for some time, then
resumed. "I'd learned some things about life in New York,
but I was still pretty much a Wyoming ranch girl at heart.
Paris changed all that. No—Ernst changed all that. The
first time I ever saw him, he was performing at one of the
Blums' Tuesdays. At that time, I didn't even know what it
would feel like to want a lover. By the time he'd finished
playing *Night and Day*, I knew."

Sally had planned to take notes on the tapes. The notes
could wait. She leaned her elbows on the table, put her
chin in her hands, and just listened. "My mother had always told me that good girls made a man wait until marriage. That women needed their rights so that they could
compel men to control their baser instincts." Meg chuckled. "The first time he made love to me, I found out a lot
about those baser instincts. I had them, too. I didn't mind
a bit." Sally laughed. Meg continued. "There was so much
more. Ernst was everything I wanted. Charming, brilliant,

passionate. He loved the mountains as much as I did. It seemed to me that he was ready for anything. He needed to be ready, and so did I. The Nazis made sure of that."

Meg described their long love affair, spanning the continent and more than a decade, and only occasionally did she descend into pure nostalgia. For four years, Meg and Ernst had lived their lives, separately and together, pretty much freely. They'd met in Paris and Nice and London and Lucerne, arranged rendezvous in Germany and Austria and Italy. They were planning to be married. But everything changed in 1933, when Hitler came to power. They put off the wedding, because Meg refused to become a German citizen, and Ernst didn't feel that he could leave the country permanently. They still managed to find ways to be together, but they knew wherever they went, the Gestapo might well be watching.

"I didn't understand how he managed to go and do whatever he wanted, when I knew all too much about what the Nazis were doing to the German people, turning the Jews into outlaws and murdering them wholesale, terrorizing anyone who might sympathize or resist, watching and striking fast, crushing any spark of humanity. Most of the time, we couldn't talk about it. We never knew if a hotel room might be bugged, or if the person sitting at the next table at a café might be Gestapo. The only times we could speak freely came in remote places—on the tops of mountains, or far out in the countryside, where we'd go for long walks, or take horses, and get far away from all signs of human beings. There, I could ask questions.

"But Ernst didn't give many answers. He insisted he had never joined the Nazi Party, and never would. Yes, he was under pressure to become a party member, but his family was so rich and influential that their position gave him a lot of protection. He had important friends in the foreign office—that was how he could travel. He said there were many people in and out of Germany who were working to make Hitler fail, but he couldn't say who or where they were, or what they planned to do. He could do more good, he said, by appearing to cooperate than by fighting them openly. He'd tell me that he didn't want to endanger me by telling me anything the fascists might want to torture out of me later.

"A hundred times, he looked in my eyes, and held me, and begged me to trust him. I loved him. What else could I do?"

Sally had no idea.

"When the Germans invaded France in 1940, I had choices of my own to make. Paul and Marc immediately went into the Resistance, but Giselle wouldn't leave her parents. I could have stayed and fought with them, but Giselle begged me to take Ezra to America, and promised me that she would find a way to follow. I had to go to Wyoming. My mother was very ill, and I wanted to be with her. I said I would find a way to get the boy out of the country, but I didn't have the faintest inkling how I was going to do that.

"Ernst was supposed to have been in Berlin at that time, but all of a sudden he turned up in Paris. Somehow, he got false papers for the three of us. I was sure we'd be caught, but he had an enormous amount of money to bribe any official who got too suspicious. He was also carrying a gun. I made him swear that if they tried to detain us, he'd use the first bullets on Ezra and me, then shoot himself. We couldn't relax until we had docked at New York and gone through customs inspection. At the time, of course, American officials were refusing to give sanctuary to European refugees, and I was terrified that if they found out who we really were, they would be cruel enough to send Ezra back."

Sally stopped the tape, got herself a second cup of coffee. A hell of a trip, she thought to herself, and not exactly a hero's welcome when Meg got home.

"My father's letters had made his ugly opinions clear for years, but I assumed that he would be glad to see me, that my mother's illness would make him want my help. I hardly expected the vicious reception he gave us when we reached the Woody D. He took one look at Ezra and screamed that he wouldn't have 'some Jew bastard' in his house. He said he was going to call the immigration authorities in the morning and have the kid deported. And he said more. I couldn't listen. I took Ezra in with me when I went to my mother's room, leaving Ernst to try to reason with my father. My mother lay in bed, ghost-pale and emaciated, weeping and pleading with me to forgive my father, to ignore what he was saying, and to stay. She needed me. She knew what she was asking of me, she said, and she was asking anyway. I couldn't refuse her. I had to find a place for Ezra, then come back and nurse her until she died."

What choice could she have made? What would Sally have done?

"I didn't know how he did it," Meg went on, "but somehow Ernst had gotten my father to calm down enough that by the time we left, he was able to keep silent. I asked Ernst what he'd said to him, and he told me that all he'd done was to appeal to Mac, businessman to businessman. He didn't elaborate, and I was so relieved to be out of there, I didn't push. All I could think about was finding somebody to take care of the boy, keeping him out of my father's reach, and getting back to my poor mother. And of course I knew that my time with Ernst would be short. I couldn't convince him to stay in the United States, marry me, become an American. He said he couldn't abandon the work he was doing. He had to go back.

"Do you know," Meg said with wonder, "on his last day in Laramie, Miss McIntyre and Miss White informed us that they would be going to Cheyenne for the night, but that we were welcome, of course, to remain at their house? Ezra had gone with the Starks. We were alone. They had put us in separate bedrooms, of course, but we spent the night together in the single bed I'd been sleeping in. I have never made love like that in my life. I was sure I would never see him again."

The tape clicked off. Sally turned it over.

"But then," Meg continued, "I did. He'd promised he would return, and so he did, in 1943. I can't imagine how he managed to get himself out of Germany and into the United States at that point, what kinds of connections he was able to make in countries in the middle of a fight to the death. Well." She sighed. "Ernst always was good at making connections. Obviously he was involved in espionage. I assume the Nazis were confident he was working for them—that's why they gave him so much latitude. I assume also that he was involved in some capacity with the American OSS or British SOE"—the countries' two main spy agencies during World War II—"and that they considered him, oh, what's that John le Carré word? An asset. Yes, a very valuable asset.

"My mother had died the year before, and I was living in Laramie and teaching at the University. It was summer, so I was at home, writing. I had no idea he was coming. He knocked on the door of my house, wearing the disguise he'd worn when we left Paris and came to Wyoming. I have written at least a dozen poems trying to describe what I felt at the sight of him, but none of them have been any good."

Sally thought for a moment. There were poems about reunions with a lover, but Meg was right. They were not Meg's best work. She could write about sex, about anger, and about loss, and could render complicated emotions into remarkable images. But joy was not her forte. Maybe because you could count on joy to blow up in your face, Sally thought cynically, half-hoping that she didn't really believe that herself.

"I'd never seen him so thin or tired. He wouldn't talk about the war, about what he'd been doing for three years. He said he hadn't heard from Marc. I asked him about

Giselle, and he put his arms around me and rested his chin on the top of my head. He said he believed that she and her parents had been sent to one of the Germans' concentration camps. They were probably dead. Paul had been smuggling arms to Resistance fighters in Marseilles. He was captured by Vichy soldiers and hanged.

"Ernst wanted to see Ezra as soon as possible, to know that the boy was doing well. I took him to visit the Starks, and saw Ernst smile for the first time since he'd come back. Little Eddie, as he was known, was thriving. Just the sight of that dear little boy seemed to refresh my old lover, to restore some of the curiosity and energy I had missed so badly those three long years.

"Ernst had a car. I have no idea how he got it in the middle of the war. We had two weeks, and he wanted to see the Rockies. We went north as far as the Grand Tetons and Yellowstone, south all the way to Pike's Peak, hiking and staying in tourist cabins. He had more gasoline coupons than any American I knew," she commented dryly. "As long as I knew him, whenever we were together, Ernst was a master at pretending that the rest of the world didn't exist.

"Our motto on that mountain tour was 'Make the War Go Away.' We pretty much managed it. We were enough for each other. Perhaps whoever you are, listening to this tape, will wonder how I could welcome a man who was, for all I knew, a Nazi agent, into my heart and my bed. I will say in my own defense that I didn't believe for one second that Ernst Malthus was a Nazi. Nothing in his character matched up with that. Nothing in any of the actions I knew about. What I knew was all in his eyes when he saw Ezra looking like a happy little boy. I had all the reason in the world to assume that he was exactly what he'd led me to believe—too valuable to the Resistance to give up the guise of being a 'Good German.' I didn't doubt that he had been forced to make some terrible choices. You could see that, too, very clearly, in his eyes. I wanted to give him an oasis, to bury him in beauty and pleasure and what laughter we could steal. He left after those two weeks, saying not a word about where he was going, or when we might meet again."

Tape number one ended.

And tape number two began. "If I'd had to guess where he went when he left me waving goodbye from the door of my house in Laramie, I'd never have guessed in a lifetime. For a long time I held on to the hope that he'd come back. I bought a big bed. I wondered, every day, where he was and what he was doing. I tried to find out. Marc Sonnenschein hadn't seen him since early in the war, didn't know where he'd gone. I wrote to everyone we'd known who'd survived the war, but it was as if he'd fallen off the earth. Gradually, I gave up trying to find him. I assumed he was dead. Or maybe I wanted to think that he must be dead. Otherwise, why wouldn't he have come back? I didn't learn the truth for more than twenty years, and then I didn't want to hear it, particularly from the person I heard it from.

"That morning in 1943, Ernst Malthus got up out of my bed, cooked me a breakfast of bacon and eggs, loaded his grip into the trunk of his car, and drove straight to the Woody D Ranch. He went to see my father, McGregor Dunwoodie. They had a kind of business arrangement. It was not the last time they met.

"You see, by 1943, my father was helping to finance the Axis war effort. Germany was starved for cash, and a small, revolting group of capitalists around the world was making it possible for the Nazis to buy enough food to keep their death machine running. The capitalists offered American dollars and gold and silver. The Nazis offered the treasures they'd stolen from the people they murdered. Ernst was, in this case, simply the middle man," Meg finished, her voice flat.

Sally had to stop the tape, rewind, and listen again to

make sure she understood. She listened three times, and the meaning, each time, seemed unmistakable.

"Do you wonder how I learned all this? My father told me."

Sally had to stop the tape again, get a drink of water before starting it back up.

"I hadn't spoken to him in more than twenty years," said Meg. "On the day my mother died, I left the Woody D and swore I would never go back and never even mention the name of McGregor Dunwoodie again. I'd lived for two horrible years with his monstrous tongue-lashings, his bitterness and anger and abuse. Once, when he'd begun to rant about the Jews, about how Hitler had the right idea, and he still had half a mind to call up the authorities and send that little kike bastard I'd brought home back to get what he deserved, I'd gotten his shotgun off the wall and told him that if he ever, ever mentioned the child again, I would blow his head off. When I left, I told him not to write or call or try to contact me. The last thing he said to me was that he'd never disinherit me, because he'd never give me the pleasure of being free of him. 'When I'm dead and buried, my goddamn money will haunt you to your own grave,' he said.

"But he didn't tell me then about his arrangement with Ernst. That came much later, in 1966. I had made good on my pledge not to see Mac or speak to him, and he hadn't written or called. But I went to my office one day to find a message from an old family friend in Encampment, somebody I hadn't seen in years and years. He said that Mac had had a heart attack. He knew he was dying. He was at home at the ranch and wanted to see me just once more, before he went."

Click. Sally had to flip the tape.

"I don't know why I went. Maybe it was the memory of my mother. But I did, I drove over the Snowies and down to Encampment, down gravel and dirt roads I could have driven with my eyes closed. And then I was there.

"He was right there in the same bed my mother had died in. And smoking—even a heart attack couldn't stop him. He already looked like a corpse. I don't know what I expected, but I should have known that he'd called me in to hurt me one last time. He was almost too weak to speak, but he managed to whisper to me to pick up a piece of paper on his bedside table, next to his ashtray. It was a list of all his property, detailed for the executors of his estate. I asked him why he was showing it to me, and he said, 'Look under the headings for miscellaneous.' I looked, and saw that he'd listed coins and jewelry, and so on. 'Those are the presents I received for giving a little help to the Axis during the war, and things like that.'

"I just looked at him. I couldn't understand. Seeing me confused and worried gave him the energy to talk. 'You'll love looking at my trinkets when I go, my girl,' he said nastily. 'I've got some right pretty jewels and quite a few gold South African Krugerrand coins in the vault over in that bank in Laramie—'course the coins came later. Got 'em all from your boyfriend, Ernst Malthus. I gave him the cash the Nazis were needing, and he brought me some awful nice things. Didn't hear from him again until 1962, when I was asked to help out some people who wanted to change the way things were going in Cuba. That time, they wanted somebody who could get 'em some weapons. I said I probably knew somebody who could help them out, but I wanted Krugerrands in return. They said it could all be arranged, and the next thing I knew, here came old Ernst with a damn suitcase full of gold. Didn't he stop by to see you, Meg?'

"'No, he didn't,' I said. 'You're lying. Ernst had so much money when we left France, I was sure we'd be robbed. Why would he need your filthy money?'

"'What kind of money?' my father asked me. 'French francs? Italian lira? How about Reichsmarks—let's see, right about then, Reichsmarks would have been trading against dollars about five thousand to one.' He looked at me like I was something he'd spat out and said, 'Who the hell would want *his* worthless money?'

"'I still don't believe you,' I told him.

"His eyes were glittering with fever and malice. He was clutching something in his hand. 'Why honey, the first deal we ever did was that day you walked in with that little mongrel bastard. Ernst said he'd heard I had expressed an interest in aiding the defense of the Fatherland—you know how he had that fancy English the foreigners talk? Yeah, he said, he could *assist* me, but that he'd grown fond of you, and out of concern for you, he would be willing to demonstrate his intent by offering me a gift that had been seized from enemies of the Reich. That time it was a ruby bracelet. When he came again in 1943, it was five of the prettiest diamonds you ever saw. Here's the bracelet.'

"He put it in my hand. I almost couldn't look. I knew the bracelet. Giselle had never taken it off. It was inscribed inside; it was a wedding present from Marc. Why had Ernst given it to my father?

"And then he crushed out his cigarette, lit another one, and really started in. 'That man you were so fond of fucking was a Nazi, Margaret,' he said. 'Aren't you proud of yourself—whoring for a Nazi? You're so high and righteous, saving your little Jewish brat, and all this time, you've been nothing but a Nazi's bitch whore.'

"Maybe that was really all he had to say in his life. He started gasping for air, clutching his chest. I knew he was having another attack, that I should call a doctor. But I just watched. The cigarette dropped from his hand and landed on the quilt on the bed. It set the quilt on fire, just a little fire. I should have put it out. But I didn't. I watched it spread. He was unconscious—nearly dead, blue around the lips." She paused. "He might have been dead. But when I walked out of that house, with the fire moving across the bed and toward the wall, I actually hoped he was still alive. I walked out, holding my dead friend's wedding bracelet in my hand, and let him burn."

Tape number three. Sally was terrified to listen, driven to hear.

"My father burned up in his house of hate, and left me hopeless and miserable and rich," Meg began again. "I didn't tell anyone what had happened. I have always wondered if Maude suspected. But then, she had plenty on her own mind in those days besides my moods.

"At first, the money was every bit the burden Mac Dunwoodie intended it to be. All I could think of was how dirty it must be, how every penny he'd ever earned must have come as somebody else's tragedy. I kept hearing him call me a Nazi's whore. I wanted desperately to give it all away.

"But then I realized that he was dead. He couldn't touch me any more. What had been his was mine. My own gift of revenge would be to take all that he'd lied and swindled and threatened his way into, and turn it into something else. I would make it a resource for all the good things he hated. And I would do a damned good job of it. Mac Dunwoodie gave me three things: a bloody fortune, a taste for revenge, and a little talent for making money. I used all three. My mother had given me some things, too: a strong brain and body, the belief in human rights, and the capacity for love. I wanted to use those things, too.

"I had known for a long time that I would never have a husband, or another lover. Ernst had been the first and last. I forbade myself to think about his betrayal, covered the hurt with so many layers of anger that I almost forgot what it looked like. And yet I couldn't just turn to stone. It became all the more important to me to be worthy of those I loved, and those who loved justice and beauty. All the things my father despised.

"I admired and loved Maude Stark from the moment

that she picked up those measuring spoons from Clara McIntyre's kitchen table, and gave them to Ezra to play with. As I tell these stories," Meg's voice quavered for the first time, "I have had years to learn just how smart and brave and loyal she is. Maude has inspired me and educated me. She made me see the ways women have suffered injustice. Without Maude, I never would have understood how my mother could have stayed with my father, all those years. I couldn't have fathomed the ways his hatred bore down on her, how the same things happen to so many women. I hope my legacy can lift some of those burdens.

"When Ezra came back to the Rockies, I felt my real family had been reunited. I do think of him as my son, but I have never forgotten his mother. When he first moved to Denver, Maude and I went down to celebrate his return. I gave him Giselle's ruby bracelet. He was thrilled to have it, but wanted to know how I'd come by it. I told him she'd given it to me for safekeeping, and now it was his to keep safe."

Sally stopped the tape. She went upstairs, got a box of Kleenex and a Coca-Cola, resumed.

"Oh yes. And the horrid Krugerrands. Those I sold for cash, then wrote a check for the entire amount to the Simon Wiesenthal Center. It was a somewhat amusing situation. I had put an ad in the Denver *Post* offering them to coin collectors, and it turned out that the fellow who came to buy them was from Wyoming, a young Teton County rancher named Elroy Foote. He was quite a character—asked if I had any more! Imagine! I told him I had thousands, and since I didn't trust the banks, I'd buried them in a secret place. I think the fool actually believed me!"

Whoops! Stop and rewind and replay that sucker. Jesus.

"Actually, I kept a single Krugerrand. I'm not sure why. I suppose I don't believe it's possible to blot out the past entirely. Or perhaps I was just fated to do it. Because when I saw Ernst again, and showed it to him, I knew my father had really gotten it from him.

"Yes, I did see Ernst again. I was down at my place in Florida, just last year. Someone knocked on the door. I wasn't expecting anyone. And there he was.

"I had always thought Ernst would age well. He had. He stood tall and strong. His hair had turned white, and it was much thinner, but he combed it the same way, straight back. His eyes were as clear as ever. I stood for a long time in the doorway, holding the door open, just staring at him. And then, he walked in.

"I had no idea what to say. 'Where have you been the last forty years?' Or perhaps, 'I would have waited for you forever, but then I found out that you were a Nazi agent?' Finally, I settled on 'Why have you come?'

"He stood in my living room, staring at me. We could hear the sound of the waves, gulls calling. And then he said, 'You look beautiful.'

"I don't know if he could have said anything worse. 'Beautiful?' I said. 'Ernst, I'm seventy-seven years old. I'm a bitter old lady. I'm not beautiful.' But to me, he looked beautiful, damn him. 'You haven't answered my question,' I said. 'Why are you here?'

"'I have business in the states,' he said, as if that explained anything.

"I couldn't contain myself any longer. 'Business!' I said, 'I know about your business. Forty years ago you did business with my father. And again in the 1960s. My father showed me the bracelet you traded him for money for your Nazi death machine—Giselle's wedding bracelet! And this!' I went to the bedroom, to my jewelry box, and got the coin. Threw it at him. 'What was this? What have you done? How could you?' I asked him. 'You betrayed me and everything I thought you loved.'

"There is a picture of Ernst, that I took on top of Mount Pilatus, near Lucerne, in 1934. I'm looking at it as I speak these words. In his eyes there was so much love and thought and knowledge—I was never the same after seeing all those things in his eyes. He had that same look, in 1981, as we sat, two old people with everything and nothing to say, listening to the sea.

"And then he told me. 'Remember when we left—at the Gare du Nord? Giselle insisted I take the bracelet. She wanted Ezra to have something to remind him of her if . . . if something happened. I gave it to your father to bargain for the boy's life.'

"'But you knew what he was doing. You knew that he and the others were dealing with the Nazis. You helped him with those deals, sold him diamonds. Whose diamonds were they, Ernst? Did one of your friends take them from some old man in Antwerp as they shoved him onto the train to the camps? How many did you help them kill?'

"He stood then, and strode over to me, and took me by the shoulders and shook me. 'How can you think that of me, Greta? Don't you know me?'

"How should I have known him, after forty years? I just looked at him. 'My father told me what you'd done. It was his parting gift to me, Ernst. He called me a Nazi's whore.'

"Then, Ernst just looked at me. And for the first time ever, too late, he began to explain. 'Your father thought he was giving aid to the Axis, but most of the money he and the others paid me never got to the Nazis. I had been secretly raising funds for the German resistance during the '30s. In 1940, I made contact with the American OSS. I worked with them throughout the war, funneling money to anti-Nazi groups inside France and Germany. I thought that would make it possible to be with you. I begged them to let me tell you what I was doing. It wasn't possible. When the war was over, I told myself, this will all be over for me. But it wasn't. I'd been playing the game so long, I couldn't get out. I'd done things they could use on me. I couldn't get back to you.'"

Was he lying? Sally sat forward, listening hard. Meg's voice, hard and raspy, came back.

"I told him I didn't see how I could believe him. If he'd been a reluctant captive, why had he come to barter gold for guns with my father, in 1962? Surely he could have refused that assignment. 'It was a CIA operation, of course,' Ernst told me. 'I could have turned it down, but I had some foolish thought that somehow I could see you. I couldn't take the chance of seeing you before, but perhaps after. Then I met with him, and realized that I couldn't face you. I wasn't fighting any kind of good fight any longer. Apartheid gold, for guns for CIA-trained Cubans to go take back their Fatherland. I had thought that no matter what it looked like, or to whom, I'd always stayed on the same side. But by then I was just, well, in the game.'"

"'And you're still in it?' I asked him. Ernst didn't answer for a moment.

"'I retired a few years ago, and moved to Perth, in Australia,' he told me. 'I've gone back to the diamond mines. The Argyle Mine, out in western Australia, looks as if it will produce remarkable gems in some quantity. Most are of course fairly small, but some,' he said, putting his hand in his pocket, pulling it out, and taking my hand, 'some are unforgettable.' He'd put a paper envelope in my hand. I unfolded it and looked down at a pink teardrop diamond, the equal of any of the ones Ernst Malthus had sold my father on the morning I'd last laid eyes on him, made love with him one final time.

"I just looked up at him. 'When we found this,' he said, 'I knew at the very moment that I had to find you, had to take it to you. To make you understand, somehow. But you can't understand, can you? Because it's not understandable. So don't,' he said. 'But can you forgive?'

"'How could you leave me, all these years?' I asked him. 'How could you give my father the very weapon he needed to destroy me? How could you ever, ever do his work? Are you here on CIA business again, Ernst? Maybe trade a few pink diamonds to smuggle guns to some pet counterrevolutionaries for the Reagan admininstration? Still in the game?'

"For the first time, he looked like an old man. He looked at me with such sadness, and such tenderness, and so much regret, I was tempted to take his hand. But I couldn't. And he knew it. 'I want you to keep the diamond,' he said. 'It doesn't make up for all I've done, but I want it to remind you of the memory of what we once had. I've kept it alive inside me for half a century, convinced myself that it was shining and unbreakable and eternal. And I'm so sorry, so very sorry, that it wasn't nearly enough.'

"He did take my hand then, and folded my fingers over the diamond, and then walked out. I didn't go after him. I sat numb, listening to the surf and the birds and the sound of my own hard breathing. I put the diamond away with the others. I have them all, still.

"I read in the newspaper, two days later, that a man identified as Ernest Martin, aged seventy-seven, of Perth, Australia, had been found dead of a self-inflicted gunshot wound in a luxury condominium on Lido Beach. I didn't pull the trigger but I knew as clearly as I have ever known anything, that I killed him."

33

The Yippie I O Cafe

The world washed clean, on a Saturday morning in June, seven thousand feet above sea level in the town of Laramie, Wyoming. Sally Alder put on her running shoes, stretched a little, and headed out the door. Gram and Emmylou wailed in her ears. Love scars the heart.

Maude Stark had once told her that writing Meg Dunwoodie's biography would be the most important work she had ever done. Now, she knew why. Maude had not known what was in the tapes, but some of it she had suspected. And when she heard the tapes, Maude just said, "Meg was wrong. She didn't kill either of those men. But maybe she should have. Somebody should have."

That was loyalty. Misguided, probably, but loyalty.

Sally thought there were sins and betrayals in her life. Comparing the dull saga of Mustang Sally to what had happened to Meg Dunwoodie, and what Meg had done herself, was like comparing pennywhistle music to Wagnerian opera. Amid the regret and the wonder, Sally felt . . . relief. The larger dramas of the world had touched her life very little. She had never been in immediate physical danger, never saved anybody's life, never come close to killing anyone (except maybe Sam Branch—but he was clearly still alive). She hadn't written brilliant poetry, hadn't had a grand tragic passion that spread over her whole life. At least, not yet. It didn't look as if she was going back to LA, but she knew that if she did, it was good-bye, Hawk.

But being involved with Meg Dunwoodie apparently rubbed off on you. Now she'd been threatened by fanatics, scorched by fire, held a fortune in mysterious diamonds in her hand, and walked back into the arms of the man she'd been mad for, once upon a time in her wayward youth. Not bad for ten months in Laramie.

Maybe it was time to celebrate. Tonight was a private party to kick off the grand opening of Burt Langham and Frank "John-Boy" Walton's Yippie I O Cafe, Laramie's first ever real live California fusion restaurant. The space in the historic building on old Ivinson Street had been completely remodeled since its last incarnation as a fern bar (ten years after fern bars were happening). A neon cowboy rode a neon bronc above the entrance. The tin ceiling was restored to perfection. Burt had keyed the decor to a poster of an old rodeo, lots of faded cream, dark crimson, and saddle brown. There were hints of leather, high blue sky, and the occasional lariat.

The bar was an art piece Burt had commissioned from a California friend, a crescent of gleaming crimson resin resting on a Plexiglas base in which were embedded row upon row of vintage cowboy boots. A moose head with huge antlers hung on the brick chimney over the much-contested pizza oven.

Sally varied her jogging route so that she could stop in for a morning cup of coffee. Burt didn't really want to do breakfasts (although he was planning a Sunday brunch menu), but she knew they'd be there, getting ready and freaking out. She wanted to wish them luck (and see if they passed her private coffee test; most restaurants, no matter how good, didn't).

The place was already insane. A fish delivery truck

(Colorado plates) was parked at the back entrance in the alley, blocking access for a produce truck (plates ditto), and the drivers were about to get into a fight. The Albany County 4-H beef project team, meanwhile, was delivering half a prime steer, a good luck present from the 4-H president, a distant cousin of the Langhams. Since they couldn't get it in the back, they were coming through the front door. Burt was screaming at them to wait, but they were all saying howdy to Delice, who had arrived just in time to see them drop the bloody semi-steer on the spanking new tile floor.

Everyone rushed over to get the steer off the floor and out of the way, and then Delice shooed as many people as possible out out out. Sally washed the beef blood off her arms, wondered if her New Orleans Jazz Festival T-shirt was wrecked, and told Delice she looked like she could use a cup of coffee, hint hint. The coffee passed the test, easily.

Dickie showed up fifteen minutes later, and they had the weird sensation of holding an informal Wranglers' Club meeting in a place that resembled the actual Wrangler only insofar as there was already blood on the floor. But John-Boy was taking it all surprisingly well, claiming that anybody who wanted to be in the restaurant business had to look sharp when things got crazy. He even offered to fix them up a couple of eggs.

"Charge 'em $6.50 for two-over-easy," Delice hollered at John-Boy. "You can't make any money in this business giving away food."

And then she turned to her brother and Sally. "I've been so busy with all this, I haven't had time to find out—what's the latest with the Unknown Soldiers? Is that one guy still on the loose?"

Dickie looked more uncomfortable than the question warranted. "Still at large. There's been no sign of him. He's probably on his way to Buenos Aires. Hey John-Boy—can you make that three-over-easy?"

"If you want to pay eight bucks," Delice answered tartly. "What's up with you, Mustang? How's the book going?" She turned toward the kitchen. "I'll have two-scrambled-soft." Then back to Sally. "Any chance we can talk soon about getting Dunwoodie House on the Register?"

Sally thought a minute. Once the biography came out, there'd be no keeping people away. Maybe the town could make some money off it, buy the Laramie public schools some books or something. She'd talk to Maude and Ezra. "Yeah, we can talk about it. It takes about a year, right? I ought to be out of there by then, for sure." Or sooner. Maude had said that it was okay for her to move out and keep working with the papers, if she wanted. Just now, the place was feeling a little too full of ghosts.

"Find anything interesting?" Delice asked, half-distracted by the arrival of a flower arrangement that resembled a communications satellite.

Sally considered her answer as her eggs arrived, perfectly crisped on the edges with the yolk still runny, flanked by two pieces of fresh toasted brioche, a sculpted strawberry, and a tiny bottle of Tabasco. "Yeah. I found a lot interesting. John-Boy," she yelled, "will you marry me?"

"So where are the Krugerrands?" Dickie asked the obvious question.

"Read the book and find out," Sally grinned through a mouthful of fried egg heaven. She wanted to change the subject. "What are you wearing tonight?" she asked Delice.

"I don't know. Whatever anybody wears, Burt'll be the best dressed person in the place. Do you think cowboy boots or spike heels?"

"How about spike heels and gunbelts?" Sally asked.

"I'll be wearing my holster," said Dickie, considering whether he could ask for a side of hash browns. "Thought I'd come as a sheriff."

"Too farfetched," said Delice.

"Gunbelts and garterbelts," said Sally, wondering what Hawk would think. "We've got a theme."

"See you all at seven! Thanks for the great grub. Let me know if there's anything you need," Dickie Langham called out as he walked out of the Yippie I O feeling well fed but uneasy. Maybe it was coming into the restaurant and finding the dishwasher mopping blood off the floor. Or maybe it was that pizza oven that Steve Baca was so worried about. But he knew what it really was. Dickie had been in enough unstable situations to trust a feeling of foreboding. Until Danny Crease was accounted for, Dickie would watch and worry. He'd even called Bobby Helwigsen to ask him if he had any clue where his former militia associate might be, but Bobby had acted as if the question was an insult.

"It was my job to act as Mr. Foote's legal adviser," he said. "My only connection with the Unknown Soldiers was in that capacity. I made it a policy to mingle as little as possible with them."

Dickie had talked to the FBI agent a.k.a. Arthur Stopes about it. "We appreciate your willingness to assist in the apprehension of Mr. Crease, Sheriff Langham," Arthur—or whatever his name really was—had said, "but we're really not at liberty to divulge details of an ongoing investigation. If you see him, notify us at once."

Thanks a lot, guys. Putting the charitable construction on it, Dickie assumed the FBI didn't know diddly-squat.

On the night that Danny Crease had returned to Freedom Ranch after Walt Flanders, Elroy Foote's earlier attorney, had run afoul of his antelope rifle, Elroy had seen fit to reward Danny in a special way. He'd put five gold Krugerrands in his hand, and told him that someday they might find more. Danny did find five more, in a doe-hide pouch tucked under his bunkhouse pillow, after Mickey Welsh's power steering fluid ran terminally dry in Togwotee Pass. No one among the Unknown Soldiers except Elroy and Danny had been aware that Shane's rumors about Mac Dunwoodie's treasure were true. Now Elroy was out of the way, but the FBI was looking for Danny. If he had any hope of getting the Dunwoodie treasure for himself, he had to work fast.

In the days since the Freedom Ranch incident, Danny had covered a lot of ground. He'd gone out to the airport in Denver, flown to Arizona, bought a 1993 Honda Civic from a guy he knew who fenced stolen vehicles in south Phoenix, switched the plates three times on his zigzag drive north. He'd had to sell one of the Krugerrands to get the cash he needed, but he considered it an investment.

The strain of revenge postponed had begun to tell on him. He'd almost strangled a cashier at a McDonald's in Grand Junction who'd insisted that he pay the tax on his Quarter Pounder. His throat felt as if he was constantly choking down a scream.

He'd come into Laramie from Cheyenne and headed for Dickie Langham's house—what kind of cop had his home address in the phone book? But Langham's patrol car wasn't there. He cruised by the cop shop, but the only vehicle in the lot was a Blazer with a mud job that looked like it was usually driven by somebody who lived out of town.

From his earlier reconnaissance, Danny knew Dickie's sister had a restaurant on Third Street, but there were no cop cars there. He cruised downtown, and was surprised to find the squad car parked on Old Ivinson, right outside a restaurant that looked like one of those faggot places in LA. He drove by slowly, and could see Langham inside, chowing down with two women. Presumably his sister was one, and the other was Sally Alder. He recognized the bitch from the newpaper picture Shane had been waving around. The guy filling up their coffee cups was wearing a KISS THE COOK apron and talking with his hands. That figured, Danny thought. It wasn't bad enough that they'd taken over Colorado—now the Jews and the homosexuals were invading Wyoming, and Dickie Langham was with them all the way. Danny sighed. Obviously, killing a couple of illegal aliens who had the gall to drive the Snowy Range Road wasn't going to put a dent in the horde of undesirables flooding into the state. He really had his work cut out for him.

Danny parked in the Centennial Bank lot, across Second Street, where he'd have a clear view of the restaurant. He saw a florist's truck pull up (Colorado plates) and unload about half a jungle worth of tropical flowers. Must be some kind of party happening, he surmised. Then he watched Sally Alder take off at a trot, but didn't follow her. He was waiting for Dickie to come out. Danny heard him loud and clear, hollering at the people inside that he'd see them tonight. Well then, thought Danny, I will, too.

The discussion about what to wear to the Yippie I O threw Sally into a frenzy. This was an event that surely called for a new dress, not an easy proposition in Laramie. She would have to go down to Fort Collins and hit the stores running, if she wanted to be back in time to clean up and get to the restaurant early, to do a sound check with the band. Hawk was out doing field work, as usual, so he'd said he'd meet her at the party.

The Mustang hummed happily up over the pass, and Sally had a hard time keeping her speed down. But she knew the Wyoming State Police were on the job, and she slowed down and savored the drive. So much had happened since she'd pulled into town last August, fiddling with the radio, listening to exhibition football. She smiled. The Broncos had even managed to win a Superbowl.

Her luck was holding—she found a slinky black dress at Banana Republic, a pair of shoes at Dillard's, and had actually gone and gotten a garter belt and lace-topped stockings at Victoria's Secret. Sally, of course, didn't own a gun, much less a gunbelt. She would have to make up for it with other ammunition. She opened the windows and listened to the Allman Brothers all the way back, blasting *Whippin' Post* so loud she scattered a dozen antelope grazing in a meadow by the road.

It was four-thirty by the time she got back; she was due at the restaurant at six-thirty. Plenty of time to get gorgeous. She showered in the beautiful green bathroom, painted her toenails pink while she waited for her hair to dry. The garter belt and stockings weren't the most comfortable items of clothing she'd ever worn, but comfort wasn't the effect she was going for. Straight sex, she thought, slicking her hair back, clipping on the diamond tennis bracelet that had belonged to her mother.

It was 6:25 already; she was running a little behind, damn it. Sally hauled her guitar and amp out to the car and put them in the trunk. She went inside to get her purse, checked her lipstick in the hall mirror. As she was about to lock the front door, she felt something cold in the middle of her back. A voice she'd never heard, but that she knew wasn't Ed McMahon coming to deliver the check, said, "Let's go back inside for a while."

"Sally's never late for a gig," said Dwayne Langham, tuning up his pedal steel. "I wonder if something's wrong."

"Don't worry about it," Sam Branch told him, checking levels on the mikes. "She probably just has a run in her stocking or something."

"Burt, where the fuck are the champagne glasses?" yelled Delice over Sam's refrain of "testing testing, one two three." She wasn't actually wearing a gunbelt, but she looked dangerous enough without it.

"There are three racks of them on the back kitchen counter. John-Boy darling, did we remember seafood forks?" They were doing a selection of hot and cold hors d'oeuvres, and Burt wondered if they needed seafood forks for the coquilles St. Jacques.

John-Boy, a blur in sparkling chef's whites, was doing ten things at once, but he took a moment to admire Burt. His partner was decked out in a yellow suede western-cut jacket, a white pleated tuxedo shirt, a bolo tie set with the biggest piece of turquoise north of Santa Fe, pressed Levi's 501s, and red lizard cowboy boots. Wowser. "They're just hors d'oeuvre portions, Burt. We can make do with cocktail picks. Now don't bug me, baby, I've gotta finish off the pizza puttanesca."

"I wonder where Sally is," Dwayne repeated, moving over to tune his fiddle.

"Dwayne, can you come here a minute and help me with these goddamn champagne glasses? Everything has to be perfect in exactly twenty minutes, or somebody here is going to get taken out and shot!" Delice warned.

The first thing Danny Crease did when he got Sally Alder inside Meg Dunwoodie's house was to slap her in the face so hard, her brain rattled. "You and I have a little business to do, *Professor* Alder. Let's make it quick." He slapped her again.

Sally staggered, fell back on the couch. Tears ran down her face. She didn't recognize the man pointing a gun at her, but she had an idea who he was: the unclaimed Unknown Soldier. Still, she had to ask. "Who are you?" she cried. "What do you want?"

Danny sat next to her on the couch, gripping her arm and holding the barrel of his Beretta against her ear. "If you cooperate with me, *right now,* I won't kill you." Yet. "I want to know where the rest of Mac Dunwoodie's Krugerrands are." He didn't much like touching a Jew. It made him feel dirty.

Sally looked at him in shock. "There aren't any Krugerrands. Did Elroy Foote tell you there were?"

Danny hit her again, just for fun. He loved the way that little stream of blood was leaking out of the side of her mouth. He had to watch it, though. He needed her conscious for what he had in mind. "Meg Dunwoodie told him herself. Now where are they, before I change my mind and decide to kill you first and then have a look for myself." He punched her hard in the ribs to make his point.

Sally was nearly hysterical from terror and pain, and the question put her over the top. She gagged and gasped, trying to get enough air to say something, or he would surely beat her to death. "I'm telling you. You can kill me and look all you want, but you won't find what you're looking for. I know that for a fact. Meg Dunwoodie sold every fucking Krugerrand her father left her, to your friend Elroy Foote. I'm telling you the truth. There's not a damned thing in this house you'd want to steal." A man like this, some recess of her brain whispered, would not want Meg's poems, or Giselle's paintings.

"Yeah," said Danny, "Jews are famous for telling the truth, especially when it comes to money." He looked around at the fancy furnishings, the crystal and the silver, but he wasn't in the market for stuff it would be more trouble to fence than was worth his time. If she was lying, he didn't have time to find out. His watch said 7:10—he needed to get her to the restaurant before somebody came looking for her. He could have shot her there, could have spent a little time looking around the house, and then gone to the party and killed Dickie. But somebody might come looking for Alder, and he had other plans for her. It was time to make a statement.

The Civic was still parked in the bank lot. He'd grab Dickie and take him out on the prairie for a chat before he let him die. Nobody would follow. Earlier in the day, Danny had left a small package by the alley door of the Yippie I O Cafe. The package contained an ordinary pipe bomb, fancied up with a little radio transmitter. The triggering device was in his pocket. He would press it at the moment that he took Dickie out the front door. The bomb would go off right next to the kitchen—no great loss. A couple less faggots and their friends to stink up the world.

"Get up, filth," he told Sally, dragging her to her feet. "We're going to a party. We'll take your car," Danny said, reaching in her purse for the keys.

When Steve Baca walked into the Yippie I O, Delice handed him a glass of champagne and gave him a very nice kiss. Their relationship had recently transcended the pizza oven. "You're just in time. The lobster pizza puttanesca is almost ready." Having given up the pretense of not owning the restaurant, Delice returned to the place by the cash register where she always felt most comfortable. She was frantically busy, but it occurred to her to wonder where Sally was.

Steve, meanwhile, made his way through the crush. The small bandstand was empty, the music planned for later. The place was packed with Laramie citizens slamming down wild mushroom pâté and Vietnamese spring rolls. Everyone had obviously arrived on time, to be there before the food ran out. Dickie Langham had one arm around his beautiful daughter Brit, and the other cradling a plate of high-end goodies large enough to feed Steve's whole firehouse.

Steve saluted Dickie with his champagne, but the fire chief looked worried. It wasn't the pizza oven, which he'd finally approved. Both Burt and John-Boy were standing near it, looking harried but happy and awaiting what Burt called "the pizza de resistance." Steve was just a fireman in a crowded restaurant. The instinct for a spot check was too strong to resist.

One part of the kitchen, the part with the pizza oven, was out in the open, but the back kitchen, where the main ovens and preparation areas were, was in the back. Steve strolled back, found the temperature as hot as it always is in restaurant kitchens in full swing, but not alarming, and headed out the back door for a breath of cool air. Just as he was noticing the small package next to the door, he heard a commotion in the front room.

Sheriff Dickie Langham didn't see Steve head toward the back. He was preoccupied with the very good food, with wondering what kind of maniac would latch onto Brit next, and with the thought that Sally Alder would never be late for an opening night. Except tonight, when everybody else in southern Wyoming had managed to be on time. Dickie observed that even Nattie, who always liked to make an entrance, was already present, ordering Jerry Jeff to get her a refill on champagne.

"They won't give me champagne, Aunt Nattie," Jerry Jeff protested, "I'm only twelve," as his cousin Josh, two years older, snagged a bottle from the bar and dragged him off into a corner.

Hawk Green arrived a little late, still wet from the shower. He'd had a great day in the field, scouting prospects in the kimberlite pipes down on the state line, and he was looking forward to spending much of the summer there, showing his students how to look for industrial-grade diamonds. He doubted there would be gem-quality diamonds, but you never could tell. If the students found anything interesting, Hawk would probably have to cancel a trip to Alaska he'd planned for August.

The place was already packed. Hawk hadn't managed to penetrate the crowd, but the food and drink had come to him. He was standing near the front door, eating a tasty scallop thing served in a small seashell, and chatting with Edna McCaffrey and Tom Youngblood.

Hawk couldn't imagine what had happened to Sally. As he knew, she was a flake in many ways, but Sally was always punctual. He didn't have long to worry, however, as the Mustang turned the corner onto Ivinson and parked out front, in the no-parking zone.

But Sally wasn't driving. There was someone with her. Hawk wondered what was wrong with her. She was all hunched over to one side, as if her ribs hurt. Her face was swollen and turning purple, one eye puffed up half-shut, the other wide in horror. Hawk's Smith and Wesson was in the glove box of his truck. He put his plate on a table and started for the door.

But Hawk was a moment too late. Hustling, Danny Crease pushed Sally in the door of the Yippie I O Cafe, holding her in a hammer lock with the Beretta nestled up under her ear. "Nobody moves," he shouted. The place was so crowded, it took a minute for people to quiet down. Dickie Langham took in the scene in a heartbeat and pushed people away from him. He'd worn a shoulder holster under his jacket. Couldn't get to his gun, and wouldn't dare anyway.

"Danny Crease," said Dickie. "To what do I owe the pleasure?"

"Remember when you used to be a coke dealer, Sheriff?" Danny screamed. A number of the people present gasped; a number of others remembered. "Remember how you were a thief as well as a drug pusher? It's been fifteen years, Langham. You ran out the back door owing me twelve and a half grand, and you should have kept on running a little longer. But then again, nobody who cheats me ever runs long enough. I have a very good memory, and I'm here to collect every fucking penny you owe me."

The crowd began to murmur, but Danny hollered, *"Shut up!"* and shoved the gun a little harder against Sally's head. Everyone fell silent. Hawk stood perfectly still, watching and waiting. Beside him, his teammate from "Old, But Slow" was tensed like a spring.

"I'll kill this bitch, I swear it, Langham. But I'd rather have you." He rammed the barrel of the gun yet harder, knocking against the base of Sally's skull. The pain penetrated a little of her shock, and for the first time, her eyes focused and she saw Hawk. He looked hard at her and told her silently, with a very slight shake of his head, to think, and to be ready.

Several in the crowd shuffled, and Danny yelled *"SHUT UP!"* again. "I swear, anyone here makes one move, and she's dead."

Dickie's eyes had gone dull and cold, but his voice came friendly and laid back. "Let her go and I'm all yours, Crease," he said, moving slowly toward the front and wondering how he could signal somebody to create a distraction. "But don't you want to stay and try the hors d'oeuvres?"

At the mention of hors d'oeuvres, Burt and John-Boy shot each other a look of panic. Frozen to the floor, they'd forgotten all about the pizza puttanesca. John-Boy's sensitive nose caught the first whiff of burning anchovies, olives, semolina crust, and lobster morsels. The anchovies and cornmeal burst into flame first. In a heartbeat, a cloud of black oily smoke rolled out of the brick hearth, and people began to tear up and cough. Even Danny Crease felt the tears gushing out of his eyes, his lungs seizing up and spasming.

Finding some last reserve of energy and, remarkably, some remnant of a women's self-defense course she'd taken twenty years ago in Berkeley, Sally stomped hard on Danny's instep just as Hawk Green hit him with a tackle at the knees and Tom Youngblood wrenched the Beretta from his hand. The gun went off, a bullet flying through the front window, spraying a shower of glass over the street. Byron Bosworth, who was watching the whole thing from a barstool across the street at the Buckhorn, choked on a pickled egg.

As Danny went down, he decided he'd take as many of these subhumans with him as he could. He managed to get a hand in his pocket, and pressed the bomb control as people rushed out the door past him, coughing and crying. But nothing happened. When the smoke cleared, all Danny saw was Sally Alder huddling in the arms of one of the guys who'd hit him, two guys holding blackened, smoking pizza pans, and about a dozen party-goers—fine, well-armed citizens—pointing their pistols at him. The sheriff was yanking him up, pulling his hands behind his back, cuffing him tight. The bomb control clattered to the floor. The sheriff's sister, holding a Colt .45, put her face right up to Danny's and said, "We'll bill you for the damage."

Then Steve Baca came walking up, black eyes glowing, holding Danny's defused pipe bomb. "Pretty primitive device," said the fire chief to the piece of slime being hauled off the floor. "Did you leave any more of these around here?"

34

Ride Me High

"You want a beefsteak for that eye?" asked Hawk Green as he eased Sally into the big tub full of bubbles in Meg Dunwoodie's green bathroom, handed her two Advils and an extra-large whiskey, sat down on the floor next to the tub, and dipped a washcloth in the water.

"Does steak really help?" Sally asked, wincing as he gently touched the washcloth to her battered face.

"Probably not, but it has the ring of folk wisdom, doesn't it?"

Sally tried to grin through an upper lip that was split and swelling fast. She failed. Her ribs ached, but Doc Anderson, who'd fortunately been among those pounding down spring rolls and champagne at the Yippie I O, said nothing was broken.

"I think ice would be better." An arm snaked through the half-open bathroom door, holding a Ziploc bag full of ice. "Reduces the swelling."

"What are you doing here, Maude?" Sally mumbled. "It's eleven o'clock at night."

"I was watching the ten o'clock news from Cheyenne and they had a story about a 'hostage crisis' at a restaurant opening in Laramie. I called Delice, and she told me what happened. I came to see if you were all right," Maude said from behind the door. "Are you?"

"Yeah, I'm great," Sally said. "Goddamn it, Hawk, go easy on that eye with the ice."

"Yeah, Hawk. What are you trying to do, kill her?" came another voice from behind the door.

"That's right, Sheriff," said Hawk sourly. "This is her bonus day for attempted murders. Why aren't you down at the jail, beating the shit out of your prisoner?"

"I'm leaving that to the FBI. They'll be here in the morning," Dickie answered.

"Everything's under control here," said Hawk. "You can leave the flowers, candy, and bottles of bourbon in the kitchen. We're not receiving visitors."

Suddenly the door burst open, and in flew Delice Langham, all ajangle, with half a Telstar worth of red ginger blossoms, orchids, and birds-of-paradise. "God, Sally, are you all right?"

"Never better," Sally managed, tilting the whiskey into the good side of her mouth. Maude reached in and took the flowers from Delice.

Edna McCaffrey peeked her head around the door. "Hey, this is like one of those sixteenth-century French salons where everybody would come into some noblewoman's boudoir and stand around watching her drop *bon mots* while she put on her underwear," she said.

"Fresh out of *bon mots*," Sally said, draining the glass.

"Can't a man give a woman a bath around here without having half of Laramie show up?" Hawk complained.

"Get out," Sally said.

"We're glad you're not dead," Delice said cheerfully as they all began to leave. "But the Yippie I O is a mess!"

"And I was just congratulating myself on how boring my life was," Sally commented.

Considering the number of half-hysterical, armed people who had been present at the eventful opening night of the

Yippie I O, it was a downright miracle nobody got shot. There was, unfortunately, one fatality. The bartender at the Buckhorn had been unable to dislodge the large piece of pickled egg from Byron Bosworth's trachea, and he expired on the barroom floor. Bosworth's funeral was very well attended, said Edna McCaffrey, who had to go.

Sally Alder was recovering from the assault by Danny Crease, under the care of Hawk Green, Maude Stark, and a surprising number of people who considered Sally a friend. Even Nattie Langham showed up with a summer sausage giftpack from Hickory Farms (Sally suspected someone had sent it to Nattie and Dwayne for Christmas and they'd never gotten around to eating it).

Danny Crease had been transferred to the more secure state penitentiary at Rawlins. In the wake of the Freedom Ranch debacle, the Teton County sheriff had done some investigating into the deaths of Walt Flanders and Mickey Welsh, both associates of the late Elroy Foote. As a result, Danny was awaiting trial on multiple charges of murder, attempted murder, arson, and assault. Dickie was also looking into the murders of the Mexican nationals on the Snowy Range Road. He had no evidence to connect Danny with those killings, and probably would never be able to make anybody pay, in those cases. He really hoped Danny had been involved. He didn't want to think there might be somebody else out there, murdering helpless people in his county.

On Danny's second day at Rawlins, he received a bill for repairs to the Yippie I O from Delice, in the amount of $12,500.

The United States Justice Department confiscated the Harrier, the tank, and several suspicious vials found in the refrigerator at Freedom Ranch. The vials were being transported, under extremely secure conditions, to the laboratories of the Centers for Disease Control in Atlanta.

Mrs. Pamela Appley of Sun Valley, Idaho was suing the Teton County Sheriff's Office, the Wyoming Division of

Criminal Investigations, the FBI, the ATF, and the United States Forest Service for violating her parents' civil rights.

CNN and several other news outlets were suing the federal government and the estate of Elroy Foote to get money to pay off the workers' compensation claims of the camera crews and correspondents deafened by the blast at Freedom Ranch.

Brittany Langham had decided to do something with her life, but she wasn't exactly sure what. She had written for applications to the University of Wyoming School of Law, the graduate program in history at the University of California, Berkeley, and the FBI Academy.

Bobby Helwigsen had received a $250,000 advance from a major publishing house for a book prospectively titled, *Teton Thunder: My Year Inside the Militia*. He was being represented by the William Morris Agency, and was considering offers including a nationwide radio call-in program and a series of infomercials for products including the Butt-Blaster.

During the next several weeks, the Dunwoodie Foundation agreed to seek Historic Register designation for Meg's house, and to transfer the papers to the archives after one more year. Egan Crain would act as chief curator. The Giselle Blum paintings from the closet were to be the centerpieces for an exhibit of the artist's work at the University Art Museum; while Brit waited to hear from her various schools, she had been hired to write the catalogue copy. The Dunwoodie diamonds had been removed from the vault at the Centennial Bank, and sent via armed courier to a De Beers, Ltd. office in New York, to see if they could be identified.

The Yippie I O Cafe reopened on the Fourth of July. The sushi special was red-white-and-blue rainbow rolls. The Langham boys—Dickie, Dwayne, Josh, and Jerry Jeff—ate four entire rolls apiece. Steve Baca ordered the green chile chicken pizza. Delice hoped that didn't mean he was getting homesick for New Mexico.

Sally Alder's inquiry regarding Margaret Dunwoodie and Ernst Malthus was sitting in an unopened manila envelope at the State Department office that reviewed Freedom Of Information Act requests. It was somewhere in the middle of a large pile of similar envelopes.

And Edna McCaffrey and Tom Youngblood returned, for what was left of the summer, to Katmandu.

Hawk was wrestling the last of Sally's boxes out of Meg Dunwoodie's house, and into his pickup. She was finally taking a bunch of her work stuff to an office on campus. She planned to split her time between Meg's house and the office, spending the year writing the biography of Laramie's greatest poet, Margaret Parker Dunwoodie. She was moving her other stuff into Hawk's house. It would be a little cramped. They would probably have to look for a bigger place.

"Well, we don't need to look right away," Sally hedged. "What if I decide to go back to UCLA?"

"You ain't goin' nowhere," said Hawk. "Ride me high, and all that Bob Dylan stuff."

Sally looked at Hawk. He looked back. She moved toward him. He stood his ground. She put her arms around his neck. He put his arms around her waist. He leaned down and kissed her very sweetly, then very thoroughly.

"I'm moving in with you, Hawk," she murmured into his ear. "What does this mean?"

"You pay half the mortgage," he whispered back into her ear.

She looked disappointed.

"Don't worry," he said, "It's a good deal. I put down a lot of cash."

"You do love me, don't you?" she had to ask.

"Yeah, I do. I do love you. Now let's get this crap over to my house. I want a beer."

* * *

Maude Stark had decided that Meg's backyard needed a white lilac bush. There was a stand of gladioli that Meg had insisted on putting in, which had never worked out. They were taking up a space that would be perfect for the lilac.

Maude put her shovel under the spindly gladiola shoots and dug deep enough to get under the bulbs. She put them in a plastic pot, thinking maybe there was a place she could transplant them in Hawk (and Sally's) yard. It was good to get out and dig, she thought, working the dirt around the hole loose, and digging deeper, piling dirt outside the hole, making room for the roots of the lilac. Her shovel struck something hard.

Maude bent down and began sifting in the dirt with her hands. Her fingers found it, and she pulled it out of the dirt and wiped it off. One gold Krugerrand. What do you know?

Maude put it in her pocket and began to dig deeper, then thought about it a minute. The hole was already deep enough for a lilac bush. She pulled the coin out of her pocket and dropped it in the bottom of the hole. Shoveled in a little more dirt. Cut the bag off the roots of the lilac, and gently placed it in the hole. Then just as gently, she pushed the rest of the dirt back in the hole, mounding it around the trunk to support the bush. It wouldn't bloom until next year, she thought, going to the potting shed to get some fertilizer.